Dominant Business

An LGBT Submissive Romance

J. Scott

Published in the United States by Chaotic Designs Publishing,

Printed in the United States.

Cover design: MiblArt

First Edition.

Trade paper ISBN: 978-1-951902-01-8

E-book ISBN: 978-1-951902-00-1

To All those lovely friends, who reminded me what treasures truly

understanding people, could bring me.

ACT ONE

Making an Impression

Bianca cursed the lingering afternoon humidity as she walked across campus. She'd grown accustomed to leaving work in late evenings, so being outside in the late summer heat wasn't the most enjoyable way to start her first day of class.

This was a new direction for her, a chance to impact the lives of young minds. The simple agreement provided the business school instructors on up-to-date business and finance practices, and the school provided a curriculum centered on the firms long-term objectives. It was their chance to influence the future of the company before it ever graduated. For Bianca, it was a few hours out of the boardroom each week.

The cool rush of air was a welcome change as she stepped into the College of Business. Miller Hall dated back as far as the college did, Bianca was thankful they'd improved the building over the years to keep in line with more modern business concepts. Finding the classroom hadn't been hard; the Dean of the school kept the room on the first floor open for their classes. Sophomores and Juniors taking afternoon business 101 classes for three hours a week was her audience.

Teaching wasn't how Bianca wanted to spend her afternoons, especially since she started her side business of playing dominatrix to high end clientele; but the visibility from the company's point of view was worth a few hours a week if it meant rising to a senior executive level.

The classroom was empty when she arrived. Placing her attaché case on the desk, she wrote her name on the whiteboard as students began filtering in a few at a time. *This could be fun.* She thought to herself as she sat and observed the students' arrival.

Bianca eyed the students as they filed into the small auditorium style classroom. Roughly fifty students ranging from sophomores to juniors, each an individual in the way they dressed and acted. She marveled at how young they looked. *How young, how long had it been?* She reminisced about a time when she sat in the same seats so many years ago.

Looking at the time on the small diamond crested silver watch band around her wrist. *Three o'clock, it was time to start.* The flow of students stopped. Starting to stand, the door creaked, drawing her attention to the late arrival, surprised to see what she perceived as a younger version of herself enter the class.

Bianca regarded the young girl. She had long strawberry blond hair, straight laced plain features and average build, wearing the usual frumpy attire she remembered dressing in so many years ago. Hurrying down the stairs, the girl took a seat in the front. It reminded Bianca of herself in college. She hadn't found her demeanor or her strength in highlighting her natural beauty until her senior year started.

The teacher's eyes followed the girl until she sat. Realizing her eyes lingered longer than they should have reminiscing and admiring the young girl; Bianca tore her attention back to the class. Assured everyone settled into a seat, her gaze turned to the crowd gathered before her.

"Good Afternoon. My name is Bianca Ristretto. I hope you are here for Business 101, if not I'd suggest you move now." She gave any stragglers a long pause before continuing. "Great..." She clasped her hands together and grinned.

"So a little background about me. I'm an alumnus of Loyola business school. I won't tell you how long ago. I'm the mergers manager at Melantris and Keen here in New Orleans." Bianca walked along the front of the classroom, stopping for a long moment in front of the strawberry blond. "So why do you want to learn business?" She asked, looking first at the young girl, then into the crowd of students. "It's a hard, hostile world that takes no prisoners."

It was a rhetorical question, though she gave the students a chance to ponder. Bianca hadn't expected a response in this style of class. When the blond replied, Bianca's amusement with her being the first to speak up showed on her face.

"S-sorry... um... were you asking me?" The girl twisted, an

embarrassed blush realizing every eye was on her now. A pause lingered as if she was having second thoughts, then she finished her response. "Oh. I want to learn to manipulate the system and make money like all the other rich white men out there?" she chuckled at her half-ass joke.

The others in the class chuckled with her, which relieved the tension of the first few minutes. Bianca gave her a curious glance. The freshly heated flush of her cheeks gave the young girl's face an alluring glow, but spoke to how embarrassed that she was she'd spoken up. This drew a more intense expression of amusement from Bianca as she let her eyes linger before turning back to the others in the class.

"Okay, interesting…" Bianca nodded as she turned her gaze away from the embarrassed girl." So you want to join the old boy's club? You want to be rich and famous? Is that all?" She asked, looking over the other students.

"Why not?" An older-looking boy in the middle of the auditorium spoke up, taking the attention off of the young blond. "I mean what's the point of getting into business if you don't want to be rich?" Everyone nodded at his remark.

"Good point." Bianca replied, walking to the middle of the room. "So, how many people in this room believe they have what it takes to make it big in the business world?"

Her question prompted half of the hands in class. The young blond raised her hand tentatively. Glancing at the hands, Bianca let the amusement of her classes naivety show on her face as she walked back over to the blond.

"So you…" She pointed right at the young girl, compounding any embarrassment with being singled out. "Might make it big out of everyone in this room." The attention caused her to blush again, prompting Bianca to turn her attention to the whiteboard. With a blue marker, she drew a large number five and a percentage sign on the board.

"That's the number of new business students around the country every year who end up earning a hundred fifty thousand or more a year." She turned back to the class. "Almost all of you will fail within the first year, or burnout in the first three. My company hopes to change those numbers by teaching you about real, hard nose, on the ground business practices proven to succeed." A fresh murmur of conversation broke at the realization that theory and reality were not the same in business.

"This class already seems different from the others I have been too," a low voice spoke.

"Same here. So... are you in this top five professor?" Another person with a gravelly tone spoke up. Bianca listened to the low drum of conversation as it filtered from student to student. She was certain they all had imagined something different. As the others in the class looked to be mulling the numbers and wallowing in illusions of inadequacy, Bianca saw the young blond having a hard time pulling her awareness elsewhere. She chewed unconsciously on the end of her pen and stared as her mind pondered the statistic.

The silence in the auditorium told Bianca that they all grasped the nature of the industry was considerably more cutthroat than they imagined.

"Yeah, how did you get to the top? It must have been a difficult journey." The younger form of herself asked, catching her eye and giving Bianca a gentle, tentative smile that translated across her face to her eyes.

Bianca's gaze hovered, locked on those bright inquisitive blue orbs for what was a much longer time than was comfortable. Her mind pondered how to answer.

"First..." She started with a predatory grin on her face. "... please call me Ms. Ristretto. I'm not a professor. I don't have a PhD or anything like that. I'm a businesswoman." She said turning back to the class. "Second... am I in this top five percent? Yes!" She said very 'a-matter-of-factly'.

"By the end of the first year after graduation I was a junior associate, and I was making a hundred and thirty thousand a year plus bonuses. Last year my annual salary was in the ballpark of eight hundred thousand dollars, not including bonuses and commissions. I oversaw six contracts this past year, totaling over eighty million in revenue for our company." She walked along the front of the room.

While she was proud of her accomplishments and how she'd reached this point, she hated to brag about her position. Bianca considered this a teaching point, not bragging.

"As of last May Melantris and Keen promoted me to junior partner and I've been the manager of the Mergers and Acquisitions division for over a year." She regarded the faces of the students in the auditorium. It riveted most of them to their seats, their young minds attempting to correlate the numbers with anything tangible or closely resembling the reality they knew.

"When I was sitting here so many years ago as a sophomore, I was a kid from the not so affluent part of town working two jobs to pay my rent and tuition." She gauged how her story played with the class. "Drive, determination, passion, hard work, these are all noble attributes to have in the business world, but there's also a requirement to never back down or question your judgment. You need to know your business, and people need to believe you're right, even if you're wrong."

She wondered how the last part of her monologue would hit them. Today's kids weren't the type to go out of their way and do something uncomfortable and didn't like their beliefs challenged. These kids needed to realize that the real world was a constant challenge and there were never trophies for participation, you won or you lost, there was no in-between.

Bianca found her eyes wandering back to the strawberry blond in the front row as she began breaking down the syllabus for the coming weeks. It felt almost like a compass needle. No matter which way you turned, the needle always turned back to North. Something about this girl served as her version of north, and Bianca couldn't figure out why.

She could see the looks in their eyes. Many of them were having trouble with the concepts she'd just laid out. Business was a foreign language to them, and with every language you needed to learn the basic syntax first. Business was no different, learn the basics of the language first and the rest would fall into place, eventually. There was the inevitable look of dollar signs on the faces of many of the students.

The boy who mentioned getting into business to get rich had that manner, and Bianca chuckled at him. He'd follow through until the going really got tough. Then he'd find some comfy stock broker job at a dead end brokerage firm and realize twenty years from now that the world had passed him by along with the riches he'd sought.

Thinking like that made her mind switch back to the young girl. *What's your story?* She remarked to herself, making a note of her younger self's curious nervous habits and her tentativeness to engage in class. The girl caught her curiosity.

Another young girl in the back of the classroom asked about the assignments, pulling Bianca's attention back to the present. She moved to the other side of the room, removing herself from the orbit of her distraction, turning her attention to the question at hand.

"One step at a time." Bianca teased. "You'll have several small projects over the coming weeks and few small quizzes to test what you're learning." Wandering over to the desk, she pulled a folder out of her attaché case. "If you read your syllabus you'll see the appendix in the back that discusses your class project. If all of you read your syllabus before coming to class, there wouldn't be any questions on your required work."

She joked, knowing that even when she sat in those chairs so many years ago, she never read the syllabus prior to coming to class. "The big final will be a business project that I'll detail next week. You'll want a folder like this where you'll organize and develop your business. Notice… I didn't say business plan." Before she could add anything further to her directions, the bell rang signaling the end of class. "Make sure you're on top of the assignments in your syllabus for next class." Bianca called out over the ruckus of shuffling students, then started putting paperwork back into her attaché case. A text on her phone caught her eye. Plucking it up and plugging in her password, she saw a new message from her service.

TR requests the honor of your company tonight.

Bianca's eyes closed to mere slits as a predatory expression spread across her face. Thomas Rutherford was the CFO of Draid Pharmaceuticals, a well connected rich man with a weakness for powerful domineering women. She couldn't be sure where things had turned with him, maybe the night experimenting with his wife, denying him the chance to join. What she knew, he was insatiable in his need to give himself to her. On top of everything, his wife was just as malleable as he was but more interested in being used than in being submissive. The symmetry was almost perfect.

Please ask him to send a car for nine pm. Bianca replied back, accepting that she'd need to hurry home and get ready to meet the car by nine.

Who In The World Am I?

"Remember, next week we're starting on supply and demand and how that is the lifeblood of the markets. And your business plan drafts are due next week. No excuses." Bianca yelled out as students began shuffling out of class. Ruby sighed, realizing class was over again, not wanting it to end. Class was once again a pleasure to sit through, although it had nothing to do with the subject. No, that was rather dry and bland. It was much more tolerable thanks to Bianca, who was a strong, beautiful woman Ruby found it difficult to get out of her mind.

Over the past few weeks she watched admiring Bianca in almost every way. She was only barely aware of the infatuation growing toward the woman. Perhaps a part of the infatuation came from her relationship with her boyfriend ending abruptly about a month ago. She suspected he was sleeping around as things grew noticeably more tense, causing more fights. Having him walk away a week before school started only added to her suspicions.

The one aspect of the class that Ruby found difficult to reconcile was her progress. As the other students rose to leave, Ruby lingered for a moment, eyeing her latest test. The large red D stood out on the page like a scarlet letter burned on her chest. It didn't surprise her. She hadn't studied and with her other classes taking so much of her time, her focus on business slipped the deeper she went. Admittedly, when her counselor reminded her she needed business classes as part of her graduation requirements, her reaction was much less than enthusiastic.

She hadn't expected the concepts to be so difficult. She didn't understand the reason for a class that had very little to do with the medical field. On top of everything else, working extra hours to earn money for school was turning out to be a more stressful than she'd expected. Still, the grade made the pit in her stomach grow. She needed to pass this class to graduate.

Ruby rose, grabbing her test and messenger bag, making her way to the teacher's desk. Her strawberry blond hair fashioned into pigtails that hung down to either collar. She knew it made her look much younger than she was, but she'd been in a strange mood in the morning and the desire to dress cute overtook her. The white button-up shirt and mid-thigh plaid skirt gave a psuedo catholic school girl look.
This wasn't planned, it was how things had turned out. The more she thought about it as she approached Bianca's desk, the more she cursed herself for such an idiotic choice of outfit.

As Ruby approached the front of the class, Bianca had her back to her, erasing notes on the whiteboard. "Ms. Ristretto..." Ruby said sheepishly, her eyes pleading. "About my grade. I know I probably deserved the D you gave me, but I was wondering if there was anyway I could take the test again, or make up the grade with some extra credit assignments." Ruby asked with hope in her tone as she bit her bottom lip.

Ruby's tentative, mousy voice made her think she hadn't caught her teacher's attention, or that she was ignoring her. The time it took for Bianca to turn and meet Ruby's question seemed an eternity. As she turned, a heavy silence fell between them.

Bianca's eyes seemed to fight to keep from lingering on Ruby's form rather than focusing on her face. Ruby couldn't be sure, the silent blank look on her teacher's face could mean she was considering the question or annoyed that Ruby even asked, which made her almost sorry for asking.

Stepping up to the desk, Ms. Ristretto slid books and papers into her attaché case. "Ruby is it?" She asked dismissively, "I'm going over to the cafeteria to get dinner. You have until I'm done eating to convince me why I should make an exception for you and not the other students who didn't score what they 'deserved'."

Punctuating the cold response by the powerful, confident teacher, she picked up her case and walked towards the door without another word. The cafeteria sat across the quad, so the walk would be short, which sent panic through Ruby's mind. Fear, tension, stress all showed on Ruby's face as she shriveled at the ultimatum. Certain her teacher must look down on her, judging her as some entitled rich kid, or just lazy? She just stood there, a dumbfounded look on her face coupled with shallow breathing, uncertain how to proceed.

Before she knew it, her teacher was up the stairs and through the door, which heightened Ruby's fear that her teacher didn't regard her plight to be all that important. "No.. no.. no, I think you misunderstood me. I'm not saying I don't deserve the grade."

Spurned by her teacher's departure, Ruby grabbed her bag and chased after. She fought to keep her tension back, and breathing in check so she could talk and walk. Running out into the quad of class buildings and administrative buildings, the large square grassy area served as much as a park for the students as it did as the center of campus. Ruby all but ran up behind her teacher until they walked together.

"I'm asking for a chance to make up the poor grade. I've just had so much stuff on my plate this semester, ya know?". Ruby surprised herself by the sudden defense, clamoring up behind, pleading her case. She knew she hadn't given the class the attention she should.

"I'm a nursing student. I'm in over my head and the school requires me to take your class as part of my program." Ruby explained as her heart pounded in her chest. It exasperated her she even needed to make this argument. "Come on, Ms. Ristretto! Haven't you ever had like a really bad day... or, uh... month? I have so much going on…" Ruby pleaded feeling diminutive, following like a needy puppy on the short walk across the quad to the cafeteria. As if on cue, Ruby's phone rang, forcing her to reach into her bag and quickly turn it off.

Bianca was hard and confident and that energy both scared and turned Ruby on. Her limited experience in the world told her that there was much more about her teacher than she could see, but whatever it was, the energy she felt around the woman was like a charged circuit.

Stepping into the cafeteria, the older woman moved with cold purpose towards the cooler case with prepared salads. "To be honest Ruby, I'm not buying it." She said pulling a club salad from the shelf before moving towards the drink cooler. "When I was a sophomore, I was taking eight classes, and I played on the softball and volleyball teams." Selecting a bottle of iced tea from the cooler, she walked to the cashier to pay. "Somehow I don't get the impression you're that busy. So I have to wonder if everything you have going on is partying too much, a boyfriend or something else not involved with school."

Walking to a nearby bar style table, her teacher slipped up into the high chair, Ruby stood frozen next to the table. She was dumbfounded. The cool, uncaring attitude her teacher exuded infuriated Ruby and made her stomach flutter. She realized that this woman could be sweet and a major bitch, with the flip of a switch. Ruby frowned and gave a heavy sigh. She didn't want to beg.

"It's true! I swear!" Ruby shot back, surprised by the accusation. She shrugged her slender shoulders. "I don't have time for a boyfriend. I'm taking six core classes and two advanced nursing classes." Ruby brushed her long warm blonde bangs back past her ear in frustration. "I also work twenty hours a week." she went on. "I don't have a scholarship or rich parents so I have to pay my own damn way through school." Ruby spat back at Bianca. She didn't mean for it to sound mean or snappy, but it just came out that way.

In that moment Ruby wondered how Bianca might respond to her reply, having heard her story on the first day of class. How would a woman who went from the wrong side of the tracks to living on almost a million a year respond to the girl who was fighting to make it through a life she hadn't prepared for. Now she was fighting to stay afloat?

The way Ruby shot back seemed to surprise her teacher. A roguish smirk thinned out her teacher's lips before the edges turned up with her eyes. There was something in Ruby that told her that the businesswoman was pushing her, testing her to see how she'd respond.

The reason she couldn't figure out was why. Her mind chewed on the idea, wondering if the strong, confident woman believed that Ruby was meek and shy. Did she imagine Ruby would just back down being questioned or accused of not being genuine? Perhaps in the working environment that her teacher was used to, testing people was a large part of how she operated.

Bianca regarded her in silence as she forked a bit of salad into her mouth, her gaze never leaving Ruby's eyes. A mix of fear and confusion raced across her face as Ruby wondered what was going on through her teacher's mind, as the long silence fell between them. There was a curious uneasiness in her belly that Ruby was having trouble defining. Sure she was nervous, but this was something else, something deeper that both scared her and excited her.

"So there is a spark in you." Bianca's roguish grin spreading from ear to ear. She took a sip of her tea, letting the motion of drinking and putting the cap back on the bottle build the tension between them. She stared, regarding Ruby again for a long moment. "Fine. Here's what we'll do, Ruby..." Her teacher looked down at her watch. "Your business plan draft is due next week, impress me! I have an office on the third floor of the Business School. Class is at three, you'll meet me at two. You have an hour. Impress me with your plan and I'll make up the difference in your grade to put you at a C."

Bianca stood, placing her bottle of tea in her case. "Do we have a deal?" Bianca asked, putting out her hand. The look on Ruby's face could only translate as disbelief, as if she couldn't believe she actually persuaded her teacher to give her another chance. Then Ruby beamed with delight, her whole face lit up like a Christmas tree.

Ruby laughed. "Honestly, I haven't gone full bitch mode yet..so yeah." she remarked, throwing her back over her shoulder before she grasped her teacher's hand and shook it. "Absolutely, Ms. Ristretto. I won't let you down. I swear." she beamed, looking up at the teacher.

There was a strange sense of excitement growing deep inside of Ruby as she realized she'd just given her teacher, the woman who exuded confidence and strength, power over her.

True Nature

Bianca watched as the young girl beamed with excitement, leaving her to her thoughts. She felt good about her day and she realized what it was about the girl she found alluring; innocence and naivety. It intrigued Bianca. Most of the people she met in life established themselves as hard-nosed businessmen and women who had the power of life experience behind them. Sure, she met people daily who had little to zero concept of the world around them, but that was more a decision than a state of being.

Ruby was different, she lacked a level of consciousness about the world that people she knew had and somehow it was turning Bianca on. Was it the image of an unformed slate of clay waiting for the right mold, or was it the realm of possibilities she could go given the right environment?

Thinking about her situation as she drove home, it felt like the class had been going better than she had foreseen. Ruby was growing on her in a way she hadn't expected. Bianca was never one to jump the gun or let emotions impede her goals. It was hard to deny there was a new sensation regarding the girl that had a profound effect on her judgment. She never would imagine letting the girl off so easy with a grade. Was she getting soft, or was her focus on something other than the student's growth?

Running home in time to finish her salad and get ready for her client worked out well. A certain spring in her step meant smoother, more fluid movements than normal. Dressed in a very form fitting evergreen off shoulder evening gown, with a neckline that crossed the tops of her breasts. Her cool frosted stockings offset the darker green of the dress that stopped above mid-thigh, accentuating the strapped pumps that stopped mid-calf.

Her red accented blond hair hung free in a mane around her head, hiding her exposed shoulders and giving onlookers a hint of the cleavage underneath. Soft green eyeshadow accented her pale freckled skin against the green dress while a gentle coat of peach lip gloss highlighted her full lips without pulling attention away from her body.

Ready in plenty of time to meet the limo outside of her building, Bianca relaxed in the back of the private cabin. Legs crossed, one hand

11

playfully caressing her exposed leg while the other fiddled unconsciously with the ankh pendant around her neck. Ruby was a conundrum, a complication she wasn't sure she needed in life, but her mind kept going back. Something drew them together and Bianca had never been one to turn away from opportunity. *Could she be the way to fill the void?* Bianca asked herself as the car pulled up to the Hyatt Regency.

Bianca could feel the eyes on her as she stepped from the limo and moved into the lobby of the hotel. She was accustomed to being watched; men and women both looked at her whenever she was out. She always took very good care of her body, being a powerful, confident woman, there wasn't any room for half measures. Her looks were just another part of that.

Walking into the hotel bar, a slim, crooked smile pursed her lips, making her face brighten as her client appeared. Todd Jefferies, CFO of Clarion Bank, one of the largest banks in Louisiana. Bianca met him a few years before at a conference. The astounding thing was how willing most of her clients were to look the other way, knowing that the woman they were paying to walk on their arm for the evening was also an executive at a local fortune five hundred company.

"My god you look amazing." Todd said as Bianca approached. His voice full and confident but adoring in warmth. Taller than her by a few inches, his slim, active build wore the dark blue double-breasted suit like a glove. His angular, chiseled face was the product of good breeding and a well-manicured lifestyle. Dark brown eyes, and matching dark brown hair blended well with his gentle tanned skin.

"Thank you!" Bianca purred as he took her arm, leading her into a nearby ballroom filled with guests dressed in the latest fashions. The party was an opportunity for the rich and powerful of the city to see them together. She looked over at Todd, knowing exactly what the point of the evening had in store.

A little more than an hour later they made their exit, having done their due diligence circulating through the other guests at the party. Todd's urgent need to be with her turned the polite glad handing of guests into a tedious exercise. No one would think twice about a man like Todd Jefferies coming to a party like this with an executive from another company in the city. No one would blame him either for leaving early with a woman like Bianca on his arm.

Of course, there were enough people in the room who knew

Bianca as much for her business dealings as they did for her side business. Many people in the room who knew what she did in private also knew they risked exposing their secrets if her private dealings came to light.. The curious thing Bianca found about the whole situation was that with the number of people in the room who knew what she was into, it was more likely her client list would surprise them.

"You're such a dirty little bitch, aren't you?" Bianca seethed through her teeth at the man kneeling down at her feet. A black hood covered everything but his eyes and mouth. It served very well as the only clothing on the man's naked body. The hotel's willingness to let her drop a back off before class impressed her. It allowed them to could go straight to the room from the party without interruption.

"Yes, Mistress." Todd groaned from under the hood while Bianca pulled tightly on a chain leading from the back of the hood. She sat in a plush antique high-back chair. His tongue gently snaked out of the small hole for his mouth, licking the pointy dark green toe of her stiletto heels. Todd like so many other men in positions of power had a taste for being dominated and demeaned, a taste that Bianca happily fed.

It started out a few years ago after a party. Introduced to a senior executive at a company in town, she went home with him, adult consensual activities mixed with a healthy amount of alcohol were a regular thing back then. And regardless of any professed intentions, somehow they'd ended up naked in bed together.

Being naturally aggressive sexually, Bianca took control. Carefully pushing the envelope of what her date would accept eventually led to them lying naked in bed together. The conversation turned to how other men in positions like him paid good money for quality and discretion. Bianca tested the waters on his suggestion and within a year developed a distinguished client list, along with almost a quarter of a million in cash to show for it.

"If you expect to please your mistress, you need to do a better job of that." Bianca growled at Todd before the cat of nine tails lashed out and swatted him firmly on his ass, leaving a jumble of dark red lines across his soft tan skin. Todd yelped in pain, his tongue more feverishly licking along the toe of her stilettos now. "Very good." She said finally after a long moment of letting him lick her shoe. "Stay just like that." She growled, standing before the kneeling figure. She took the tip of her cat-o'-nine-tails handle, curiously shaped like a phallus, and slowly slipped it into him from behind as he kneeled before her.

Smiling when his only response to the violation was a gentle flinch and imperceptible whimper. She let the whip hang from his puckered hole as she moved back to the chair. Sitting down, Bianca spread her legs to hang over the arms, pulling the dark green fabric of her panties aside to expose a pair of full wavy lips and almost bare mound with a medium triangular patch of trimmed reddish blonde hair just above.

"Show your mistress how much you appreciate her attention." Bianca sighed as the man's tongue gently started working its way up and down her wet folds. Her mind jumped to Ruby. She wondered if the girl was working on her plan. She wondered what it would be. There was something there between them, and Bianca hoped someday soon she'd figure out what it was.

Down the Rabbit Hole

Ruby stood in front of her teacher. The calm and studious mask of confidence and poise from her teacher barely wavered as she finished up the presentation. It scared her. Ruby had been nervous for the past couple of days, going over her plan constantly. Truth be told she twisted in knots stressing over a plan that spoke to her or connected with her.

Coming up with a stellar plan eluded her all week, causing her to default to the first thing she could come up with. Working as an assistant manager at a local coffee shop gave Ruby a little insight into the inner workings of her store, but that was a tiny rudimentary part of the overall business. She hated using this as a plan but with so much pressure on her nothing amazing stood out that she could use to dazzle her teacher.

She practiced how she would present the details as often as she could. She practiced in the shower, and in front of a mirror, and even driving on the way into school. With her G.P.A. riding on this presentation, and a chance to make up her poor test from last week, she needed to do well.

Dressed to impress, trying to look as business focused as she could, Ruby went to the extreme. She wore a silver skirt and vest over a white blouse. The blouse unbuttoned to the middle of her chest to allow the shirt to emphasize the soft, supple rise of her breasts hidden beneath the vest. A pair of dark gray rimmed glasses on her eyes with her hair pulled in a tight bun on the back of her head gave Ruby a simple business look. Nude stockings accented pale legs, added a bit of sheen with simple silver two-inch heels.

Ruby feared it was too bold a look. It was more than she was used to. Her muted makeup looked professional, accented by the crimson-colored lipstick she wore. Only a splash of cherry blossom body spray clung to her frame.

"Thank you for your time, and consideration." Ruby said, offering a polite smile. Her pearly white teeth flashed briefly. She was shaking with nerves, staring across the desk at her teacher. The confidence, the strength, the self-assurance in her look, her demeanor made Ruby tremble. The scary thing was that the trembling was not from fear, rather from admiration or adoration. *No,* she thought. Neither of those words adequately labeled the feeling in her gut that made her tremble. It was a yearning. But a yearning for what, was the part that scared Ruby.

"Thank you Ruby." Her teacher said flatly, the edges of her mouth turned down in a gentle frown. Ruby could tell by the unimpressed look on her face and the way she gave her begrudging attention to the plan, that she had not hit the mark. "You're having a hard time with this class, aren't you?" Rising from behind the desk, straightening her skirt as she walked over to the front where Ruby stood.

Ruby's mouth opened to offer some half-hearted retort. Their eyes met as her teacher sat on the corner of the desk, mere inches from where she was standing. Closing her mouth, Ruby's head slumped forward in a meek nod to her question.

They stood silent for an eternity before the older woman gave Ruby a gentle half smile as her hand brushed her arm. There was an uncharacteristically soft and warm tenderness behind the momentary touch. Their eyes met as Ruby peered deep into her teacher's, holding her gaze for a moment. Something strange passed between them that Ruby couldn't put into words.

"Why didn't you do something based on medical services or products?" Bianca finally asked, breaking the tender moment as she held her student's attention. "If medicine and the medical field is something you're interested in, it makes a lot more sense."

"I didn't even think about that." Ruby whimpered, realizing how stupid she'd been. For weeks Ruby beat her head against a wall, trying to come up with something plausible. Now the mere suggestion of it by her teacher suddenly sent ideas rushing into her mind like a flood she couldn't stop. Bianca nodded at her admission, pushing off the desk and moving back to the other side, collecting her files and placing them back in her case.

"I'll hold judgement on your grade until I see the final product." The business woman said as she collected up her paperwork in preparation to head down to class. "But I'd strongly consider that drop add ends on Friday next week."

Ruby stared at her teacher, confused. The back and forth of the woman's attitude towards her threw Ruby for a loop. First she was cold and disinterested, then suddenly she became warm and almost caring, only to return to the coldness.

Ruby's mind was reeling. Not only from the confusing nature of a woman that she was quickly finding herself very drawn to, but from the assertion that she should consider dropping the class.

The words hit Ruby like a ton of bricks. She was a deer in headlights, and her heart raced. Somewhere deep inside, Ruby wanted to throw up. Already she could feel her eyes watering, she felt so defeated and low. She bit down on her bottom lip, turning to watch the teacher walk past her and towards the stairway.

No. she couldn't give up, she wouldn't. Ruby scolded herself. She needed this class for her program. *But is that all I need?* Her mind asked as she watched after her teacher, heading down to the classroom on the first floor.

"M-miss Ristretto!" she called out. The loud sound of heels clicking against the hard floor, chasing after her teacher. Ruby reached for her wrist, taking it gently, her fingers brushing along her teacher's warm skin as she circled around a silver bracelet. She didn't mean to touch her, she just had a lapse in judgement. Her eyes were watering, and her mascara was about to run.

"Ms. Ristretto, please. I worked really hard on all of this! I mean, it took countless hours staying up and rehearsing. I'm desperate Ms. Ristretto." She whimpered, pushing back tears. "I can't afford to drop this class. My G.P.A. is low enough already, and I need to get it higher if I am to apply for scholarships next semester. Please, I need another chance. I'll do anything." Ruby was only dimly aware of how close her teacher was now.

There was an intoxicating aura around the woman that Ruby soaked up as her eyes went large with a pleading puppy dog look to them.

Bianca looked down at the Ruby's soft watering eyes. There was a flicker of something in her teacher's look before the cold mask returned to her face.

The other hand rose slowly, the back of her fingers brushed tenderly against Ruby's soft cheek. Her hand drifted toward the back of her head. The intimate touch was almost sensual. It sent a warm shiver along Ruby's spine. But there was something in her teacher's face that was far from sensual.

The sensual aspect of that movement vanished in the blink of an eye as her hand briskly grabbing the bun at the back of Ruby's head.

Bianca pulled her head back abruptly. Leaning in so their faces were a mere inch apart, those full pink red lips dipped toward her face, stopping near Ruby's ear.

She could feel the warm breath upon it. It was an odd contrast to the sound of Bianca's cold voice. Ruby's mind was racing. A mix of fear and desire coursed through her body. She could smell the combination of her teacher's perfume and bath soap, she was so close. For a second, the scent overpowered Ruby as she felt her knees weaken.

"Be careful what you promise Ruby." Her teacher whispered, letting the comment hang in the air for a long moment. Still holding Ruby in her clutches. "If you won't drop out, then I will find a way for you to make it up. But realize your success in the class is now in my hands. I will find a way for you to get through, but on my terms."

Bianca Ristretto exuded power. Ruby understood this the first day in class. The way Bianca held herself, walked, smelled, looked and acted. Everything seemed to scream power. And now, here she was, close to Ruby and wearing what could easily be mistaken as a smirk had the situation not been more dire.

Ruby's heart thudded in her chest, making her feel so nervous and slightly excited. *Why was that? Why did she get all discombobulated with her teacher so close?*

Her hands trembled as she stood there, wide eyed and mouth slightly ajar. Had this been some guy she would have screamed rape or fought back? But no, this was Bianca Ristretto, a woman she both admired and now feared. She hesitated and felt her throat go dry.

"I… I don't know what you mean." Ruby fought through the fog, feeling vulnerable under the woman's piercing gaze. There was a conflict raging through her body and mind while she hung there in the clutches of Bianca. The look in the woman's eyes was almost predatory, if not mildly lustful, which only made Ruby more confused at what was going on.

Just as quickly as she had grabbed her, Bianca let her go as her open hand again brushing Ruby's soft face as the girl backed away.

"You will spend an afternoon at my office with me next week." Bianca finally said in a calm, soft, almost tender tone. "I don't care what day. But you must be free until I say you're done. You tell me which day you want by the end of class."

She looked at her watch, prompting Ruby to look up at the clock in the hallways, realizing they only had a minute left until class started. "Business attire. Look professional. I'll pick you up at twelve on whatever day you pick. You'll be working for me at my company, so you can see how it really works." She left Ruby standing frozen on the stairs without further words.

Considering Danger

'The rest of class was quick, Bianca's mind on Ruby, and not so much on the short five-minute presentations that each student had for their business plans. Most of the plans were just as rudimentary as Ruby's, causing Bianca to wonder if she was being too harsh on the girl. But Ruby was the focus of her mind, not her grades. It dawned on Bianca that the grades were the vehicle she could drive into Ruby's world.

Thoughts wandered regarding Ruby. This girl touched her in a way she never felt before. Bianca couldn't understand why it burned in her core. Ruby was adamant that she could wow her with the business model draft. The disappointment was there. It also opened a door Bianca wasn't sure she should open.

She chuckled softly to herself as she considered suggesting that Ruby lick her pussy to work off the grade deficit. Quickly pushing that idea, trading grades for sexual favors was not a great way to gain a reputation that involved her returning next year. She needed to keep things level regardless of the strange draw she was feeling towards Ruby.

The surprising thing was how distracted her mind was over this younger version of herself. Even this past weekend, her evening with Todd turned into more than a party and after party games. Waking up Sunday morning naked in bed with him when she meant to spend Friday evening, said a lot about the time they spent together.

Bianca never got into a habit of spending that much time with a client. Though well compensated for her time, both financially and emotionally, she kept work and feelings separate with strong boundaries. Sometimes one of those clients came along that forced the wall between the two to fall.

The curious thing about Todd was how opening her mind and body emotionally during a weekend with him freed her mind to think about Ruby. Unlike most of her clients, Todd was the closest thing she had to a boyfriend, and he tended to touch her in ways others couldn't.

The moment in the hallways at the top of the stairs kept her thoughts from the presentations. She walked a fine line in that moment, trying not to push Ruby too hard, but she'd wanted to see how she would respond to being challenged. *How far would she go?* Bianca scribbled doodles on her sheet, half-listening to the business plans.

She wanted to see what kind of grit Ruby had; to test her and the creeping feelings, Bianca had about her. Power over another person was a very delicate game to play, a game she'd had years of practice in. While there was a huge difference in the power exerted over a person in the boardroom and the bedroom, the concept was the same. Remove their options and hold all the leverage.

She wondered at the look in her eye at the top of the stair, her head firmly ensconced in Bianca's grasp. She could almost see the contrasting emotions running through her body.

Was she scared or turned on? Did she feel helpless or angry at being treated like that? Equal parts tenderness and strength. For everyone, the formula was different, but they all started out with a certain need for approval and a secret desire to submit to control.

The trick was finding the balance.

Playing out the hunger growing in her belly would mean stepping into waters Bianca knew she should steer far away from. But something about this drew her to Ruby, as she could see her inextricably drawn to Bianca as well. That was power. Power and control were more than physical commands. She needed Ruby to feel that she was the only person who could put her world right.

She'd use the weekend to plan how to do that.

The bell pulled Bianca from her thoughts abruptly, her eyes going to the young version of herself sitting off to her left. There was a tender meekness about the girl that only fed the desire. "See you all next week. We'll be discussing supply chain management, so read up. Have a good weekend." Bianca called out to the class as her students scrambled to leave and start their weekends.

"Ms. Ristretto. I have Tuesday free if that works for you." Ruby was doing her best to stand up to her tormentor as she declared the day she was available. Obviously unwilling to give up, Bianca nodded in approval to her young protégé.

"Sounds good. See you Tuesday, Ruby." Her tone was soft but self-assured. She'd done enough to intimidate Ruby, now she needed to show her that acceptance or compliance brought reward.

Collecting her materials, Bianca exited the Business school building, immediately pulling out her cell phone, quickly sending a text. *'Need a supportive ear, you free for drinks?'* Ashley would always be there for her. A girlfriend from college and a long-time friend, Ashley knew almost everything about Bianca. If anyone could answer questions about what she was feeling, it was Ashley.

'Sure, 7@usual spot?'

'See you there.'

The Sovereign Pub was a local haunt of theirs through college and over the years. At least once a week they met for drinks after work, a tradition that dated back over ten years. Bianca smiled as her mind turned back to the look in Ruby's eyes in the hallway outside her office. She could see the fear and uncertainty in the girl's eyes, like an animal caught in a trap she wasn't sure was actually dangerous.

Bianca wondered if she would contemplate dropping rather than be the subject of whatever sinister ideas Bianca could come up with. She was sure Ruby must have peed her pants after grabbing her in the hallway.

Her mind wandered, driving through the city not only on Ruby, but now what she would tell Ashley. The one big thing Bianca needed to be careful of was to make sure she didn't cross that line. Class over the past month turned out better than she'd expected. The freedom of her business curriculum gave her the opportunity to really press the students hard about how the real world works. Real world business verses how the college wanted the school of business taught varied and the young minds were eating it up like candy.

Her boss stepped into class the previous week to watch and gave her nothing but resounding reviews on how well engaged and hooked the students were to the upside of their business.

This was turning out to be a much better job than she originally expected when they suggested it. The last thing she needed was an assault complaint derailing it. To do this right, she needed Ruby to come to it on her own.

Bianca grinned widely as she entered the bar, seeing her friend already arrived and ordered. "So... what's so damn important you need to cry in my martini?" Ashley asked as Bianca approached the booth. Black shoulder length hair, her face long and angular, Ashley's build and looks were less pronounced than Bianca's, but she was no less attractive. Dressed in a silk blue blouse and white skirt, suggesting Ashley just came from work. Bianca slid into their booth, greeted by a waiting Martini.

"A woman who has caught my interest." Bianca said, holding up the glass in a toast before taking a long sip of the clear liquid.

"Sounds serious..." Ashley responded. Bianca began shaking her head as she bit through the alcohol of her drink.

"Don't know yet. But I'm having trouble figuring her out." Ashley giggled to herself for a moment.

"Why do you need to? If you think she's right, just tie her up and play with her. If she doesn't respond like you think she should, she runs away and you find another." Bianca's head tilted softly to the side, her eyes squinted for a moment as she considered Ashley's words.

"I guess there are worse ways to find out what I want to know."

"If you think she has what you're looking for, she'll accept it, eventually." Bianca looked across the table at her friend. She'd been one of the first to allow Bianca to test her limits. The bond between them was beyond anything Bianca shared with anyone else ever. Ashley was the only other girl Bianca ever dominated, and Bianca wondered if the effect on girls differed from the effect on men. *How would Ruby respond?*

"I assume this isn't some woman you work with?" Ashley pried, curious to understand the apprehension more deeply.

"No." Bianca shook her head, taking a long sip of her martini.

Ashley could read Bianca's cryptic responses better than hers sometimes. The, *and who is she,* look in her eyes told Bianca there was no dancing around the answer. "She's a college student."

The assertion caught Ashley's hand mid-drive as it carried her own drink to her mouth. It hung half open, as if working out how to properly respond before closing slowly in to a thin, twisted expression. Ashley knew that Bianca taught at the university, and while she had shared none of the details about the class up to this point, it wasn't hard for Ashley to figure out what was going on.

"Is this wise?" Ashley dug more, trying to understand her friends thought process in putting herself in what could be a very precarious position if not handled correctly. Being a lawyer, Ashley always made her questions about Bianca's decisions seem more dangerous than they might be.

"Probably not." Bianca replied with a bit of a giggle.

She knew it wasn't wise, but what could she do. The funny part of the whole situation was that the scenario was so appropriately something out of a trashy romance novel, but the reality of the situation was anything but a fantasy.

"She's in a bad place grades-wise, if she keeps up the way she's going she'll probably fail my class. It all started out so innocently." Bianca smiled at that statement. *Of course it did! When did it ever not start out innocently?*

"Has anything happened yet?" Ashley was hooked now, she would follow the line wherever it went until she had the whole story.

"Aside from a very domineering moment outside of my office in an attempt to impart on her how dire her situation was; and how that situation's outcome hung in my hands. I don't think she could claim anything other than me being a bitch." Bianca replied, laughing softly as she thought about that moment again.

A warm tightness grew in her belly as she remembered that look in Ruby's eyes, fear and desire all at the same time. She'd seen the look before, but this had been the first time in a long time the look had turned her on like this.

"Well, if anyone can make someone want to do something they know they shouldn't, you're high on that list bee. Whether I think you should is not for me to say."

While their talk did little to persuade or dissuade Bianca from her intentions, it aired some critical questions that made her think. Spending the weekend in the seclusion of her apartment, enjoying the summer warmth without distractions, gave Bianca time to reflect and understand what she was doing.

Was it right that she was thinking of testing the waters with a student in her class? She was using her position to take advantage of a situation. She never considered something like this being a bad thing, until realizing it could impact not only the target of her interest, but also her. On the flip side, she really wanted to see if Ruby had what it took to succeed. Maybe this was the only way.

Ruby stood outside Bianca's campus office awkwardly, her dark green pencil skirt clinging to her lower half. It stopped just above her knee, soft cream stockings she wore matched well with the dark green heels. She didn't have a lot of business outfits, so her top was just a thin white blouse, with two buttons undone showing a conservative bit of cleavage from her average sized breasts. Long strawberry blond hair pinned up off her neck, made her neckline seem much deeper. She had a small kanji tattoo for perseverance on the back of her neck. Friends she knew who understood Japanese looked at it more than once to make sure it said what it should. Under her outfit was a matching dark green bra, panties and garter belt that held her stockings up.

In her right hand was her iPad, with a purse slung over her left shoulder. Makeup done up light and conservative and she wore the same bright red lipstick she'd worn for the presentation the week before. When she entered Bianca's office, she reflected on the last time being here. The way the woman grabbed her hair, pulled it and whispered, sent shivers down her body. She wasn't aware why, It just did.

Ruby found her teacher in her office eating her lunch and doing work on her laptop when she walked in."Hello Ms. Ristretto." Ruby said. Her voice wasn't weak or timid, but audible and more confident. Ruby faked the confidence, intimidated by the powerful woman's presence. Despite sounding more bold, Ruby stood awkwardly and tucked a stray strand of hair behind her ear. She wore black-rimmed glasses, giving her a more studious look. "I hope I'm not too early." she said, holding up her iPad. "I'm super eager to learn. I can't tell you how little sleep I got. I'm excited to prove I'm more than some girl with a silly dream."

Suddenly realizing she was rambling, her mouth snapped shut. Bianca looked up at Ruby with a friendly smile, almost as if actually happy to see she was making an attempt.

"Hello Ruby, no, you're just in time. I was just finishing lunch." She replied, crumpling the paper for her sandwich up as she stood. Tossing the paper in the basket before walking over to Ruby, her eyes swept along her body. The look sent a tension along her skin following her teacher's eyes. *Why were her eyes so intense?* She stood there thinking.

The mere presence of the woman made Ruby weak in the knees. She was intimidating, sensual and just plain attractive. Although Ruby had trouble reconciling her attraction, she stood there, feeling like a piece of meat as her gaze washed along her body. So enthralled was Ruby that she failed to feel her cheeks flush red.

Bianca stepped up to Ruby still with a smile on her face as she gently took each arm in a hand, holding her away to get a good look.

"Very good. This will work." Giving Ruby one last brush on her arm before grabbing her case. "Ok, let's go."

Excitement was building, and Ruby curiously wondered if she had somehow found her way into her teacher's good graces. It would be a welcome change.

Bianca led them to the parking lot where a navy blue BMW sedan waited. "Wow. Nice car." she said, admiring the vehicle. Much like her teacher, the BMW was splendid and sleek, truly a luxury sedan that screamed power, success and money. Ruby melted into the passenger seat and crossed her legs, the skirt riding up a bit and giving a view of the top of her stockings and garter straps.

"You are helping me with some paperwork on a case I'm working." Her teacher explained, starting the car. She couldn't be sure, but Ruby swore her teacher gave her thigh a sidelong glance before pulling out. "You'll need to sign a non-disclosure agreement before we start. Are you ok with that? Let me know now and I can turn around and take you back." She pulled out of the lot and onto the city roads.

Ruby shrugged her shoulders. "I have no problem signing." she remarked casually. Ruby didn't have any reason to think this was anything but a business meeting or even an internship for the company that Bianca worked for. She noticed as they drove every second or so her teacher looked over to see how Ruby might respond. She tried to gauge the look on her face, the tension behind her eyes.

"Good, I'd hate to lose you because of a silly legal form." Her hand went from the gearshift to Ruby's knee in a reassuring squeeze. This caused Ruby to jump slightly. Looking down, she realized that her skirt rode up more than was proper, exposing the edge of her stockings. The skin tingled at the feeling of her teacher's warm hand on her knee. Ruby wasn't sure what drove her to do that, but the physical connection only made her confusion worse. Her body responded in way's she never experienced from the touch of a woman before.

The rest of the ride was quick, the office not being far from the campus. Bianca offered some small talk about what the company did and how the department she managed focused on buying out and selling smaller companies. Leading Ruby into the building and up the lift to the tenth floor of the building, Ruby trailed Bianca through the floor of cubicles and conference rooms to a room at the far end encased in glass on three sides. A secretary sat outside the office door at a workstation.

Inside the office was a desk and cabinets, with a couch and a few chairs at the front of the desk. To Ruby's surprise, there were warm family pictures, pictures of friends and trophies from what she assumed was softball. The woman suddenly became more real, more human, more normal as the decor gave her cold demeanor more depth.

The main wall opposite the door was all glass, looking out at the city of New Orleans spread out below. Another half wall of glass and to the right of the door they entered separated a small conference room from the office. Through the door Ruby could see a rectangular table with chairs and a pile of unsorted files spread out. Glass encased this room on three sides.

"Put your stuff anywhere in here." Bianca signaled toward the conference room table with a hand before lowering a set of blinds that exposed the conference room to the outer offices. Now the only view in was from the skyline outside.

Ruby placed her purse and iPad down on the edge of the large table as Bianca opened a red folder that was sitting nearby. Inside it was a non-disclosure agreement with the company's letterhead.

"This just legally binds you from speaking about anything you may see, hear or do inside these walls. We have proprietary business dealings that go on in here, and sharing those with someone on the outside might hurt our business." Bianca placed a very expensive looking black ball-point pen on the paper.

Ruby looked at the presented document and shrugged her shoulders. There wasn't any reason she shouldn't sign it, especially considering she had no intention of having anything to do with Bianca's business outside of her class participation. As far as she could tell, it was a long page of legal looking words that would more likely get her in trouble than anything, but what could she do. Not even taking time to read it. She was just content to be in a friendly environment with Bianca.

"Sure no problem." She chirped happily, taking the expensive-looking pen and quickly signing the agreement.

The next few hours involved Bianca walking Ruby through the intricacies of how she was helping and what each of the files meant or dealt with. As far as Ruby could tell she was helping to collate files, sort entries, basic intern work. The one thing she found curiously out of place was how Bianca made it a point frequently to gently touch, or brush

Ruby. The touches were innocent enough, but there was a perceived undercurrent of more intimacy with them.

At first Ruby thought it was just her friendly nature. A touch on her back, or her arm made sense. But then it increased. A stray strand moved away, or a hand on her hip as her teacher leaned over to explain something.

The closeness made Ruby uncomfortable. Especially when she felt the graze of the woman's breasts against her back. *If the touches are uncomfortable, why do I want more of it?* Her mind spun. When she did something right, Bianca was affectionate and encouraging, but when Ruby messed up, or filed something wrong, the teacher was harsh, cold and almost belligerent.

It was confusing. Subconsciously Ruby tried desperately to please Bianca in any way she could, just for more praise. But when she talked down to her, it made Ruby weak in the knees and she felt her heart race more quickly.

The strange rollercoaster of perceived intimacy and power worked over Ruby's senses, and she found it harder and harder to focus her attention on her work. Nothing Bianca did appeared overly flirtatious, but whether it was meant to be, Ruby felt the draw pull her closer and closer. Ruby realized the worst part was that as she drew closer, the harsh response to something innocuous didn't push her away as much as it pushed her to try harder.

The experience was nice. And the corporate setting wasn't nearly as daunting as Ruby thought it would be. What made it awkward was Bianca. She was having a hard time gauging Bianca and didn't know if this was how she normally treated her employees or if there was some strange game she was playing.

As the day wore on, Ruby felt more emotionally exhausted than ever before. The constant reward and punishment from Bianca made her head fuzzy. The past hour being the worst, seemingly more punishment than reward.

"Oh, for crying out loud Ruby, how many times have I told you that assets and liabilities don't get filed together?" Bianca berated her again for what Ruby had finally come to realize was an over-blown response to a fairly worthless mistake.

"Fuck this!" Ruby finally groaned, throwing the pile of papers she had in her hand down on the table. "You've been riding me all day for stupid mistakes expecting me to understand any of this. You don't like the way I file your stupid papers then do it yourself."

In an almost terrifying way, Bianca rose calmly from her seat, walking around behind Ruby. One hand grabbed Ruby's hand while the other one grabbed the back of her head like the time outside of her office.

"I guess it's okay to make stupid mistakes when millions of dollars are on the line, right? Doing it right every time isn't that important, I guess." Bianca stood over Ruby, staring down into her large almond-shaped eyes. She could see the conflict in her eyes. "It's time you decided about what is important to you."

Before Ruby could respond, Bianca twisted the girls head slightly to the side by her hair as she leaned in. She aggressively pressed her lips to Ruby's with an open mouth kiss. The kiss was more Bianca trying to eat Ruby's lips than kiss them.

Her confusion flared, puzzled by the abruptness of the act and the electricity that passed between them as Bianca kissed her.

Eyes widened. H*er business teacher was kissing her hungrily on the lips!* Kissing a girl only happened one other time before for Ruby, being more of an experience, then actual interest. Ruby remembered it being nice, but it was nothing like this.

"W-woah! What the hell?" Ruby pulled back, wiping her lips. Her lipstick smeared a bit.

"Straighten this up." Bianca broke the kiss suddenly. "We're going to go get some dinner." Her tone returned to a rather heavy coldness as she walked back into the main office. Her teacher had just sexually assaulted her and then was suddenly acting as if nothing happened. Ruby knew she should be angry, storming out of the office in a fit of rage. She stood there, dumbfounded.

The protest didn't even seem to register with her teacher. Ruby didn't know what to do. Bianca seemed so calm about the whole situation, and strangely, it kept Ruby in check. A part of her wanted to report the incident to the school, watch the teacher get fired and then go back to her crappy little life. She didn't do any of that. Instead, with a look of puzzlement, Ruby did exactly what her teacher told her, straitening up like she was told.

When she was finished, Ruby walked into the larger office, looking down at her teacher. "Are we not going to talk about what just happened...?" she asked. "I'm not like... you know. That." she said referring to same-sex relationships. "And... you're my teacher. That's like abuse of power, or something..."

Ruby tried to portray a stout, unbending visage for her teacher as she confronted the woman about what had happened, but her head was swimming, her knees were weak and there was a warm knot twisting in her belly that seemed to grow by the minute.

Bianca looked up as Ruby came out of the conference room. Neat piles of files sat on the table with all the random paperwork collected up and stacked away to the side. Ruby realized regardless of how Bianca treated her she was doing exactly what she asked her to do, and doing it without question. Bianca only smiled as Ruby came at her about what had happened. Grabbing her purse and keys off of the desk, she moved towards the door.

"Are you coming?" Bianca stood at the door without answering. She waited for Ruby to collect her things, making sure not to show to the girl in any way that she would talk about what happened.

Once Ruby exited the office, she closed the door, locking it, leading Ruby back to the elevator. There wasn't any conversation. She wanted Ruby to wonder what was going on, why the silence. Bianca didn't want to talk about something of this nature in public, it wasn't the place. They would talk about it, in her time, on her terms.

Bianca's mind was spinning in sixteen different directions as the tingle of Ruby's lips lingered on hers. A warm knot appeared in her gut, a knot that had been nothing more than a soft tingle in the past weeks. Something about the kiss threw fuel on a smoldering fire that Bianca couldn't understand. Now that she'd taken the first step, her body responded by telling her exactly what she was feeling about Ruby. It was about influence over her, but there was also an attraction much like there had been with Ashley so many years ago. The only problem was that now it was more than just two girls exploring each other's limits.

This was Bianca being in a real place of power over someone and using that position to influence decisions. In reality, Bianca was just as much under Ruby's control, and she was willing to do almost anything to push deeper.She could tell the girl was uncertain about where things were between them. She saw the fear and confusion in Ruby's expressions, in her movements. The outburst became the tipping point.

The emotional rollercoaster of rewards and punishment pushed Ruby. Instead of leaving or complaining, she tried harder and harder to do things she thought would please, only to have some of her efforts fail, bringing on a more profound response from Bianca. A strange strength filled her whenever Ruby bristled at an acknowledgment of good work, then she almost crumbled whenever Bianca admonished her for doing something wrong.

The reality of the situation was that nothing she could do to the files in this room would affect the outcome of the deal one bit, but putting Ruby through the paces, letting her see how things work and using it as a vehicle to bind the girl was worth the trouble.

Reaching the parking garage and her car, Bianca drove them both through the city to a small Cajun restaurant on the north-east side of town. She was fairly sure this wasn't a place that Ruby had ever been, but it was close to her apartment and she hoped the location might turn advantageous.

Once seated, and the waitress provided them with two large glasses of red wine, Bianca's face warmed as she looked across the table at Ruby. "Do you really want to talk about what happened in the conference room. Or would you prefer to talk about what you're feeling?" Bianca left the topic purposefully vague, knowing it could send Ruby in any direction she wanted. Hoping it would take the girl where she knew she wanted to go.

Ruby seemed to flush with embarrassment as she sat across. She wasn't sure if it was the way Bianca watched her. The young uncertain hands quickly picked up the glass and drank half of it. Bianca sat patiently waiting to see how her new toy would respond.

"Um...yeah. All of it?" Ruby finally said aloud. Her tone was more questionable than firm. "What is going on? Why are you all over the place with me?" Ruby leaned in, whispering." You talk down to be, but then you're kissing me. I mean, you can't do that shit. You're my teacher. I could get you fired." Ruby's tone became more confident. "And I'm not even into girls. If this is some mid-life crisis thing, then..." she trailed off, looking away. "I mean, you're like... old enough to be my mom." she finally said.

Bianca's cool demeanor never faltered as Ruby chided the way she'd acted towards her. Twisted curls at the ends of thin pursed lips gave the impression to the young girl that Bianca found something about her argument enjoyable or amusing. Bianca wondered if Ruby might find more enjoyment in the whole experience, had she not been so flustered and wrapped up in her own fears and needs?

She couldn't help but snicker at Ruby's assertion that she wasn't into girls or that Bianca was going through some mid-life crisis to be. *Does she really think I'm that old?* She watched Ruby gulp down the last of her wine. It was lucky for both of them that the city always seemed to be more lax on drinking. Bianca didn't worry so much about that, she'd been drinking since she was sixteen and never made much of a deal about it. She wasn't about to start now.

"I'm sad to hear you say you think I'm old enough to be your mom." Bianca pouted playfully. "I'm barely ten years older than you." Bianca's pout turned to a grin as she took a sip of wine. She enjoyed the way the red liquid felt rushing across her lips. It was reminiscent of the taste of Ruby's lips on hers, the heat, the spice, the way it tingled even after it faded.

"You're free to go Ruby." Bianca nodded towards the door dismissively, her smile twisting the edges of her lips more as if she'd said something she found internally amusing. "If you feel I stepped over the line, then say something." They were edging closer to the line. The question was whether Ruby accepted the push or pushed back.

Bianca's hand pulled the drape of bouncy reddish hair back over to one side of her head. Leaning forward on the table she looked deep into Ruby's eyes. "But something tells me you want to see how this plays out..." She spoke softly enough the make the words intimate and personal. "... to understand that hook deep inside that seems to pull you towards me, that reason your heart is racing right now and your uncertainty is making your head spin."

There was a look in the girl's eyes that told Bianca she was almost there. A soft nudge in the right direction and Ruby would give Bianca power over herself without so much as a sigh of protest. Ruby paused for a long moment after Bianca finished.

The teacher wondered where her mind was going. *Was she considering the offer? Had she mis-judged Ruby's response.* She could see the fight-or-flight in her eyes, and she couldn't help but feel the hook was pulling deeper even now. Then she noticed Ruby softly chew on her bottom lip, crossing her legs and looking off to the side. She seemed to watch a waitress deliver drinks and food to a nearby table.

Ruby was still wrestling with logical answers to illogical questions. She thought there was a simple answer to this question. She didn't realize how much deeper this went. Bianca's eyes never left Ruby as she turned to look off at the other tables.

Finally, she leaned in over the table, supporting herself on her elbows, looking to Bianca. Her voice was more demure than earlier. "Ok. So I get this is some kind of blackmail thing. Do you want me to sleep with you to get my grade up? Is that how this works?"

Even as the words left those sweet innocent lips, Bianca noticed a change in the way Ruby looked at her, as if some sense of a jolt of excitement or fear shot through her body. The question that finally came out of Ruby's mouth was not unexpected. Bianca's grin grew wider. Her tongue slid slowly across her upper lip, licking the wine from the rosy skin.

Bianca was telling the truth. Ruby was free to go, but what started as getting a better grade was now turning into some weird power play, and the girl was quickly losing. Ruby had absentmindedly toyed with one button on her blouse as Bianca let the silence linger between them. Bianca grinned as she sipped at her wine.

Ruby was so close.

She listened to the way Ruby talked, the wavering tone in her voice, the uncertainty in her thoughts and the slowly simmering desire in her eyes. She could sense that somewhere deep down in some dark region of Ruby's consciousness, she wanted to drop to her knees and give herself to Bianca. - Ok, maybe that was Bianca's dark wish, but she was close to getting it.

"Do you believe that is what we're doing here, Ruby, blackmail?" Bianca finally asked, letting the tension grow between them. Her words were soft, sensual. She spoke over the top of her wineglass, her eyes locked onto Ruby's. "This ends whenever you say it does." Bianca reminded her.

The true nature of power was making other people believe it was their choice. Making the other person believe they either want to or have no other choice. Bianca was banking on the idea that Ruby wanted to know more than she wanted to walk away. She'd been wrong before, but she'd grown so much since then, it was worth the chance.

Ruby blinked. "Yes. I do. I've seen the news. Teacher blackmail's a student for sex to get a better grade." the young girl said, crossing her arms over her small chest. Her eyes looked directly into Bianca's eyes. She was feeling brave now, a state Bianca attributed to the glass of wine.

"You can walk out that door right now and never look back." Bianca replied, barely reacting to the girl's assertion.

Ruby shook her head. "I could. You know. Just walk out of here, go see the Dean of the school and tell him you sexually assaulted me." she whispered. Bianca could see the uncertainty in Ruby's eyes.

She didn't think it was so much a point of whether she thought anyone would believe her as much as it was a point of whether she wanted to. "If that's not what this is, then what is it? I'm confused." she said, admitting defeat to knowing what the teacher's motivation was. Her body turned away only slightly, as if trying to hide her feelings from Bianca.

The defiance she saw blossom in Ruby when she huffed up, crossing her arms across her chest made the warm knot in her belly flare. In reality, all Bianca had done was give Ruby a kiss in a moment of passion. It wasn't the best in a line of decisions, but one they were likely to overlook considering how much money her company was giving to the business school to manage the future of their business students.

Bianca let her grin linger as Ruby threatened to speak with the Dean. Her defiance was cute if not misdirected and misplaced, but what could she do. Human instinct when cornered or uncertain of one's surroundings was to run or fight. Ruby had obviously picked fight.

"Very well... You know, you're absolutely right." Bianca leaned back, pulling her purse out. She pulled two twenties from her wallet, tossing them nonchalantly on the table. "That should be enough for a cab to take you back to campus." Picking up her wine glass Bianca drank as she stared across at Ruby. "I'll let Dr. Bruner know you withdrew from my class in the morning and see if he can transfer you to Dr. Ransen's Business 101 class."

Without further word, Bianca called the waitress over, giving her an order for a single entrée and another glass of wine. Ruby stared down at the money on the table, then back up to the teacher. *Had she misjudged the young, naïve girl?* Bianca wondered to herself as she saw the conflict in Ruby's face, staring down at the money lying on the table.

No, this had to happen. Bianca reminded herself, sitting back in the chair with the same grin still on her face. Ruby was feeling it too, she just wasn't sure how to process the information her body was giving her. There had to be new and confusing signals coming from her body as she realized that Bianca called her bluff.

In a huff, Ruby grabbed her purse and slipped out of the chair. "I don't need your money." she said coldly and turned around. She looked back briefly to Bianca and frowned. "Lady, you're crazy."

Bianca sipped at her wine as Ruby left the table. There was fear in her voice, fear that she would lose control, going to give in to her desires without knowing why. As soon as Ruby left, Bianca picked her phone up out of her purse.

'She's fighting it.' She texted to Ashley.

Placing her phone back on the table she took in a deep breath of the wine before drinking some, her mind raced over the last few hours. Did she miss something, some indication that Ruby really wasn't where she needed to be? Had she moved too fast, too soon?

'Give her time.' Bianca's phone buzzed. Turning it over, she grinned. Yes, she needed time to let the ideas smolder and heat her need. Eyes focused on nothing in particular as she swirled the blood red liquid in the glass. She reminded herself the draw that power created.

Bianca finished her dinner in peace, occasionally trading comments with Ashley about the direction her plans were going, or about how she was learning lessons from the past but needed to make sure she put them into practice. By her accounts the day had been good, but hadn't ended how she expected. Normally this would have bothered her, but Ashley's insistence to stay patient and let Ruby come to it on her terms drove Bianca to simply relax and let it play out.

After walking home, Bianca got comfortable, all but naked except a pair of boyshort panties and a sports bra, something she rarely had time to do lately. A glass of wine and some electric swing in the background she walked out on her balcony. Surrounded by the sound of the city, the lights in the distance, the smells of the early fall air and all the scents that made New Orleans what it was. Tension flowed out of her body as a warm breeze brushed across her naked arms and legs. She was sure her neighbors had seen worse than her standing on the balcony in a bra and underwear over the years.

A gentle buzz drew her attention to the phone lying on the kitchen counter. She hadn't expected further conversation with Ashley, so random texts interrupting her evening were not welcome. Two more buzzes in quick succession drew a curious scowl to her face as she picked up her phone.

'Are you there!? Yes, ok. I liked the kiss. But I don't like not knowing what you want from me. Oh. This is Ruby, BTW.' Her mouth twisted up in a gri*n. Ashley was right, as usual.* Giving her the chance to decide on her own had worked. Now it was necessary to seal Ruby's fate. If she was willing to take the next step, Bianca knew she had a true power over Ruby.

'Are you done with the accusations and the threats?'

'I guess. I mean yes.' The quick change from passive agreement to confident agreement flared the warm knot in her belly. She could feel it now, as Ruby moved deeper into what Bianca knew was an unbreakable power over her.

'If you're truly ready to understand what this is all about meet me at Fritzels European Jazz Club on Bourbon and St Ann. Ten thirty tonight. Dress to impress.' The text was vague enough, but confident enough to let Ruby know she was coming because she wanted to, not because Bianca was holding something over her. It wasn't hard to see she was, she was holding the power, but Ruby didn't need to see that.

Bianca looked at her watch, nine o'clock. She wouldn't move until she knew Ruby was coming. She considered inviting Ashley to watch, but didn't want to get her hopes up. She needed to let things work themselves out first.

'Sure.' The response came almost twenty minutes later. Bianca just about gave up on Ruby when the phone buzzed one last time. Sure it was a weeknight, but the day of the week only meant they would get a different audience, and the audience Bianca wanted wasn't one that involved students from school in the off chance they knew Ruby. With the agreement made, Bianca walked into her bedroom; she'd need to put on something that would make Ruby unwilling to walk away.

Drink Me

Still confused and infatuated as Ruby sat in the back of the taxi headed toward god knew what, she felt as if she was Alice, tumbling down a rabbit hole that she now needed to see to the end. She sighed. *What did her teacher have up her sleeve? Wouldn't she be worried about being seen with one of her students?*

Truth was that regardless of what she felt about everything that had happened, there was no denying what she was feeling. The kiss kindled something. *Curiosity*. She was curious how, and why Bianca seemed to have some weird power over her. Her heart was thudding in her chest by just thinking about her.

Fritzels European Jazz Club was an odd name for a club, but who was Ruby to judge? Never coming here, she preferred more conventional clubs that her younger friends went to. Doing as she was told, though uncertain why, she dressed for a club atmosphere. She wore a black halter style backless dress with a drooping neckline. Thankfully, her breasts were firm and small enough that she could wear an outfit like this without a bra running across her back.

The bottom of the dress only came down to her bare mid-thigh. If she bent over, it would ride up and reveal the red lace thong she wore. Not having a lot of time to style her hair, she did a simple curl and let it hang across her bare shoulders and back. She'd gone easy on the makeup, focusing more on her eyes and lips than the rest of her face, letting her natural tone underscore the contrast. To match her small dress, she wore a pair of strappy heels that gave her another two inches where the straps stopped just above her ankle.

Ruby stood outside of the club, staring up at the sign above the door. Several men and women checked her out as they passed. Something in the back of her mind didn't care that they knew they were checking her out. The whole situation was rather embarrassing, but she also took some small measure of pride in it. *What are you doing?* Her mind raced as she stepped up to the door.

Before she could answer herself, the sound of footfalls on the cobblestone streets caught her attention, but the honey sweet voice that caught her ear made her turn. "Well, aren't you just gorgeous tonight?" Bianca came up behind Ruby. She was self-assured and sultry in her movements. Her body swayed with fluid sensuality in her strapless red dress.

The red fabric crossed her chest like some streamer across her ample cleavage, and her full hourglass figure stopping mid-thigh filled out the dress as if painted on her body. Tan, knee-high boots with four-inch heels matched her own light reddish blond hair that hung in a wavy curtain over her shoulders. Full red lips with gloss accented her dress but didn't take attention away from it. Ruby suddenly yearned to feel them again. Bianca's very light makeup did little to take away from her naturally piercing green eyes, she let the red dress emphasize them.

Placing a soft hand on Ruby's shoulder, she gave her a quick look up and down. "C'mon inside." Bianca finally said, leading the way.

To say they were making an entrance would have been an understatement. Ruby couldn't help but notice that every man and most of the women in the bar were watching Bianca lead her through the small crowd, headed toward the back of the bar. She sat on a well-worn sofa along the back wall of the large open room. The dark, laid back decor spoke to the long history of Jazz in New Orleans, and the atmosphere helped her relax and gave off a sense of confidence. The music was at a fairly comfortable level, just enough to have a conversation but not so quiet everyone else knew what they were saying.

Bianca sat back against the worn sofa, one leg crossed over the other, her arms on the back of the sofa as if she was reclining at home. Ruby took a seat to the side, keeping a safe distance from her teacher as not to raise any suspicions.

As they sat, a waitress in a short black skirt and a black polo shirt approached asking for drinks. "A vodka martini with a twist of lemon and whatever she wants." Bianca said waiting for Ruby to order and the waitress to leave before turning her attention to the girl.

"Um. Same as her." Ruby ordered as the waitress nodded and left, Ruby looked to Bianca.

"I'm glad you came." Her teacher said, laying a hand gently on Ruby's thigh. The club had a smooth, sophisticated look to it. Something that Ruby wasn't used to. She had mostly been to the loud, over the top clubs that encouraged a lot of sweaty dancing and dark make out corners.

Her heart raced suddenly as she felt the rather warm hand on her leg. The simple touch made her feel weak and excited all at the same time. Ruby's eyes took in the soft features of Bianca's face and those lips that had kissed her earlier.

Ruby couldn't help but stare at Bianca, she was envious of the woman's curves, breasts, hair and overall confidence. She felt a blush on her cheeks as the waitress came back with their drinks and set them down. Bianca handed the waitress a twenty-dollar bill after she set the drinks on the table. She didn't seem to mind Ruby staring; it was almost as if she wanted Ruby to enjoy looking at her, as if to feel the need to be closer to her.

Ruby quickly took the drink and swallowed almost all of it within seconds. When finished, she looked back to Bianca. "Sorry, about the accusation shit earlier. I guess I just get weird when I'm not sure what someone is expecting of me. Becomes hard to meet standards, you know?" she looked down briefly. "You're kind of intimidating. You have this whole powerful business persona, but you're still a hundred percent feminine, you know? You make me feel rather inadequate, and excited at the same time." She looked away to the bar around them once she realized she was rambling.

Ruby noticed two men in suits eyeing them from a distance. They seemed to discuss something between them.

"I sense a bit of affection in that comment Ruby. I know you said you're not into women, but I get the feeling you're developing an attraction to me." She picked up her glass and took a long sip before continuing, her fingers balancing the glass between them. She gave a soft smile, her hand still on Ruby's thigh, inching gently towards her hip.

Ruby tensed a bit, feeling Bianca's hand go higher. "No, I didn't mean I'm not. I don't have a lot of experience with... girls." she said, but then quickly added. "I usually date guys, you know."

Bianca knew she had Ruby on the ropes and confused about a lot of things. She felt as if the room was much smaller than it was, and her heart was racing from the attention. Her legs remained together at the knees, trying to save some sense of propriety.

Looking at Bianca was like looking at the sun. She was bright, beautiful and ultimately gorgeous. Her eyes would steal glances of the woman's exposed cleavage, not even registering that the hand on her thigh was dangerously close to exposing her red panties to the bar. "So you've told me how you feel about me. Tell me you are here because you want to be, not because you believe you need to be."

With everything else overwhelming Ruby's mind and body, the question finally registered after a long moment. It was an odd request, one that Ruby wasn't sure she could answer appropriately. She was here because of her grade in Bianca's class, but more so it seemed like she wanted to be here. Maybe it was just subconscious, but it was there. Ruby quickly swallowed the rest of her drink and sat back in the booth.

"I am here because I want to be." she said flatly, the alcoholic beverage giving her more confidence. Her eyes met Bianca's, and she gave a polite smile.

Bianca removed her hand from Ruby's leg, she pushed her hair back, drawing the full curtain of red locks around her head to hang down the side opposite Ruby. This one action gave Ruby a full view of her bare shoulders and ample cleavage. When she finally admitted that she was here with Bianca because she wanted to be instead of feeling she had no choice, Bianca gave her an open mouth grin.

"Good, good..." Bianca nodded her head. She took another long sip of the martini before putting it back on the table. "... Ruby, you're confused about why I'm treating you the way I am. Please believe me there is a good reason." She placed her hand back on Ruby's thigh, this time fairly close to her hip, her fingers lightly petting the soft skin on Ruby's inner thigh just at the edge of her panties. "I want to show you an amazing new world, but to do that I need you to be with me for you and for me, and I need you to trust that I will never do anything to hurt you."

Ruby's cheeks were probably as red as Bianca's hair by now. She felt the heat in her cheeks as soft fingers slipped up her leg. The edge of her dress pushed up and suddenly Ruby felt incredibly vulnerable and exposed. Ruby's eyes looked away briefly. *Her teacher was totally hitting on her!*

"I'm flattered. Really! Is this like a weird sex cult thing?" Ruby's mind was fluttering about like a butterfly in a breeze. "I'm not sure what you expect." she sucked in a sharp breath of air, feeling Bianca's hand go slightly higher.

Again Ruby felt that excitement she hadn't felt in forever. The full pert globes of her breasts rose and fell under the free flowing halter top as her breath quickened and her heart raced. Her eyes seemed heavier, as if they were being drawn into Bianca's.

Her teacher's lips looked so full and red, and in that moment Ruby wanted to kiss her. A small image of them together in an expensive bed appeared in her mind, and she could only imagine what that would be like. The knot in her belly tightened, as a soft heat grew between her legs.

Finally, Ruby's right hand shot down to Bianca's hand, resting over it. Whether she was trying to stop Bianca's hand from going higher or to encourage her, not even Ruby knew.

"A weird sex-" Bianca repeated what Ruby had asked, finally stopping with a laugh. A soft smile and a giggle on her lips as she leaned closer to Ruby, putting more weight on her hand resting on Ruby's thigh. "... dear god no Ruby."

Her mouth was so close now, inches away as that sultry voice whispered just to her. "I don't know what your experience with sex is, but I don't think you could include weird or cult in my intentions."

Bianca let her previous comment hang in the air as she lifted her glass to drink. Ruby felt her mouth go dry as she watched Bianca lick her full red lips, their eyes never breaking contact as she drank and put the glass down. The connection suddenly became stronger, the smoldering heat in her belly grew hotter.

"You're cute..." She smiled. "Why do I feel college isn't giving you what you want or need?" Bianca pushed. Ruby shook her head quickly.

She couldn't believe the conversation she was having with her teacher.

"Oh, my god! Totally not your business." she quickly realized it wasn't a denial. *Fuck!* Bianca had a way of drawing out answers to questions that Ruby had no desire for sharing. Blushing, she glanced away, and waved the waitress down for another drink. *Why was she so parched?*

As they ordered, she watched the waitress leave giving her a chance to collect her thoughts. Turning back, she noticed her teacher looking up at the two men Ruby noticed earlier. They still stood at the edge of the bar. Every once in a while as they talked, Ruby's eyes turned to them when she needed to break herself away from Bianca's spell. They always seemed to watch them talk.

"What would you say if I offered you to those two men as a gift for you to pleasure for the rest of the night?"

Ruby nearly fell off of the sofa at the suggestion. Sure, the men were handsome, but much older. Probably in their early 30's. Ruby flushed as she looked to the men and then shook her head.

Deep down she remembered a fantasy about being in a threesome. But that was it, *only a fantasy right?*

In reality, it was scary.

Her heart thudded loudly in her small chest. She was certain Bianca could hear it.

"Ms. Ristretto!" Ruby tried to keep her composure with a hushed voice. "You have got to be kidding me! I'm not some slut." She argued, realizing quickly that Bianca likely had already planned this out ahead of time, meaning she needed to stall. "Picking up random guys is dangerous. They could be murderers. Or maybe they have some STD, and not to mention pregnancy and all that shit." she said. Once again she was only dimly aware that she had not come out with a simple and solid *'no'*.

"Please Ruby..." Bianca chided, her hand gripping Ruby's thigh more aggressively, sliding more towards the inner thigh.

It was obvious that Bianca enjoyed watching Ruby squirm as she responded. "Do you not think I haven't considered all the angles?" She whispered into Ruby's ear. "If I'm there to keep these men in check..."

Her hand drifted ever so slightly up Ruby's inner thigh until it was softly teasing the inside of her panties. "... You would experience a realm of pleasure few women ever do, nothing you've ever experienced before."

Her mouth was very close to Ruby's ear now. Her voice soft and sensual as her fingers teased closer and closer. "I'm offering you a chance to open your mind to new and exciting things. All you need to do is trust that I will keep you safe."

Thump. Thump. Thump. Ruby's heart banged a mile a minute inside her chest. The knot in her stomach tightened as her teacher's finger caressed her pelvis. She could feel her sex respond to the touch, even if she wasn't actually touching it.

Her body responded, but it wasn't fear or stress. Her nipples hardened under the soft velvety fabric and her lips swelled between her legs, letting small drops of moisture soak into her panties. She could have clamped her legs shut, or pushed her teacher's hand away, but her legs moved on their own, parting only a bit.

She exhaled slowly, feeling Bianca's breath on her ear. Her bright red panties were in full view of the two men at the bar, and by the look on their faces when her eyes flicked up to look, they were enjoying the show.

"Sleeping with strangers isn't what I imagined...." Ruby started, her own lips suddenly dry. She licked them absently, feeling herself falling deeper down a rabbit hole. She never even imagined getting into this kind of crazy sexual activity, never overly sexually active before. But now, with Bianca, everything seemed murky. It was true that her love life was lacking. Nothing she'd tried recently seemed to fill that pit in her stomach.

"I don't think…" she began to say, head turning to Bianca, lips mere inches from her teachers.

She knew she had to say *no*. She couldn't give into this woman who has teased her for months. But, looking into those emerald green eyes, she couldn't possibly say no. She couldn't finish her sentence. Her body coursed with adrenaline. Slowly she nodded in consent.

"That's my girl..." Bianca said with an affectionate grin. Leaning in, her free hand caught Ruby on the torso under her arm, her palm barely brushing the girl's small pert breasts. Her warm skin on Ruby's chest, skin on skin, she was sure Bianca could feel her heart racing inside.

She pulled Ruby closer as her lips pressed softly against Ruby's. Her tongue slowly snaked into Ruby's mouth, sliding along the inside of her teeth for a second as her lips suckled eagerly at Ruby's.

The kiss! God, that kiss was magic. It was the first 'true' kiss that the two of them shared. The luscious lips, the warm wet tongue and the pure surprise that she didn't pull away or try to leave ensnared Ruby. No, her mouth opened and accepted it willingly.

God, it felt great to submit to the beautiful kiss.

Then there was the hand under her arm, the soft cupping of a petite breast. She couldn't stop herself from moaning into the kiss briefly. Her dress was just a thin garment that covered her supple young frame. How easily exposing her to the world would be if Bianca pulled it aside. The tantalizing thing was that at the moment, Ruby wouldn't have cared.

"So...“ Bianca said, pulling away until she could see Ruby's eyes again, a small trickle of saliva broke between their lips. "I want you to go over to those two men and tell them I am offering you to them for the evening. But, they must abide by my rules without question or argument."

Ruby's eyes glazed over with lust and alcohol, and she looked flush. The request from Bianca seemed almost like a dream for a long second as it took her mind a moment to process what she was asking. "I...I can't do that...“ she said, biting her bottom lip, embarrassed. "I'll look like a whore."

Bianca's words were firm and the look in her eyes was powerful but demanding, and almost authoritative. Ruby opened her mouth to protest further, but found that she was already standing up. *What the hell?* A part of her looked on with sober horror as she turned around and adjusted her dress and hair before approaching the men. She sauntered over, her body nearly trembling as she approached the men in suits.

"Hi.“ she said, almost bashfully. "This is going... I mean, this is kind of crazy.. but..” she paused. She shouldn't be doing this. *This was wrong. For fuck's sake*, she was nineteen, and these men were well in their thirties. Her mind raced, trying to find a reason to back out.

She glanced back at Bianca, as her resolve faltered. That powerful look in her teacher's eyes filled her resolve once more. She turned back to the two men. "What I mean to say is... I'm... I'm supposed to offer myself to you for the evening. As long as you follow her rules." Ruby said, flush with embarrassment as she pointed to Bianca. *Oh god! What have I done!? I need to get out of here!* Ruby thought. This was a bad idea, yet incredibly exciting.

Bianca leaned back on the sofa, crossing her legs as her eyes watched Ruby. There was timid uncertainty and a need to look confident. Ruby was trying very hard to please her, and Bianca found it alluring. She bit her lip softly as she watched Ruby stand up and expose herself to the realities of what she was doing. She submitted to Bianca with very little protest and did exactly what she had asked.

Ruby adjusted her dress and walked over to the men like a woman who felt sexy and powerful even if she was uncertain and feared for what may happen. Picking up her drink, Bianca watched with amused interest. Ruby hesitated. She couldn't blame the girl for that. She was about to do something incredibly outside of her comfort level. Bianca's every confidence knew that Ruby would do exactly what Bianca asked. Almost two months of testing, two full weeks of pushing and tenderizing and one night of bliss put Ruby exactly where she wanted to be.

Not hearing what Ruby was saying over the music, Bianca let her approval show in the amused expression in her body. The look on the men's faces told Bianca everything she needed. Intrigue filled their eyes along with a little concern. New Orleans had a bad reputation for safe sex activities. Both men were clean, respectable types. She'd seen them in here a few times in the past, always drinking and talking but never approaching anyone. Their clothes said they were corporate types and their demeanor told her they were relatively sane. Several years working and playing in this world gave her a good eye for the crazies and those not.

Bianca watched as both men seemed to look at each other for a long second before turning back to Ruby. When she noticed them both nod and verbally agree to the terms, Bianca pulled a twenty out of her wallet, dropping it on the table as she grabbed their belongings.

"Good Evening Gentlemen. I'm Victoria, has Jennifer explained to you my proposition?" Both men nodded. Bianca placed a hand around Ruby's hip, her arm running down the girl's warm back. She pulled Ruby close as they talked. "I assure you there is nothing untold or devious about this. We are not propositioning you for money nor do we have nefarious intentions." She said it more for Ruby's comfort than the men. But in New Orleans, working girls and vice officers pretending to be working girls was not unexpected. "I have a place close to here. If you would like to follow us, I'll explain everything on the way." Bianca led Ruby out of the bar as the two men paid their tab.

Walking out of the bar and across the street, she pulled Ruby to her, pressing the trembling girl against her supple body as she looked down at her new toy. "You were very brave Ruby." Her teacher pushed a strand of hair out of the girl's face.

She could see the look. She felt like she was spiraling out of control. The world was upside down, left was right, up was down and her mind fought to bring order to the chaos. The look behind her eyes yearned to know what to expect, or what Bianca had in mind.

As Ruby's mouth opened to utter what she imagined was a last ditch protest, Bianca's mouth was on hers. She kissed her deeply, longingly on the lips. Her tongue slid along the young girl's soft lips before breaking the kiss. "Now..." She started pulling back from the kiss, pressing a finger to Ruby's lips to silence them. "Trust me. You are perfectly safe and perfectly free to do whatever you want, but I promise if you listen to me and do as I say, you will never imagine how amazing this will be."

Ruby answered with a shaking head after. "I shouldn't be doing this, Ms. Ristretto. It's… Its wrong." she said. Bianca could see behind her pupil's eyes how powerless she felt to stop any of this. As the men approached, Bianca softly brushed Ruby's cheek before turning to the men.

"Follow me, please." Bianca said, turning down Bourbon Street, Ruby beside her with a hand firmly pressed against the small her naked back as they walked, providing a reassuring pressure to keep her moving forward. The two men walked behind them, both whispering to each other down the street.

Bianca pulled Ruby closer, having heard her protest from before the men approached. "I told you Ruby, you don't have to do anything you don't want." She looked from her then to the men as they approached. "If you want to turn them away we will, but it's up to you." When Ruby didn't immediately stop and back out, it emboldened Bianca to continue.

The walk was short, only ten minutes of winding through downtown streets before Bianca walked up to a floor level door to a multistory apartment. The winding walk was more to throw off any return engagements. She fished her phone out of her purse. Opening an app on the phone, she typed in a code on the app and pushed a large orange button. A second later the round red light on the door turned green with a resounding click. Bianca turned the knob, opening the door to a small lounge furnished with a few chairs, sofas and tables. A flat screen monitor hung on the wall to the right of the entry door, and another door across from that were the only other fixtures.

"Gentlemen, please wait here." Bianca said, pressing another button on her phone that opened the second door. Bianca escorted Ruby through, allowing the door to close with a click. She led Ruby down a hallway to a room on their left.

Low red and orange colored lights around the edges of the room and dimmed lights from lamps in the corners created a warm intimacy for the room. In the middle of the large rectangular space lie a thick knee low cushion, large and square and covered with lots of pillows and blankets. On the edges of the room were other contraptions and pieces of furniture that Ruby was certain came out of hardcore porn videos.

"I don't understand. What is all of this stuff? Do you own this place? Who exactly are you?" Ruby said, an obvious fear and uncertainty in her voice.

Bianca smiled softly, placing a hand on either side of her face before planting a long lingering kiss on her soft lips. "Stay here, get comfortable. I'll be right back. Don't worry." Bianca didn't answer as she broke the kiss. Instead, she pressed a button on the wall under a small screen that sat near the door. The screen flickered to life. She turned the corner and walked back towards the main door.

Alone in the room Ruby could see Bianca on the small screen, move through the door back into the lounge, the camera obviously in the ceiling above the door. She could see Bianca and both men. "Gentlemen, I don't care who you are, but know that I have you on video." Her hand pointing back to the camera. "The video is for security and safety reasons to protect you and us. In no way is the video saved or edited once you leave. You are free to leave if you like."

She waited a second to see what the men would do with the knowledge. "I ask nothing of you for this except to be respectful to my friend and give her a good time. There will be no penetration of any sort without a condom. I will decide where, and how and I will guide and lead the experience. You will do as I tell you or you will leave." Her tone was stern and confident that if they didn't follow her instructions, she had the means to enforce her stance.

"You will not take any liberties with her. If I tell you to stop, you stop. Please do not think that I am some naïve defenseless woman either. I control the doors in and out of this building and I have a security detail that is no less than fifty seconds from breaking down that door if they receive any sign there is something wrong. Do we understand each other?" Bianca's stern, confident tone never faltered.

Both men turned and spoke quietly with each other for a moment. Bianca stood, her arms crossed over her chest. Finally, the men turned back, giving her a nod.

"If you wish, there are masks on that shelf. The door is controlled by me, so you can leave your stuff in here. Please give us a few minutes to get things ready. When we're ready, the door light will turn green and you may enter. We are in the first room on the left." With that, Bianca turned back through the door, which locked immediately after it closed.

Walking back into the bedroom, a sensual, alluring sway to her stride. Stepping up to her scared deer in the headlights, Bianca softly ran a hand through Ruby's hair, amazed at how feathery and natural it felt. She stared softly into those young, scared almond-shaped eyes with a level of stoic tenderness. "If you stay and enjoy yourself, I'll explain all of this..." She looked up with a nod to the room setup. "... later. But for now, please trust me, Ruby. You won't be disappointed and I won't let any harm come to you." Bianca could tell by the look in her eyes she was uncertain what she'd walked into or whether she should run out the door.

Ruby looked to Bianca and gave her a pleading look. "I don't think...I mean, I can't. Two men...I mean. I can't do this. Please..." she whispered. Shocked at how the last part of her sentence seemed to sound like she was begging, Ruby demurred. Bianca gave Ruby a long hard look as she listened to a girl drone on about how she didn't think she could do it. She pleaded against being offered to two strange men, how she wanted to release from whatever agreement she'd given those men.

"Listen to yourself, Ruby..." Her tone growing harder. "you sound like a little kid." Bianca finally said after a long pause where her eyes stared into the heart of her new toy. "If you want to leave, then leave, Ruby." She said as she reached up behind her, pulling down on the zipper that held her dress against her body. "I told you, it's your choice. You decide."

It dawned on Bianca that this would be the first time Ruby had seen her with almost no clothes on. She worked the fabric down until it reached her curvaceous hips before she let the dress fall to the floor. Stepping from the bundle of red fabric on the floor, Bianca turned her attention back to the scared little girl on the bed. Wearing nothing but a sheer black lacy bodysuit, she stood in a way that projected power, being very close to Ruby, making sure she had to look up along her frame to see her face.

"I have two men in that room willing to do exactly what I say for a chance to pleasure you, to show you a level of excitement I'm sure you've never felt." Bianca leaned down, her abundant cleavage struggling to stay close to her chest with the bodysuit.

"I don't even know who they are! They could be dangerous, Ms. Ristretto." she said, her body shivering from excitement and nervousness.

"Who cares who they are, Ruby?" Bianca said, realizing once she'd said them that the words were cold; colder than she had planned, but she could see Ruby's resolve fading. "If they are dangerous, I have ways of dealing with that." Bianca didn't want to tell Ruby she had some local muscle on call in case of issues such as those Ruby brought up. Thankfully, she never needed to use her muscle for anything other than some simple coercion. There was always a first time for everything.

She took Ruby's chin between her forefinger and thumb, pulling her face up to lock their gaze. "If you want to walk away, you go tell them you changed your mind." Her tone was cold and calm. She didn't show frustration, or anger, that's not what Ruby needed. She needed control. That was the power Bianca held over her, and that was what she needed to assert.

Ruby chewed her bottom lip timidly. Fighting to keep eye contact with Bianca, as if she felt ashamed that she had scorned Bianca's gift. Slowly she spoke, her voice shaking as her eyes came back up to meet Bianca's. "I'm sorry. Okay… I can do this…" the last part seemed more of a question than an answer.

Bianca watched as the fight and the uncertainty melted away, leaving Ruby in her most submissive position yet. A crooked grin curled her lips. Grabbing Ruby gently by the hair, pulling her head back up much like she did that day at the top of the stairs. "Good girl." Her words came out as a heated whisper, as her mouth found Ruby's.

Velvety pink lips mashed hotly together, her tongue shot into the girl's mouth. She sucked hungrily on Ruby's lips and tongue. Her hunger grew as the kiss shifted and jumped. Her other hand reached down, sliding along the torso until it slipped between her legs. Her fingers palmed Ruby's sex through her thin underwear. She could feel the warmth there. *She's ready.*

Finally, certain she'd given Ruby enough of a taste to keep her focused, Bianca broke the kiss with a loud gasp of delight. Her pet moaned softly, as if upset the kiss had ended prematurely. A string of saliva hung between them as she pulled her head away.

"Now, get naked." She commanded, hands still on Ruby's head

and crotch. "I want you on your knees in the middle of the bed." Bianca let her go gently. Ruby was panting, her pale cheeks flushed red with embarrassment or excitement, Bianca couldn't tell. Her body trembled.

Bianca watched with delight as Ruby followed her commands.

Moving to the middle of the bed, her movements to undress were erratic and nervous. She softly traced a finger along her own swollen lips under the lace outfit as she watched Ruby reveal herself to her new mentor. The young body was slim but with gentle curves. Her breasts were small but full, round like ripe oranges with thick pink nipples and a matching quarter size areola.

Both breasts stood firm against her torso with a nice roll of cleavage between them. She struggled with removing her thong panties, as if she was uncertain about exposing herself to Bianca. Working them down her legs, Bianca walked the edge of the bed as she watched Ruby remove her panties. "So beautiful." Bianca whispered, hunger in her eyes. She gave Ruby every reason to feel confident about her decision.

Turning toward an end table near the wall, Bianca picked up a black length of fabric, dropping it in front of Ruby on the bed. The fabric formed mask like something she might wear on an airplane to sleep, but the ends and edges were large enough to wrap around the head cutting off any light to the eyes.

"Put this on." Expecting a protest, Bianca cut it off before it could start. "I will be in the room with you. You need to trust I know what I'm doing Ruby."

She was glad to see that any protest about the mask ended before it could form in her mind as she started tying the fabric while she tried to hide her private parts from sight. Stepping onto the bed, Bianca produced a second strand of soft fabric bundled up in her hands. Pulling Ruby's hands around to her back once the blindfold was in place. Tenderly tying the fabric around those young trembling wrists, and between her hands and arms until she created a dark blue cross against her faint white skin.

"Ms. Ristretto..!" Ruby protested, a protest that cut off quickly when she realized exactly how powerless she was at this point.

Firmly securing hands behind her back, Bianca leaned in to the side of Ruby's head, her hand reaching around to apply a subtle pinch to one of her erect nipples. "That's a good little slut Ruby." Her mouth nipped at those sweet innocent ears. "From now until I tell you otherwise, you call me Mistress." She ran a finger up between Ruby's trembling inner thighs until her finger brushed the folds of her sex. "Since we didn't really have a chance to discuss this. In the event you need or want to stop, you will either show three fingers on your right hand or call out Hatter. That is your safe word to stop. Once we use it, the activities end completely." Her finger dipped between Ruby's folds, enjoying the dichotomy between her young pet's apparent arousal and her protests. "Do you understand?" Bianca asked softly. Ruby nodded tentatively. "Good. Now, how about we see how far you're willing to go to please me."

Bianca backed off the bed, settling into a large red antique chair with dark cedar accented edges that sat in a corner of the room where she could see everything. Her finger pressed a button on the edge of the chair that unlocked the door for the men.

A moment later the door to the playroom opened. "Please come in gentlemen and take off your underwear. I want you naked." She watched as both men stepped into the room. Their eyes hungry on Ruby as they let their underwear drop to the floor, each of them growing hard as they approached the bed.

"Mouths and tongues only Gentlemen. Explore her body. The only thing you can use your hands for is to change her position." Bianca ordered with a grin. She was certain that Ruby's heart was racing with the unknown right now. There was a desire deep inside to give her young pet something else to get her heart racing.

"W-wait..." The soft whisper of protest escaped Ruby's mouth as both men moved in. Without question both men kneeled on the bed like a pair of vampires, their mouths open as they licked and sucked along every inch of her body. Nipples, breasts, neck, arms, torso. It didn't matter, they ate at her with diligent obedience. Before long they had Ruby lying on her back, with her legs spread as they explored.

She could hear Bianca's voice. Smell her perfume, but could not see what she was doing. Her voice was haunting, teasing and as always commanding. Ruby shivered, making her nipples swell even more. She could feel the butterflies in her stomach, and she was only dimly aware of how hungry she was. Fear and excitement filled her. Her skin was hot to the touch, her body flush with arousal. Nipples engorged and aching, her flower bloomed with nectar both out of fear and desire.

Here she was, tied up and naked, exposed for two men she just met. She could hear them. They were talking... *about her!* Then the sound of rustling fabric pulled along skin. She felt a pang of panic. *No. They were about to rape her!* She felt too vulnerable. *To open. Too naked! Oh god, what had she done?*

Then the bed pressed in. She couldn't tell which of the men was in front of her. But she felt lips on her neck, then on her back. She felt herself struggle, then felt them lick her back, her ass. One of them forcefully took a nipple into her mouth and suckled on her. She could feel their hot skin on hers.

One was behind her, his erect organ against her leg. Gasping for breath, afraid he would mount her from behind. *He didn't.* He only nibbled on her ass. She felt her ass cheeks open, her little anus, and naked sex exposed before the man.

The other man was kissing her now, forcing her mouth open. Unable to object, taking his tongue into her mouth.

She should have found it revolting, but moaned instead. The other man behind her licked her nether lips. Ruby's body rebelled against her mind and pushed back into the warm tongue.

Turned onto her back, arms pinned behind her and legs spread open. She couldn't tell who was looking at her. She was naked and open, her sex girlish and tight and exposed to them.

"Mistress..." Ruby whispered, heart racing. Fear, arousal, confusion circled her mind.

"MMmmmm....that's right, boys, go slow, let her feel your hunger, feel your desire."

Her teacher- her *Mistress* barely registered her objection. She was still there, watching, enjoying.

The kisses plagued her body like little hot butterfly wings. She couldn't object or tell them no, or even put up a fight. *Or was it that she wouldn't? That she didn't want to?* She was at the complete mercy of the men and the woman who watched, yet Bianca said she could leave at any time, just had to say the word. *What was the word? Hatter?* It seemed a strange word to say stop. *What would it mean if she used it? Her teacher said all activities stopped.* The implication terrified Ruby, while at the same time it aroused her.

Her rational mind rebelled at the touches, the kisses, the teeth that bit and suckled her nipple.

"P-please…" she choked out between ragged breaths. The more aggressive man had her legs pulled apart. She could feel him slide between them. His mouth was on hers, his throbbing organ engorged and resting against her entrance.

The rough kiss made her weak and discombobulated. The aggressive man was passionate and needful. His constant organ swollen between his legs, sliding along Ruby's body. She could feel its heat, its girth, and its firmness. She could tell he was large, and the thought covered her body with chills.

She squirmed, wanted to pull away. *Was she ready for something like this? How could she be?* Somewhere deep inside, Ruby knew this was something she wanted. The thought ashamed her, made her feel slutty and gross.

The two men worked at her body. One was more aggressive than the other. She wondered if it was the clean cut dark hair man. His demeanor gave him the look of a gentleman with good breeding, but this one seemed a more hungry animal. The other man seemed scruffier, more muscular than the other. Was he the more gentle and exploratory one? The aggressive one pushed his way into her mouth, kissing her.

The less aggressive man traced his tongue around her small left breast. It left a saliva trail. She felt the sensation of heat and cool wet against her skin.

He seemed infatuated with how firm and nubile Ruby was. He shared his appreciation a few times already with his friend. They made small talk. Each one talking about who got to fuck her first, or who would get sucked off.

In truth, Ruby didn't want to do any of it. She knew Bianca was watching. She could hear the woman breathing faster. *This aroused her teacher?* Secretly, Ruby took pride in getting her teacher worked up.

"No more kissing gentlemen, mouths on her body please." Bianca called out, her tone cold but even. The words startled Ruby, but she found them comforting. Something about the way the men shifted based on her teachers… her mistresses direction gave her poise.

The more aggressive man pulled away from Ruby's mouth. He sucked, licked and nibbled his way down her frame as the other man suckled at Ruby's breasts. The aggressive man moved between her legs, his mouth hungrily nibbling at her folds while his tongue lapped up the trickle of moist dew clinging to her lips.

"Dark hair on your back. Blond hair, please lift her up and set her on his face so he can lick her. Then I want you to gently let her suck you." Both men seemed to hesitate at the directions. Grumbles and groans, whispered protests between them told Ruby it frustrated them at being told what to do.

Ruby felt the mattress move. The man between her legs, rolled onto his back. She felt the other man's hands on her arms, lifting her up.

"Mistress... I can't..." she whispered hotly, her lips flushed red, smeared from the kissing. The muscular hands gently, but firm adjusted her position. Paying little attention to Ruby's whimpers.

He guided Ruby up easily. Her skin bristled with arousal and glistened with saliva. Most of her upper torso and engorged flower tingled of drying saliva from being licked and nibbled on. Her already spread legs settling on either side of the dark-haired man's face.

Her flower was now in full bloom, as she settled down onto his mouth. She gasped, then bit her bottom lip as his nose brushed her sensitive nub and his lips sucked at her folds. Her pearl peeked from its hood, meeting his mouth, hard and throbbing, yearning for attention. His hungry mouth was more firm than the other. His tongue quickly slipped past her folds and darted up into her. Ruby sucked in harshly as he penetrated her tight slit. Her breath was ragged, gasping for air with each lick. She could feel the bed move again. The other man moved up in front of her, standing on the bed. Feeling the tip of him on her lips, her body tensed.

Her mouth partially opened from fighting for air. She feared he would push into her mouth, forcing himself into her. To her surprise, he waited patiently for her to open and accept him. She cried out briefly when the hungry tongue dove into her canal.

She instinctively fought the suggestion of taking the man. Her mouth closed, the muscular member against her chin. The tip was bulbous and leaked tangy drops

"That's right pet, show me how you like to pleasure him."

Ruby couldn't see anything, only hear, smell, and feel. But now she was about to taste. The fat tip pressed softly against her lipstick stained lips. She didn't want to open her mouth, but Bianca's words struck a chord in her. She wanted to make the woman happy. To feel her kiss again.

Slowly she opened her mouth, and without wasting a second the man penetrated her. She could hear him groan in pleasure. The first inch was easy, but the second, third and fourth nearly made her gag. He was greedy, sliding back into her mouth, forcing it to her throat. She could feel him sigh with relief as the soft warm confines enveloped him.

It amazed Ruby at how much she liked this. How she felt when her head bobbed up and down on him. How she enjoyed the sounds the man made, and how his pubic hair brushed against her nose.

He was using her now. Not in a sensual way, but in a purely sexual need. Her mouth was just a hole for him. His heavy sack gently swayed against her chin as her tongue traced the thick veins of the underside. When he pulled out briefly, Ruby could taste him on her tongue. She hated it. But also found it curiously arousing. Then she felt his hand on the back of her head and once more he plunged into her.

Meanwhile, the dark-haired man's tongue penetrated, stabbed repeatedly into her and tasting the juices that were pooling with each intense moment. Somewhere in the distance, as if in a dream, Ruby could swear she heard Bianca moan quietly as she watched Ruby's body respond to the attention. The dark hair man ate hungrily at Ruby, his tongue working its way in between her folds as much as he could. The noises coming from his throat said he was deeply enjoying her tight wetness.

The other man throbbed in her mouth. Ruby struggled to remain perched upon the man. Accosted from the front and down below, her body quivered. The dark-haired man lapped up every drop of her nectar, replacing it with his saliva.

"You like this don't you pet?" Came a soft honey tinged voice moving closer. The bed pressed in more and the warmth of a womanly body pressed against her back. Ruby shuddered. She moaned with excitement. "You certainly seem to enjoy this attention." Bianca whispered softly against Ruby's ear, her face an inch away, the hot breath sent shivers along her spine.

One hand slipped down Ruby's side along her ass while the other slid around her chest, pinching and pulling gently at her erect nipple.

The warm breasts against her skin through the light fabric of her teddy, erect nipples poking through added to the heat of Ruby's desire. Bianca's mouth nipped earnestly at Ruby's earlobe, then softly suckled the lobe. "Are they driving your body crazy, making you wet and excited?" The words touched something deep inside Ruby's chest. Her teacher's words flashed through her mind from earlier as dark hair's tongue brushed over her needy pearl. *Experiencing a realm of pleasure few women ever do. A chance to open your mind to new and exciting things. All you need to do is trust that I will keep you safe.*

Inexplicably Ruby realized that despite her fearful recriminations and protests, her teacher… her Mistress kept every promise she ever made till now. The paradigm shift broke through Ruby's mind like a rock through glass.

Bianca's hand slid up along Ruby's back, over her shoulder and up along her neck until her hand was on the back of Ruby's head, replacing the muscular man's hand. She held Ruby's head, pushing her gently forward as the man pushed into her.

"Take him pet, I love watching you being used like this. Show him how much you love pleasing me." Bianca's words held power over Ruby, even though she didn't want to admit it.

She breathed heavily from her nose as her head bobbed up and down on its own, saliva running down her chin to drip over her swollen breasts. She felt embarrassed that her desire to please Bianca cored so deeply.

Bianca's fingers pulled harder at Ruby's nipple as she licked at her ear, her tongue tracing the lines before she began working her mouth along the lobes and Ruby's jawbone. The sounds of choked wet thrusting grew more intense coming from her mouth. When the man pulled out of her mouth, she gasped for air.

"Please… too much." Ruby said, but before she could object again Bianca's hand intertwined in her tangled reddish locks, forced her back down onto him. He moaned out, feeling himself near his limit. Ruby dimly was aware how he commented her ability to swallow.

Licking along Ruby's neck, her teacher savored the sweaty salty heat of her skin. She seemed to enjoy the aroused, nervous energy surrounding Ruby. Bianca moaned softly.
Ruby's mind swam with the ecstasy of the moment. Her body quivered under the assault as her mind fogged over.

Bianca was right in that she wanted to please her. She'd slowly slipped over a threshold she hadn't even known was there until now. She was ready to simply do without question, without protest.Ruby's breath came faster. Erratic breaths drew her chest in and out against Bianca's hand. Fingers pinched and pulled at each of Ruby's breasts and nipples.

"Mmm.... yes Pet, that's it. Tame him." Bianca whispered

approvingly as Ruby unconsciously took charge of the forward motion of her head down along the swollen shaft. The slurping noises coming from her throat filled the room as she willfully took every inch of the offered phallus.

As Ruby swirled and fell further and faster down the rabbit hole, her mind slipped back to reality by Bianca's voice. "Ok, gentlemen. Please step off of the bed for a moment." Groans from both men at being stopped so abruptly broke through the fog in her mind. Ruby's body reeled at the sudden change.

The muscular man slid out of Ruby's mouth, a long string of thick saliva broke and fell down along Ruby's chest. Dark hair made some muffled verbal protest before extricating himself from between Ruby's legs. Both men walked off of the bed, quietly mumbling between themselves.

Still stayed kneeling on the bed, her body humming with energy, covered in saliva, sweat and her own juices. Ruby breathed heavily. Her eyes still blindfolded, she couldn't see what was happening. That didn't decrease the level of intensity she felt in all this.

She was weak, near orgasm before being yanked back from that edge.

"Now Pet, do you remember your safe word?" Bianca whispered in her ear opposite the two men. Ruby nodded. "I want you to say it, whisper it to me." Bianca insisted.

"Ha… hatter." Ruby fought to get it out as if saying the word would bring the world she was now living in crashing around her shoulders.

"Very good pet. I need to know you can remember it and say it when your mind fogged like this." Her hand slid down Ruby's slim, sweat drenched, back to her tied arms. Fingers deftly untied the silk fabric around Ruby's arms. "Why don't we give these men what they came here for." Bianca said in a sultry tone, giving Ruby one last pull on her nipple. She guided Ruby gently from her legs to her hands and knees, pussy in the air.

Bianca kept her body near Ruby's face, kept the connection close as if Bianca felt Ruby would need the safety and reassurance with this next level. "Ok, gentlemen, there are condoms on that shelf. Dark hair, you are first. You will start out slow until she's accustomed to you." Her tone turned deep and predatory. "There is one caveat..."

Ruby was keenly aware of the fact that Bianca's growing list of orders and restrictions surely wore heavily on both men. Her doubts built again, making her squirm to get up. "I can't do this…" she whispered to Bianca as the woman gently guided her onto all fours. Bianca didn't even respond to her protest.

"… No coming. If you come, you're done until I say you can come back onto the bed." Bianca leaned across Ruby's body. "If you desire to use your safe word pet, you end this here and now. There's no shame in saying no." Bianca whispered in her ear. The words didn't just fill her senses with a heavy honey sweet power, it pierced her soul. Ruby felt her body relax at the suggestion that she had the choice to end it with one word. *Hatter.*

Ruby's mind chewed on it. Some dark, scared place pushed it to her lips but somehow the rest of her body fought the urge.

Bianca's hand swept long and slow up from Ruby's thick swollen sensitive areas, along her wet spread folds, and finally slid across her puckered rear. Drenched wet like this It was impossible to hide her desire despite her protests. Bianca could tell it wasn't from the severe licking she'd received, but arousal. Regardless, Ruby knew her body was ready for what was to come next.

A sound of tearing. Helplessness in her eyes behind the blindfold. The anticipation of what was to come overtook Ruby. Her breathing grew ragged as the sound of latex stretching echoed into the room. Soon the bed sunk in more and she felt the tip of a man pressed against her folds.

As he stepped forward and steadied the tip at the entrance to Ruby's lips, her teacher leaned back, cupping Ruby's face with one hand. "This is very exciting pet. I'm so happy you decided to share this with me." She said as Ruby felt the first man push into her. Bianca pulled Ruby's head back by her hair gently enough to arch her back, but not enough to really pull hair as her mouth pressed against Ruby's. Their tongues danced into Ruby's mouth as their lips locked together.

Pulling her hair changed the angle of penetration. Her face in a position Bianca could enjoy the long sensuous kiss. Bianca's mouth was on hers then, kissing her deeply, encouraging Ruby to take it and enjoy it. Bianca made everything better, and Ruby kissed back.

The kiss shrouded the penetration. Gave her no time to brace herself for the quick stab of pain. He pushed deeper past her folds and buried himself to the hilt. Ruby groaned into Bianca's mouth as the first guy filled her.

The man exclaimed with satisfaction, commenting on how virgin tight she was, and that she was like a vice. He stretched Ruby open, and the feeling of pain and pleasure mixed like a wild and delicious cocktail.

She never felt so full inside. It was an odd sensation. Her inner walls clenched and molded around the man. His hands went to her hips, while thrusting slowly in and out of her.

He took great pleasure in taking long, deep thrusts, nearly pulling himself out before plunging back in. Her young ripe body tensed, dark hair was giving Ruby a steady rhythm of deep thrusts without letting himself get out of control. The moaning and whispers of enjoyment coming from him said he wanted to go free, to remove the shackles, to tear into her like an animal.

It wasn't time; she wasn't ready. "Don't come!" Bianca reminded him breaking the kiss with Ruby. The dark-haired man was grunting hard, his breathing growing ragged. Ruby felt the bed move behind her. She wondered if the other guy stepped up, tapping him on the shoulder for his turn.

A bestial grunt preceded dark hair's withdrawal. The head broke the threshold with a pop as it pulled out between her folds. The absence brought a whimper of relief, but also a surprising whimper of disappointment. As good as it felt, the ever nagging presence in her mind was condemning her as a whore and she would suffer for her transgressions. It also kept telling her how she's a slut for enjoying this the way she was. The darker part of her mind screamed for more, to tell them to fuck her silly and make her sore.

Poor Ruby's mind was a battlefield. She was breathing heavily, but thankful that the bed she was resting on was soft. Still blind to all transpiring around her, it enhanced every sense, especially touch. She felt the muscular man's hands on her hips.

"Take this pet." Bianca whispered in a way that flushed warmth along her already bristling skin. The feel of a needy erect nipple pressing into Ruby's mouth pulled at the maternal strings in Ruby's mind. Like urging a baby to nurse, Bianca created an undeniable intimacy between them in such an erotic moment.

"I want to feel you nurse on me." She whispered, as the second man grounded himself deep into Ruby's sex. She cried out, feeling the second man force her inner walls apart and plunge into her depths. She found it a delicious pain.

Her teacher's breast pressed against her lips as a hunger grew in Ruby. She couldn't see it. The nipple hardened against her tongue and she instinctively opened her mouth wider, licking lovingly with her hot tongue. *Fuck! She was suddenly in heaven!* Ruby's mind raced. Her lips wrapped around it tightly and she sucked hard, as if expecting Bianca's milk to be there. *This was by far the highlight of the night!*

Soon the man was grunting, and the sound of his hips slapping against her rear made Ruby moan in pleasure and embarrassment. Her mouth opened to object, to tell her teacher she had enough, but Bianca's sweet voice was there to encourage her. "That's it, pet.... mmm...." Bianca moaned gently to Ruby as the warmth of her mouth surrounded Bianca's nipple. "... you're almost there." Bianca whispered through a moan of arousal. Ruby's mouth continued to suck on the firm nipple, her moans pressing into the ample tit flesh of her teacher. She could smell Bianca's sex, and it was like an intoxicating drug. The last dam had broken inside of her mind. She was grunting with excursion, pushing back against the ravaging fuck.

Some primal thing inside of her had awakened and there was the intense need to fuck…to breed became the only thing on her mind.

Her sweat drenched reddish blond locks were held back by Bianca as she dug her hands into the bed sheets of the soft bed. Being fucked on all fours, like some animal became incredibly hot to the broken Ruby.

She no longer cared about any preconceived notion of right or wrong. Only thing that mattered was to be filled in any way she could. She pulled her mouth off her teacher's breast to exclaim in pleasure before clamping down once more on Bianca's awaiting breast. She suckled on the offered boob as desperate childish desire for her mother's milk over took her mind.

Pulling the breast away, in one more act of denial of pleasure, elicited a groan of displeasure from Ruby. On the bed, hands and knees, her mouth open, she moaned deep and carnal as she breathed erratically through each hard thrust. Bianca slid her fingers into the girl's mouth, her palm down. "Taste how pleased I am with you pet."

Ruby's mind swam at the taste of slick sex on her hot tongue. It was slick, pungent, with a bit of spice. Her groans of displeasure quickly changed into a lustful moan of pleasure. Her lips closed around the fingers. Her teachers dripping sex on her tongue flared shivers along her spine. Fingers lingered in her mouth. She sucked on them, replacing the nipple, Ruby let the push of the man behind drive the fingers deeper and out again. The loving juices of her teacher's approval lingered on her tongue, but the idea of her teachers approval overpowered any last bits of protest she might have.

While Ruby's experience with girls was limited, there was something intoxicating and powerful about the way Bianca tasted. Her mouth slurped at those fingers hungrily, desirous of more as her body was rocked again and again by a hard swollen manhood buried deep inside.

59

Ruby groaned as Bianca pulled the fingers from between her juicy lips. Standing above her student, watching the muscular man's rhythmic thrusts deep against those milky hips.

"These are the gifts you get when you obey me little slut." Bianca said with a cold sultry edge to her voice before pulling the blindfold from Ruby's eyes. Her stared along soft tan legs and the apex of Bianca's inner thighs revealing wet swollen lips with the fabric of her teddy pulled to one side. She stood above Ruby, A finger brushing tenderly along the edges of her sex, the soft folds barely dropped below the outer lips, her pearl poked attentively out of the top of her hood. A faint trickle of moisture hung from the lips as rivulets of liquid ran down her inner thigh. A small thin triangular patch of dark red fur sat just above.

Bianca grabbed Ruby by the hair one last time, pulling Ruby into her, setting her mouth against warm wet lips. "Now I'm going to let these men have their way with you." She continued coldly, holding Ruby's mouth to her dripping flower. Too long removed from a female lover, Bianca enjoyed the feel of Ruby's velvety tongue and mouth on her. Ruby looked up. Those needy blue eyes staring up along Bianca's luscious womanly body. The lusty expression on Ruby's face told Bianca she'd lost her young pet in the moment as the brown-haired guy stepped up to relieve his friend. Frantic animalistic grunts pushed her nubile body deeper into Bianca's moist slit again and again.

Her expression was warm, approving as she watched. Finally, after a short moment, Bianca pulled Ruby's face away. Kneeling down, running her tongue along Ruby's chin.

"If you give them what they want, I will let you pleasure me." Her eyes stared deep into Ruby's as she ran her tongue around Ruby's mouth. She could see the need in those eyes. It was approval in the most assuring way. "Boys, she's all yours. Do what you want, but don't hurt her or you answer to me."

She let Ruby's head go dismissively, walking back to the chair. Letting the teddy slip off as she sat down in the high back red velvet chair in the corner, her expression was back to predatory. One leg up on the arm, Bianca softly played with herself as Ruby stared, body rocking back and forth with each deeper thrust.

At the suggestion that they were free to use her body, muscular guy stepped up beside the brown-haired guy and whispered something in his ear. Whatever the suggestion was, judging by how brown hair promptly pulled out of Ruby, Bianca knew it would be interesting. With nothing holding her up or keeping her moving, Ruby collapsed onto the bed, her ass in the air. Bianca knew that look. A contented, sexualized high that fogged her young mind with swirls of color, scents, noises and images. Ruby was calm, stoic in her arousal.

Her eyes stared up at Bianca sitting nonchalantly in the chair, fingers gingerly caressing the twisted pink lips between her legs. Bianca saw the goosebumps, the way Ruby's body shivered gently, like there was a soft electrical current running along her skin. Ruby's breath came out erratic, broken, but there wasn't the slightest bit of fear or protest in her eyes like before. There was serenity in her face.

Bianca watched as the men talked. Curiosity twisted her mind. This was the first time trying this. There was a risk, there was in everything she did. Leaving these men to their own devices has its problems and possibilities. She watched as eventually they carefully lifted Ruby up off of her belly. The muscular guy's hands cupping each of her breasts as he lifted her like a rag doll into the air. Brown hair lay down in her spot on his back, his bulbous head like a mushroom on top of a thinner shaft standing at attention.

Positioned like some inanimate sex doll, Ruby straddle brown hair, pushing once again into her dripping sex. Ruby moaned loudly now as he filled her. His hands went to her pert round breasts. She accepted her position and started to slowly ride him, enjoying the sense of him moving inside her. Her moans, the moans of a woman actively enjoying her lovers, came out faster as she gyrated back and forth on his hips. Her eyes closed she'd lost track of the other guy.

Muscular guy slipped up behind, hands on her hip and back. He was straddling brown-hair too, his tip brushing against her ass cheeks. Before she could protest, before her eyes could even open, Ruby went forward until she was hovering over brown-hair.

Suddenly, Ruby's head spun around, eyes wide as she felt muscular guys sleek uncut head press against her backdoor. Ruby turned back to look at Bianca, a pleading look in her eye as she moaned through her growing pleasure. Inch by inch the warm rubbery tip of his condom encased member tempted her hole. Ruby's body was uncertain, shifting between pleasure and pain, tensing then relaxing as Brown hair thrust up into her in time with his friends next push. Fear and uncertainty filled her eyes. Bianca wondered if it was a fear of being hurt or a fear of the unknown. The calm was still in her face, but uncertainty too.

In that moment Muscular guy pushed past the ring, Bianca could see it. That shift in her young student's body, the tranquil acceptance. It spread through her body again. Ruby's eyes bulged, her mouth opened, body clenched as she felt him push until sheathed inside her. Ruby caught Bianca's expression. Her teacher felt a dark arousal seeing her accept this as the way she was. It was impossible to know if Ruby read the foxy grin on her face as lust or pride.

Before muscular guy could start pumping, Ruby let out a moan that echoed from the walls. Her body flushed with an orgasm that pulled her spine back into the man on top of her. By the look on her face, Bianca wondered if the young girl ever experienced an orgasm like that in her life.

"Gawd… oh phuck!" Brown hair exclaimed against clenched teeth. Bianca could only guess a combination of the two men rubbing together deep inside, separated by the thinnest of membrane in her bowels, lit a fire deep inside her that threatened to consume Ruby. Her body visibly clenched hard as she rode both of them with utter abandon.

All sense of control or regard fell away from Ruby. Her body writhed uncontrollably. There was a look of utter loss of reality in her face as they filled her so utterly.

She clenched and milked at both swollen members until both men groaned with her, in what would have easily been a deep breeding had they not been wearing rubbers.

The orgasm ripped through her body for an eternity. Bianca's expression turned lustful as she watched time and space crash down on Ruby's mind, her body exploding with energy then suddenly collapsing against Brown hairs chest.

Soaked in sweat, her breath more ragged. She fought for every breath. Numb with pleasure, barely flinched when Muscular guy collapsed behind her, ripping himself from her hole. Hair matted with sweat, stuck chaotically against her face, Ruby looked up at Bianca, her eyes half open like she was high. There was a new expression on her student's face as she regarded the woman sitting and watching. There was a look of realized and accepted position.

What did she see now? Her teacher, her mentor, her mistress?, Bianca let the question float around in her mind like a butterfly as she considered their new relationship.

Eventually she rose from her chair and walked over to the bed. "Thank you gentlemen. I trust you enjoyed yourself. There is a bathroom through that door and on the other side a door back to the foyer." Brown hair slipped out a while ago and Muscular guy lay on the bed panting. Brown-hair merely pushed Ruby to the side and rose from the bed.

She reacted like a ragdoll, her mind shrouded by fog, showing in her apparent lack of concern with being pushed off like a piece of meat. Both men picked up their discarded underwear and walked into the aforementioned bathroom. As the door closed, there came a resounding click leaving Ruby on the bed in a heap with her teacher naked standing over her, a lustful smirk on her face.

"You did well my pet." Bianca finally said after a long silence, sitting on the bed beside Ruby, her hand pulling the tangled, sweat twisted, reddish hair from her face. Reaching down between her legs, Bianca ran her fingers along the folds of her lips, cupping some of her sticky juices between her fingers. "Now it's time to please your mistress." She breathed into Ruby's ear before slipping her slick, juicy fingers into Ruby's mouth, smearing her arousal over those full pink lips. "Follow me. Leave your clothes."

Ruby's mind was numb. All she wanted to do was sleep, to get some food and sleep, but there was a burning desire in her that urged her forward. Sitting up on the bed, she pushed herself up. "No, no, my pet. On your hands and knees."

Bianca scolded softly.

Ruby wasn't sure what game she was playing, but there was a look in her teacher's eyes that said doing what she asked would be amazing.

Without argument, Ruby dropped to her hands and knees and followed Bianca. Eyes glued feverishly to the full round globes of her teachers buttocks swaying side to side as she followed. The soft sway of her hips hid the treasure between them, just barely giving a glance here and there. Bianca led her down the single, dimly lit hall in the opposite direction until they reached a door.

The door opened to reveal an elevator. It was small, large enough for two adults standing side by side. Bianca stepped in, tapping her leg like she might a dog to come forward. Ruby followed, Bianca's hand softly caressing her head as she pulled Ruby's face in between her legs. "Sit and sniff, it's not time yet." Bianca reminded her, as Ruby sat on the backs of her ankles, her face a mere inch from the treasure between her legs. The scent of Bianca's arousal was overpowering as it flooded Ruby's senses, causing her to swoon. Her pussy ached, the tension of her raging abuse suddenly gone.

The ride was quick, a minute, maybe less, then the door opened to a large studio apartment. Full walls on the right and left and a half wall in front of the elevator hid the sparse, well-decorated space from view. The decor spoke of clean, wealthy tastes. Most of the furniture was white or silver, black marble counter tops in the kitchen and a matte black high dining table surrounded by tall high-back chairs. Cool white tile spread across the expansive floor of the main rooms. A large glass wall along the far side of the apartment showed the lights of old town New Orleans and the Mississippi river in its entire splendor.

Her hand still on the back of Ruby's head, Bianca led her pet to the balcony. Opening the sliding glass door, the cool moist air of early fall tickled both of them, running along their sweat drenched skin. A waist high frosted glass railing ran along the edge of the long thin patio.

Bianca walked over to a padded lounge chair with high square arms and sat down.

"Take your reward, my pet. Please me." She ordered softly, spreading her legs wide, with no concern for their surroundings.

Ruby felt the uncertainty slip back into her mind. *What if someone saw them, what if they got caught?* Her mind raced, but as she looked from Bianca's wet, inviting lips to her eyes, Ruby's fear dissolved. She crawled forward until her face was against the inside of Bianca's thigh. Her tongue snaked out tentatively, lightly brushing the tip against the swollen pink lips. Each lip glistened in the light of the city around them.

"It's not an ice cream. Eat me out slut or I'll find something less enjoyable for you to do." The word hit Ruby like a ton of bricks. Images of what she'd just endured ran through her mind. How she'd allowed two strange men to take her made her feel used and dirty and slutty. But then something inside reminded her of the chances she had to walk away; of how much she wanted it, enjoyed, and accepted it.

Just as she'd resolved herself to the idea that eating out Bianca on the patio of her apartment was the least of the things she'd done, her teacher's hand grabbed the back of her head and pulled. "I said eat me." Her tone was cold again, powerful and demanding.

Ruby's mouth descended on her teacher like she was thirst parched. Her mouth ate hungrily, licking every drop from those twisted pink folds. Her scent surrounded Ruby, penetrated her mind, as euphoria fell over her consciousness.

Bianca moaned with pleasure, so loud Ruby was certain the city had heard it.

Licking and sucking at her sex, pushing her tongue between the folds into her teacher's deep canal, Ruby cherished every second until finally Bianca's thrust her hips forward. and groaned in a deep throaty appreciation. Her body shook. Her hand held Ruby down, not letting her mouth leave its spot as her legs twitched and flexed.

Finally, free of the spreading pleasure across her body, Bianca released Ruby's head. Gasping for air the young girl continued to kiss and lick at her prize, savoring every drop. Ruby kissed along Bianca's inner thigh and licking errant drops of juices escaping her lips, listening to her mentor's breathing slow. Bianca finally touched the side of her cheek with the tenderness she'd used earlier trying to calm Ruby.

"Come here." She urged Ruby to up onto the chair, pulling her face up. She held Ruby's eyes with a intent gaze as she rose, until Bianca could lean forward. Their mouths met as lips connected in a passionate dance. The kiss was sensual, as both women shifted and changed, suckled or nibbled at each other's lips and tongues.

Bianca eventually broke the kiss, her eyes still holding Ruby in her spell.

"You'll spend the night with me tonight. I promised I would explain, so in the morning I will explain how this works." Without further comment or entertaining questions, Bianca stood, taking her pet by the hand and leading her to the large airy bedroom. The bed was big enough for four people, but Bianca pulled Ruby close as they came together under the sheets. She wasn't sure what had happened, or what would happen from here on, but Ruby knew tonight she was in heaven.

Sleep came fast for Bianca as she'd laid in bed curled up behind Ruby. She enjoyed the feeling of her new pet's ravaged body at peace pressed against her own. They'd fallen asleep with Bianca softly caressing her arm and playing with her soft strawberry blond hair.

Sleeping with someone who wasn't a client, rarely ever happened anymore. Bianca enjoyed the difference being close to Ruby brought. There was something different about Ruby, and suddenly realizing the this was more than a game surprised Bianca.

Ruby brought something out of her that only Ashley ever could, and Ruby did it unconsciously, where her relationship with Ashley took months to form. *Maybe it was the euphoria of the moment* she considered? Bianca dismissed the thought almost as soon as she heard it, accepting that there was more growing between them.

Considering the night they spent together, Bianca would have happily spent the morning enjoying the warm comfort of closeness as they slumbered together. She might have given into that if not for the soft stir beside her in the bed. The sense of someone else in bed was strange enough; to feel movement while she was half asleep with her eyes still closed broke into her consciousness like an alarm.

Her mind shot awake, urging Bianca to open her eyes to see where her young pet was going. Just as she did the sensation of tentative softness of Ruby's hands on her thighs caused her to purr gently. Hand's tenderly pushed her thighs apart. Bianca's thighs parted, exposing the warm apex to the cool chill of the morning air.

A gentle dance of fingers caressing the insides of her thighs drew another purr as they eventually explored the edges of her nether lips. Bianca lay back, pretending to sleep as she spread her legs further allowing closer exploration, enticing Ruby to follow her desires.

Never one to deter enthusiasm of her pets at serving her, Bianca knew at this early stage in her learning and development, Ruby needed encouragement to seek opportunities to pleasure her.

It only took a few minutes before the exploration turned from fingers to tongue and lips. Her mouth opened, letting a sharp wanton sigh escape as she felt Ruby's warm breath hit her lips, followed closely by the heated wetness of her tongue brushing against her more sensitive parts.

It didn't take long for her body to respond. The tip of her eager tongue played attentively along her folds. The night before, Bianca insisted that Ruby aggressively suck and lick her, but today she let the newness and fascination with the experience guide her new plaything. She wanted Ruby genuinely find enjoyment in exploring and pleasuring her mistress.

Before long, Ruby's warm thick tongue broke in, spreading her petals, exploring the inner edge of her quickly moistening flower. Bianca felt her breasts tingle, firmness swelling them as her nipples grew erect. Ruby's mouth descended around her lips, sucking at them, drinking at the moistness forming along the edges. One of Bianca's hands found her breast, mashing the pillowy flesh, pinching the hard nipple. Her other hand reached down, fingers spreading tenderly through those strawberry blond locks.

"Yes pet, just like that." She prodded, her hips gently twisting with the tongue to increase the range traveled between her folds.

A muffled moan came from below, pulling her attention to the girl between her legs. The angle was odd, but by the way her hips were moving Bianca concluded that Ruby was playing with herself and enjoying what she was doing with utter abandon.

"No coming my pet." Bianca ordered as she felt her own orgasm starting to build. Delaying or denying gratification was one of the best, most powerful forms of domination a woman like her could use, and she needed to make sure that Ruby understood who controlled that now.

Ruby's hand slid out from under her young firm body, reaching up as her thumb brushed the swollen nub at the top of Bianca's petals. Bianca pulled the hand from Ruby's hair, grabbing sex smeared hand pulled from between Ruby's legs and pulled it up to her own face.

She could smell the sweet tangy scent of Ruby's arousal on those fingers long before they reached her face. Supporting herself on an elbow, Bianca's mouth encircled and sucked Ruby's fingers, savoring Ruby's juices for the first time. She moaned through closed lips around her pet's fingers at the combination of fresh wetness in her mouth and the attention her pet was giving her slit.

That hungry tongue sliding across her swollen pearl lit the fuse that quickly ran up through her belly and threw Bianca into the throes of an intense orgasm. Falling back to the bed, her hand grabbed Ruby's hair, urging her selfishly into her needy honeypot, holding her attention at one spot as electricity of carnal release tore along her skin. Limbs bucked and writhed violently as spasms clenched her legs all the way to her toes.

Ruby held on for all she was worth, licking and sucking through it all as Bianca growled like a caged lion at the intensity pushing up from her belly to her head.

Finally expelling the orgasm with an exasperated sigh that would likely scare small children, her body went limp. "Oh… my… gawd… little one." Bianca fought for words, full flush breasts heaving up and down. Her body shook, mild tremors centered on her core kept the tension in her muscles. "Come here."

She invited Ruby with a hand on her chin, guiding her up to her Mistresses mouth. With a sultry lick, Bianca's tongue collected up a few errant drops of her juice hanging below those young tender lips before pulling Ruby into a deep passionate kiss.

It was amazing to taste herself on the mouth of someone who so eagerly attended to her body. Their tongues danced for a long moment as Bianca pulled at Ruby's with her lips, sucking it like a small flexible phallus.

A hand-held Ruby close from the back of her head, even though she made no move to pull away. Sated with the kiss, Bianca let her young pet free, her hand slipping down along the soft supple shoulder to the pert swollen mounds on her chest.

"Did my little pet enjoy that?" Bianca asked in a whisper as fingers worked the small pink nipple between them, slowly applying progressive amounts of pressure as her eyes watched Ruby's response.

There was a distinguishable progression of pleasure in her eyes as they half closed. Her mouth opened and her breath grew more ragged. She answered with a nod. "I didn't hear you pet, did you enjoy pleasing your mistress?" Her young apprentice's mouth opened as if trying to respond as a throaty whisper drew out between her lips. "I didn't hear you." Bianca said, her other hand slipping between the moist folds between Ruby's legs, two fingers pinched Ruby's swollen pearl between them. Her young body jolted at the feeling, her mouth hanging opened as a mix of pleasure and pain coursed through her.

"Yes…. Mis… Mistress." She finally said in a much more audible throaty reply.

"That's my good little slut." Bianca replied, giving her one last bit of pressure on both regions before releasing her. "Now go into the shower and clean yourself up. You had two strange men using your body last night and you smell like a whore." Bianca said in a soft dismissive tone, that likely didn't match the warm adoration in her eyes.

She could see by the look in Ruby's expression that she was having trouble reconciling the the tone and words with the shared moment. The long pause before obeying told Bianca that Ruby was still questioning what she'd gotten herself into.

Finally, crawling across the bed toward the door leading to the bathroom, Bianca watched her slender body move with fascination and something more than mere carnal attraction. "No playing with yourself in there. I'll know if you do." Bianca called after her, before taking a moment to stretch herself to the extent of her still tingling relaxed muscles.

As soon as she heard the water running, Bianca pulled herself out of bed. She twisted her hair up into a bun on the back of her head and threw on a thigh length silk robe as she walked to the door to the bathroom. Leaning against the frame, Bianca watched through the quickly fogging glass as steam filled the large octagonal enclosure. Inside, Ruby washed herself diligently without a word or question. The edges of her lips curled into a grin. With a bright twinkle in her eyes, watched with admiration, arms crossed over her half exposed breasts.

Certain that Ruby would follow her instructions and refrain from any indulgences, Bianca walked through the open floor plan studio apartment to the kitchen. She moved through the kitchen, pulling sliced fruit and some bread from the refrigerator. Her untied robe swayed and swung, exposing her naked body, though exposing nakedness to the world had never bothered her.

Tossing a coffee capsule in to her European coffee machine, the soft churn of hot water being pushed through shrouded the sound of the shower in the other room. Just as her coffee finished, a very uncertain young woman wearing nothing, but a towel wrapping her torso stepped into the kitchen.

"Ahh… good. You're done. Are you hungry?" Bianca asked, walking around the bar at the front of the kitchen where Ruby was standing. Ruby nodded quietly. Bianca found her uncertainty warming and only made her more curious about pushing her new toy as far as she could. "Stay here." Bianca ordered before walking back into the bathroom.

Reaching into a drawer near the door to the bathroom, Bianca pulled out a large peach colored dildo. Embedded into the base of the dildo was a flat white plastic suction cup.

"Here, sit down." Bianca ordered, pressing the dildo down onto the seat of a hard dark wood chair on the front side of the bar. Ruby blinked up at her in confusion. Resistance and trepidation hung behind those gentle, soft blue eyes. There was tension in her arms and shoulders. Bianca wondered if she wanted to disobey, to run away, to leave this behind. Her mouth half opened to say something.

Something changed in her expression. Mind and body, right and wrong, fought a conflict. As if realizing two men ravaging her body was just a taste of what she might experience. Bianca recognized the look on her face, that look that if she walked away, she would close a door on something that would change her as a person and she'd never be able to get back in.

There was a long silent moment, as if time stopped as she stood still, staring at the large thick vertical dildo. Bianca didn't move or say a word. Her expression unchanged. Her stone cold demeanor and the warm insistence in her eyes refused to show any glimmer of change to her young apprentice.

Finally, likely deciding that doing as Bianca asked was the least of what might happen to her, Ruby stepped up on the stool, her crotch hovering precariously over the soft pink phallus. Pulling the edge of the towel up, she spread her lips with two fingers before dropping slowly along the soft fleshy shaft.

Bianca was uncertain if she was wet from the shower or still from playing in bed, but Ruby showed no discomfort or hesitation as the firm dildo impaled her belly. Her eyes half-closed and mouth fell open as a silent moan escaped her lips. Within a moment, her ass pressed down onto the chair, accepting the fullness of the intruder.

"Good girl." Bianca said finally, reaching and pulling the towel from her body, leaving it sitting on the counter. Ruby sat on the chair staring at her like some wounded Doe, trying to figure out how to get away but realizing she couldn't.

Bianca returned to her breakfast preparations without further discussion, letting the moment simmer between them. She stopped Ruby playing with herself in the bed, leaving the young girl yearning for a release. It would only be a matter of time before those hips gyrated on the thick dildo.

Pulling a large pitcher of orange juice from the fridge, pouring two full glasses, then spooning two hearty servings of cut fruit from a bowl onto two separate plates, Bianca went about setting up breakfast as silence fell over the kitchen.

"So I imagine you're wondering what's next?" She finally asked, placing a piece of toasted bread on each plate. Setting a plate in front of her naked pet and a plate at the side of the bar, then setting a glass of orange juice and silverware at each plate, Bianca waited for Ruby to reply.

She purposefully kept moving to discourage the young girl from giving a non-verbal response. Grabbing the coffee she'd made before and a plate of chilled butter, Bianca sat so she could see Ruby. When no response came, Bianca remained silent, quietly sipping at her coffee.

Those young blue eyes stared down at the food before her, tortured uncertainty in her expression as she came to terms with her situation. The curious twist was the soft, almost imperceptible movement of her hips flared her arousal. Her taut naked breasts and the straining nipples at their tips grew flush and Bianca could tell Ruby was enjoying this as much as it conflicted her.

"Am I your slave now?" An almost incoherent murmur finally escaped her lips as Bianca picked at the fruit on her plate.

"I'm sorry, what?" She asked, her voice still cool and emotionless as she pushed a large piece of cut cantaloupe between her lips. Her eyes never left Ruby's face, watching every movement, every expression. She was gauging, testing. She could see the conflict raging inside her mind, her body and soul fighting an epic battle.

Up to this point, fear, curiosity and pleasure kept her malleable. That could change in an instant if Bianca couldn't capitalize on the strides she'd made before logic and reality overpowered desire and need.

"Am I your slave now?" Ruby answered with a more resounding tone in her voice as her hand gradually reached for the glass of orange juice, raising it to her lips. Bianca put the fork she'd used on the melon back on the plate, her hand reaching out to firmly tweak one of Ruby's hard nipples between her fingers. The motion caused her pet to jump at the unexpected move. Ruby's body must have clenched against the dildo impaling her as Ruby sucked in breath sharply, trying to stifle a moan.

"Slave? No. I don't take slaves." Bianca replied dismissively, her fingers releasing the now red throbbing nipple to reach up and take Ruby's face by the chin and turn it to her. "Slave implies you are here because you don't have a choice." She said, her voice softer and warmer than it had been before, hoping to give Ruby a lifeline to hold on to. "You are here by choice, my pet. You can leave whenever you want." She said, their eyes locked in understanding. "However, if you leave out of fear or anger, when I haven't dismissed you, you'll never return."

Her fingers released Ruby's chin. They gently slide down along her shoulder to the swell of her breast and along the rolling edge of her firm mounds. They traced the back of her fingers along the underside of those ripe supple globes.

"If you dedicate yourself to me, I will open to you an amazing world that will truly show you who you really are." She could see the tension in Ruby's chest as her heart rate picked up. The bulbous dildo piercing her belly was becoming hard to resist, and the attention on her breasts wasn't helping.

Ruby clumsily forked a piece of melon and pushed it into her mouth. She was quickly losing the battle her body waged, and she knew it. Bianca watched her chew. A finger barely caressed the underside of her breast with a feather touch.

"I guess if I leave you'll fail me or kick me out of class?" She finally said after chewing through her melon. The assertion caused Bianca to sigh visibly. She rolled her eyes, then reminded herself that she needed to reassure the girl not demean her. There would be time for that later. Getting her to stay on her own accord was necessary for this to work.

"Ruby darling, you dealt with your grade last night when you arrived at the bar. You said you were there because you wanted to be. As far as I'm concerned, you've shown more commitment to this class than most." Her hand shifted from the breast to the girl's upper arm, giving her a reassuring caress. "Everything you did last night was something you wanted, right?"

Bianca pushed, subtly reminding the young girl she was free to stop at any point if she wanted to. "I want you with me. I want to show you your limitless potential and the freedom that brings, but you need to believe that you're here because you want to be, not because you owe me something." Her hand went back to the fork on the counter as she ate a few pieces of fruit, letting her words germinate in her young apprentices mind for a bit.

"Yes, Mistress." was all she said. It was all she had to say to tell Bianca that she was ready for the next step. All she could do was sit and stare in admiration at the strength and conviction Ruby was showing in that moment.

Here she was sitting naked on a stool, impaled by a thick fleshy dildo, bared and vulnerable to the world around her, and she accepted it as if this were what she'd always wanted. Bianca smiled like a proud parent.

Standing from her seat she moved closer to Ruby, a hand wrapped behind her head, pressing their lips into a slow lingering kiss. Her other hand slid down Ruby's taut belly, past her pelvis to the swollen pearl between engorged spread lips.
Her finger tenderly pressed and rolled the swollen nub between two fingers as her tongue explored. She felt Ruby moan into her mouth, her body responding to the caress.

Breaking the kiss, Bianca held her eyes in a thoughtful gaze, her fingers played a minute longer. The pleading desire in those young eyes was powerful and needy. Her breath quickened with each flick of the nub.

"I didn't give you permission to come yet." Bianca reminded her softly as she twiddled Ruby. Fingers wet with her juices, slid down and pried the suction cup from the flat of the chair. "Hold on tight. If you want to orgasm today, you'll keep this inside you." Bianca ordered as she took Ruby by the hand, easing her out of the chair.

Ruby's hand reached down to catch it before Bianca chastised her with a swat to the ass, leaving a quickly fading red hand print. "Clench down, Keep it in without hands. Now walk." Bianca hissed softly, leading her pet back toward the bed.

The tension in her pelvic muscles would make walking slow and arduous. Not wanting to wait for her tentative slut to reach the bed, Bianca walked ahead, keeping a wary eye on the progress till she reached the bed.

Reaching into the lower drawer of her nightstand, Bianca pulled out a black fabric harness with an embedded attachment at the crotch. She slid the harness up her legs, tightening the straps at her waist as the duckling finally waddled her way to the bed. "On your hands and knees, ass in the air." She ordered coldly.

Ruby could see the harness she wore as the robe she was wearing dropped from her arms to a bundle on the floor. Walking behind Ruby, she placed one hand on the base of the dildo protruding from her twat as the other grabbed the white suction cup. With a tense pop, the tip of the suction cup pushed up into the dildo came free.

Those young legs quivered as they strained to keep the thick intruder between her dripping lips. Slick juices ran down the inside of her thigh. Bianca ran the tip of the suction cup along the inside of those firm quivering legs, slathering Ruby's arousal all over it.

Without so much as a warning, Bianca gradually pressed the ridged tip of the suction cup attachment against Ruby's puckered rear hole. A quiet groan of protest started but quickly stopped as the tip slipped inside her, held at the edge of her ass by the large round disk.

Her legs shook harder as Bianca pulled her close, lining up the black tip on her harness that was a replica to the tip of the suction cup. Pressing deep, eliciting a lustful moan from her obedient slut, the tip pushed into the hole at the back of the dildo, locking it onto the harness. "This is what you want isn't it, pet. Getting fucked like some dirty slut." Bianca teased as her hips began pulling the dildo to the edge of her canal, only to press it to the hilt again and again.

"Yes Mistress, please fuck me!" Ruby moaned between thrusts. Bianca picked up the pace slowly until she was sawing deeply into the slit once or twice a second. All she heard from her pet were groans and moans mixed with the sound of slick slurps as the fleshy dildo pumped into her.

"I didn't give you permission to come yet." Bianca reminded the young girl as familiar sounds of a growing orgasm overcame the other moans of pleasure. "If you want to come, you need my permission." Bianca asserted as her finger applied pressure to the white rubber ring pressed against her anus, her intensity slowing to long deep thrusts every second or so.

"May…. I… come Mistress?" Ruby groaned through ragged breaths, her mind fighting to resist the urge.

Bianca smiled. *How quickly she learns.* She thought to herself before leaning down to grab those pert globes of flesh in each hand. Pushed in to the hilt, the older woman pulled Ruby up off of her hands until she pressed against Bianca's body, her full voluptuous globes against the young muscular back. Hips still thrusting against the insides of Ruby's tight walls.

"Tell me you want to be mine." Bianca whispered into an ear as she softly nibbled on the lobe.

"I am yours to use and command Mistress." Ruby replied breathlessly as her body shuddered to resist any further.

Bianca moaned. She loved hearing her young pet say that.

"That's not what I asked you." She growled, her finger abruptly mashing each nipple between them as she bit down hard on the soft lobe in her mouth, her hips still thrusting hard and deep.

"I want to be yours, Mistress. Please may I be yours?" Ruby fought to get the words out in a coherent sentence. She was trying to sound certain and confident in the wake of everything that warmed Bianca and reignited that feeling of pride in her chest.

"Now you may come my pet." Bianca said after a long moment.

On cue, Ruby's body erupted and shook like a torrent. Hours of pent up need ignited in her belly and spread through her like wildfire. Slamming her head back against Bianca's shoulder. Holding her close, she let Ruby's young body deal with the intruders in its own way as her hips bucked and writhed against the thickness inside.

A throaty mind splitting groan erupted from her chest, escaping through her mouth, the force of her orgasm riveting through her body into Bianca's. Holding her tight and secure, Bianca held her close until the full force passed. Finally, feeling Ruby go limp, Bianca leaned back to the bed, letting her drop to the firm padding.

With a sloppy pop, the slick, cum drenched dildo fell out of Ruby's overworked canal. A stream of milky white film smeared across the head. Feeling satisfaction in earning the trust and submission, Bianca lay on the bed on her side, her hand tenderly caressing and tracing the accented curves of her young lover's body. Ruby lay quiet, still on her belly, the only sign of life was the soft rise and fall of her back against the mattress.

They must have laid that way for twenty minutes before Ruby stirred, her head turning along with her body until she was facing her Mistress.

"So now what?" She asked eventually. Like a crystal clear pool of water, her soft blue eyes looked as if someone pulled a great shroud from her sight. "Do I come live with you or you keep me chained up in your dungeon downstairs?" She added with a bit of a curl on her lips and a jovial tone in her voice that made Bianca match her expression.

"In public unless I specifically designate the event, you are my student and you will act accordingly. I know you have a busy life so I don't expect you to always be available."

Bianca's gaze swept up and down Ruby's naked body, drinking up the events of the previous day with relish.

"There are nights I will not be available. But when you wish to see me, you will ask me before you come over. You are welcome to spend the night, but there's no guarantee you'll be sleeping in my bed." Bianca reminded her she was a pet, not a lover. "There may be an event I want you to join me. These events may come up with little notice. I will never demand that you sacrifice work or school work to join me, but if you do, I promise you you will enjoy it and will be well compensated for your time."

The plan had never been to involve Ruby into any of her business. After the last night with the two men, it dawned on Bianca how having a submissive pet to join a few select clients might be beneficial to her training and to her financial issues.

"Wait, what?" Ruby asked, pushing herself up on her arms, having caught that there was now a financial component in this.

"It's too soon, forget I mentioned it." Bianca dismissed the suggestion.

"Please Mistress, tell me how I can serve you." Ruby said, reaching out a hand to softly cup her arms in her young palm.

"I will never order you to do this pet. But I have a select group of… friends who are very generous when a woman can give them a certain attention and discretion that they can't get anywhere else." Bianca tried very hard to be as vague as possible. She knew there wasn't any chance that Ruby would turn on her, but the fear of Ruby finding out what she did on the side and breaking the very fragile bond they had just built was very real.

"You're an escort?" She asked after a long thoughtful silence, a mischievous grin on her face as she lay on the bed, her head supported by her arm. Her young taut breasts hung to the side, but barely lost their shape.

"After a fashion yes. I am a Dominatrix, but I attend clients in public and private as a part of the service." The look in Ruby's eyes changed slightly as her mind processed. Those young innocent eyes roamed her body for a long minute without changing or answering. It dawned on Bianca because Ruby hadn't stood up and walked out, that there was a real possibility that she was considering the offer.

"And you would have me do what? Like we were last night?" Her tone was more inquisitive than incredulous, like the night before when Bianca suggested she offer herself to the two men at the bar. Staring down at that young uncertain face, Bianca reached down and ran the back of her fingers across Ruby's full pale cheek.

"First my pet, beyond last night, as long as you are with me, you will never be in the company of strangers. Every one of my clients I research and vet before I ever meet them. Second, most of my clients prefer to being dominated, so you will be as much a plaything as you will be an instrument of my domination."

Her hand left Ruby's cheek and recounted its earlier journey to her breast, rolling one of the small pink nipples between her fingers. "Third, if you agree to join me, while you will enjoy some financial freedom you could never have found by yourself, you will do whatever I tell you to do without question or hesitation." She finished with a rough pull on the small tender flesh. The action brought a groan of mixed pleasure and pain to her young face, her eyes half closed and her mouth half open.

"I will join you mistress if you will have me." Ruby finally said after a long silence.

The answer had been almost as profound as when she'd said 'Yes Mistress' after being given the choice to leave or stay. Pleased with the answer, Bianca's hand slid back past her pets belly to the moist patch of skin between her legs. She leaned in as her fingers rubbed the edges of Ruby's slit.

"I will have you many, many times my pet." Bianca said in a sultry whisper before her mouth and fingers descended on their targets. Like at the counter, Bianca kissed her new toy passionately while playing teasingly with the swollen overworked clit.

She felt her girl swell up at the touch like her hand applied a live electrical current to her skin. Just as her young lover fell into the attention, Bianca pulled away to a very disappointed moan.

"I'm hungry. Come, eat your breakfast." She said, standing from the bed, letting the harness slip from her hips to fall discarded to the floor. Bianca walked naked and fluid into the kitchen. She could feel Ruby's eyes on her as she walked. It only fomented the decision that she'd made the right choice in this girl.

I can't go back, I was a different person

Ruby lay on the bed watching her teacher walk back into the kitchen, the sun creating a warm glow along the edges of her lusciously curvy body. Still numb from the power of the orgasm and the constant state of arousal she'd been in for the last day, Ruby barely moved when Bianca had suggested she come eat breakfast. As far as she could tell, it was a suggestion, not an order, those had been obvious up to this point. That the woman was walking around the apartment nude as the day she was born wasn't lost on Ruby as she realized she'd lost track of her clothes. The last she could remember she'd taken them off in the room where she'd become a fuck toy for two strange men.

Everything the past day presented regarding experiences excited her beyond anything that she ever imagined. There was a nagging doubt in the back of her mind, that she would get herself into something terrible that would end up ruining her reputation or turning her into some pariah. Looking around at the lavish apartment this woman owned, to include the sex dungeon in the basement, Ruby couldn't help but think she was very good at everything she did, even convincing men to pay her for a service.

Pushing herself up off of the bed, tentatively testing her legs as they felt like rubber bands below her weight, Ruby eventually worked her way into the kitchen, approaching the seat she'd been in. She eyed it tentatively, before looking back up to Bianca seated in her chair, eating naked to the world.

"You miss the dildo? I can put it back?" Bianca said with her head slightly cocked to the side, her eyes half closed in a predatory stare that was becoming familiar. Her voice, uncharacteristically jovial, made the expression seem playful.

Ruby gave a meek smile, shaking her head softly at the suggestion before pulling herself up into the chair.

It felt curiously absent of something as she sat. *Now that's just weird.* Her mind wrestled with the sensation as she picked up the piece of toast. Slathering butter over the cold toasted bread then biting into it. The fascination of food after so many hours without seemed to fill a hunger inside her that had taken a back seat to other hungers driving her.

"Do you have class today?" Her teacher asked before forking a piece of fruit into her mouth. Ruby looked around the kitchen for a clock. *9:30?* It took her mind time to remember what day it was. The last twenty-four hours were such a fog of constant lust, desire and hunger she'd forgotten the day.

79

"I missed physics. I have chem three at twelve then I have your class at three." She replied finally recalling the day and the schedule. Missing physics would hurt considering her professor only allowed two absences a semester. Thankfully, she had chemistry three later which meant she didn't really need to study. The scary part of everything was how much she wanted to simply stay here and let Bianca have her way.

Ruby never considered herself to be a submissive person. She knew she didn't have an aggressive personality, but that wasn't the same as far as she knew. It was intriguing how willing she was to let herself go to be with Bianca.

"I'll give you a note for physics." Bianca said over the top of her cup of coffee that had to be room cool by now. "You were being interviewed for an internship at the company and this was the only time we had. We would have given you enough notice to work a plan with your professor, but the timing was short." That all of that had seemed so off the cuff surprised Ruby, having not realized where this arrangement with Bianca would reach.

"Thank you, Mistress…" Ruby was tentatively uncertain where the line between their situation and real life intersected. The reply seemed to please Bianca though based on the soft smile crossing her face at the comment.

"You'll need to figure out a couple of days a week that you can fit in some time at my office." She said dismissively, as if it had been a foregone conclusion. Of course it wasn't, and Ruby's mouth dropped open in surprise at the suggestion.

"Wa… wait what?" She finally worked out of her mind enough to produce only those two words. The suggestion that she missed class for an internship interview was one thing, but being brought on to actually be an intern went way beyond what she had expected this arrangement entailed.

"You thought you were just going to be my plaything, and that's it?" Bianca asked, an inquisitive look on her face. Her tone changed to match, as if she was testing Ruby's answers with a more sardonic tone.

"I… I don't know what to think. I'm still not sure how to act or how to be around you." Ruby replied, her tone docile.

Bianca watched Ruby, letting those emerald green eyes stare deep into her soul as she chewed on a piece of toast.

"You're right, of course. I need to set some ground rules for you, don't I?" She finally suggested, taking the glass of orange juice and enjoying a long sip. "Ok, so… when you are here in the apartment or the rooms downstairs you refer to me as Mistress." She started, her eyes holding Ruby's in a firm commanding stare. "The only clothes you will wear in the apartment are clothes that I will give you. When you come to the apartment, you will enter through the rooms downstairs, strip naked and await instructions." Her eyes continued to hold as she drank more juice, then continued. "When we are in public, you will act normal as if we are acquaintances only and you will refer to me as ma'am or Ms. Ristretto. In the event I introduce you to a client or a friend, you follow that same construct, ma'am in public, Mistress in private. Do you understand so far?"

Ruby nodded. "Yes, Mistress." her response was more assertive but obedient. The way this was playing out differed greatly from anything Bianca imagined.

"Starting mext week you will join on at my firm as an intern working for me. You will do what I tell you and if you're very lucky, you will learn a great deal about many things simply by watching." Bianca continued spelling out the enormity of the situation. "After your time at the office, if you're not working or studying, you will come here and be my plaything. If you would like to come here and study, that is welcome, but if you're going to study, you must keep yourself from being distracted."

The suggestion of studying here had never even crossed Ruby's mind and mentioning it, while enticing as it was, elicited exactly the thoughts she assumed Bianca's rule meant to stop.

"You will need to come up with your own safe word, something innocuous that only you would know but not something you would use in normal conversation. While you are here under my control, that will be the only way that I will know if I am pushing you too far, or too hard, or hurting you in a way that you are uncomfortable with."

While her mistress gave her a safe word and insisted she use it, the implication at the time was a way to stop. Ruby's mind now whirled at the implications. She read enough romance novels and even several trashy porn novels to know that allowed for someone to get extreme with the person being dominated.

Bianca must have seen the change in her expression. A hand reached out and took Ruby's arm, firmly but in a reassuring way.

"You remember how I promised you last night I would protect you and make sure no harm came to you?" Asking in a very tender motherly tone.

Ruby nodded. "You may have given yourself to be my pet, but I promise you that your safety and well-being are paramount in my mind. I will never put you in a situation I don't feel you can endure." Ruby saw the strength and commitment in the older woman's eyes. There was something else there that she couldn't gauge. *Attraction, affection, love?* Ruby's mind tried to put a name to the emotion she saw on her teacher's face before she leaned back in her chair, her full firm breasts hanging against her chest.

"If you intend to join me and my clients, you will need to be comfortable using your safe word if things get out of hand." Bianca said, crossing her arms over her naked chest. "All of my clients are contracted to abide by certain rules. That includes anyone I might bring into the scene." She said with a nod toward Ruby. "Do you have any questions for me." Picking up her cup of coffee, her expression softened, turned more motherly again.

Ruby nibbled absently on a piece of melon as her mind processed everything. Her body tingled along every inch of her skin. Her nipples stood erect and throbbed at the memory of what she'd been through and what the days and weeks ahead could bring.

"Am I required to come at your beg and call? Or do I have freedom about my life?" She blurted out the only real question that rolled through her mind. It was still chewing on the information her teacher gave her like she chewed on her melon.

Bianca smiled, pulling a strand of reddish hair from her face, tucking it behind her ear.

"You are still who you are, Ruby. As I said, you are not my slave. I will never demand your presence. I will request your presence, and if you can make time then while we are together you will be mine to command." Bianca slid out of the chair, stepping closer to where Ruby sat. The scent of sex, her skin, her shampoo, her breath swirled around Ruby as the energy of the proximity became heady and filled her again with desire. Bianca's hand slid up along her face, fingers brushing her cheek as she took a strand of the more strawberry blond hair and tucked it behind her own ear. It was more an act of affection than an act of help. Her hand palmed Ruby's jawbone, turning her head up to look into those deep green eyes.

"My sweet pet, I understand the cost benefit analysis of this may seem a bit off to you right now. But if you trust me and do as I ask, you will find the benefits far outweigh any cost you may pay. But remember, you can walk away anytime you want without question or retribution."

Her closeness, her touch heated Ruby's body, twisting her belly. *What is it about her that has this power over me?* Ruby swooned as she looked up into those green eyes. They looked into her, piercing her soul. Ruby felt herself swell with power and determination.

"Yes Mistress. I understand." She said with genuine obedience as she leaned in and softly suckled on the full erect nipple mere inches from her face.

"Good girl." Was all she heard as a hand lightly caressed her hair, pulling her into the supple flesh, forcing her to suckle like a babe.

After her new pet spent a good while nursing on her breasts, Bianca took some time to prepare an official letter for Ruby's missed classes . She enjoyed the way Ruby tried to please her without being told. Taking some time to get ready while Ruby retrieved her clothes from the playroom, Bianca was feeling good about how things worked out.

Dropping Ruby off at her dorm, having offered her t-shirt and a pair of sweats so she wasn't walking back into her dorm in the middle of the day in a club outfit; Bianca messaged Ashley inviting her to lunch. The one luxury she had with being the manager of her department was the flexibility of schedule. As long as the contracts and project were on schedule, no one questioned, especially when the young female executive calls in at eleven thirty in the morning and cancels the rest of her appointments and meetings for the day.

Ashley's face lit up when Bianca walked onto the restaurant's patio, the midday sun warming her already reddish tan highlights.

"You're glowing!" Standing to give a kiss of greeting on the cheek before Bianca sat down. "Something happen last night?" She asked as a waitress set down a glass of water and offered a menu.

"You could say that…" Bianca replied vaguely as she looked through the menu, eyes hidden by the folded laminated paper.

"That wasn't vague." Ashley's half-closed eyes glared inquisitively as Bianca finally put down the menu. Her best friend would know that the glowing look of contentment on her face was enough to speak how the evening went. Knowing the plan to seduce Ruby to like Ashley did, like any girlfriend, she wanted details.

"Blackened Catfish, a Caesar's salad and a glass of rose wine please." Bianca gave her order to the waitress, then waited for the young girl to smile and walk away. Taking a long sip of water, emerald eyes watched the pain of anticipation growing on Ashley's face. "She's more than I could have imagined looking at her in the beginning." Bianca said, leaning forward, her elbows on the table to keep the conversation between them.

"The last I heard from you she'd left the restaurant and you were going home." Ashley reminded, her head softly tilted to the side with an inquisitive look. "Something changed?" Bianca was good at cold expressions and keeping her emotions in check, but she'd never been very good at hiding her feelings around Ashley. The twinkle in her eye, the expression of mischief on her face gave her away before she ever said a word.

"She came back, didn't she?" Ashley's questioning expression was full of mirth.

"I brought her to Fritzels to talk and things kinda spiraled from there." Bianca whispered, her hand laying atop Ashley's, a thumb gingerly running along the skin at the back of her hand.

"Spiraled?" Ashley asked, the curiosity growing with every word. Bianca took a second to let her eyes scan the area before continuing.

"I was eventually able to get her to offer herself to a couple of guys at the bar."

"What!?" Ashley gasped incredulously, her eyes wide as eggs.

Things certainly spiraled out of control with that situation, and Ruby accepted it all like a champ. "You convinced some new girl you know nothing about and someone who by your own admission was likely very innocent to any of this, to walk up to two men at a bar and offer herself for sex?"

She whispered the last part almost through her teeth to keep others around from hearing. New Orleans was a very progressive town, but that didn't mean they needed to be spreading their news among the public. Bianca nearly nodded, a toothy Cheshire cat grin spread across her face.

"Not just offered." Bianca added, marking the shocked stare in her friend's eyes and the gradual change back to that naughty curiosity she'd had minutes before.

"You took them back to the playroom didn't you?" Ashley shook her head.

It was no wonder; Ashley suggested the apartment in the first place. Close enough to the French Quarter for enjoyable evenings, the addition of the playroom was a bonus. The building went up for sale as a whole in expectation of some business buying the lower part for a store with the upper part being leased for offices or apartments. Being well-known among realtors in town, Ashley got wind of the sale before it went on the market, giving Bianca the chance to bargain before the realtor fees went into effect. Considering the business Bianca was in, having a controlled environment to entertain clients outside of a hotel room seemed a good investment.

"She was incredible. It took her a bit to relax and realize I wasn't going to let them do anything that would hurt her. By the end she was begging for it." Bianca explained in a level proud tone she knew Ashley was used to by now. "In the end, she took everything they did without argument, and even accepted crawling on her hands and knees up to the balcony to finish me." Bianca added, softly biting her lower lip at the memory of seeing Ruby crawling after her through the apartment, then happily attending to her needs on the balcony.

"You took her to the apartment?" Ashley asked, the tone in her voice telling Bianca leery of accepting they'd moved so fast that quickly.

"She slept with me, woke up to her mouth on me. She's insatiable, Ash." Bianca purred.

Ashley sat back in her chair with a look of utter shock on her face. The break in conversation timed perfectly as the food arrived. Both women sat and stared at each other with knowing glances on their faces while the waitress placed the plates of food and asked if there was anything else they needed. They both shook their heads and thanked the girl, wanting quickly to return to the conversation.

"So, what now? Do I get to meet her?" Ashley asked as the waitress walked away.

"You want to play with her." Bianca corrected knowing her friend well.

Ashley could tell that there was more to this girl than some conquest. There was an attraction in Bianca's eyes and voice, and that meant that she needed to gauge how reckless Bianca was being in bringing this girl into her life. Only a few times in their history together Bianca took a lover or became involved in a relationship, and while all of those eventually ended in pain, Ashley always stayed an anchor.

"No, I want to make sure you're not going to ruin your career or life over a girl who's playing with you for a good grade." Ashley teased. Quickly her expression became more animated. "Of course I want to play with her. But I also want to make sure you're not setting yourself up for something dangerous."

"So I guess you'll tell me I'm crazy for hiring her as an intern?" Bianca asked, half laughing at her friend's change of demeanor.

"You are crazy." Ashley barely let Bianca get the words out, shaking her head, then interrupted herself, shaking a fork at her as she chewed. "Actually, that's probably a smart move. Gives you an excuse for being so close."

"It's not that Ash. I don't want this to be just some strange sexual game." Bianca picked absently at her fish. "I see a lot of myself in her, that scared hunger. I guess I want to give it a vehicle to express itself."

"You're in love with her, aren't you?" Ashley said picking up her glass of wine, talking over the rim, her eyes never leaving Bianca's. Bianca shook her head almost immediately with a half scowl on her face.

"It's not like that."

"Yes, it is."

"Ash… Ok, so I'm attracted to her in many ways yes, but there's fire in her I want to mold and fan." Bianca knew there wasn't any hope of hiding her feelings, Ashley knew her well enough she could read the attraction without hearing her say the words.

"Next you're going to tell me you've considered introducing her to your clients." She said with a sarcastic tone, picking at her salad. It took a minute for her to realize the knowing look Bianca was giving her in her sudden and palpable silence.

All Ashley could do was softly laugh to herself and shake her head before taking a bite of her salad. Bianca chewed her catfish in silence, letting her friend process all that they'd discussed. "How would that even work?" She took a sip of her wine.

"I have a few clients that would allow it and would happily submit to her attentions." Bianca explained. The look on her friend's face told her that wasn't the answer she was looking for.

"I mean most of your clients are subs, she's your sub, how would that work?" She clarified causing Bianca to sit back in her chair, arms crossing her chest as she balanced her wineglass between her fingers.

"Honestly Ash, I hadn't thought that far ahead. It just came out that I was essentially an escort while we were talking after I fucked her on my bed." Bianca paused. "She pushed. I wasn't even going to mention it. When I did, she bit." Bianca's eyes lingered on something in the distance as her mind mulled over how she would broach the subject with her clients.

"How does this mold or fan her fire?" Ashley asked finally, realizing Bianca hadn't explained how this would help Ruby in the long run.

Bianca took another bite of her fish and chewed, letting the question hang in the air while she planned a thoughtful answer from the broken ideas floating in her mind. The reality of the situation was that all of this happened way faster than she expected, and Ruby turned out to be way more malleable than she foresaw. That threw a monkey wrench into her plans. Granted, they were good problems to have, but problems.

"A few of my clients are in the fields that would be of interest to a young girl like her to have connections. Remember how vastly my fortunes changed in the business world when I started dating Randal?" Bianca didn't mean to bring up her ex-fiancé, but unfortunately the comparison was fairly apt.

"Randal was a prig. The only reason you got half of the connections you did was because all of his college and work buddies wanted to fuck you." Ashley replied with a scowl on her face. Ashley never liked Randal and vehemently opposed the suggestion of marrying him.

Unfortunately, at the time Bianca was young and fresh and hungry to move up in business and Randal provided that. At least until she caught him fucking his secretary in their living room. That was the first, and only time Bianca dedicated herself to the idea of destroying someone.

Much to Ashley's enjoyment, by the time Bianca finished with him, Randal became such a pariah, a move to Chicago was the only way to get far enough to find work.

"Exactly, and how is this different? I'm going to help her make an impression on some of the industry's top executives. Since they have as much to lose as she would if anything ever came out regarding what she may or may not have done in private, she'll have some powerful references when she graduates."

"In theory." Ashley added, prompting Bianca to shrug and smile at the suggestion.

It was a sound theory. Bianca gained a bit of influence in the business world because of her connections, so why couldn't that influence carry over to her young protégé?

Before either of them could say anything else, Bianca's phone buzzed in her purse. Seeking the sleek metal device, she held it up to see the message. sly adoration spreading across her face.

"What?" Her friend recognized that devious look immediately.

"She wants to know if she can be of service after class." Bianca replied.

Ashley laughed out loud this time.

"You're kidding, right?" She rebuffed the idea until Bianca turned the phone so she could read it. "Mistress. I wish to serve you tonight after class if you wish it." Ashley read the text with surprise and enjoyment. A soft twinkle in her eyes caught Bianca's attention as she looked from the phone to her friend. "She learns quick. Well?" Ashley's expression took on a similarly devious look.

Bianca nodded, pulling her phone back.

"Hello Pet, I would love for you to attend me tonight." Bianca relayed what she typed on her phone. "I have a friend who really wants to meet you. Be ready to go after class." Bianca looked up as Ashley gave a reassuring nod, prompting Bianca to press send.

"You can't be surprised when I'm tender but firm with her." She said putting her phone down and taking another sip of wine.

"It's how you always were with me." Ashley replied with a twisted smile.

She was right of course, there was something about how Bianca approached Ruby and the way she and Ashley were together in college that was far different from how she was with men. Maybe it was a *men are sturdier* mindset or something else, she couldn't say, but Bianca was certain that there were only two women in her life that she'd ever dominated and Ruby was the second.

The two of them spent time as lovers after the curiosity of domination wore off, but never lost the enjoyment of role play. Now that they were best friends, the absolute trust established during those episodes only bound them closer.

"I won't say what I know you're thinking." Bianca said before returning to her food. Ashley's look had been the same as when she'd asked if her friend was falling in love with the young girl. It would definitely be interesting introducing the former pet to the new pet, Bianca thought as she ate, as Bianca and her best friend were surely both thinking of fun ways to test Ruby.

To say the last day had Ruby distracted would be an understatement of historical proportions. She'd walked into the wrong Chemistry room, making her late for class. She left her lab book at home, and had to sit in the quad for an hour because she'd mis-read her physics professor's office hours to deliver Bianca's letter. Thankfully, he'd accepted the letter with congratulations, reminding Ruby that while internships were an important part of school, they didn't take priority over class and studying; a point that she politely accepted.

Then there was Business 101. How she ever imagined siting in class with her Mistress standing only a few feet away without getting distracted was beyond her limited understanding of what was happening. She might as well have been a hundred miles away for all the relief it gave Ruby in being able to focus or make sense of the intricacies of their relationship.

Bianca barely gave her notice outside of the cursory greeting she gave all the students. They were working on supply and demand logistical problems, which meant small groups, leaving Ruby to hang on the edge of the group, pretending to listen while her eyes were on the woman who had turned her life upside down in the space of a day.

It was a good thing they left her from the work schedule tonight, she knew she'd never be able to focus on running the store. She only hoped that things would make sense soon and she could turn her mind back to life again.

"Okay, you've got about five minutes left until class is over. Remember, you have a quiz on supply-side economics next week." Bianca called out to the class as the different groups finished up their assignments. "Ruby. Can I talk to you for a minute about your project?" Bianca walked up behind her. Ruby jumped with surprise, not noticing her teacher move up behind her so quickly.

"Uh, sure. Sorry, I didn't realize you were there." She said apologetically as she picked up her notebook and walked with Bianca to the desk at the front of the room. There were no other students nearby with everyone else finishing up projects.

"I would like you to be at the downstairs door at 7pm. I will send you a code to access the door." Bianca mumbled, looking around the room to make sure everyone was busy doing other things. "Once inside, you will go into the room you were in yesterday, get undressed. There will be a few items on the bed for you. Put them on and wait, kneeling on the bed until we arrive." Bianca gently put a hand on Ruby's arm. Warm skin tingling against her own arm sent goose bumps across her body. "Do you understand me?" Her tone was warm but stern, and Ruby nodded in obedience.

"Yes Mi… Ma'am." She said catching herself. She noticed the soft smile on Bianca's lips at the realization that she had caught herself.

"Good Job Ruby." She continued louder. "We'll see you next class." Ruby nodded, then walked back to her desk to pick up her things. Pulling her phone from her purse, she had little over an hour to get dressed and reach the door. Her roommate, likely off with her boyfriend somewhere, wouldn't bother her getting ready or start asking silly questions.

After running back to her room and taking a long shower to include some well-needed grooming, Ruby tossed on some fairly plain clothes and ran to the street near her apartment to hail a taxi. It would be easier than getting her car, and losing her spot. Taxi's into the edge of the French quarter were cheap from campus, and Ruby stood outside the door a good fifteen minutes early.

Even though she did not understand what Bianca planned, Ruby was fairly certain trying to enter the building early would only bring out the cold hard bitch and not the tender sexual deviant she admired. Not to mention the code to enter the building was missing, so trying to enter without it seemed a bad idea.

Uncertain how to proceed, Ruby walked along the street. A reminder of the night before and the uncertain walk from the bar to the apartment they traveled with two strange men in tow. How the events of the past night seemed so much like a dream now, considering how real and powerful they were at the time. While Ruby still struggled to understand exactly what was happening, she now held a better idea of the threat and the thrill involved.

Bianca swore she would keep her safe. Amid being at the mercy to two very strong, very horny men, Bianca kept her word. Not only keeping her word of safety, but also showing her a level of desire and arousal she'd never felt. The most amazing realization that hit her later in the day, after almost missing her second class, was that in all the attention she was getting, somehow Bianca kept her on the verge for so long without an orgasm.

Lost in her thoughts, meandering along the street, the ding of a message arriving turned her attention back to the phone. Uncertainty and exhilaration spread across her body.

Follow this link. Enter 6547132 and wait for the light on the door to turn green. Do as I asked Pet and you will enjoy tonight immensely. Ruby stared at the message for a long moment, something in her mind still holding back. Conscious thought fought back as she heard the battle rage inside her mind. The overarching argument being that Bianca lived up to every promise made and never endangered Ruby.

Taking a step forward, another after that was enough, she finally won out over indecision by walking back to the door and committing to a course of action which in itself felt amazing. Even that small victory felt good to a girl who leaned on indecision and timidity in the face of uncomfortable decisions.

Perhaps that was part of the lesson Bianca was trying to teach her. The last night Ruby accepted because she thought her grade was on the line or her teacher's approval was on the line. Today she was accepting because she wanted it, and no bit of her usual fear would stop her.

Following the link as requested, a webpage loaded on her phone. A large red circle with a place for the key code beneath waited for her input. A frustrated scowl crossed her face when she realized she couldn't paste the code into the boxes.

Flipping back and forth between Bianca's message and the page, she eventually filled the space with the long sequence of numbers. Pressing on the large red button, being the only place to *send* anything, a green line ran around the edge of the red circle until coming full circle. As if her phone sent the command itself, the green button on her phone and the green light on the door clicked at the same time, along with the door.

The last time she walked through the door as a fawn following the wolf into its den, uncertain of her future. Today she walked under her own power and decision and the trepidation of the night prior now gone, replaced with anticipation and exhilaration. Sure, there was fear, but fear of the unknown, not fear of danger, and there was a profound difference in that.

The inside door was open already, leading her down that long hallway. Plainly decorated in warm lavender, a strange detail that her frightened mind failed to latch onto the night before. Walking into the big room, Ruby still found the large mattress in the middle.

On the mattress, three items lay at the edge with small tags tied to them. One she recognized from the night prior as the length of cloth Bianca used to tie her arms and blindfold her. The tag said put this on. The second looked like a black leather collar with soft metal studs and a ring at the center. The tag mirrored the first with… the ring at your neck, as the only difference. The third was a skinny strap with a ball in the middle. While never seeing one in person, it didn't take much for Ruby to figure out it was a ball gag.

What Bianca could want her to wear this for, Ruby didn't understand. Thankfully, there weren't any tags with instructions on the ball gag, so Ruby left it.

Stepping up to a small dresser against the wall, she stripped, folding her clothes and laying them on the top. Being naked felt curiously liberating as she walked back over to the bed, her eyes on the three items. Lifting the collar up, she placed it around her neck as directed with the ring in the front at her throat, slipping the soft leather through the metal buckle until it was snug on her neck but not choking her. Climbing onto the bed, she lifted the blindfold next over her eyes, tying it around her head.

She kneeled obediently on the bed, naked and alone, her senses compensating quickly for losing eyesight as her ears tried to identify every noise and the hairs on her skin reached out for the slightest change in temperature or air flow.

Ruby wasn't sure how long she kneeled on the bed before she heard female voices moving down the hall. Goosebumps rippled across her electrified skin as her body reacted to the newfound anticipation. *Female voices? Two?* She realized. Did they made her wait for a reason? Ruby wondered as she felt her body tremble.

"Oh my, you weren't kidding, she's adorable." A new voice she didn't recognize caught her mind, her head turning to follow the voice. Ears tried to follow the new noises in the room, but they were moving in different directions. "I can see why you're so taken by her. It's almost as if you taught her to be this way."

The new voice sighed, growing closer until Ruby felt pressure move the mattress behind her. Like an electric current coursing across her skin, her body responded to the presence behind her as she felt her breasts firm up and her nipples harden. Heat warmed her pelvis at the first touch of a new hand on her body as she softly sighed into the touch. The hand slid along her hip, following the curve to her torso then around the front of her belly until softly cupping her full round breasts.

Shock shot through her, followed by a sharp gasp as she went weak at the hard pinch her nipple. The power of that simple act made her weak in the knees, but desirous of more for some strange reason.

"Are you going to be our willing play thing tonight?" A wickedly warm female voice whispered into her ear from behind, another hand gradually working its way around from the other direction but diving between her legs to her moistening sex.

"Yes, mistress." Ruby choked out over the pain on her nipple. The pressure intensified as soon as she answered.

"I'm not your mistress. I'm Miss. Ash. Do you understand little slut?" she asked as her fingers found the young wet lips swelling up between her legs, her aroused nub poking out of its hood with need.

"Yes, Miss. Ash." Ruby moaned through a mix of the pleasure of Ashley's fingers on her applying pressure both to her sex and pinching her nipple between them.

"Good girl. I think you are going to please me very much." She said, her tone even more warm and soft than before.   Suddenly Ruby found herself released from the tension of pleasure and pain as the new woman released her. She found the absence painful in itself having almost grown to enjoy it.

"She's curiously wet and excited by all of this. I think she'll be a fun toy." Ruby heard Miss. Ash say as she moved away from the bed.

"I'm glad you like her." Ruby heard Bianca whisper before what sounded curiously like kissing. "She's all yours, but first we have one last thing to take care of." Bianca said, her voice moving closer. Ruby could smell the smooth scent of her skin, a scent she'd grown to know well in the past day. A pressure on the bed in front of her as the rustling of skin on fabric.

"So my pet, did you come up with your word yet?" She asked in a low, teasing tone.

"Yes Mistress. Apple." Ruby replied thinking about the requirements for the word.

"Are you sure?" Bianca asked quietly into Ruby's ear.

"Yes, Mistress." She answered with conviction.

"Very well. Apple it is. If ever there is a time when you feel like it's too much, you will say Apple. That will stop whatever we are doing. Do you understand?" Bianca asked, her mouth close enough to her ear that she could feel the heat of her breath and smell the woman's hair near her nose.

"Yes, Mistress." Ruby trembled softly. The anticipation of what was to come weighed on her senses, but that she might need a word to stop from pushing too far almost frightened her.

"Good. Open your mouth now. If you need to speak your word while something blocks your mouth, you will put three fingers up on your right hand and that will tell us you need to say something."

Without waiting for Ruby to open her mouth fully, sudden pressure of a hard rubber ball pressed between her lips, eventually forcing her jaw open as Bianca ran the strap around her head. The ball completely blocked her mouth, forcing her to breathe through her nose, which took her a minute to get under control.

Before she'd had a chance to get used to the gag and the change in her breathing requirements, a firm pressure pinched down on one breast, then another. Ruby let out a muffled yelp from behind the ball. The pressure was intense, more intense than Ash's fingers pinched her earlier, and more constant.

There was also a slight weight to them, as if something hung between them. Just as the pain dulled something pulled sharply on whatever it was hanging between her breasts.

"Come with me slut." Ashley's voice, biting and sharp, enticed Ruby to move forward on the bed by whatever it was hanging between the clamps on her nipples.

She eventually found her feet, dragged along like some uncertain animal until abrupt, silky hands turned her around, her back pressed against something firm, cool and metal. Those same hands guided one foot then another up onto platforms slightly higher than her ankles. A buckled strap wrapped around each ankle tightly, clasping them in. Next her hands, raised up above her head, buckles strapped down her wrists leaving her hands left free to hang limp.

"How about we start with five?" Miss. Ash said thoughtfully if not absently vague. Ruby soon understood what five meant as something small yet weighty pulled down on the clamps connected to her nipples, a cold hardness of metal banging against her chest bone.

A shutter along her skin at the mix of pleasure and pain drew a muffled yelp. "Does that hurt a lot slut?" Ashley asked, a wickedly happy tone in her voice. Ruby shook her head gently, not wanting to prompt further weight but not wanting to lie. It was a strain, but it didn't hurt, *not yet.* "Good. Now I want you to feel something else."

Next came a sensation so surprising, Ruby jumped with a moan part from pleasure and part from surprise. Many firm strips of cloth or leather bounced along her bald, moist pelvis.

"Do you like that?" Her new tormentor continued lightly swinging the strips, gently against her mound.

Ruby nodded, moaning softly. It felt nice the way it tickled at her pussy lips and inner thighs. That all ended when the soft gentle tickle became sharp stinging smacks. Yelping through the gag as the strips came up between her legs and struck sharply against her sensitive areas.

Her body jumped in response as the second hit came, then the third.

Eight or ten even tempered and timed strikes assaulted her already swollen and excited pulsating core. Each strike enhanced the sensation. Sharp stinging pain shot through her body. Just when anticipation told her to prepare for another strike, nothing came. Leaving her on edge she waited for the next one, not knowing what would happen next.

Instead of leather strips, fingers rubbed along her womanly center.

"She's wet even after that." Ashley's fingers pushed aside her young soft lips. Ruby's body weakened in the restraints at the change in sensation, causing her to moan deeply.

"I think she likes it." Bianca seemed appreciative in the background before she felt fingers press against her nose. Slick wetness spreading across her obstructed lips and nose. The scent of pungent, tangy arousal filled her nostrils.

"You see how hot you are for me whipping you slut? Shall I stop?" Ruby heard the words, but before she could respond logically she felt herself shaking her head.

Before she knew it, the whipping started again, followed closely after each by a lustful moan. After another batch of ten, instead of fingers, Ruby felt a mouth lick the juices from her abused mound. Her knees buckled, leaving her hanging at the feel of a soft tongue slipping between her slippery softness. Her body trembled with pleasure she'd never experienced before as the mix of pleasure and pain fogged her mind of all but the moment.

"You don't get to come until I say so little slut." Ashley ordered, realizing that Ruby's breathing picked up as her body fought to stay in control.

"Let me see how wet she is." Bianca drew closer. There was a quiet minute where nothing happened aside from the sound of plastic moving across the floor, then suddenly she was there, pressed close, their body touching, the older woman's warm breasts mashed against her own young perky globes.

Ruby felt something brush across her sensitive body as Bianca pushed closer, then without warning a soft and rigid intruder pierced her lips, pushing all the way back as Bianca's pelvis pressed tight against hers. Remembering the dildo from the morning, Ruby groaned through her gag as it filled her and impaled her all the way to her womb.

"Oh yes. She's drenched." Bianca marveled as she pumped into her young pet. "Do you like what Miss Ash is doing to you pet?" She whispered, one hand on Ruby's hip the other on her shoulder. The young student moaned and nodded emphatically, enjoying the feeling of her teacher pressing her body so close.

All Ruby could think about was the heat in her belly and the lingering pain on her pussy and nipples. The weight between her tits bounced and jerked every time Bianca thrust into her or pulled out causing a soft mix pleasure and pain to fog her mind more.

Growing close, but uncertain how they would respond if she came without permission, Ruby's mind fought the urge. Thankfully her mistress stopped, pulling out, leaving Ruby feeling empty inside.

"Wow, she's loving this, I can tell." Bianca's voice trailing off as she must have turned away from her. "I'm thirsty, should we go get some wine?" Her teacher suggested to her friend, absolutely disregarding the naked, tortured girl hanging on the wall.

"What do we do about her?" Ashley finally asked, a jovial tone in her question before silence fell over the room. All Ruby could hear was her breathing as her body trembled at being brought to the edge of orgasm and left the linger.

"I have an idea." Bianca blurted. There was the sound of movement and heavy things shifting about or opening. Ruby couldn't make sense out of the sounds because neither of them said a word while they worked. Before long her arms and legs came free as someone coerced her down off of the step by what connected the clamps on her breasts.

"On your hands and knees slut." Ashley ordered, guiding her down with a hand on her shoulder until Ruby was on her hands and knees like a dog. With a couple of swats on her firm ass cheeks coaxing Ruby forward, a hand guided her head until she felt smooth padding under her hands and knees.

The scent of metal all around, and her arm brushing against a metal bar rekindled fear in her mind as she moved forward. Hands adjusted her position from both ends. She rested on her elbows with arms bent and wrists locked down with metal restraints. At the same time restraints locked down her ankles, her knees and elbows rested on soft padding.

The sensation sent chills along her spine. the feeling and sound of metal locked around her neck intensified her fear. Pressure against the collar made her situation very real. Hands fiddled with the weight hanging between her nipples as a heavier weight filled the void she'd slowly grown accustomed to.

The final piece of her subjection came with the sound of a metal door closing and the unexpected protrusion of rigid plastic in both her pussy and ass. Neither was as thick or filling as the dildo Bianca used, but their presence became noticeable, especially when they vibrated ever so gently.

"Enjoy your cage slut. We'll be back in a bit to see how you're doing." Ash's voice came cold as she wiped a string of saliva from Ruby's chin. "Remember, no coming till you ask my permission." Without a further word, Ruby listened as both women walked off, chattering quietly to themselves.

She had no idea how long they'd left her for. Darkness and silence while immobile with a dildos penetrating and vibrating deep inside her forced Ruby to focus on keeping her orgasm at bay. She was certain knowing what she did about the video surveillance in this play room that they were likely watching her and would be very upset if she tried to orgasm and hide it.

So she fought it.

Her body ached with desire and tension. Her breasts throbbed from the weight hanging between her nipples, and her moistness dripped down her legs. The strange thing for Ruby was how her body became accustomed to the sensation, like wearing in a pair of new shoes.

As if they knew that her body was quickly losing the fight against an orgasm, the sound of laughter and women chattering filtered down the hall. Ruby perked up.

"She's a superb slut. But I think she's going to pop any minute." Miss. Ash's voice came from behind her. "Wow, look how wet she is!" Her arousal barely registered until they brought it up. Ruby suddenly realized the seeming endless trickle of liquid down her inner thighs.

"Should we just let her, that way we can punish her for not asking." Bianca's voice was in front of her, close enough that she could be kneeling near her face.

"That would seem rather unfair since she has a gag in her mouth. We can't punish her for not asking permission to cum when she can't speak." Ashley joked. Ruby felt the dildos push in further, threatening to drive her over the edge.

"Very true." Bianca's voice joined a pair of hands on the back of her soft red locks. They began unlocking the strap holding the gag. Ruby gasped as the gag pulled away, a stream of saliva slipped past her lips before she could close her mouth.

"Miss. Ash, may I come?" Ruby pleaded in a broken gasp, trying hard to make her jaw work again.

"Not yet, little slut. We still have plans for you." She replied with a sharp tone. Before she knew what happened, a hand lifted her chin up and a familiar soft rubbery friend pushed past her lips into her throat. At the same time the dildos penetrating her slipped out to, quickly replaced by a much larger dildo pushing her moist lips aside.

Ruby groaned, unceremoniously impaled from both ends. Unable to move or shift, Ruby accepted her fate as she became the fuck hole in the room.

"That's such a good little slut. Take it all." Ashley moaned from behind. Ruby felt the cage shaking a bit every time the dildo behind her pushed deeper. She imagined Miss. Ash supporting her weight on the cage. "Don't come yet, little slut. You need to take more of this first." Bianca's friend ordered her, realizing the soft moans coming from Ruby were her on the verge of losing it.

The weight between her breasts swung back and forth, pulling at her, adding a tinge of pain with each alternating thrust. After the time she'd been kneeling here, the sensation of the weight dulled, but now it flared with increased activity.

Reaching a point of tension she was having trouble fighting, both women stopped their assault on her body. Both pulled out at the same time as if they'd sat upstairs that whole time coordinating their attack. That possibility was likely, Ruby also realized, it was likely they knew each other well enough they didn't have to.

Aside from the soft rustling sounds of movement in the room, Ruby couldn't tell what they were doing since they weren't talking. Eventually a pair of hands grabbed either side of her face, lifting it up and holding her still, a thick rubbery tip pressed against her mouth. Willingly accepting, she marveled at the scent and taste of her molten need on the dildo.

She was so horny, she tasted heady and pungent with need as it spread across her tongue. She couldn't fight a groan as a dildo pushed into her tight behind. Both intruders found a similar rhythm again, pushing into her body at the same time as to press her in the center with each thrust.

Ruby could feel the drool running out every time the dildo in her mouth pulled back, and she could feel the heated dampness dripping as she hung on the edge of orgasm. It was only a matter of time before she lost control completely with or without permission.

"What do you think?" She heard Bianca ask in between fevered grunts as they both fucked long and deep at their respective holes. Lost in the moment's rhythm, trying to force herself to hang on just a moment longer, Ruby groaned as the dildo in her throat slid out, leaving her empty. The hands on the side of her face were tender but firm as they turned her head up as if she was looking at Ashley.

"Well, little slut. What do you think? Would you like to come for me?" Bianca's thrusting stopped, leaving the rubber intruder buried deep within her rear.

"Yes Miss. Ash, please may I come?" Ruby choked out, her mouth raw and wet from the abuse.

A long minute passed then Ash's hands let her head free. A moment later there was a muffled thud as something fell to the floor near her. The hands came back, guiding her face up, but this time instead of a rubber dildo, the taste of moist flesh pressed against her mouth and nose as the sweet aromatic scent of a woman's delicate softness filled her nostrils.

"Do a good job licking my pussy slut and I'll see what it's worth to you." She said, pulling herself into Ruby so she couldn't do anything other than eat at Ashley's most sensitive spot.

Her sore mouth went to work as her lips and tongue sucked and licked Ashley's downy mound. Desperation to get Miss. Ash off drove her like a woman in a desert trying to suck liquid from one lone fruit. Ashley's hands went to the back of Ruby's head. She humped and ground her folds against the hungry mouth.

"Oh yeah, you dirty little slut, that's it, eat me up." As Ruby's mind went numb with desire to prove she was worthy of coming, the dildo in her ass slid out. A moment later it sheathed itself inside her. Bianca began gradually building her thrusts into a steady, heavy intensity.

Each thrust forced her more into Miss. Ash, her tongue pushing deeper and deeper in between those folds. Moans of pleasure matched Ruby's as Ashley grew more and more wet on her face. A silent moment must have passed between the two women as Bianca's thrust's turned more pronounced and powerful, just as Ashley's attention turned back to her plaything.

"Come for me, slut. Show me how much you enjoy the way we treat you." Like a dam breached with explosives in her core, Ruby's body lurched in her cage, restrained at her arms and legs, but her body writhed within the confines of her world. Clenching down on the thick dildo inside as tongue and mouth attached themselves to Ash's folds like a remora.

Ruby's body trembled.

The orgasm rippled across her skin in shock waves from her pulsating core to her head and back, straining every muscle and pushing her consciousness to the limits. Confined as she might be in her current position, her mind was free as a blissful tranquility finally chased the tension and strain away.

Locked in place in her cage, her mouth still held to Ashley's sweetness as the orgasmed poured into her mouth. She shuddered uncontrollably against Ruby's face, drenching her mouth with a gentle trickle of warm juices. Finally letting go, Ruby went as limp as she could in the restraints that held her. Ruby's body collapsed, dead to the world.

She wasn't sure how long the numbness took over before the movement of being gently removed from her restraints roused her mind. The world seemed a fog, the only thing she recognized was the closeness of her teacher's body, the warm softness of her skin against her back. As the fog lifted, surprise pulled at Ruby's reality, finding herself lying in Bianca's bed at the center of the two women's attention. Their hands gently caressed her skin as sanity and reality slowly returned to her mind.

"Welcome back." The voice pulled her attention to a woman laying on her left. The woman next to her seemed softer, more gentle that the woman who had been her tormenter for the evening. A curtain of long dark hair hung behind her head to the bed, her olive skin and soft angular face accentuated Ashley's slimmer build and smaller breasts. She was a vast difference from her teacher, but no less attractive as she lay caressing Ruby's leg just above her inner thigh. Her attractive angular face, full lips formed in a gentle arc, sultry orange brown oval eyes that turned slightly down excited Ruby, understanding her teacher's attraction to the woman.

Another finger softly caressed the soft roll of her bosom where it met her ribcage, turning Ruby's attention to the other side. Bianca lay at her side, tenderly caressing her breast with a finger. "Mistress, I don't understand." She said trying to guess at their intentions.

"Miss. Ash enjoyed playing with you so she thought it would be nice to have you join us tonight. She is very fond of you and truly felt you showed a lot of spirit and commitment to pleasing her." Bianca said, shifting her eyes from Ruby to Ashley with a grin before turning her attention back to Ruby.

"It's only fair that you get a chance to show her how much you enjoy pleasing me without the role play."

Ruby looked from her teacher and mentor to her friend. Until recently Ruby never considered herself attracted to women or turned on by being with them, but she couldn't deny, there was something amazing about lying in bed with two beautiful women whose only desire was to have her please them.

Without further words, Ruby turned to her left, her mouth seeking Ashley's medium sized round breasts, sucking the nipple into her mouth as her other hand trailed down the woman's flat belly and over the soft patch of trim fur at her mons before slipping between her legs. Ashley lay back, letting Ruby explore her body. Ruby took her time, kissing along Ashley's belly, licking the soft line of hair at the center of her belly. Her fingers kneaded Ashley's breasts as her mouth worked across the taut stomach and down between her legs. Ashley's spread her legs, welcoming Ruby as a sigh of contentment escaped her mouth.

"She really is a treasure" Ashley said as Ruby's mouth descended, kissing her tight vertical lips. Her tongue spread the folds, seeking out the hard pearl she'd felt against her mouth and tongue earlier. Looking up, she saw Bianca move closer, the two women shared a passionate kiss as Bianca's hand tenderly teased her friend's breasts.

Unlike before, Ruby's mind lost in a fog of sexual tension and her face mashed against Ashley's moist lips, barely had time to enjoy the moment. Now her tongue explored, savored every inch and every sensation. Her fingers pulled the edges of her warm damp entrance aside, to expose the lips as her mouth suckled at each. Her tongue flicked against the pearl under its hood, enticing it out so her lips could wrap around it and suck gingerly.

Ashley's back arched when Ruby's mouth found her button, causing Bianca to look down and watch, feather light caresses of her finger along Ashley's small perky brown nipples. Ashley's hand found Ruby's strands of strawberry blond locks, but this time instead of forcing her face into her, she caressed it lovingly as her body grew closer and closer to orgasm.

Bianca's mouth worked down along the slim woman's collar and across the soft rise of her chest, taking the round pert breast in her mouth. Her tongue worked the edges, Ruby watched with curiosity and desire as she poked her tongue in along the edge of Ashley's deep crevice. She was writhing on the bed now, mere inches away from release. Ruby didn't remember if she'd set Ashley off when she came, but she could tell the woman was close now.

Surprise hit Ruby when Bianca's face appeared near hers. Her tongue working at Ashley's button while her student gently explored her lips with the tip of her tongue. Being the first time she'd shared anything like this with her teacher, and it made her swell with attraction to see her helping please Ashley.

Ashley didn't last long after that. Her body tensed as she moaned loudly without care of who might hear her. Back arching as she grasped at the sheets for something to hold on to. Bianca and Ruby continued the assault on her lips and swollen pearl until she finally collapsed back to the bed exhausted and spent.

Smiling, Bianca turned to Ruby, moisture beading on her chin as she leaned in and kissed her intensely. Their tongues, coated in the juices of her friend danced in Ruby's mouth, spreading more of Ashley's taste across her mouth until they both broke the kiss breathless.

Surprised as she opened her eyes to see a warm longing in Bianca's expression. They gazed across Ashley's hip at each other. "Come here, pet." Bianca urged in a whisper, her finger under her students chin as she crept back toward the head of the bed, almost sitting on the pillows next to her friend. "lay here." She patted the bed just below the pillows beside Ashley. Ruby did as she was told, partly because that was why she was here, and partly because she found the excitement of being told what to do and how to do it comforting.

Both women nestled on either side of her, returning to the way things had been when Ruby awoke with Bianca and Ash pressed close on either side, their hands and fingers gently caressing her young nubile body.

"I think she's going to make a wonderful plaything." Ashley finally said as the euphoria of lightheaded bliss finally subsided. They were talking over her, not to her, and Ruby understood the dynamic. The contentment of being in the same bed with them was enough now. "You listen to what your mistress tells you and learn from her my little slut." Ashley turned to Ruby, kissing her on the lips and rising from the bed.

"Yes, Miss. Ash." Ruby responded obediently as Bianca also crawled out of bed, trailing after her friend as she dressed.

"You can't stay?" Bianca asked Ashley, placing a hand on the small of her back, their naked bodies looking so different together but yet so perfectly matched.

"I wish I could. I have court in the morning. I can't afford to spend all night with you two fucking." Ashley teased, looking back at Ruby lying prone on the bed. Bianca nodded with a longing smile in her eyes.

"Pet, please get a bottle of water from the refrigerator and grab Miss. Ash's purse from the counter." Bianca ordered. It took Ruby a second to realize she'd been talking to her before she started moving without question. Under normal circumstances she might be miffed at being ordered to fetch something for someone, but considering what she was being shown and the potential benefit she saw, a little polite fetching couldn't hurt.

"Yes, Mistress." She replied padding across the kitchens cool stone tiles on naked feet. The chill was a strange feeling compared to the heated warmth of the past few hours. Grabbing two bottles of water from the refrigerator and grabbing the small black clutch from the counter, Ruby sauntered into the living area at the edge of the sleeping area where they stood.

Quietly waiting, she watched. Ashley was now dressed in a simple black dress that wrapped around her chest, leaving her shoulders and arms bare. She'd twisted her dark silky hair up into a fairly neat bun atop her head with strands of hair sticking out the top. Last came a pair of medium height heels when Bianca turned to see Ruby standing patiently to the side.

"Such a good girl." She gave a grin and a sharp but easy smack on Ruby's right ass cheek.

Barely flinching, Ruby accepted the praise and the slap for what it was.

"Thank you. You're such a sweet thing I'm almost jealous." Ashley gave her a soft kiss on her lips before taking the clutch and a bottle of water. Bianca and her friend shared a simple kiss with hugs before turning to the door. "I'll call you tomorrow. Get some rest." She said giving Ruby a sidelong glance before opening the door.

Bianca stood silently staring at the closed door for a long minute. Eventually, she turned back to her pet, standing patiently behind.

"Come with me." She finally said walking out through the living area to the patio. "Kneel there pet." She said pointing to a place on the patio just outside the door. Ruby did as she was told. Just because she'd been party to the personal connection between her mistress and her friend, Ruby didn't have any illusions she was not an equal of any sorts in this arrangement, "Did you enjoy tonight Pet?" Bianca asked, pulling the patio chair close to where she was kneeling and sitting so she could look out over the city.

Ruby hesitated for a second, uncertain how she should respond. *Would enjoying herself mean she wasn't taking this seriously?* She wondered silently before answering.

"Yes Mistress, did I please you?" She added, hoping that showing she considered her position would temper any wrong answers. A smile turned up her teacher's lips, a sight she caught even at the angle looking out of the corner of her eye.

"Yes pet. You pleased me very much. Miss. Ash is quite taken with you, which bodes well for you." Bianca replied with a wink. Taking a moment to look, Ruby could see the affection in her eyes, telling her that the two women were more than close friends at one time. "I want to introduce you to a client I think would like you very much. I believe he may take great interest your future." Bianca turned to Ruby, placing a gentle hand on her shoulder. "But I will not tell you what to do on this matter and your answer will not influence how I see you or the relationship growing between us." Ruby took the chance and looked up into her mentors eyes. She could see the sincerity in those dark green eyes, even in the shadow of her dark patio.

"I am yours completely, Mistress. If you believe it is what is best for me, I will join you." Ruby was feeling an undeniable sense of devotion and commitment in her submission to Bianca. Her thoughts barely questioned or hesitated in the answer. Under normal circumstances she'd find this surprising considering her personality. She didn't know what it was about the influence Bianca's control had that made her so decisive and committed, but she found the new sensation pleasing.

"If that is your choice, you need to understand that you are accepting whatever happens without question. And outside of the parameters for using your word, you will accept and respond without hesitation. Do you understand?" Ruby heard the weight in her words. She knew they were about to step into a new dimension of the relationship they were building by the tone her teacher took.

"I do, Mistress. I am yours." She said unequivocally, her eyes holding those green emeralds without hesitation.

A smile brightened Bianca's expression, as she looked down, pride swelling up in her eyes. An open palm reached down and pressed against Ruby's cheek, a touch so soft and tender Ruby leaned into the warm palm as fingers spread out across her jawbone.

"You're more than I could have hoped for little pet." Bianca confided. "Now, I want you to go downstairs and get dressed. I will have a car waiting on the street to take you back to campus. I will send you instructions for meeting my client. It will probably be the Saturday night after next." Her teacher leaned in and gave Ruby a long tender kiss before releasing her without further word. Watching the Bianca walk away, Ruby felt a yearning pull at her body that she couldn't reconcile.

Obediently, she stood and walked to the elevator door at the front of the room next to the main apartment door. It dawned on Ruby that she'd never entered the apartment through the front door. The ride down the elevator and the time it took her to get dressed left her lost in thought, considering the events of the night.

Her eyes finally free to examine the cage they placed her in, a hard black metal box surrounded by bars and shackles. *Is this to be my purpose?* Ruby wondered to herself as she pulled on her clothes. Nothing that happened to her in the short time with her teacher ever hurt or scared her, but the idea of being caged like an animal for their pleasure weighed heavily on her mind.

True to form as Ruby walked out the door and down the street a sleek black car with tinted windows and a man dressed in a very smart gray suit waited for her. He already knew where she was going and, aside from a friendly greeting for the late hour, barely spoke to her. He showed her a class deference, as if she was someone important, and Ruby wondered if that was what people who could afford cars as opposed to taxis expected.

Returning to her apartment gave Ruby such a sense of how small and plain her little world was. She experienced so much in the last two days it seemed almost painful to try to settle back into a routine of school, work and life outside of Bianca.

Questions

"You okay?" The question didn't initially register with Bianca until Clay Richards walked around the side of her desk and leaned down into her field of vision. Staring off into the distance of the random downtown buildings and the New Orleans skyline, Bianca zoned out. The events of the past few days running through her mind like mice on a wheel and she lost track of the world around her. At least until Clay stuck his head into her office. Clay was handsome in a very plain way, sandy blond hair styled short, roundish angled features with grayish blue eyes and a nose with a gentle slope. His mouth always seemed to have a smile on it, underlining a narrow chin that made his smiles seem to dip more at the center. He dressed in his usual gray suit with some variation of a purple or violet shirt, with gray or silver tie.

"Huh…? Oh, yeah, sorry I got lost in thought there." Bianca answered, pulling the end of her pen from between rosy red lips. "What's up?" She asked, turning back to her desk.

"I was curious if you wanted to talk about the Peterson account… and you have a visitor." He said, his eyes tracking back to the door. Bianca turned to see Ruby standing at the door dressed smartly in a dark skirt and maroon blouse, her tablet clenched against her chest under two arms crossed. Her hair was up in a bun and she wore a pair of thin dark wire-rim glasses that made her look every bit the young business executive.

"Ruby!" She cried happily, standing at her desk. "I'd completely lost track of the day. Is it already twelve o'clock?" She asked turning to Clay who could only nod, his usual grin spread from ear to ear. "Clay Richards, this is Ruby. She's my new intern, one of the kids from the class I'm teaching. She shows great potential." Bianca beamed a bit, introducing her protégé to Clay.

He had no idea about her private life, even though they'd been partners for almost two years. "Ruby, Clay here is my right hand in the division. Probably one of the smartest financial minds I've ever worked with." She smirked, realizing that Clay was not only blushing, but could not take his eyes from Ruby since she'd stood up. "Clay, I'll come find you in a few minutes, let me get Ruby settled first." She gently pushed her partner from the office so she could bring Ruby in.

"I'm sorry ma'am, I didn't know the protocol. We never talked about what to do, just the days." Ruby uttered as if she'd intruded on something.

"No, never mind that. I completely lost track of time."

She led her into the conference room they worked earlier in the week. Instead of the piles of folders and files, there was one box, a chair and several pens and highlighters. "Put your stuff where you want." Bianca stood and watched Ruby walk to a table and put her purse and tablet down. She didn't realize how much she missed her in the short time apart. "I'm so glad to see you pet." Bianca whispered as she slid a roaming strand of hair back along the girl's ear.

Ruby's eyes looked up with an expression of contentment on her face, the cool blue eyes warm with emotion at being near her.

"Okay, so, first things first, there are several files in this box." She said putting a hand on the top of it. "I want you to go through these files and find any reference to Peterson or Witherspoon. You have highlighters and pens. If it says Peterson, you put them over on the right side. If they say Witherspoon, you put them on the left. If they have both, put them in the middle. Highlight where you see the name and mark a P or a W at the top right corner." Bianca explained the plan, her eyes going back to Ruby as she did to make sure the young girl was tracking. "Any questions?"

"No, ma'am." Her student shook her head confidently before moving to the chair sitting near the box.

"I'll be down the hall talking to Clay. There's a woman outside my office named Theresa. She's my secretary. If you need anything, ask her and she'll find me." Bianca said before giving Ruby a reassuring squeeze on the shoulder. With a nod, she turned out of the conference room back into her office to pick up her tablet before walking down the hall to Clay's office.

At the other end of the conference room where Ruby sat and worked sat Clay's office separated by a door much like the layout of Bianca's office, the only difference was that his door was closed leaving the young girl alone from all but prying eyes outside the building.

"An intern? When did this come up?" Clay questioned looking up from his desk when Bianca entered and sat in one of his comfortable arm chairs.

"It's part of the program. We take on a couple of students that show potential as interns for the semester or the year and hopefully one or two of them will learn enough for recruitment right out of the college." Clay laughed softly to himself, picking up a bottle of water and taking a drink.

"I don't remember them looking like that when I was in college." He finally said.

"Of course we looked like that in college Clay, that was like ten years ago." Bianca laughed.

She agreed, Ruby was attractive in her own way and her partner would likely lose his mind if he knew what they were doing together, but it didn't matter, he would never find out. "So what's going on with the Peterson account?" Bianca asked, sitting forward in the chair.

Having spent more than an hour in Clay's office talking over account issues then being called into an end of the month partner meeting, Bianca barely got back to her office by five thirty. She stood silently swelling with pride at the door to her office, watching Ruby diligently working away at the files.

Every fiber of her being wanted to go in and close the door and throw her over the table, to ravage her body. Despite her urge, Bianca found the need to resist stronger, knowing what was happening between them.

"Oh pet, I'm so sorry, I totally forgot you were in here." Bianca finally said walking into the conference room, placing a hand on the young girl's shoulder. "Why don't you grab your things. It's late, let's grab something to eat." She said with a warm smile.

This was a different environment for her to experience being with her young protégé. She couldn't really be domineering but she could be much more free in her company. There wasn't like to be many people they shared connections with in this part of town.

"It's ok ma'am, I was in a zone." Ruby replied with a smile that lit up her face.

Bianca's head cocked to the side with a raised eyebrow at the sign that her young student had gotten into her assignment. Granted, it was a rather mindless mission that only removed the burden from one of the young paid assistants, but she was glad that Ruby took to the task so willfully.

"Do you like sushi?" She asked walking back into her office, grabbing her purse and coat. Even though it was the late September, the evenings were cooling off quickly and she had no illusions that they would be out past sundown. Ruby nodded in agreement, prompting Bianca to escort her out of the office and lock the door behind her. "Theresa, go home already." She teased with the young administrative assistant that was still diligently working through something on her computer. The girl waved with a smile on her face as Bianca realized she was on a call, phone pressed to her ear by her shoulder.

She waited to say anything else until they were outside the

building, not wanting anyone to think their relationship extended any further than a work or school connection. Ruby was obediently quiet without there being an awkwardness hanging between them. Bianca enjoyed the connection.

She's learning fast. She thought to herself, wondering if this was a natural propensity for being submissive or if she was trying her best to understand. There was a fire in her heart, Bianca saw it. That fire attracted her to Ruby in the first place.

She saw the yearning in those eyes many times over the past week, the desire to be more than a plaything. The night Ashley joined them, the burn in Ruby's eyes said she yearned to be an equal between them. Of course that level of connection in their relationship would take time, but it proved to Bianca, based on what she'd endured already, Ruby was willing to do anything to get there.

"I hope all the sorting and filing wasn't too boring for you. Unfortunately, that's what interns usually get a lot of in the first few months, it's meant to prove they can do menial work without too much direction before being given more responsibility." She snickered. "You'd be surprised how many don't make it that far." Bianca said as they stepped out onto the busy downtown streets.

Growing up in the city left a love in her heart for New Orleans, the local flavors, the charm of the culture, the smaller winding streets. A city laid out in a simpler time where space was at a premium.

"No, ma'am it's okay. I actually rather enjoyed it." Ruby responded wholeheartedly. The brightness returned to her young face now that they were out of the public eye. "I'm glad to have the opportunity." She added.

Bianca was certain the last thing Ruby expected from all of this was an internship. This all started out as a bad idea based on bad grades and quickly spiraled into something much larger and potentially more dangerous if anyone ever learned of their liaisons.

"Ruby, I want to take this opportunity to give you a chance to speak honestly. For the rest of the evening until we are done with dinner, you are free to say what you want without fear of judgment or reprisal, do you understand?" Bianca knew from her time with Ashley and her clients that constantly being under the collar had a tendency to chafe the wearer. The only way to get a spirit like Ruby's flying in this environment was to give her a chance to feel she is free.

"Yes, ma'am." Ruby replied with her usual obedient deference to their relationship, but Bianca could see her release brightened the glimmer in her young student's eye just slightly.

"So what's on your mind, pet?" Bianca asked after a minute of walking together silently down the street. It wasn't as if she removed a gag from the girl's mouth, but still the silence felt comfortable, like that energy between two people who need not talk to be in each other's company.

"Why does this have such a powerful hold on someone?" She asked suddenly, prompting Bianca to break out with a hearty laugh. The look of confusion on Ruby's face caused the teacher to catch herself. It wasn't the first question she expected to come out of Ruby's mouth, which caught her off guard.

"My dear Ruby, the only power is in the person being held, that's what makes it so powerful." Bianca replied finally catching her laughter as they approached the restaurant.

She held the door as her protégé entered as a medium height, slender Asian woman escorted them to a table. She's frequented many of the restaurants near her office over the years, giving their wait staff a good idea of where she liked to sit. Usually if she was alone, she'd eat at the bar, but entertaining a client or a coworker she'd sit further away from the main crowds to give them some privacy. Today the waitress seated them behind a trifold bamboo separator.

The restaurant wasn't overly busy for the time of evening since most professionals in the financial district preferred to go home before going to dinner. The waitress handed them menus and walked away, giving Bianca a chance to think through her answer.

"Tell me, how many times I told you it was your choice, or that you were free to leave." She asked, lifting a glass of cold water up to her lips as her eyes watched those cool blue eyes contemplate the question.

"I don't know." Ruby replied with a shrug, her mind still trying to process why it mattered. "Why?"

Bianca watched, letting the synapses in Ruby's mind fire back and forth for a second before she answered. She wondered if Ruby would latch onto the answer to her own question. She knew deep down inside Ruby thought it an impossible choice and her question didn't answer the question.

"When I said you were free to leave at the restaurant, what did you do?" She reframed the question, hoping the answer would present itself.

"I left." She replied tersely. Bianca remained silent, seeing the thoughts working through her line of questioning. "And then I messaged you." The sudden reply brought a smirk to her face.

"Yes, exactly, and every time I've told you it was your choice or your decision, what did you do?" They were forming the lines of logic that would be her student's first foray into why this game worked the way it did.

"I stayed, or went along with whatever you had planned." She responded. The softer more drawn out way she answered the question and the way her eyes seemed to focus off in the distance, told Bianca she was seeing the answers now.

"So now answer your question; why does this have such a powerful hold on someone?" She reiterated the question, uncertain if Ruby forgot what she asked in the short time her mind chased the answer.

Her smirk grew slightly as she saw Ruby's eyes softly widen after a long minute of thinking.

"Because I give you the power…" She started,

Bianca's smirk faltered as those young eyes widened in awareness.

"… because I am choosing to stay." The response brought her smirk back as she started nodding at the realization.

"Yes pet. You surrender to my control of your own free will, trusting I won't abuse that trust, but in the end it is your free will that holds you. The other night with our two friends, you could have stood up and walked away at any point, why didn't you? And don't use the excuse that you thought it would affect your grade."

Ruby blushed at the suggestion of their first night together. She'd took a leap of faith most women would never consider because something inside let her, and only that reason would allow her to realize the depth of the hold, the trust that no matter what happened she would be safe.

"Because I wanted to please you." She said, her tone slipping back into the meek, subservient whisper.

"Ruby, we're being open and honest remember, that includes to ourselves." Bianca chided, knowing the deeper answer but knowing that the girl needed to accept it.

"Because I wanted to." She said just as the waitress arrived for their order. Bianca ordered a couple of rolls and a couple of plates of various raw nigiri sushi. As the woman left, the teacher turned her eyes back to the student.

"And how did that feel? Not the act, but the decision?" She asked noticing there seemed to be more behind her eyes that her mind wanted to say.

"It…. it felt powerful, I felt confident. All the doubt, the fear, the apprehension vanished, and I was just there in the moment."

"Now do you understand pet?" Bianca asked, her hand reaching out, tenderly taking the girls soft dainty hand in her own. The touch was more intimate than any time in the past week, and she could see the way those cool blue eyes stared down at the touch.

"I think I do." Ruby was thoughtful. "Is this how you became the way you are?" She asked, turning her eyes up to catch Bianca's.

"No pet, but in a rather round-about way it's how Miss. Ash became who she is." The teacher replied with a soft squeeze on her hand. They explored with this world during their relationship in college, and Ashley found a natural draw to it like Ruby.

Unfortunately, the seduction for Ashley came from a man that fed her submissive side, at least until the abuse started. She'd learned quickly the difference between submission and power, and she'd also learned quickly how the two were not necessarily one in the same. Having a father who was a lawyer and being brought up to stand up for herself put a quick stop to the abuse, but unfortunately the damage was done. "I helped her, but she found her own path as you have to."

"Why do you do it?" Ruby became inquisitive, which surprised Bianca. She watched as Ruby's finger played with the rivulets of water on the outside of her glass. Ruby turned her other hand to lock fingers with Bianca's but her eyes down-turned, her mind seeking answers in the questions she asked.

"Honestly…" Bianca replied thoughtfully. "… I enjoy that people trust me enough to open up a side of them that few see, and become who they really are deep down when no one is looking. There's an inherent power in that. I also enjoy the physicality of it, the sexual power it brings."

Ruby looked up, her eyes bright as if the suggestion of sexual power threw gas on a simmering fire. Before she could say anything, the waitress returned with multiple plates in hand. Placing their order on the table along with a steaming pot of green tea, the woman stepped back with a smile before turning away.

"Do you enjoy using me?" She asked as the waitress walked out of earshot. The question wasn't in an accusatory tone the way she asked, but more that of a young girl looking for approval. Bianca stared into those cool blue eyes for a long second, curious what brought on the question.

She thought perhaps her suggestion of sexual power caused Ruby to question how much plaything she was or made her wonder if there was more to this than sexual control. Realizing she would need to be very careful about how she answered the question, she reached over and poured two small cups of tea for the both of them before her eyes returned to Ruby's.

"Is that what you think I'm doing Ruby?" Bianca asked in a warm, affectionate tone, hoping to delve further into how Ruby truly viewed what they were doing together.

"I mean don't get the wrong idea, I enjoy it, I'd have to, seeing as how I haven't left yet; but isn't that what I am to you, a plaything?"

Bianca lifted some nigiri into her mouth with chopsticks to hide the smile in her thoughts. While that was a very simplistic way of looking at what had happened up to this point, it was certainly not how Bianca saw her young protégé.

"You most definitely mean more to me than being my plaything, Ruby." She'd set the rules for dinner requiring openness and honesty regarding everything they talked about, so she couldn't hold back her feelings. Telling Ruby her true feeling could have a detrimental effect, but she needed to abide by the rules if she expected Ruby to as well. Trust was built on honesty and she trusted Bianca with little hesitation up to this point. It was time to repay that trust.

"I see a young woman who has the potential to be strong and confident. I want to give that woman every chance to explore the things that are likely to make her grow and succeed." Outside of blankly admitting her attraction, Bianca did her best to give Ruby that sense without saying it. "I guess after all that you have seen and done to this point, I should have asked you, what do you want pet?"

Those young pink lips opened to accept a piece of sushi roll as Bianca asked the question. A long silence hung between them as Ruby chewed and the question simmered in her thoughts. Bianca almost wondered if Ruby slowed her chewing rhythm to consider her answer.

"I want to be more like you." Ruby's reply struck Bianca with a strange sense of wonderment and pride. "Ever since that first day in class you intimidated me. I didn't fear you, you drew me to you, to your strength and poise. I want to know what that's like."

"Well Ruby, I'm honored that you feel that way about me." Bianca exclaimed approvingly. "But strength, poise, confidence, they all come from knowing who you are and accepting that person. Once you decide who you are, you can have all of that and more."

"How did you find out who you were? I mean, I heard you describe your story when you were in my shoes back in college. How did you go from that girl to this?" The question surprised Bianca. It was fairly deep and astute for a girl her age, but that trait drew Bianca to her.

"Well pet, after some very jarring failures in my life, I decided I would never let anyone tell me no or tell me I couldn't have what I wanted." Bianca answered, picking up her tea, deciding how much she wanted to share about her past with this young impressionable girl.

There was a difference between being honest and opening your life to someone, and Bianca wasn't sure she was at that place with her young protégé yet. "After that, it was a matter of sticking to my principles and not compromising." She could see by the look on the girl's face as she ate and listened that she was processing and trying to understand what that would look like for someone like her.

"Doesn't what we're doing counter that stance?" Ruby's question caught her teacher off guard.

"What do you mean?" Bianca questioned.

"I mean the focus of what we are doing seems to be about denying me or making me do something that goes against my desires." She could tell Ruby was having trouble trying to articulate her feelings in a way that described her point.

"Is that what I'm doing pet? Or am I giving you an environment where you can freely test and understand your limits and your desires? Remember what we talked about earlier, you have the power to stop whenever you want." Bianca gave her a stern look, reminding her of the boundaries of their agreement. "If you believe I'm making you go against who or what you are or want, all you need do is walk away." Her tone had grown gradually colder, hoping to remind Ruby that this wasn't a game nor a joking matter.

The trap with what they were doing was always the fear of walking away and losing everything. There was an equal measure of depravity and pleasure for that simple reason. It was human nature to endure strain and tension, to enjoy the pleasure or the inverse of enjoying the pleasure of knowing that strain and tension may follow.

Bianca looked up, surprised to see a bit of fear in those young naïve eyes. There was no telling if Ruby thought she would end this or if the young girl finally realized that she controlled what was happening to her. There was a discernible fear behind her eyes though. However, instead of inquiring at what she saw, the teacher held her gaze, not letting on that she'd seen the fear, or the distress, whatever it was.

"I understand now." Ruby finally said in a low acknowledgment, her eyes turning down to the table.

"What do you understand pet?" Bianca asked curiously, wondering what revelation her young protégé had in that moment.

"You are trying to help me understand who I am." She said after a long pause, her thumb playing unconsciously with the condensation on the side of her glass, her eyes following. "I thought this whole time I was doing this to please you, but you're right, I don't know who I am, but with you there's no indecision, no hesitation." She finally looked up to her teacher's eyes as she shared the epiphany.

"Why does that scare you?" Bianca asked.

Ruby's eyes flashed, understanding that she had in fact caught the fear in her eyes. Those young hands picked up her teacup. Lifting it, Bianca saw a hint of a tremble on her velvety pink lips. Bianca watched as she sipped at the hot liquid, her eyes full of questions, concerns, the fear all but gone now.

"Because I could never imagine myself as someone who might accept this role in my life, yet I know in my heart it's the right path." Bianca could see the clarity in her eyes now as she realized what they were doing truly was the path she needed to walk.

"What scares you more, that you never imagined doing something like this or that you enjoy it?" Bianca asked with a fairly serious tone.

Ruby looked up from under hooded eyelids, a rather wry look on her face before a smirk spread across her face. "That I like it." She said rather frankly, which caused Bianca's face to light up with amusement. Of course she resisted in the beginning, but that was because it was something so outside of her comfort level that she had no frame of reference from which to understand what was happening. Now that the trust and the world opened up to her, Bianca could see the light in Ruby's eyes at the idea of going deeper.

"Good pet." Bianca's smirk matched the one on Ruby's face as she spoke. "Now, are you ready to take another step forward?" She asked, realizing that opening this door for her pet was likely a very dangerous gamble. Ruby nodded without hesitation, which made her teacher's smirk grow into a toothy grin. "Very well, Saturday evening at nine, one of my clients is having a small party at his house for several colleagues and business acquaintances."

Bianca knew she was taking a chance without preparing the ground before their arrival. She was trusting in her client's emotional response to make this happen. Showing up with Ruby in tow without details about her guest would not only create a shadow of mystery but would guarantee her client's response was genuine. "You'll come to my apartment at eight and we'll get you dressed. Don't worry about the dress, I have that covered." Knowing work or studying for class needed to be a priority for Ruby, Bianca asked Ashley to join her in finding an outfit that would dazzle, but make enough of a statement he couldn't resist the offer.

"I've never been very comfortable in classy social situations. Will I be expected to talk with people?" Her question was assertive with a timid tone. Bianca couldn't blame her for being anxious, the first time at something other than a college frat party more than a year after graduation, and she was a wreck following Randal around like a scared puppy.

Eating a piece of nigiri Bianca let her mind chew on the comment while her mouth chewed on the raw fish. "Don't worry pet…" She replied finally after swallowing. "As you'll be a showpiece for my client, you will need to play the part, which means being your charmingly subservient self and only responding when asked a question. Do you understand?"

"Yes, Mistress." She said in a very low tone that only Bianca could hear. The action brought a warm smile to her face. Ruby had learned so much in such a short time. Ashley's surprise mirrored her own. Ruby quickly took to her role with uninhibited acceptance of their dominance.

"And while I expect nothing to happen during the party, if he wishes to sample what I am offering, you will submit yourself for his pleasure without question." Ruby nodded in acceptance.

The rest of dinner turned to less heavy subjects. They discussed how Ruby's internship would help her understand the business world. It was important for Ruby to gain a better foundation for future enterprises as she became more involved in her nursing program. Bianca found the exchange to be rather comfortable and relaxed, something she rarely had with most people. But then again, most people she dealt with were looking for something or trying to find a weakness in her hard cold exterior. Ruby was different, she was doing this because she wanted to. Her desire to be with Bianca to find herself through submission had changed the tenor of their relationship drastically.

The rest of the week became a blur of class and work leaving Ruby very little time to consider the discussion with Bianca over dinner. To be true, it really didn't matter. In her mind she was now more committed than ever. Ruby finally came to understand the true nature of their relationship and what she was doing with Bianca.

Ruby had little time to see Bianca outside of her internship as her Mistress already had a client scheduled on Ruby's night off. She spent all day Friday in class and the evening studying, then opening the coffee shop instead of closing. The request to attend her prompted a last minute change to Ruby's work schedule. To say she spent the day in anticipation of the party that night would have been an understatement.

Ashley called at her lunch break to verify Ruby's waist measurement and shoe size, but nothing more. She gave no indication what the plan for the evening was outside of what Bianca already shared. Ruby wondered if this client's special tastes enticed her Mistress to dangle her in front of him, or if there was some special connection that would be beneficial to Ruby.

What she knew was what the expectation was, and that brought a certain sense of order to life she missed before now. For the first time in a long time, Ruby felt centered and driven.

Bianca expected her to focus on her studies and understanding the business aspects she was trying to teach first and foremost with extracurricular activities as a secondary interest. Ruby did everything she could to meet that expectation without question.

She was certain her roommate must have thought Ruby joined a cult with how little time at the apartment they shared in the past weeks and her constant running in and out. Today was no different as Ruby went straight to Bianca's apartment from work rather than home first. She'd covered the first part of the later shift they moved her off to accommodate the other assistant manager accomodating the last minute change. Stepping from the taxi, her fingers shook with nerves as she approached the door to the downstairs playroom. Bianca had given no alterations to the standing rules, so Ruby followed procedure until told to alter. That meant entering through the downstairs door, stripping naked and waiting until she came for her.

On the bed sat a square jewelry box with a note attached to the top that said bring this up stairs pet. Inside the box sat a shiny ornate silver band with artistic patterns carved along the outside. A small blood red ruby hung from a small ring at the front. The back of the band closed into two small clasps on either side of the band with a gap in between. At the center of the box, in the middle of the ring of silver, sat a small heart-shaped lock with a high horseshoe shaped clasp and two small silver keys embedded into the satin cloth.

Regarding the piece of jewelry curiously, Ruby closed the box before walking down the long hallway to the elevator. Pressing the button for the apartment, Ruby stood straight and proud, holding the box out in front of her.

When the door opened instead of finding a proud, smiling mistress waiting for her, the scowl on her face could have frozen steam in a heartbeat. "Why aren't you on your hands and knees?" She growled at Ruby. Embarrassed and uncertain again, the girl's eyes turned down as she started to kneel. Before she reached the floor, Bianca stepped up, grabbing her by the hair and pulling her forward. "Come with me pet." She growled in frustration, ignoring the soft yelp that escaped Ruby's mouth.

Bianca pulled her out of the elevator by her hair, dragging her across the apartment into the bedroom, Ruby fought to stay upright and keep her balance until Bianca pushed her down against the front edge of the bed. "Stay there." She scolded as Rubye kneeled at the foot of the bed.

Her teacher walked to either side of the bed, pulling long leather straps up from the frame of the bed before locking Ruby's wrists in the hard leather cuffs at the end.

Before she knew what was happening, she found herself spread across the bottom half of the bed, arms restrained by straps and her legs locked into cuffs by leather straps around the supports at the foot of the bed.

Bent over, her legs as wide as they would go without making her fall over, her hips, belly and breasts pressed against the bed as Bianca tightened the straps connected to the head of the bed.

"I'm sorry Mistress." Ruby pleaded softly just as the leather bite of her cat-o'-nine-tails streaked across her exposed ass. A second later the leather bite tore across her pubic area, causing a stifled yelp. Two more blows from above and below assaulted her sensitive areas before her mind caught movement behind her.

"What do you say pet?" The voice demanded from behind as she leaned in over top. Ruby could feel her body so close.

"I'm sorry Mistress." Ruby whimpered, only to receive two more strikes the same as before.

"You say 'Thank you Mistress'. Thank you for teaching the proper way to accept punishment." Her voice was cold and hard, sending a shiver along Ruby's spine. This was the darkest Bianca ever, and suddenly her mind reeled that maybe she'd made a mistake. Two more strikes came before Ruby caught on.

"Thank you, Mistress" She cried through soft tears streaking down her cheeks. Her body shook with a combination of fear, adrenaline and the scariest of all, pleasure. Bracing as anticipation tensed her body for another strike. She was more surprised when a hand grabbed the back of her hair and jerked her head up and to the side so she could see the face of her tormentor.

"Understand pet, obedience will be rewarded, I will punish failure when you don't do what I expect of you." There was confusion in Ruby's mind as she looked up into Bianca's eyes. Her voice was cold and harsh, while her eyes burned with a heat that threatened to consume her.

Before Ruby could answer, Bianca leaned in and forced a hard kiss on her lips before letting her head go with a jerk. "Don't move. I have something for you." She said, her voice trailing off into the apartment.

As if she could move, Ruby wasn't about to risk enduring more of that to even shift a foot without permission. A minute later, the sound of bare feet padding across the tile floor into the bedroom caught Ruby's attention. Not that it mattered, her soft reddish blond hair fell over her face and she couldn't see what was happening.

"Okay, listen pet. Do not let this fall out. If you do, what you just endured will be a fraction of the whipping I will give you." Concern crossed her mind again at what it could be she would need to keep from falling out. As soon as the thought crossed her mind, Bianca's hand pulled her left ass cheek to the side as a cold metal pressed against the dark puckered opening to her rear.

There was a cool, slimy sensation with the metal as it slowly spread her small tight ring. Ruby gritted her teeth as whatever it was being pushed into her body spread her hole to the edge of its limits. Then almost as quickly as it spread, her body relaxed as it accepted the new intruder, closing around it until something thin and metal kept the hole from closing completely.

"What's going on?" Asked a second voice Ruby immediately recognized as Miss. Ash behind them. "Oh, that's pretty. I always like new jewelry." She said, her voice growing closer. Something pressed against the intruder in her ass, making it shift slightly. "Is she being bad?"

Miss. Ash walked around the side of the bed. "What did you do my little slut?" A crooked smile on her lips she pulled Ruby's head up by her hair removing it from her face.

"I was disobedient Miss. Ash." Ruby responded flatly, a remorseful strength in her tone.

"I see that. Have you learned your lesson?" She asked, her voice sweet with a light spice of sarcasm to hammer home the fact that she really didn't care as much as her sweet tone might imply.

"Yes, Miss. Ash." Ruby replied obediently. On the other side, Ruby felt the bed move until she saw Bianca's naked leg cross over her head.

"Good, show me how appreciative you are pet." Bianca interrupted. Ruby lifted her head to find Bianca on the bed above her, legs spread on either side of her head, supporting her weight with an arm. The free arm grabbed Ruby's hair from Ashley, pulling her head until those moist pink and purple lips sat before her face.

Using her strawberry blond locks as a handle, Bianca guided her face down until Ruby's mouth and tongue hungrily sucked and licked at her Mistress' heated furnace. The scent of arousal filled her nose as her tongue slid across the hard nub peeking out from the top of her lips. Bianca's lips dripped. Her sweet and tangy flavor carried a heady bite of desire that tingled in Ruby's mouth.

Ruby could hear Bianca pant softly above as her tongue worked along the inside folds and explored the inner edge of the her damp, needy mound. Without warning, another lite strike of leather broke across Ruby's flower, causing her to yelp into her Mistress.

The strike was nowhere as bad as what she had endured already, but it still sent a shock through her body. A second and a third strike followed closely behind the first, but instead of fear and anxiety, Ruby's body tingled at the sensation.

Again and again, each time the strikes grew gradually sharper, but each time she found her body responding with eagerness until she could sense an orgasm growing from each hit.

"I think she likes this." Ashley said from behind, hearing Ruby beginning to moan with each strike. Her attention on Bianca blossomed too, until her teacher was writhing in the bed, her hand holding Ruby's head down as her hips bucked and shook with a long lingering orgasm.

Before she knew what had hit her, one last strike from the leather against her quivering soft flesh sent her into orbit, matching the woman under her mouth. Her legs strained against whatever solid surfaces they could to brace for the ripple of excitement along her skin. Lite hit after lite hit continued as her body shuttered against the orgasm piercing her belly.

Bianca's hand finally released her hair, as Ruby's body tensed, throwing her head back in an animalistic groan. Arms strained against the straps, as did her legs. Her body unable to respond on its own found the only way it could to release the tension, thrusting it out through her mouth in a heavy cry

Finally collapsing onto the bed, her head between her mistresses legs. Her own legs weak with release, she tried to hold herself up. Her mind almost lost track of the now warm hard metal inside her ass and clamped down on it as she felt the muscle relax.

"See, I told you she was a natural. It took me six months before I could come from being whipped." Ashley joked, her hand tenderly rubbing out the soreness in Ruby's abused skin with the juices forming on her outer lips. "She's dripping now,"

"Did her jewelry fall out?" Bianca asked from further up the bed.

"Nope, started to slide, but she still holding on tight like a good little slut." Ashley said as Ruby realized she no longer found Ashley's use of that pet name hard to hear.

Am I a slut because I enjoy being called that? Ruby thought to herself as she fought to get her heart rate down and stop the quivering in her legs.

"You two need to get ready." Ashley had concern in her voice. Although Ruby lost track of time, she arrived early, which meant they should have time to prepare.

"Pet, once Miss. Ash releases you, go into my bathroom and take a shower. You are free to use whatever is in the bathroom to make sure you are presentable for our client." Bianca commanded as Ruby felt her feet suddenly release from the restraints. A moment later her hands came free, the weight of her weakened body now unbound slid to the floor until she was kneeling at the foot of the bed. Without thinking, she began walking on all fours around the foot of the bed and into the bathroom.

She heard Ashley giggling behind her.

Once there, she lifted herself up using the counter and staggered weakly into the large shower. The water felt refreshing against her tender skin, releasing much of the tension she held onto during the ordeal. A lather of soap left her skin feeling tingly and soft and a razor smoothed out the day growth on her legs and trimmed the small patch of blond hair between her thighs.

Her mind wandered between the way Bianca responded in the elevator to the reaction of her body to the whipping Ashley gave. The anxiety to the way Bianca responded quickly faded as Ruby realized regardless of how roughly her teacher treated her, she'd never hurt her. Still holding true to her long-standing promise from the first night in the playroom.

The more perplexing reaction swirled around the arousal to being whipped. Granted, the way Bianca whipped her in the beginning seemed harsh, but the fear and uncertainty of the moment drove much of the anxiety in the act. Ashley on the other hand was less hard with her strikes, yet each strike drove Ruby closer and closer to an orgasm.

She found her hand wandering down across her belly until fingers fondled her swollen lips, her mind lingered on the memory. Every time they pushed her limits a little more and every time she found pleasure and enjoyment in where things ended. As she admitted to Bianca the at dinner, the scary part was that she was enjoying everything that happened. *Is that the trap?* Ruby questioned to herself when a commanding voice from the bedroom broke her attention.

"Pet, get out here. We need to get you ready." Bianca ordered.

Ruby turned off the water and toweled her body off. Stepping in front of the mirror, her eyes went to her ass and the silver outline of a heart with a bright red jewel embedded in it sitting plainly against the inside of her cheeks. She marveled at the decoration, having never imagined something like this being a decorative accessory. Her hand lifted the towel to her hair as Bianca's voice broke the moment.

"We'll worry about your hair in a minute." Bianca added sticking her head into the bathroom to watch her young protégé dry off.

Ruby hesitated, wrapping the towel around her body and walking into the bedroom. "Come here." Her teacher ordered. She stood at the foot of the bed in a very alluring sheer lace bodysuit that hugged her voluptuous curves from the tops of her breasts down to the top of her thighs. At the foot of the bed lay a whole ensemble of clothes. A pair of black faux leather string panties. A pair of sheer black stockings and a dress with a stretchy top and an attached faux leather skirt. Beside the outfit, the box she'd brought up from the basement sat with a matching set of silver bangle bracelets and hoop earrings.

"Please get dressed pet while Miss. Ash and I figure out what to do about your hair." Ruby obediently nodded as her fingers picked up the panties first. The thin fabric converged at the top of her cheeks, barely filling the crack of her ass. The fabric left the decorative jewel uncovered.

Next came the stockings. Carefully slipping the perfectly fitted fabric up her leg, she tested their fit, realizing they likely wouldn't slip at all. Ruby marveled at how well Ashley and Bianca fitted the clothes to her as she picked up the dress. The material was stretchy on top as she wiggled her ass into the faux leather skirt, drawing the spandex material up her body.

"Here, let me help you." Ashley warmly stepped up behind, pulling Ruby's wet hair out of the way to slip the faux leather collar around her neck to attach the hooks together. A finger pulled the zipper up along her back and Ruby marveled at how it fit against her body. It held like a glove, even holding her perky globes firmly against her body.

"He's going to lose it when he sees her." Ruby heard Bianca say from the wall separating the bedroom and the living areas.

"I wish we had more time. I'd love to put a bit of a braid in her hair. It would make this work so much better." Ashley grumbled as Bianca walked around in front of Ruby, now wearing a skintight red strapless bandage dress that stopped mid-thigh and emphasized the voluptuous cleavage. A pair of light brown knee-high boots gave her a few extra inches of height. The boots perfectly accented the reddish blond hair hanging down along her shoulders.

"We have a little time. Braid it to the back loosely. I want to bring attention to the jewelry." Bianca had a hint of desire in her eyes as she looked Ruby up and down.

Without further word Ashley pushed Ruby into the kitchen, urging her to sit in one of the bar stools. A moment later she brought out a hair dryer and a brush with which she promptly brushed out her soft reddish blond hair and started loosely braiding it to the back of her head. It ran down the back of her neck and over her right shoulder where Ashley secured the braids with a silver cuff at the end.

"Such a vision." Ashley stepped back to look her over as Bianca stepped forward with the flat square jewelry box in her hand. Her teacher opened the box, placing it on the nearby counter, stepping up in front of Ruby. She slipped the metal band around her neck. Surprise overcame Ruby, feeling how snugly but well measured the band was to her neck. Bianca stepped around behind her. With a slight pressure and a discernible click of metal, she felt the band tighten into place.

"Since you were so committed to being mine the other day, I'm accepting your request." Bianca held up the small key before placing it on a clasp connected to the bracelet she wore. "You cannot take that off without the key. While most people will see that as a beautiful piece of jewelry, the collar signifies to others, you are my submissive. Do you understand?"

"Yes, Mistress." Ruby said, her head falling forward to look at the floor. It surprised Ruby to find a finger pressing up against her chin. Before she knew it, a tender, moist pair of lips pressed against hers. "Tonight you will stand tall and be proud. You may be mine, but you are mine because you choose to be. Show it." Ruby nodded. "Let's get some makeup on her and her shoes and we'll go." Bianca said, looking at the small silver watch on her arm.

Ashley's masterful work perfectly accented Ruby's natural colors, bringing out the silver of the necklace, the earrings and the bangles against the dark gray dress and her strawberry blond hair. The limousine that Bianca ordered sat patiently for an extra twenty minutes, but the value made it worth the wait as both women slipped into the back ready to turn heads.

"You look amazing pet." Bianca said, giving her thigh a tender squeeze, her eyes holding Ruby's in a desirous glance.

"Thank you, Mistress." She whispered more out of appreciation and desire than weakness.

"I think our host will like you very much." She said before breaking the connection of their eyes.

"I hope so. I want to please you." Ruby replied seeing Bianca's attention turn to the open space between them and the driver. Pressing a button on the panel of the door, a tinted glass pane rose between them, providing a small bit of privacy.

"Our host is Mr. Mulroney. What he does or who he is doesn't matter to you right now. All you need know is that he pays very well for my attention and my discretion and since you are with me that discretion, and attention transfers to you." Bianca's eyes caught Ruby's again to make sure she was paying full attention to what she told her. "You will not answer personal questions from anyone. You will stay close to me at all times unless I tell you to stay where you are. I do not mind if you enjoy a drink or two, but you represent me while you are here and I need you to be in control." Her hand slid further up Ruby's leg, exposing the lacy top of the stockings and pushing the short skirt further toward her hips.

Ruby's eyelids shuddered slightly and her lips parted as Bianca's fingers pressed her swollen button beneath the faux leather panties.

"How does your jewelry feel?" She asked, her tone soft, sultry as her eyes watched her face. The curious surprise in Ruby's eyes told Bianca that she forgot about the bulbous intruder in her ass until reminded of it.

"It feels good Mistress." She replied under labored breaths as fingers rubbed harder against her swollen nub.

"Do you like your collar?"

"Y… yes Mistress. I am thrilled you gave it to me." Ruby was growing closer with every bit of pressure applied. Bianca wondered how much teasing and control Ruby could muster.

"Good. I want you to know what you mean to me and giving you that collar means that I am as committed to you as you are to me. It's a reminder to both of us of the bond we have." Young, tentative fingers unconsciously went to the small ruby that hung at her throat. Bianca knew from experience how the symbol of the collar changed submissive attitudes. The cool metal that now circled her neck; the heart lock at the back became a reminder of her purpose in the world.

Bianca said *bond,* but she wondered if Ruby read anymore into that. It was obvious there was affection between them. It caused Bianca to wonder if she could ever say the words to Ruby. This type of relationship was very new even to Bianca, but it was reasonable to wonder if maybe someday their bond would transmute to something more.

Just as Ruby's body reached that pinnacle, Bianca pulled her hand away without so much as a word.

Ruby stifled a whimper of disappointment. She closed her legs, pressing them together to work out any lingering sensations of arousal on her own. She wouldn't come, that was for Bianca to direct, but she could savor the sensation a bit longer.

"Straighten yourself up." Bianca was cool again as the car began winding its way down a long driveway.

Ruby gasped faintly as the large house came into view. Warm light filled the air around the house, surrounded by a forest of trees. Ruby pulled the skirt down along her thighs, over the top of the stockings, using her hand to spread the fabric down across her legs. Bianca watched out of the corner of her eye.

From the tinted window of the limousine, looming above them on a hill sat a familiar Victorian style plantation house, well known for this part of the country. It had a wide porch and columns on the front with two separate floors.

Several silhouettes stood or sat on the porch as they approached. They all dressed with fairly classy outfits, not the dress or fashion you'd find at a college party, which made Bianca grin. Realizing this was likely nothing Ruby ever experienced before, Bianca wondered if it was a good or bad thing to bring her here. Bianca gave Ruby a reassuring squeeze at her hand, causing her to look over. Bianca stared back with a warm, confident smile on her face.

"You'll be fine pet. I'm right here beside you." Ruby smiled and nodded happily.

Kieran Mulroney was old money Irish whose family came to the country in the mid-nineteen hundreds, working their way from the docks of Boston to the upper crust of New Orleans. The grandson of a docks foreman from the late nineteen hundreds, the son of a heart surgeon and his lawyer wife, Kieran knew about hard work and success. He owned one of the biggest medical technologies companies in the southeast, a beacon of the community and the audacity of the American spirit.

Standing in the door with a glass of scotch balanced in his hand, Kieran watched quietly as Bianca and Ruby stepped out of the limousine. Waiting till they were up the stairs to the house, he kept his laid back stoic visage, the air of the sort of man who earned everything he has.

Tall compared to both Bianca and Ruby. He wore a light blue button-up shirt and khaki slacks that fit comfortably. His appearance gave the impression of a man who would be just as comfortable in the boardroom of a fortune five hundred company as he was standing on the porch of his house. Soft smile lines at the edges of his mouth and even softer lines radiating out from his eyes. He seemed the type of a man who spent a great amount of his life smiling, and the smirk on his face at the approach of the two women only confirmed that assumption.

His fairly round head and large bright eyes drew the eye to the center. Flat pointed ears and a mixed mane of gray and light brown hair with lighter gray hair near the ears, framed his face, adding to his seasoned executive look.

"Bianca my dear, such a surprise to see you." Stepping forward finally as they approached, a light mix of an Irish and Cajun accent in his voice. Truly a man who'd lived in New Orleans most of his life, he gave off a welcoming laid back air about himself as Bianca stepped up and gave him a soft kiss on the cheek.

"Kieran, it's been too long. I'm so sorry I never responded to your invitation, I'm teaching at Loyola now and between that and work it slipped my mind until just a few days ago." Kieran cocked his head gently to the side as he listened, his smile barely slipping with Bianca's apology. It didn't take long for the man's eyes to turn to Ruby. From the corner of her eye, Bianca realized every person standing on the porch was trying their best not to stare at her. To Bianca's surprise, Ruby stood quietly behind her.

"And who is this?" He asked without turning his attention from Ruby. Bianca turned to admire her protégé happily before leaning in.

"This is Ruby. She's my new pet. I have a proposition for you which I think will be beneficial for all of us." Her voice barely carried beyond his ear. Bianca couldn't be sure, but the way his already large bright eyes lit up, what he heard was a welcome surprise.

"Well Miss. Ruby, welcome to my home." He finally said after a careful moment of consideration. He stepped up and took her hand to kiss the back. Ruby flushed across her face at the attention as Kieran turned back to Bianca. "Can I get you a drink? I get the feeling we'll need to talk at some point?" Bianca nodded

"That would be wonderful. For both of us please."

He led them into the house, Ruby obediently following behind Bianca as Kieran handed both of them crystal flutes of golden champagne. "Pet, sit here while I talk with Kieran." Bianca asked Ruby to sit in an armchair near a front corner of the room. She and their host sat on a smaller sofa further back into the room. Bianca watched as she took her seat, quietly sipping at the champagne while watching the guests in the house mix and mingle. Bianca wondered where Ruby's mind was. *What was she thinking or hearing?* Bianca knew the random bits of conversation she picked up as they pretended not to notice her sitting by herself could raise her awareness of the situation she was in.

As time passed Bianca circulated through the house, always with Ruby following close behind. As directed she only answered questions as best she could when approached directly. It seemed curiously out of the ordinary to Ruby that people would be so unconcerned about an anti-social and subservient woman at a party such as this.

In the short time at the party, several guests quietly filtered out, until Ruby realized that only about eight people, including herself, Bianca and Kieran remained. That number quickly changed as the last couple, an older man and woman said their goodbyes, leaving the three of them, two women and a man who appeared to be a professional in his upper thirties.

The two women appeared to be friends or closer. It was hard to tell, but they were never far from each other the whole party. One was older, likely in her late forties or early fifties, and the younger looked to be in her thirties. Both looked classy and well groomed, and spent a large amount of time since they arrived at the party eyeing her.

"Come with me pet." Bianca whispered from behind. Ruby didn't notice her mistress walk up behind after going off to talk with Kieran. Ruby turned obediently and followed. There was a look in her eyes that Ruby couldn't place. *Was it desire, hunger, or admiration?* Whatever it was, she was about to find out.

Guided into a small ante-chamber with another door and just enough room for two or three people to stand close together, Bianca stopped her with a touch on the shoulder. Little passed between them about what might happen on the other side of the door. The only activity was her teacher pulling a silk mask from a shelf between the doors.

The concept of blindfolds and experiencing her domination from the point of view of other senses was becoming an expected and almost welcome feeling for Ruby. Something about not seeing what they would do to her made the anticipation greater and the fear less.

"This is more for the discretion of our host and his guests than for you pet." Bianca explained, slipping the soft black mask over her eyes and tying it back around her braided hair. "Please know I argued for you to face this without."

"It's okay, Mistress. I'm happy to do whatever is necessary to put your friend at ease". Ruby said confidently as darkness overtook her.

"That's my good pet. Remember our agreement regarding doing what they ask of you and this could be very beneficial for us." Bianca reminded, planting a soft kiss on Ruby's lips.

"Yes Mistress. I will serve as requested." Ruby replied without hesitation, feeling strength and confidence swell inside of her.

Looking the way she did went a long way to making her feel more confident in the face of strangers. Knowing Bianca was near and supporting her helped immensely. There was a soft click and the sound of murmurs from in front of her as scented warmth tickled her skin and teased her senses.

The murmurs dissipated as Bianca guided her into the room. Ruby was uncertain, but she could swear she heard a hint of low moans coming from somewhere near to where her mistress stopped her.

Once stopped, hands took hold of her wrists, gently clasping what felt like leather cuffs around each with some sort of buckle. As they cuffed both hands, they raised them above her head, then connected her hands to something. Ruby felt herself pulled upward until she was almost hanging from the floor by whatever clasped her hands together.

Her feet still barely touched the floor, but her arms strained against the weight of her body. A hand at the back of her neck released the clasp that held the top of her dress against her front. At the same time the zipper on the back slid down, exposing naked skin while the tight lycra front fell away exposing her naked breasts.

Free of the soft pliable fabric, her breasts firmed, her nipples peaked with arousal. "Very nice." A female voice moving around in front of her whispered. The skirt of her dress eased down along her hips to the floor at her feet. Ruby hung naked besides the leather thong panties, stockings, boots and the jewelry still intruding on her ass.

"You have some exquisite jewelry." Ruby heard the female voice say as something pressed absently against the warm metal heart and ruby protruding from her rear. "You're beautiful." The voice circled her. Someone started removing the boots on her legs, pulling them off from behind, taking the dress with them.

"Are you an obedient little slave?" A male voice from behind interjected. He was very close, almost touching her shoulder, but just far away she could feel his energy but not his touch.

"Yes, I am." She replied. Almost immediately a snap of leather arched across her back, causing Ruby to flinch and yelp softly.

"Yes, I am Sir" the male voice reminded her harshly, tweaking one of her nipples.

"I'm sorry,, sir. Yes, I am, sir. I'm an obedient slave." Ruby cried out from behind the pain radiating from her nipple. The level of pain was far beyond anything that Bianca subjected her to.

"Very good. I'm glad to see you learn fast." The male voice said from behind as a finger played with the leather thong in front of her. It was very obvious to Ruby that the hand was not the man's but the woman's as she heard quiet sighs come from where the owner of the hand should be.

"What do you think?" The woman's voice came from in front. Ruby was uncertain who she was talking to as the man did not respond and no one else in the room made a noise.

A moment later, now almost naked aside from the stockings, panties and jewelry, a pair of hands grabbed at both her back and front as whatever held her up released, lowering her to the floor.

They urged her back a foot or so until her ass pressed against warm wood and cool metal. Eased onto her back, laying on a long wooden bench that barely reached from her shoulders to her hips. This left her head hanging back against the leading edge of the bench, pressed against a pad. The pair of hands worked quickly to secure the cuffs to her wrists on the sides of the bench as another raised her legs up to the point where her hips barely lifted off the bench.

Cold metal against the inside of her knees and cuffs wrapped and secured around her ankles left her folded in half and exposed, legs spread wide.

"Can I take this out?" The female voice asked without answer, the jewelry in her rear moving gently. "Relax little one." The woman's voice gently tried to ease Ruby's nerves as she felt the jewelry move and slowly slip out of her. "Very good. Now this may feel a bit uncomfortable." The woman's voice came as a new cold metal intruder pressed against her tender puckered hole before slipping in. Cool metal attached to her round intruder pressed against the crack of her ass leading along her back.

"Open your mouth." The male voice ordered. Ruby did as she was told. A round piece of plastic pressed between her lips, around the edge and against her teeth, forcing her mouth to open. Hands tied a strap tightly around her head as a second set of hands tied something to the straps of the gag and the blindfold.

Hands were everywhere on her, and Ruby felt pressure pulling on the intruder in her ass, as her head moved. This forced her hips to draw closer to the bench to relieve the pressure on her ass. Increasing the pressure on her legs natural tendency to bend in a certain way. By her estimation, there were several counter balanced restraints on her body that would work in unison to add to her discomfort.

"I think she's ready." The female voice said with a gleeful tone standing off to the side. A long uncomfortable silence permeated Ruby's world as all activity around her ceased. Her senses strained to capture something that might tell her what was going on, but to no avail as the only discernible sound was that almost imperceptible moaning somewhere in the room and the rustling movement she couldn't place.

Finally, after what seemed an eternity the pain of something cold and plastic clamping down against her erect nipples caused Ruby to flinch. A second pinch on her other nipple caused her head to jump, pulling at the connection between her head and the intruder in her ass.

"Now little one, your Mistress tells me you have a word and you understand its use. If this is true, please give me a thumbs up on your right hand." The woman's voice was stern but warm as she established ground rules.

Ruby obediently replied with a thumb on her right hand without the use of her incapacitated mouth.

"Good. If at any time you feel the need to stop what is happening to you, you will put up three fingers on your right hand. That will be our indication that you wish to speak, and we will remove the gag. Do you understand?" Ruby replied with a thumb again. "Such a good slave."

The woman's tone was hard to place because just as she registered the comment, a stinging snap of leather bit into her inner thighs and pelvis, causing Ruby to jump. The reality of the intricate combination of restraints they had connected around her became very apparent as the torrent of the lashes forced her body to jump and flinch each time. The lingering pain and discomfort tormented her more absolutely than Ruby ever felt before. Every aspect of her body was being restrained or tortured in some way without actually torturing her.

After what she could have sworn was twenty or thirty lashes, her attention from the pain on her body quickly shifted as the sensation of something warm and fleshy pushed into her mouth through the gag. What she hadn't realized with the gag had been the hole in the middle, perfectly sized for the man who was now holding her head on the sides as he pushed himself deep into her throat.

Gagging uncontrollably, Ruby fought back any reflex to vomit as he pierced the back of her throat. Holding her head on the sides removed the strain against her ass from the front, but that strain changed to a relentless slow methodical intrusion of her mouth and throat.

Ruby fought to breathe through her nose as her body endured the assault. She felt herself grow dizzy with either a lack of oxygen for her rapidly beating heart or an overabundance of oxygen flooding her mind.

Whatever the situation, Ruby's mind told her she should scream out, stop this intrusion.

Even knowing she could put up her fingers, she found she could only moan into intruder. A familiar tension of arousal in her belly fought against a desire to run.

"Wow. Did you know how much this turned her on?" The female voice asked further into the room from below, leading Ruby to believe she was the one torturing her with the lashes. "Slave, get over here and give her something to put those dripping lips to good use." The woman ordered. Ruby found herself both curious and frightened by something and by who the other slave could possibly be.

Was it their host? Was it someone she hadn't seen still in the house?

Ruby's fought to keep logic and pleasure equally circling in her mind as not to lose herself. The only assault on her body being the hot throbbing shaft in her mouth, gave her a moment to collect her thought, but only a moment.

Without warning, the something the female voice suggested became very real as a very thick intruder pushed deep into her tight wet womanhood. Her hips clenched at the flood of surprise and pleasure as her moist lips barely resisting the intrusion.

Her shifting hips pulled at the intruder in her ass and yanked her head back into the shaft in her throat. The whole situation sent a wave of pain mixed pleasure across her body.

While while the intruder was warm like skin, it felt hard and rubbery, pumping back and forth, in and out of her almost mechanically. She hated to admit it, but her body was moving quickly toward an orgasm brought on largely from the lashes. The surprising thing was the assault on her mouth was quickly starting to turn her body on more the longer she grew used to it.

"Pull the slave away. I'm going to take off the gag. I want to feel her lips when I come." The male voice said urgently as the pumping of her heated core stopped. Hands at the back of her neck released the restraint connecting her head and her ass as the gag pulled away from her mouth.

Almost in unison, the intruder slipped from her rear with little remorse. To Ruby's surprise, the removal didn't hurt at all as she felt curiously accustomed to the abuse. "Have the slave fuck her ass so you can whip her some more." The man's voice said before he pressed the tip of his thick head against her lips, forcing Ruby to open her mouth and accept him. "Oh yeah, that's perfect." He groaned as he pushed into her mouth back to her throat.

At the same time the hard rubber from before pushed passed her relaxed and loose anus until the thickness of the member filled her to the edge of comfort. A new torrent of lashes struck out at her inner thighs, her pelvis and her chest, just barely brushing her nipples and the device clamped to them. The now dull pain flared back up with renewed attention.

She was again being assaulted on all sides. Her body flushed with contrasting sensations, it made her reality swim. "Don't let any slip out." The man ordered, bringing Ruby back to reality for a second as she tried to figure out what he was talking about. Immediately realization hit her as she felt him swell in her mouth, followed closely by a flood of warm wetness spilling into her throat.

Ruby locked her lips around his mouth, understanding that if she didn't do what he said, the consequences would not be fun. At the same time, the assault on her ass pushed her closer to an orgasm than she realized she was.

Concern filled her mind. Doing as she was told by not letting any of his seed escape and not letting her body release into an orgasm meant she couldn't ask permission. The tension pushed Ruby to a point of control she'd never known she had. Her mouth focused more on the seed now flooding her throat, turning her attention from the growing threat of orgasm.

Swallowing what she could in her precarious position, she fought to keep the gooey liquid out of her sinuses as she felt his release slow. Swallowing for the third time, she locked her lips around his shaft as he started to pull back, letting them sweep along his warm vein bristling skin until the thick ridge of his head pulled her lips apart.

"Very good little one." He said, patting her on the cheek.

"May… may I come sir?" Ruby croaked through saliva and jizz in her throat in between ragged breaths brought on by a body that was a hair width away from collapse.

"I'm sorry, I didn't hear you." The man teased, forcing Ruby to swallow again and pull a bit more confidence in her voice.

"May I come, sir?" She asked desperately.

"Oh, you want to come?" He asked coldly. "She wants to know if she can come." He asked the room.

"Wait." The woman's voice said as another torrent of lashes streaked across her inner thighs and pelvis, brushing her swollen sex.

"Slave, take that off. Show our guest how good you are at eating pussy and clean those drippy lips." The woman ordered in between lashes that were bringing Ruby dangerously close to the inability to control her own body. Just when she worried the sensations had reached a pinnacle, the feel of a warm wet, tender tongue on her oversexed folds and throbbing button almost pushed her over the edge.

Ruby writhed as much as the restraints allowed her body to move. She fought mercilessly to keep her body from tipping over the edge.

Lips suckled at her and licked deep into her, lashes landed over and over on her torso. Her head swam, she saw black spots in her sight when she heard the command.

"You may come now little one." The woman's mouth above Ruby's face, her warm breath washed over young skin as she released control. Ruby's body shuddered, the scent of arousal filled her nostrils as wetness met her mouth. Without question or hesitation, her lips locked around the sweet warmth presented to her. She groaned like some caged animal as her body exploded, overflowing with sexual tension. She bucked and clenched as much as she could, considering the level of absolute restraint her body was under. Her tongue lashed out and gave no consideration for how hard or aggressive she was. She sucked and bit at the lips in her mouth as a response to the fullness of her orgasm.

To her surprise, she felt the woman above her groan and tense at the same time, grinding against her mouth. They came together in throws of the sexual overload they just put her through.

Unfortunately for Ruby, that was the last thing she remembered as a dizzy darkness overwhelmed and shut down her mind.

ACT TWO

Dynamic Shifts

The surprise for the evening was less how well Ruby endured their abuse; and more the fact that she passed out from all of it. She barely stirred the whole time they dressed her, placed her in the limousine and brought her back to the apartment.

Bianca leaned on the rail of her porch, staring out at the city below when Ashley walked in, quietly checking on their young friend before joining her.

"She's still out?" Ashley was both surprised and disbelieving as she walked onto the porch with a large round wine glass and a bottle of Bordeaux wine that Bianca left waiting on the counter. She topped off her friend's glass before setting it on a table and leaning in next to Bianca.

"She'll probably sleep through the night." Bianca said dismissively. She was still wearing the red dress from the evening, even though the boots came off hours ago.

"Were they that rough on her?" Ashley asked after licking her lips clean of wine.

"Not really." Bianca shook her head absently, her mind still running through the events of the night. "Honestly, I expected things to go differently. I was kind of concerned when Kieran told me what he wanted to do."

"Why did you? I didn't get the impression that was the plan." Ashley could seeing the thoughtfulness on Bianca's face.

"It wasn't. But at the time it seemed the best option if I wanted to move forward with her." Bianca wanted to keep Ruby from anything that intense, there was a chance the couple involved would push her too far and ruin any path forward Bianca hoped to achieve. To her surprise, Ruby endured with grace. "They actually took it easy on her for what they are used to. But I have to admit, she did well. You said it, she's a natural."

Bianca sighed with a gentle nod of her head to Ashley before taking a sip of her wine.

"I'm glad they weren't too hard on her. That would have been unfortunate." Ashley admitted.

"Oh, I didn't say they weren't hard on her. She did well despite how they treated her." Bianca corrected.

When they arrived at the party and Bianca saw who was in attendance, she knew off the bat that there was a chance things could go south fast. Kieran got off on watching the harder side of fetish lifestyle and attracted those who shared his desires. Bianca told him she didn't think Ruby was ready for that level of action, and Kieran did his best to ease her concerns.

It was a strange dynamic for Bianca when considering Kieran's natural tendency to do and get what he wants when he's in charge, but when he relinquishes that authority to Bianca, he's one of the most submissive men she ever worked with.

This was Kieran not relinquishing his authority. It was also Bianca agreeing in payment for accepting to bring Ruby into the fold if she passed his test. In reality, all the relationships with her high end clients were strange. Most of them refused to accept Bianca's position as the Dominatrix outside of the privacy of their playrooms or hotel rooms. It didn't help, most of them were high-powered alpha males in positions of power in the community. In that she couldn't blame them for not wanting to look weak in public.

"Did it work?" Ashley finally asked, realizing that Bianca's mind was still working through the events of the night.

"I think so. Kieran seemed satisfied, as did Vanessa and Cain. Hell, even their slave seemed to enjoy not being the center of attention for once." Bianca said with a snicker.

"I've only really enjoyed playing with them once." Ashley admitted. To their credit, Vanessa and Cain toned things down a lot since the time when Ashley was more active in the fetish world. Timing of events in her life coincided poorly with her last real interaction with them and things went bad.

One of the fun attributes of being acquainted with Kieran was his inclusion of people of like minds into monthly gatherings. These allowed a few select people to find new experiences and make new friends they might have never run into.

"I don't think you'll have to worry about seeing them again. This was a onetime thing. I almost feel for her. If I'd known they would be there, I would have waited." Bianca took another sip of her wine, hoping the strong floral tones would lighten her spirit some.

"What was the point of meeting Kieran versus any of your other clients?" Ashley asked, having not really been in on the thought process as much as the planning process. Bianca considered the question for a long minute. There was a very valid reason for pointing towards him first over any others, but talking about it in the open like this made her question her logic. Perhaps sharing it with someone she trusted, she could test the validity of her plans.

"She's a nursing student. His ties to the medical community could be invaluable to her, given the right situation. It made sense to give her something that she could see as long-term gain to keep her focused." Curiously saying it out loud, Bianca didn't sound as sure as it had in her mind when she'd worked it out the first time.

"That could work. But Kieran isn't the type where he'll actively involve himself in playing with her." Bianca quickly remembered how much Ashley knew about some of her more prominent clients. Several of them came to her through Kieran's gatherings, which meant that Ashley was familiar with them. It didn't hurt that her friend was a lawyer and acted also as her lawyer, which meant any discussions they had about her clients gave her protection.

"That was probably the one other positive that came from watching those two; I saw how she worked with her slave. She was rather good and with the right tools Ruby could do the same for me with my clients." Ashley pursed her lips into an almost pouty droop as her head nodded gently to the side with a thoughtful acknowledgment.

"During the party the two seemed like close friends or lovers, talking and sharing closeness without being overly apparent of their situation. Once they were in private the girl changed into a most demure and obedient slave. She reminded me of Ruby, seemingly content with her position of being ordered around and demeaned. Watching Vanessa and her slave interacting both in public and private gave Bianca a new perspective on how to interact with Ruby. .

"So what now?" Ashley asked after a quiet pause.

To be honest, Bianca's thoughts beyond the evening never really formed. Regardless that nothing played out how she'd expected. It reminded her that sometimes having a plan wasn't necessarily always a good thing. She never planned on having Ruby sound asleep in her bed after a long night of being abused and pushing her limits beyond anything Bianca ever expected.

"I don't know Ash." Bianca shook her head, her reddish blond locks falling down over her face as a hand moved to push them back. "What do you think?" Those soft, thoughtful green eyes stared over at her as Ashley considered the question. If there was anyone who could sort through this objectively, regardless of her attraction to Bianca or her fondness for Ruby, it was Ashley.

"How much more time do you have as her teacher?" Bianca could see where this was going. Unfortunately, it was too late for Ruby to drop or move to another class, which meant there was a critical conflict of interest going on with them.

"About eight weeks, around which time I have a plan to meet Kieran."

"Is she ready for that?" Ashley knew that the situation with Kieran was a relatively new development.

"Probably not." Bianca replied with a scowl on her brow. "I'm not even sure I'm ready for that, especially after seeing Vanessa with her slave. There is a new dynamic there I hadn't considered."

"How so?" Ashley asked, walking over to a nearby chair and sitting, her legs up on the arm of the chair as she sat sideways, the glass of wine balanced on her knees. Bianca joined her, sitting so they were looking at each other.

"Vanessa and her slave had this almost sensual connection in public, but a very domme-sub connection in private." Ashley's cool orange brown eyes stared across at her friend as she pulled unconsciously at a strand of dark black hair.

"Like they were lovers?" She asked curiously of Bianca's impressions.

"Yeah, very close." Bianca nodded, her eyes lost in thought. "I've felt a draw very much like that with Ruby, but I'm not sure it's what is best for this situation."

"Bee, I don't know if there is a 'best for this situation'." Ashley replied wholeheartedly before taking a sip of wine. Bianca could tell she was using the pause to form her next response. Ashley's eyes never left hers. "You need to be careful and take this slow bee. You're already way beyond crossing the line with her." Ashley leaned forward, placing a hand on her arm. "You know I want you to be happy and fulfilled. But is this worth your career or your reputation?"

Ashley was right. There was more going on here than a simple budding relationship between two women. "As usual Ash, you're here to keep me centered." Bianca placed her own hand on top of Ashley's.

They stayed on the patio for another hour; the conversation turning toward a new client of Ashley and the intricacies of the case attached to that client. In all their time together, Ashley always found creative ways to discuss the intricacies of her cases and clients without compromising the integrity of the client relationship, a skill Bianca grew fond of.

In the morning the feeling of a soft tongue lapping intently at her sensitive folds awakened Bianca. She opened her eyes to a reddish blond mop of hair bobbing gently against her warm inner thighs. The attention to her moistening depths drew a growing, passionate moan from her throat. Considering her semi-conscious state, it didn't take long for her body to respond to her protégé's attention with a gut clenching orgasm.

As the haze of heat faded from her eyes, Bianca found her hand tightly gripping the locks of reddish blond hair, holding her close as her body came down as quickly as it had shot up. "You're very attentive pet. It's good to see your ordeal last night didn't diminish your spirit." She said pulling Ruby up along her body by her hair until her mouth was close. Bianca leaned up, giving her pet a tender probing kiss. Her tongue worked the ridges of those young lips, collecting the remnant of her own bodies scent and flavor as they kissed. "Stay like that." Bianca ordered Ruby, who was on her hands and knees on the bed. She straddled Bianca who gradually extricated her legs and arms before sitting up on the bed next to Ruby.

Reaching for the nightstand, she picked up the silver butt plug with the ruby heart. Sticking the large tapered bulb in her mouth for a second, Bianca then pulled the saliva laden metal bulb from her mouth. Turning to Ruby's rear, she slowly pushed the tapered end of the plug into Ruby's puckered hole until it vanished. The plug quickly disappeared into her dark canal. "Go wash yourself up." Bianca said with a smack to the firm round ass of the girl kneeling before her. "Find me in the kitchen when you're done."

"Yes, Mistress." Ruby gave a sheepishly unquestioning reply.

Without further word, Bianca crawled from the bed and padded into the living area of her apartment toward the kitchen. Ruby did as she was told and walked into the bathroom. Soon the sound of water in the shower filled the silence of the large studio apartment. Setting some freshly ground coffee to steep in a glass French press carafe, Bianca walked into the living room.

Pulling a large black half circle cushion attached to the wall with a power cord from behind the couch, Bianca placed the apparatus on the floor in front of the couch. With a small black remote from a nearby coffee table, she tested the machine with a few button presses. On top of the half circle, a long thin skin colored strip with nubs and ridges began to hum softly.

Happy everything was ready, Bianca walked back into the kitchen, pressing her steeped coffee. Placing a small assortment of bread pastries on a large square plate, she added a small bit of butter and jam just as Ruby stepped into the kitchen with a towel wrapped around her wet body. "There you are. Good." Bianca said with a grin, walking around the counter of the kitchen to take her by the hand. "Come here pet. We need to talk."

Leading Ruby into the living room, Bianca pulled the bundle of towel from between her breasts, causing the large fluffy white fabric to drop uselessly to the floor. "Squat down please." Bianca instructed, guiding Ruby's legs to straddle the machine as she kneeled until her legs spread and the the skin pink strip pressed firmly against the bare flesh at the apex of her legs. "Wait there." Bianca ordered, pressing one button on the small black remote she'd tested a few minutes earlier. Suddenly the muffled hum broke the silence, followed quickly by a weak whimper from her young pet. Set on the lowest number, to keep the experience slow, a torment of pleasure to keep Ruby off balance as they talked.

Bianca gathered the plate of pastries and the coffee from the kitchen, placing them both on the coffee table to Ruby's left. Still naked herself, Bianca sat on the sofa less than a foot from Ruby, her eyes focused on her nakedness as the torment of the vibrator teased her body.

"Is that okay pet? I don't want you to feel the need to come until we've talked."

"Yes, Mistress." Was all she said in reply, her breath heavy and steady as she fought against the sensation assaulting the cleft between her legs. Bianca picked up the remote, pressing one button which caused the muffled vibration to intensify slightly.

"Good. Now, first I want to tell you your dedication and resolve impressed and touched me last night. You went above and beyond my expectations and held fast to your promise to do whatever they asked of you." Bianca had a warm smile on her face as she talked, eventually leaning forward, tenderly touching Ruby's face, pulling her into an easy, intimate kiss. Her lips pulled at Ruby's full pink lips, letting the kiss translate her adoration.

"Thank you, Mistress." Ruby replied as Bianca broke the kiss, leaning back on the sofa. She could tell that Ruby was fighting hard to keep her composure regardless of the sensations between her legs. Her eyes held her mistress's gaze, a promise of undivided attention.

"That being said pet, we need to cool down this relationship slightly until we are no longer in a position where it looks like I have undue influence over you." Bianca watched Ruby's eyes and body flinch at the statement. It would be hard for anyone to hide surprise in the face of that statement normally, but naked and exposed while being teased by a vibrator was definitely not a situation where you can hide a reaction. But Ruby's composure surprised Bianca.

"I'm sorry, Mistress. Did I do something to displease you?" Ruby asked through ragged breaths as she felt the strain of the building pleasure in her body.

"No pet! You please me more than I should allow. Which is why we need this." Bianca said, leaning forward, her hand softly brushing along Ruby's flush naked skin. "We have eight weeks left for class. I compromised my objectivity already deciding to pass you regardless of how the rest of the semester grades play out." She was certain the assertion that she would pass the class regardless of her performance would be just as much of a surprise, but what could she do? Ruby had done everything and more of what she had asked of her.

"Can I see you, Mistress?" Ruby asked sheepishly, her breathing becoming more beleaguered. Bianca's hand reached up as she pressed an open palm to Ruby's cheek, her thumb sliding softly across partly opened lips as her young protégé fought each breath for control.

"Yes baby. You will still join me for your internship. In four weeks we will go to a private party where you will join me with a client so we can prepare you. The week after our last class, you and I will attend Mr. Mulroney by himself." Continuing to talk, Bianca reached over and pressed the remote once more as the intensity of the hum from the machine nudged up. "You impressed him very much and is eager to see you again, but he is out of the country on business and wants see us again when he is back."

Ruby's body began to visibly fight the growing pleasure. Her skin flushed as small beads of sweat formed in the soft valley between her pert, round breasts that rose and fell with greater frequency now. Her breathing grew faster to keep up with the racing heart.

"Don't worry pet, I am not letting go of you." Bianca's fingers went to the ruby on her collar swinging erratically with Ruby's growing arousal. "I gave you that collar to signify as much the commitment you've given to me as the commitment I give you. But we need to be careful if we want to continue. Being seen together in public while you are my student and I am your instructor at college could have lasting consequences for both of us."

"I understand Mistress." Ruby said with a soft nod, her senses fighting to stay composed. Her nipples stood like arrow tips along the soft roll of her round breasts, straining against the growing need. "I wouldn't want to do anything that might keep me from you." She finished, the devotion in her comment ringing in Bianca's ears, mirroring her own sentiments.

"Does being with your Mistress please you pet?" Bianca asked, her tone more sultry and playful now as she reached out. Taking one of Ruby's erect nipples in between her fingers, she abruptly twisted the nipple, pinching down on it.

"Yes, Mistress." Ruby replied following a whimper muffled behind a lip biting groan. Her eyes teared up and glazed over slightly as Bianca kept up the pressure on her nipple, causing Ruby to gasp for breaths between increasing waves of desire.

"You will keep your jewelry in place at all times except in the event you need to use the bathroom. You will take it out and wash it thoroughly every morning and then replace it. Can you do that for me pet to show me your dedication to what we have together?" Bianca asked, reaching up and tweaking the other nipple, pulling Ruby forward so she could softly nibble at the young velvety lips.

"I… will do… as you ask… Mistress." Ruby replied with difficulty, her body starting to shudder as she fought to keep the orgasm back until free to let go.

"I know you will pet." Bianca said with a look of tenderness, their faces mere inches apart as she looked up. "Would you like to come now my obedient jewel?" Bianca whispered, their gaze locked onto each other with an intensity only comparable to the desire in Ruby's body for release.

"If you wish it Mistress." Before Ruby would have asked for permission to orgasm. Now she was deferring to Bianca's desires. The teacher beamed at the progress she and Ruby made in such a short time.

"Yes, of course, pet. Come for your mistress. Show me how much pleasure being with me brings you." Her hand gripped the small remote, pushing the intensity up another two notches as Ruby's body thrust backward. Like a jolt of electricity delivered through the machine, Ruby's body stiffened, back arched, uncaring at the strain Bianca's fingers created pulling back on her nipples. Her small frame shuttered and writhed as the buzzing grew louder. Her skin grew flush red, sweat spread across her curvy chest as an eruption of pent up need ripped from her chest through her lungs to her mouth. Ruby growled like some caged animal, hands and arms supporting her arched back, pressing against the black machine's rounded frame.

Without warning, Ruby's body sprung forward, collapsing in on itself, falling into Bianca's waiting arms as she fought for breath and composure. Bianca realized in that moment with her young pet weak in her arms how difficult it would to be so distant over the next few months.

Who...Are...You?

The first few weeks of their new relationship were intense and overwhelming. But by comparison to the next four weeks, they were a mere fantasy in relation, at least for Ruby. She'd spent the first few days of seclusion on cloud nine having realized the true nature of her feelings for Bianca. This went way beyond adoration or idolizing a strong, confident woman, and was much more than a simple crush or infatuation. There was a power that her teacher had over her that went way beyond a sexual desire or some misguided need to please her.

The bulk of Ruby's thoughts circled over the first week. Her conscious and subconscious mind fought to come to terms with what brought them to this point. She wanted to understand what she was feeling for the woman who threw her world into a tailspin. By the second week, desire and need shifted to a painful yearning. While there were opportunities to be near Bianca, the closeness meant proximity, not connection.

Ruby wasn't sure if the distance and detachment was part of being in the work environment or if it was part of Bianca's training like the first time she came to her office. She understood the need to keep any suggestion of their relationship hidden to the world for a time, but the sudden shift did little to reassure Ruby that things were still warm between them. Needless to say, by the time Ruby arrived at Bianca's office the beginning of the fourth week, she was needy and frustrated.

The past few weeks focused on breaking down the business plan of a company that the firm was in the process of buying out in order to breakout the component parts. They only ever referred to it as the 'Peterson account', and judging by the records, they were closing in on a final decision.

Regardless of everything else going on, or not going on in her life, Ruby couldn't deny she was definitely learning a lot about how businesses worked, grew, prospered and died. That was the case with the Peterson account. The business in question was hemorrhaging capital, and they were trying to find a way to stop the bleeding. Once the blood's in the water, the sharks circle, which is what had happened with Bianca's company. Seeing a viable investment, they began circling, and every day they grew closer to the kill, a kill that Ruby would have a hand in.

It had started out simple enough, sorting parts of the company, breaking out the individual departments and divisions. The past week focused on sorting through the business plans, breaking down the revenue streams and products lines to find the weak points to break off. Ruby wondered if the employees or investors for this company had the first clue what was happening.

"Ruby!" Bianca's voice broke into her thoughts like a ball peen hammer shattering the fog around her mind. "Where are you?" She added as Ruby blinked, turning to acknowledge the call.

"I… I'm sorry. I was just thinking." Ruby grumbled, turning back to the sheets of numbers and names sorted out in front of her.

"What were you thinking about?" Bianca asked in her cool business tone that Ruby had become very accustomed to over the weeks.

"I was thinking about the employees, the investors. How they likely don't have any idea what is happening to their company." Ruby could tell by the stifled sigh and how Bianca's shoulders dropped that she was about to get another lesson in how businesses ran. Many such lessons became a regular part of their time together recently. While Ruby appreciated the education, she deeply yearned for the other lessons that were a large part of their earlier relationship.

"It's normal to feel a level of compassion for the people affected by the outcomes of these situations, but remember much of the damage is done. It's business Ruby, they are born, they grow and they die."

"But you're profiting from that death." Ruby argued.

"Actually, we are profiting from their rebirth." Bianca shot back quickly, a response that both surprised and confused Ruby.

"What do you mean?" Ruby replied sharply. The tone in her voice and the look on her face surprised Bianca as much as her response surprised Ruby. A quick moment of frustration flashed across Bianca's face before she caught herself. Ruby could see the moment she took to compose herself as a thick silence hung in the air between them.

"Think of the company as a dying body…" Bianca took a sheet of blank paper and laid it out on the table. Using a black marker, she drew a very crude outline of a human body on the paper. "… we're identifying the parts of that body that are still viable. The heart, lungs, kidneys. You get the picture." She drew a few small circles around in the places where the body parts she rambled off should be on the outline of a body. "We also identify the parts of the body that are failing, ones we can't salvage. When we're done, we invest in other companies by transplanting those useful parts hoping they will make the new body thrive."

"And what happens to the unsalvageable parts?" Ruby asked, a tone of uncertainty still in her voice.

"We do what we can to be as surgical as possible in making sure that we lose no viable parts in the transfer. As with everything in life once something reaches a certain point of entropy, you can't fix it. Some people who make those viable parts work will continue to make their parts grow. We will lose others. As it is with an organ transplant, there's always a risk of rejection."

That Bianca took the time to create a visual in a medical context that touched on her studies, Ruby could suddenly relate easier, which went a long way to settling Ruby's mind. In the process of understanding the imagery, Ruby didn't notice Bianca stand. She walked around the table and sat on the edge so she was practically touching Ruby. Her teacher stared down, forcing Ruby to shift her attention up, the way Bianca liked it.

"What's wrong pet?" Bianca asked, putting a crooked finger under her chin. The warmth of the touch sent a wave of heat through Ruby's body. The first time in weeks Bianca had showed her any warmth of connection. "This isn't about what's happening to the company."

Ruby shook her head softly, looking down submissively, feeling embarrassed at how she let her emotions color her attitude. The truth was, deep down she wanted Bianca to throw her down on the table and punish her for being insolent. The problem was how do you articulate that to a strong and confident woman like Bianca?

"I miss you, Mistress." Ruby whispered almost imperceptibly.

"What did you say pet?" A soft joking tone in her voice as she leaned in closer so Ruby could speak her mind without fear of exposing them.

"I miss you Mistress." She repeated, a bit louder. The wry grin that formed on Bianca's face told Ruby exactly what she had wondered. How did her teacher want Ruby to express her desires?

"What exactly do you want?" Bianca asked, leaving the door open for whichever way Ruby wanted to take her next words.

"I… I want Mistress to use me however she desires." Ruby replied quietly, fighting through the nervousness and uncertainty in her voice. She expressed these desires in the past, but those expressions of need generally came in the throes of very tense emotional and physical events. As far as she could remember, she never freely admitted her yearning for giving herself over to her teacher's control.

Ruby could see by the bright proud look that spread across Bianca's face that something about her comment either surprised or pleased the woman. She leaned back on the table, staring down at her.

"Well, isn't this a nice change?" Bianca finally said, her hand reaching out to take Ruby's in her own. "When I first met you, you could barely articulate why you should get a second chance on your grade. And now you're able to articulate a desire for something most people could never admit to themselves, let alone openly admit to another person."

Bianca seemed genuinely happy with the shift, which seemed to surprise Ruby more than anything. It was hard to recognize the difference, but once the woman she came to respect and desire pointed it out, the reality became obvious.

Without further word her teacher's finger and thumb pulled up on Ruby's chin, tilting her head up as she leaned in and gave her young firm lips a prolonged kiss before pulling back.

"Now we just need to inject a little confidence into your spirit." She whispered, their eyes locked in a gaze before the business woman stood and walked back to the other side of the table.

With doubt and concern removed from her thoughts, Ruby found clarity in her work like she'd not felt before. She cleared the files for the account earlier than either of them expected, leaving her without a task almost an hour before her usual stop time. There was an obvious shift in the way Bianca regarded her the rest of that day, a shift that only seemed to bolster Ruby's confidence more.

"Wow Ruby, this is good work." Bianca said, walking back into the conference room from her office and looking over the packet of Ruby's files. "I'd have to say looking at these that you've come a long way from the business plan outline you presented when this started."

"Thank you, ma'am." Ruby replied happily, her teacher's appraisal filling her with elation.

"Would you say you've learned something about business helping me here?" Bianca asked, taking a seat in the chair at the head of the conference table.

"It definitely makes more sense to me now, but there is more I want to learn." Ruby replied honestly. Her appetite for learning about business grew considerably since that first day of class when all she wanted was credit so she could graduate.

"Good. I'm glad to hear you say that. Your progress has validated my faith in picking you for this internship, which helps diminish any suggestions of impropriety." Bianca pushed up out of the chair, taking the files and stacking the many thick folders together. "Can you be here in the morning on Thursday, say nine thirty?" Bianca asked, held the stack of folders against her perfect full bosom.

"I have Trig at ten on Thursday ma'am." Ruby countered, feeling sad that she might miss out on whatever event her teacher wanted her to attend.

"Are you doing okay in that class? Can you miss one day?" Bianca asked, checking something on her phone as she spoke.

"Yes, I have a high grade and our final review isn't until next week." Ruby replied.

"If I give you a note, I'm certain your professor will let you miss one class. I really want you here Thursday." Bianca replied before turning and walking from the small conference room into her office. Ruby followed as her teacher sat down at the desk and quickly started typing something on her computer.

A moment later the printer came to life, spitting out a white sheet of paper with printed text on it. Bianca picked it up off of the printer and subsequently signed the bottom of the sheet with the expensive pen she'd had Ruby sign the NDA so many long weeks ago.

"There, that should do." Bianca said handing the letter to Ruby. It asked for her to be excused from class on Thursday to attend a meeting crucial to her success in the internship and business class. While the relationship with her trigonometry professor was in no way like the relationship Ruby had with Bianca, her already above average production in class and friendly connection would go a long way to her professor not questioning.

"Thank you, ma'am." Ruby replied happily that Bianca was taking such an interest in her growth as a person. Taking the note, she placed it in her purse.

"Thursday morning you will be here at nine thirty. We'll talk through our understanding of the account so we are comfortable with the details." Bianca stood at the desk, stepping around to Ruby. "At ten we will have a meeting with the team to make sure we are on the right track with the direction we are taking with the company. You will get to see how we make these decisions."

Bianca stopped and brushed Ruby's face with the backs of her fingers. The movement was light and sensual, but affectionate enough that it sent a wash of heat and energy along her skin. "Thursday afternoon you'll have free to do whatever you want before class since you'll be with me in the morning. Saturday you will be at the apartment promptly at six thirty so Miss. Ash can prepare you."

"Prepare me Ma'am?" Ruby asked more assertively this time, feeling that perhaps considering her mistress' mood she might gain more insight to the future of their interactions.

"Miss. Ash will explain pet." Bianca murmured with a methodical tone that told Ruby further inquiry would garner little more information. If there was one thing she'd learned about Bianca at this point was that the woman held her cards close. Whether it was a defense mechanism or her personality, Ruby may never understand, but it was an aspect of her personality she would need to grow used to.

Bianca leaned on the conference table, taking one last minute to look over the numbers for the Peterson account when Ruby rushed into her office looking frazzled and winded. Strands of hair in her usually immaculate bangs hung freely in her face, and the pink tint to her natural pale skin gave Ruby a warm glow that Bianca felt a yearning for. She looked down at her watch. *Five minutes late, perfect.*

"I'm sorry I'm late ma'am, traffic delayed the car picking me up." Ruby offered, having been told the same by the driver. Bianca fought to hide the smirk on her lips. The car had been late picking her up, she'd told the driver to arrive a few minutes later.

"No matter. You're here. The meeting has moved up to nine forty-five and I need you to talk to the conclusions." She could almost see the red flush from Ruby's skin at the suggestion that Ruby would brief the team on their aspect of the account without any preparation.

"But… ma'am, I'm… I'm not.." Ruby stopped, uncertain how she could argue the point. Her eyes stayed locked on her mentor as the gears behind her eyes worked on how best to approach the subject without drawing the ire of the woman before her.

"What's the problem Ruby?" Bianca turned, her hand firmly on the soft gray blouse fabric on her shoulder. Fingers pressed lightly into that skinny arm as Ruby's mind raced. "You've been studying these files for over a month. You know them better than anyone in this room. Just assess the value of the information you have and give a recommendation."

Bianca's voice was steady and firm. "Think of it this way…" She continued, moving closer to Ruby until her mouth was barely touching her ear. Bianca was certain the warmth of her breath brushing that soft pale lobe would spread heat all across Ruby's skin. Her tone softened and her voice became a whisper. "It's no more threatening than giving yourself up to two strange men and letting them ravage your body in front of your teacher."

The hand on her young skinny shoulder slid down Ruby's arm. Bianca's palm brushed along the full round globe, so pert and tender beneath the silky softness of Ruby's blouse. She could sense the demeanor shift in Ruby. Her exasperation at being thrown to the wolves faded and the strength and determination she'd shown so many times during their extracurricular activities surfaced.

Ruby stood straight and looked into Bianca's eyes. "Yes ma'am. I'll do my best." She finally said, strength with an undertone of anxiety carried her as Ruby stepped up to the table and pulled together the master file on all the parts of the Peterson account.

"Of that I have no doubt pet." Bianca smirked.

A moment later the team filtered into the conference room, taking seats around the table, all eyes on Ruby who sat straight and confident to the right of Bianca. Most of the team, Ruby only met in passing. Connected with this account long before she arrived at the company, each was an executive or junior account manager. She knew each held a stake in the outcome of this account and Bianca knew her young protégé was likely thinking the same thing as she sat quietly. Anxiety in her eyes, the only sign of uncertainty in her body language.

"Good Morning everyone." Bianca started as everyone settled into the chairs and took their seats. "Martin Coumes needs to decide on Peterson before Wednesday of next week to keep the offer price point competitive, so I want to go over each of your assessments of the various areas you're working." She paused for a moment to gauge each of her team member's reactions to the suggestion of an end to their current project.

The man hours and time spent dealing with each major contract such as this tended to have a deep psychological effect on the team. Bianca tended to push for closure as early as possible on each account to help the team cope.

"To start Ruby will set the table regarding the overall assessment of each division, then each of you will have a chance to break down your division and argue any points you may not agree with." Bianca was firm, cold, but her team was used to the cold impartiality of their business.

Without further word, Ruby stood, walking around the table to hand each member a printout of their assessment from the past few weeks. Bianca could see the strain in her posture, her movements. The young girl was far outside of her element, her comfort zone, but there was a strength in her demeanor that made Bianca's expression beam with adoration. Ruby was far from that timid, uncertain girl she met so many weeks ago.

"As you can see from the assessment before you…" Her voice started out uneasy and shaky. "… Peterson's eight separate divisions together as a single entity represent a value of barely three point eight million dollars. Human resources, Manufacturing, Supply and logistics and Executive Management are the largest draws with the least value." As she talked, Bianca heard the confidence of knowing the material push the uncertainty and uneasiness aside. "Research and Development, Sales, Product, and Financial Management represent the largest value."

Her teacher's eyes watched the table, slowly moving from person to person as they listened and checked Ruby's facts against the information on the assessment she handed out. The curious aspect of the whole situation was that Ruby made none of the determinations she was discussing, Bianca did. Ruby represented each of the points as someone who directly influenced each assessment.

The level of confidence and pride in her voice resonated with the members around the table as Bianca realized they didn't see her young mirror as a naïve intern. Regardless of her status among those arrayed around the table, Ruby had found her groove and was giving it all she had. There was a powerful change going on inside that mind, so torn with the way things had always been and the way things were now. Bianca could only smile with pride.

"Of course breaking up divisions such as product and manufacturing or supply and logistics would make them more difficult to package, the question we need to ask is how can we justify the loss in value if we don't remove the dead weight?"

The last question came from Bianca's assessment, having discussed the very issue the last day Ruby was at the office working on the account. Bianca was surprised, and impressed that Ruby remembered the point. Bianca didn't see any benefit in taking credit for the question. It was an opening salvo for the rest of the team to assert their positions, and the way Ruby presented it only helped establish her credibility in the discussion.

Walking back around the table to take her seat beside Bianca, Ruby never let her demeanor slip. The strain and anxiety of being required to present without preparation was over and now. The responsibility to run the discussion fell to Bianca. She was happy to take the pressure from her intern after having showed the resolve she had.

"I agree with her assessment." Clay Richards, spoke up first; his gray-blue eyes never leaving Ruby's face until it was time to speak his mind. "We keep everything except Human Resources, supply and logistics and Executive Management. Manufacturing is already tooled for the product and the people who run the manufacturing are experts on the setup." That Clay referred to her assessment regarding Ruby's report sent a tingle along Bianca's spine. Ruby asserted herself and having Clay recognize the youthful intern in front of the team gave her credibility, which Bianca knew would go a long way to establishing confidence with Ruby.

"Alicia," Bianca asked, turning to a younger team member sitting across from Bradley, her wild dark brown hair and glasses giving her a very soft nerdy look that curiously attracted Bianca. "How would keeping manufacturing impact our price point calculations?"

"Manufacturing is probably the only one we could bundle without a significant impact on price point." Alicia responded, adjusting her glasses as she looked over the figures. "Most of the equipment is already calculated into the asset liability. The bulk of the drain on value in manufacturing is depreciation of the equipment and the salary for specialized technicians to maintain the equipment."

The mousy dark-haired girl's eyes anxiously jumped between Ruby and Bianca. The executive couldn't tell if she was seeing interest or jealousy from Alicia, but she made a note to watch future interactions.

"Does anyone else care to argue why we should keep or break off their division?" Bianca asked to the gathered team. Those who hadn't spoken up were those who either accepted that the division they assessed was on the chopping block or not. Based on the information they gathered over the past few months, it wasn't a surprise that the others had nothing further to add.

"Very well, we'll present this to Martin tomorrow and let him decide if he agrees with our assessment. Good Job everyone, as always, you've made our division look good with your stellar diligence on another account."

As if by some unwritten rule the gathered team took her praise as a dismissal, Bradley first followed closely by the rest as he stood. The junior executives left the conference room through the back door while Clay stayed, his eyes looking down at Ruby as she sat proudly but quietly in the chair to the right of Bianca.

"I'm impressed, Ruby," Clay finally said after everyone had left. "Good job. I'm curious to see how you survive Martin." The senior executive said with a teasing tone as he stood and walked toward Bianca's office, a hand gently squeezing the shoulder closest to his path before he walked out.

It took her a moment as Clay left before Ruby's face turned bright red. Her cool blue eyes turning and reaching out for any support she might find in the woman beside her.

"Don't worry Ruby. I'm still debating if I want to throw you to the wolves just yet." Bianca answered the growing concern on her face, laughing softly.

"I'm not worried ma'am as much as I'm concerned about failing you." Ruby licked her dry lips.

"Oh, pet." Bianca's voice now a whisper. She leaned in closer, a hand softly caressing her warm pulsating cheek. "You were astounding today. I was very proud of you and how far you have come from that young timid girl in the cafeteria arguing for her grade. You never have to worry about failing me if this is how you will respond to stressful situations I put you in." Bianca wanted desperately to press a kiss to those tender pouty lips, but the threat of a team member returning unannounced kept her distanced as much as was possible.

Ruby seemed to sense the need in Bianca's eyes as her face lit up with elation. She was too well trained to let her emotions get the better of her, but the teacher could see the power of her adulation in Ruby's face and it made her heart race. "How much I want to kiss you and show you how appreciative I am of you, my pet." Bianca whispered sensually, her thumb sliding across Ruby's full lips before standing at the table.

Walking to her desk, Bianca dialed a number on her phone and waited for the ring to turn into the voice of a woman on the other end. "Janet. It's Bianca. Can you let Martin know we're still working a few details on Peterson and I plan to brief him on Tuesday at twelve?" The older womanly voice on the other end of the call was sweet but all business as she confirmed the meeting time. In reality, they had never made a plan for her to brief Martin or the senior partners in the firm on the account. Bianca wanted to make sure all of her ducks were in a row. Now that they were certain of the direction they wanted to go, putting Ruby in front of Martin, hoping to push her a little harder tempted her. Ruby's performance this weekend would decide how much she wanted to push.

"Was the meeting ever actually at ten?" Ruby questioned, stepping up to the front edge of the desk, her fingers restlessly drawing invisible circles in the dark wood. Bianca reset the receiver. Her eyes went to those restless fingers.

"No." She said coldly, shifting her demeanor as a reminder that confidence and obedience were two different things.

"So the car was late on purpose too?" Ruby questioned, her eyes up, holding her teacher's gaze with intensity. Bianca steeled herself. She could sense there was more of a need for understanding than anger or frustration.

"Yes pet. I wanted you stressed and anxious." Bianca replied before turning and pushing the door until it closed.

Those questioning eyes never left her as she turned back and walked until she was only inches away. The intensity of the energy between them rippled across her skin. A hand reached up softly to push an errant strand of hair from intense eyes. In a blink of an eye, that hand snatched at the back of Ruby's hair, pulling her head back until she yelped softly at the movement.

"Never forget…" Bianca spoke in a soft cold tempered tone one step above a hiss that only the girl in front of her could hear. Two fingers from Bianca's free hand pressed between the cold metal collar and Ruby's throat. The skin was warm, and Bianca could feel the pulse racing in her neck. "… you chose to be mine, and I promised to train you in whatever way was necessary for you to become the person you want to be. Never question how I choose to train you."

Her eyes were intense and locked, then those cool blue orbs dropped in submission, staring down at Bianca's chest.

"Yes, Mistress." Ruby replied submissively, her voice raspy, fighting against the pressure her teacher's fingers placed on her throat.

"Good." Bianca released both her head and her collar. "You're released from class tonight. I want you at the apartment at six-thirty sharp on Saturday night." Bianca ordered moving back to the desk and sitting. She barely looked up at Ruby as she fought to settle her heart rate. "Dress normal. I've taken care of things for the evening." She finished before turning her attention to reports on her monitor. "I'll have a car downstairs waiting for you."

Ruby stood in silence for a long moment at the cold dismissal as Bianca worked, before picking up her messenger bag. She watched Ruby from the corner of her eye. There was uncertainty again in her movements. There was a torrent of emotions circling inside that nubile body and mind. Bianca found it curious after everything she'd been through in the past few months, Ruby still hadn't fully realized the ebb and flow of the power of their relationship.

Before her mind wandered off onto other things, Bianca picked up her cell phone from her desk, her thumbs quickly dialing in Ashley's number. The vibrant thrum of the call going through became almost soothing as she waited for the other end to pick up.

"How'd it go?" Ashley's voice asked as soon as she picked up the line. The two of them discussed a way forward in how to test Ruby. Ashley knew her friend well enough to know the call would follow the event closely. It was the nature of their relationship.

"She did good, but she seemed distressed at the point that I planned to put her on edge." Bianca replied with an exasperated sigh. She could be hard and cold to anyone in the world, but there was something with Ashley that broke through that fasçade almost immediately; it was likely the reason they never established a true dominant/submissive relationship.

"How did she know you planned it?" Ashley's tone turned sharp.

"I may have mentioned something about her thriving in any stressful situation I put her in." Bianca groaned into the phone. She pushed errant bangs back out of her face and along the back of her head as she turned to look out the window. "I never thought she'd draw the connections between the time change and the late arrival. But it shouldn't matter." She added with frustration in her words.

"It shouldn't, but you know how people respond to being tricked or thrown into situations they aren't ready for or expecting." Ashley's voice became softer, more tender. "Up to this point Ruby has known what she was walking into and followed you regardless of the circumstances.

"But choosing to be mine, she should understand everything I do is in her best interest regardless of whether or not I tell her." Bianca retorted sharply.

"Does she know that?" Ashley questioned. The question rang in Bianca's mind, leaving a long silence between them. Thoughts of the events of the past months and the discussions they shared ran through her mind. Bianca realized the constantly changing environment of their relationship likely left Ruby uncertain, but she was certain that she spelled out the intent for what they were doing fairly well.

"Yeah, we've discussed the boundaries of the relationship. I worry maybe this newfound confidence is causing her to question." Bianca let the thought manifest into words. She knew Ashley was used to being her sounding board and could generally be counted on to see the things hidden in her thoughts.

"I think that's natural Bee. I know I did many times, but I never faltered no matter how crazy things got." Ashley liked to remind Bianca of who they were in the beginning and how those people grew up learning from experience together.

"I want to push her Ash." Bianca replied curtly.

"Aren't you already?" Ashley replied. Bianca stood up, walking to the window that looked down on the city below. The question was fair and made Bianca pause for a moment. *How was she being pushed?* Bianca thought to herself. More than a month past since her experience with Vanessa and Cain. An experience that was likely the most intense sexual encounter her nubile body knew. Since that time very little sexual contact took place and all the pushing came regarding learning the business side of things. Bianca and Ashley never found the pain side of the fetish life exciting, at least not as much as they had been into the intensity and psychological aspects of it. So Bianca would never push Ruby in that way. She needed a push in a way that solidified the connection to the relationship and bolstered her self-worth and self-esteem.

"Not the way she needs to be pushed. What type of experience is likely to feed her connection to me, but also bolster her confidence towards the person she wants to be?" Bianca asked uncertain how her plans to use Ruby as a tool to play with Todd Jefferies could serve that purpose.

"I have an idea, but it might require burning a favor to find a way to get Todd to join you." Ashley replied cryptically peeking Bianca's curiosity.

"What are you playing at Ash?" She asked cautiously, wishing very much that she and her friend had met for lunch instead so she could see the look on her face.

"I know you trust me, so I won't insult you by telling you to trust me. Let me make some calls and once I'm sure I can do what I want, we can work out the details." Cryptic Ashley rarely ever came out, but that was because Bianca knew what her friend was thinking as she thought it. Somehow, the woman she knew better than anyone in the world, had her sitting on the edge of her nerves wondering what grand scheme she had planned. Whatever the plan was, Bianca knew Ashley's plans never blew up in her face, so all she could do was wait and see.

Ruby thanked the driver in the waiting car for offering her a ride. She turned up the sidewalk, aimless determination in her stride as she let the adrenaline power her in whatever direction the world around her pushed. That was about as free and unburdened about her life as she'd felt in the past few months and somehow the longer she walked, the more she felt the warmth of the metal ring around her neck radiate through her thoughts.

It wasn't anger or disappointment that drove her as much as it was anxiety of the power she'd surrendered to Bianca. The control of her life that most people would accept as chance. The hardest part about the whole situation was that Ruby knew deep inside that she asked for this, welcomed the control and power her teacher represented.

She wrapped herself in the blanket of the confidence and poise, strength and self-assurance Bianca represented all in hopes of one day being more like the woman wrapped around her.

By the time Ruby pulled herself out of her thoughts to figure out where she was, she found herself deep in the French quarter walking down old narrow streets peppered with restaurants, shops and businesses. The location reminded her of the first night, the night she gave herself over to two strange men out of a desire to please her teacher. Her mind traveled back to the confusion and uncertainty of that night. To the scared, timid little girl who walked up to two strange men and offered her body to them.

How far in such a short time? Turning towards the canal, Ruby's thoughts wandered. Walking let her mind sift through every moment of the past few months. The level of torment her body and mind endured and the ever-increasing level of intensity Bianca subjected her to. All the while Bianca kept her promise that first night, *I will never let any harm come to you.*

The words echoed in her mind and warmed her heart. Ruby's hand unconsciously went to the metal ring around her neck and the red ruby hanging at the base of her throat. The small gem swung and tapped against her throat, like a pulse reminding her every day of the connection between them.

The longer she walked, the more the trick became trivial to the overall situation. It didn't take long for Ruby to understand. Using a late car and a meeting change to put Ruby off balance, then asking her to brief the team didn't differ from Bianca using sex and desire to push her into propositioning strange men for sex.

In the end she'd shown Ruby exactly what she needed to see. The things limiting her were her mind telling her she shouldn't or couldn't do something. In a way her teacher always gave her the chance to say no, but never let her get away with saying no. In the grand scheme of things all of this changed Ruby into this new girl she barely knew but respected much more.

A taxi back to campus and a warm bath helped focus her mind more, putting Ruby in a place to study and catch up on classes. Falling behind while working with Bianca broke the trust, and she needed to do everything to live up to her end.

Removing the requirement to attend class in the evening created a welcome break, giving Ruby a chance to catch up. Her Friday and Saturday work schedules ended up eating more hours than she planned. Thankful she finished her class work Thursday evening, Ruby got off work with just enough time to run home, shower and eat before she met the car Bianca sent to pick her up. The ride across town made Ruby tense. While she came to terms with the trick on Thursday, no chance to talk to Bianca arose since. Ruby hated that they hadn't parted on the most friendly terms. On top of everything, her tension stemmed from no idea what the plan for the evening was.

Bianca said arrive and Miss. Ash will be there to prepare her. *Prepare me?* Ruby came to trust her mistress without question, but uncertainty was not questioning, and there was always an abundance of uncertainty with the way things played out between them.

The car pulled up on the curb near Bianca's apartment; the driver helping her out seemed friendly enough. She couldn't tell if he'd driven them before, but she always had to wonder what the drivers thought about what they saw come out of this apartment.

Walking around the back side of the ground floor from the main door, Ruby pulled out her phone and unlocked the keyless knob. As the handle flashed green, she pushed open the door, anticipation flooding through her body at what she would find as the event of the evening.

The interior door stood open and a warm light came from the dressing room across the hall from the playroom. The warm chatter of two close friends echoed down the hallway as Ruby approached. Before crossing the threshold into the hallway, Ruby quickly stripped naked, folding her clothes into a pile and setting them on the table near the door.

How strange she thought it would seem to an outsider to see her, strolling submissively through the hallways with a hand-crafted collar around her neck and a bright red ruby heart pressed between her ass cheeks.

"There she is." Bianca said in a bright happy tone as Ruby's naked figure silhouetted in the doorway to the dressing room. Miss. Ash stood in the back of the room looking over a pair of dresses hanging from a rack as Bianca stepped up. "I've missed you pet." She said, an open palm cupping her jawbone. That palm pulled Ruby into a long, heated kiss.

Not wanting to draw conclusions, she swore she could feel more emotion and passion in the way Bianca kissed her than ever before. Maybe it was the time apart, but there was a definitive change.

"Thank you, Mistress. I've missed you." Ruby replied solemnly as the kiss broke.

"Miss. Ash has an audacious plan for you tonight." Bianca beamed, looking to Ashley before turning back to Ruby, taking her slim shoulder in strong hands and holding her with warm green eyes. "I hope you are up for this pet, I need you to be the confident self-assured woman I saw in the boardroom on Thursday." Ruby knew this wasn't business, but Bianca wanted the woman she'd become while presenting business assessments to the team.

"I'll be whatever you need me to be Mistress." Ruby was confident. She could tell in Bianca's reply that any concerns about the incident at the office vanished.

"I know you will be pet. You're becoming the woman you want to be, and I'm very proud of how far you've come in such a short time. Whatever you think about the plan tonight, I need you to trust Miss. Ash and I." Bianca reiterated, even though she knew there wasn't any reason. Judging by the way Ruby was responding and acting, there was likely nothing she could ask her to do tonight that she wouldn't do.

"Okay, come sit down Ruby." Ashley ordered coming up behind Bianca. "We need to do your hair and your makeup first."

"Wait, Ash…" Bianca interrupted, her hand tenderly caressing the gradual 'V' between Ruby's thighs. "She needs to clean this up if she is going the way we want her." Ashley inspected her and started nodding.

"I'll take her to the bathtub here. I have an idea." Ashley said with a crooked look on her face before taking Ruby by the hand and leading her to the large bathroom off the side of the dressing room. "Sit on the edge right there." Ashley directed, still holding her hand while Ruby stepped into the large whirlpool tub and sat on the corner closest to the faucet.

Ashley turned the water on, testing the temperature with her hand, but her eyes and the knowing look stayed on Ruby. The older woman's hands spread her legs as a trickle of warm water rained down over her exposed crotch. Ruby watched with desire at the caring way Ashley worked the cream over her mound, massaging it into the light reddish hairs.

Her fingers worked every exposed inch of pale pink skin around her lips until only a soft patch of reddish blond hair on her mound remained. She traced a small triangle in the cream. Pulling out a straight razor, Ashley carefully scrapped the edge of the trace until the only hair between Ruby's thighs was a tight reddish triangle starting just the apex of her lips and extending about two inches up. Ashley's diligent eye and steady hand removed the rest of the hair from her crotch and around her lips.

"There. How's that feel?" Ashley asked, prompting Ruby to run her hand over her crotch. The intensely smooth sensation not only made her skin tingle, but caused a shudder along Ruby's skin. A smile immediately Ruby's face at how soft and bare she felt. Standing in the tub and drying her thighs off with a towel, Ruby stepped out of the tub and walked to stand in front of the full-length mirror.

Her eyes followed the soft reddish triangle between her legs as she turned.

"Is there a reason you left the patch?" Ruby asked inquisitively, having never felt much need to do anything other than shave it all or let it grow.

"You'll understand." Ashley replied with a cryptic look. She slid a hand down along Ruby's naked side and hip. "Let's finish getting ready so you can see the reason." The older woman prompted her to follow back into the dressing room.

Sitting her down at the vanity, the assortment of items Ashley set out surprised Ruby. Various vials of paints and colors, brushes, the table looked more like a painter's palette than a makeup artist. How the plan included paints and expansive makeup, Ruby couldn't fathom,

Ashley spent the better part of an hour working Ruby's hair up into a collection of strands all braided to the top of her head. The braided up-do kept her neck exposed and left random strands to hang down. Several small pins with pearls on the ends held certain sections together. Located strategically around the crown of her head they accented the hairstyle.

"Baby you're an artist. She looks amazing." Bianca beamed from the doorway, watching. Her teacher worked some of her own magic, putting her hair into a style that bunched at the back of her head. Bianca's style gave her enough fall and curl to cover her right collar and shoulder. Stepping up behind Ruby, still naked and sitting before the vanity, Bianca leaned in and kissed her on the neck.

"You're going to make quite an impression tonight pet." She whispered after a prolonged kiss along the tender skin of her neck. Ruby mewled into the kiss, a longing in her heart and body at the touch drawing a soft murmur. "How long do you need Ash?" She asked pulling away. Ruby's eyes follow her mentor in the mirror.

"Probably an hour. We're not on a timetable, are we?" Ashley never missed a beat as Bianca pulled back and shook her head. Happy with the hair, Ashley settled down in a chair between Ruby and the vanity. Watching in the mirror as Bianca turned and walked away, Ruby didn't catch Ashley pick a small paintbrush from the vanity.

"You need to sit perfectly still till I'm done." Ashley pressed the brush into a pallet of white, gray and black colors. Before Ruby could respond, the brush's soft bristle began tracing along the edge of her temple. Cool slickness from the paints chilled her warm skin. A sensuality of the smooth movement and the intimate closeness to Ashley teased Ruby's simmering arousal.

Unable to control her body, she bit her lower lip as her nipples hardened, her breasts tingling with taut firmness. So intent on her work, Ruby hoped Ashley missed it. The tension in Ruby's face, trying to control her growing arousal, drew attention to the changes in her body. Ruby noticed a glimmer in Ashley's orange-brown eyes as a curl turned up her lips. She continued to paint around her eyes and nose.

"Does this arouse you little one?" Ashley's face twisted up into a devilish smirk as her fingers touched a placed along her cheeks. Ruby nodded meekly, hating being caught.

Ashley laughed to herself. Her hand moved with precision and purpose. Ruby could only guess at the patterns the brush painted on her face. She felt a pool of arousal growing in her belly the longer Ashley worked.

"That should do it." Ashley gave a contented sigh as she looked over Ruby's face. The paint wasn't hard or crusty, but moved with her skin. Standing out of the way, Ashley let Ruby see herself in the mirror.

Her mouth dropped open as the visage appeared.

Ashley stepped back with a gratified look in her eyes as she watched the response. Leaning to get a better view, Ruby's breath caught in her throat. She studied the soft feathered design spread from temple to temple, covering her eyes, eyebrows and nose with white and gray feathers accented in black lines.

Her finger floated above the paint, tracing the lines.

"Oh my gawd, it's beautiful." Ruby gushed, seeing the look of adulation on Ashley's face. "I don't understand why, but whatever you have planned this is incredible." Ruby turned her head from side to side to catch various angles. The mask covered any trace of identifying features and even drew the gray in her eyes to cover the usual cool blue tones.

"It looks good, and I think it's all going to flow very well." Ashley said with a smile, her hand gently resting on Ruby's shoulder. Her cool fingers tenderly caressing Ruby's flush skin, sending waves of heat coursing in every direction. "Come here, let's put it all together." Ashley softly guided Ruby towards a dress rack where an opaque white bag hung.

"Okay, now I want you to close your eyes. Keep them closed until I'm done." Ruby did as she was told.

The next few minutes did little to help cool her down. Ashley's hands constantly on her body, she guided Ruby around as she worked. Ruby could only wonder at the very light, form fitting dress sliding over her naked body. Ashley hadn't put on either a bra or a pair of panties which concerned Ruby. She stood quietly trying to sense the movements of the hands on her.

A few minutes of pulling and smoothing, Ruby felt the dress tighten even more against as Ashley pulled the zipper up along her spine.

"Not done yet. Keep your eyes closed." She reminded. Hands once again slid along her torso, smoothing down the light fabric against her skin. Those hands moved to Ruby's ears as earrings filled each of the holes in her ears and then vanished.

Ruby heard rustling and movement in the room, but stood silent, her body marveling at the feeling of the dress as it clung to every curve. The very sensual touch of the dress on her naked breasts and erect nipples sent shudders of heat across her body at the smallest movement.

Even her virtually hairless crotch wasn't free of the tender touch of the fabric on her freshly cleaned skin. She felt her lips tingle and swell with need.

"Final touch." Ashley's whisper surprised Ruby being so close. Her thoughts so focused on the sensations along her body, she'd lost track of the woman's movements.

The touch of cool metal sliding along her temples and against her face caused Ruby to tense. Placed across her face, over her eyes and set on the bridge of her nose, the metal pressed softly into her forehead and cheeks as she felt hands at the back of her head, pulling at what she could only guess were straps.

Hands now firmly on the back of her shoulders, Ashley guided Ruby gently forward a few feet. "Tell me what you think little bird?" Ashley's hands affectionately holding Ruby's shoulders as her eyes opened.

The first image caused Ruby to breathe in sharply. Her mind tried to reconcile what it was seeing. A sensation of admiration, desire and anxiety flooded her body as she came to realize what she was seeing.

In the mirror before her stood a woman shrouded in a sheer fabric dress. White embroidery sewn into the fabric gave her the image of being covered in white icicles. The white embroidery, strategically placed, hid her private parts, but just barely. Depending on the angle, it wasn't hard to visualize or imagine what was there. The dress covered her from shoulder to the floor. It opened into a soft flowing bell that stopped just above her feet. Strapped to her feet, were short white heels with thin bands of leather that wrapped around her calf for support.

The dress below her hips revealed almost all of her hips and leg to her heels. The articulate, fancy mask on her face, curved and flourished like some old world masquerade mask. Starting with a point resting just above the tip of her nose, the mask spread to either side in a flowing triangle to either ear. It covered almost half of her face and reached more than halfway up her forehead with more flourishes and decoration. The paint underneath accented the mask perfectly, removing any distinguishing features under the thin metalwork.

"I…. I don't know what to say Miss. Ash." Ruby finally found the words to speak, awestruck as she was, the sensations of arousal and anxiety still swirling under her skin. Something inside of her found the audacious nature of the outfit powerful despite essentially being naked and exposed to the world.

"Oh gawd Ash, you have outdone yourself this time." Bianca's voice pulled their attention from the woman in the mirror to the woman in the doorway. Her hair still up as earlier, but now fully dressed in a black gown that clung as if painted to her body. Similarly sheer, the gown separated into two panels. The right and left were different, but accented each other with their design and the exposure of skin underneath.

The right side held more vertical lines, starting at the breast in a cup and running down along the body to the ankle. At the right angle, the casual observer could easily visualize aspects of Bianca's body from the sheer nature of the fabric.

The left panel looked of vines curling their way up along Bianca's body from the flowing dress at her ankles, then up along her belly and torso. The vines rose over her left breast and up across her shoulder to wrap around her neck. A cut just at the intersection of the two panels, allowed her toned naked leg to slip out as she walked.

On Bianca's face, on top of eyes painted if not as fully and articulate as Ruby's, Bianca wore a black masquerade mask that looked almost the negative twin of the one Ruby wore. The glint of light as Bianca entered the room spoke to the metal wire woven through her hair to the back of her head.

"She's a vision." Bianca gushed, stepping up as the back of her hand slid down the front of Ruby's body. The touch came lite as a soft breeze caressing her skin. "Is she ready?" Bianca asked, her eyes lingering heavy on Ruby's body.

Unable to turn her own eyes away from her mistress, Ruby finally realized she didn't care where she went or how she looked as long as she was by Bianca's side.

The fact that they had gone to this level of time and trouble meant the world to Ruby. Whatever the evening held for them, it only resolved Ruby of the commitment she and Bianca made to each other.

"Ready as she'll ever be. I'll put her clothes in the bag and have the driver put it in the car." Ashley moved toward the door before stopping and turning back to Ruby.

"We're both very proud of you little one." The older woman said, giving Ruby a soft kiss on her cheek then turning to the hallway. Bianca walked to the rack of clothes and pulled a long black and long white cape from the rack. Stepping up to Ruby, Bianca shrouded her body with the white cloak, carefully covering the masterful hairdo with a hood before doing the same with her own cloak.

"You ready pet?" Bianca asked with more tenderness in her voice than she'd spoken to Ruby in a long time.

"Yes Mistress. I'd follow you anywhere." Ruby replied confidently with a smile, a smile quickly mirrored by her mistress.

"I'll explain things in the car." Bianca said before gently pushing at Ruby's back for her to lead the way toward the door. Both women walked out into the foyer where Ashley stood waiting.

"Enjoy yourselves, you two." Ashley said as they walked up. Bianca leaned in and gave her friend a kiss on the lips that always seemed more than friendly.

"Thank you for everything Ash." Bianca whispered as she pulled back and opened the door. They needed no answer between them. There was a bond there that went way beyond words, and Ruby felt it the first time she'd met Ashley.

Transition and Revelation

Walking to the car, the same driver who picked her up waited by the door, still dressed in his tailored suit. "Evening ladies." He said as they approached and slipped into the car. The back was larger than a usual car, a short limousine, rather than a sedan. The dark privacy glass already raised as they drew together in the smooth leather seats. The door closed behind them.

The look of surprise on her pet's face seeing the bottle of chilling champagne set into a wall-mounted bucket, hinted at an astounding change from previous experience. As the car moved, Bianca took the bottle and filled two glasses, handing one to Ruby.

"Miss. Ash was very true in her words to you pet." Bianca held up her glass. "When I look at the woman you are now, compared to the young girl I first met in that classroom so many months ago, I have to say I'm very proud of you." The warmth spread along her skin. Her chest swelled with pride, flowing with the sincerity in her tone. A discernible swell of emotion showed as Ruby breathed in deep before tilting her glass and softly touching them together.

"Thank you Mistress." Ruby replied, putting the glass to her lips accented in soft gray and white lip gloss and liner. Bianca's gaze followed as she drank.

"So…" Bianca started pulling the half empty glass of champagne away from dark red lips outlined in black. "We are going to a very private and very exclusive party. A friend of Miss. Ash did her a favor so I could give you a chance to step out of your comfort zone even more." Bianca paused for a minute, her hand going to the tie at Ruby's neck, pulling it away so the cape opened to expose her torso. Her eyes trailed over her for a long minute in silence.

"When I say private and exclusive, I want you to understand that there will be things going on at this party that may seem rather outrageous to you. There's a reason we made you up like this. Do you know what it is?"

Ruby sat silently, letting the question hang in the air. Bianca could see the answers forming behind the hidden blue in her eyes. She knew why, but knowing it and articulating it confidently were two different things.

"As you said Mistress, to put me out of my comfort zone." A hint of uncertainty as the direction of Bianca's question.

"Yes, that's part of it. But why this way?" She questioned more inquisitively.

"Because I'd never go out in public dressed like this, exposing myself to people in this way. You want me to understand how beautiful and powerful I can feel exposed to the world like this." Bianca felt the emotion behind her eyes swell more. She fought back against it for fear of ruining the makeup.

"Exactly pet. You will walk in, and all eyes will be on you. Men and women alike will desire you, but you will be unattainable to them. We will join a man I know, someone I have worked with in the past, someone I trust implicitly. He has agreed to help me in your training. During the evening we will retire to a private room with this man."

Bianca drank slowly at her champagne, letting Ruby's mind process the information. The emphasis on the words she used made it very clear that this man was a client, not a colleague. The implication of a new style and a new venue without a name spoke to it, not having anything to do with Kieran.

Ruby knew that Kieran was out of the country on business. Bianca wondered what was running through her mind. She made a point of keeping the tenderness in her demeanor. Now was a time for Ruby to feel safe and free to understand.

Fear and uncertainty only clouded an already intense situation. Tonight wasn't about domination, at least not to begin. Tonight was about building confidence.

"Am I to act as I did the last time we went to a party mistress?" Ruby's question almost seemed to grow from Bianca's thoughts, which caused a gentle slant to her head in curiosity. Only in Ashley was Bianca able to sense thoughts to the point of finishing them.

"No, pet." She set her hand on Ruby's thigh, watching a shudder run along Ruby's skin. The heat of her touch spreading even through the light sheer fabric.

"While we are at the party, you are free to enjoy yourself. You are here *with* me and I want us both to enjoy being together. You will still show your usual deference to me, but relax and enjoy yourself. Remember, you still represent Miss. Ash and I, so how you act is very important to our reputation with this friend. Once we move into the private room, I will explain to you the rules. You will know when the situation has changed."

"Yes Mistress. I understand." Ruby seemed excited at being free to be with Bianca as a friend or a lover and not her submissive. The anxiety from earlier transmuted quickly into desire and confidence.

"I find it very difficult to keep myself from you, pet." Her hand trailed along Ruby's thigh, enjoying the relative protection and inherent tease the fabric created. "Miss. Ash outdid herself tonight. You are more beautiful than I've ever seen you." Even under the fabric, Bianca could see the flush in her young skin.

Bianca's attention aroused Ruby, but the way she bit her lip and held her breath, it wasn't hard to tell her heart raced. The subtle way she started pressing her thighs together, trying to hide it behind the sheer fabric, spoke to a fire smoldering between her legs.

Bianca could see the impact her praise on the growth in confidence, and poise meant to Ruby. She grew exponentially in the past few months, but being appraised by the very woman she claimed a desire to emulate seemed to set her protege off.

"I appreciate you saying that Mistress." Ruby wavered. "When I first met you, I just wanted you to notice me, now here I am and I'm overwhelmed with my emotions for you."

"You're no different now than that quiet, timid girl in class, Ruby." Bianca said, her hand reaching up to brush the soft edge of Ruby's jawbone. The touch was sensual and she could see the shudder radiate out along Ruby's skin.

The backs of her fingers trailed along her neck until her hand brushed over the metal ring circling Ruby's thin creamy neck. Bianca's finger curled under the ring while her thumb playfully tapped on the red jewel hanging at her throat. "You've always been this young woman, you just needed someone who could bring it out of you. I'm just supremely happy to be the one to share this journey with you."

Bianca stared into her eyes from behind the mask. The reality of her tone and where the words came from struck Bianca more than she imagined. While she admitted an attraction to Ashley weeks ago, the true feeling behind how she felt about Ruby always simmered below the surface. Being a person who strove to keep her emotions hidden and in check, Bianca suddenly found it hard to hide it from the young woman in front of her.

"I don't supposed it would be too bold to assume that your feelings for me have evolved beyond the relationship this represents?" She asked, softly tugging with a finger on the collar at Ruby's neck.

Ruby flushed. Emotion already swelling in her showed behind the mask. Bianca considered the cryptic vagueness of the question. She didn't want to lead Ruby into anything; she needed to articulate her own words, not repeat her teacher's.

There couldn't be any question though that Bianca just asked if Ruby's emotions went beyond the training relationship they established. Ashley reminded Bianca of this when things started with Ruby, a reminder of so many years past that almost tore the two friends apart. The trap with these situations being how the intense emotions of submission confused with more meaningful emotions.

Was Ruby as resolute in her feelings as she was in her commitment? Did she questioned the origin and the nature of her feelings for Bianca? In fairness, the past few weeks didn't make it easy to understand or accept there was more than a simple training relationship. And Bianca admitted her actions surrounding the staff meeting did little to bolster any feelings of closeness or admiration.

"Yes, Mistress." Ruby finally replied, the long silence in the cabin not an unfamiliar thing between them during discussions. The admission surprised Bianca, pulling her from those questions in her mind. "I have deep feelings for you and the connection between us." Bianca could hear the hesitation in her voice like she was trying carefully to not say she was *in love* with or falling for her.
It was almost as if Ruby wanted to leave the door open for the two of them to come to the word on their own time. Bianca's eyes stared back in silence with an affectionate warmth she couldn't hide.

"Would you say that you are falling for me?" Bianca asked as if she'd heard her student's thoughts. Ruby only nodded, with a solemn seriousness to her face. Bianca found the response amusing, almost as if Ruby didn't trust herself to say it out loud for fear she might say something that would ruin the moment.

"Miss. Ash asked me when this whole thing started, if I was in love with you. Of course I denied it then because I wasn't sure what I was feeling. But now I would say that we are drifting dangerously close to something resembling that my pet."

The admission seemed to surprise Ruby by the way her eyes and face flinched ever so softly. A certain bit of tension in her body seemed to melt away, possibly due to the uncharacteristically warm way that Bianca talked with her. It was safe to say the dynamic between them changed. The more sinister side of Bianca urged her to show Ruby that there was still a cold, domineering side to their relationship, but she quickly dismissed the idea.

Tonight was about building confidence and comfort. She reminded herself. Somehow Bianca recognized in that moment that even if she turned on Ruby, whatever happened, it didn't matter as long as they were together.

Before either of them could say more, the car turned abruptly and began an uphill climb along a circular drive. A glimpse out the dark-tinted window revealed a large Victorian residence coming into view along the right side of the car. The structure itself was immense, resembling a mansion more than the usual Victorian style homes found in New Orleans. Flames in sconces outlined the outer perimeter of the house's expansive porch, which wrapped the front and much of the upper floors.

Very few windows around the residence showed light through them. The only light around the residence besides the torches was the front entrance, lit up in a deep red light along the walk and around the door. A pair of large, sharply dressed men stood at the entrance, one at the door and one at the foot of the stairs. No other people were about outside the house.

The car pulled up in front of the stairs, prompting Bianca to pull Ruby to her with a crooked finger under her chin until she planted a soft kiss on velvety pale gray lips.

"Here we go pet. Remember, how beautiful and powerful you are. I want you to portray that in how you move and act." Bianca said with a soft but powerful gaze in her eyes as her hand took Ruby's in her own just as the door opened on the right side of the car.

Both women stepped out of the car into the gentle cool of late fall. The chill traveled Ruby's skin like a thousand small pin pricks reminding her how naked she was. To her surprise, she didn't shrink at the thought. Instead, she stood tall and proud, letting her pert full breasts and erect nipples push firmly at the tight dress's limits. She hid nothing about how exposed she was, instead proudly displaying it along with her pride at attending her mistress in such a way.

Bianca handed the man at the foot of the steps a small envelope with very ornate calligraphy on the front. The man opened the envelope and read the card inside before turning to the man at the top near the door and nodded.

"Come, pet." Bianca urged warmly and loudly enough for anyone within earshot to hear as they both walked up the stairs, hand in hand black and white contrasting each other perfectly.

"Enjoy your evening ladies." The large black man with a bit of a Cajun accent at the top of the steps said, opening the large red door, ushering them inside. The lighting inside was much like the lighting outside, dim and warm. Candles and oil lamps flickered in the main hallway.

A long classically styled foyer with wood paneling, long antique looking carpets and décor that looked like it dated back a century filled the hallway. A few groups of people clustered around in the foyer. Small groups of men and women, just women and just men, sat on benches or whispered to each other in doorways as Bianca led Ruby along the hall. Everyone wore similar masks, and while most wore fashionable evening gowns or cocktail outfits, some more hidden groups were missing various articles of clothing.

Ruby caught her breath as they passed a small alcove where two half-naked women and a man were engaged. One woman in the middle faced the other woman braced against the wall as she sucked and licked the large round breast of the woman in the middle. Her top loose around her torso gave the other woman access. The back of her skirt bunched up around her hips by the man as he pressed against her back. The motion of his body pushing into her suggested more. Her expression and the moans quietly filling the alcove added power to the scene. Ruby felt herself blush as she walked by.

Both women turned and watched with wicked grins as Ruby and Bianca passed. There was a heavy hunger in their look, like predators feeding on a kill but sensing even fresher meat near. The electricity of the look rippled over Ruby's skin like a current. A firm squeeze of her hand from Bianca, looking straight ahead, brought Ruby's attention away from the threesome.

At the end of the hallway, a warm orange hue filled the large open gallery. The flicker from a multitude of burning lamps washed the walls with ever shifting shadows. The room was warm, the difference obvious to Ruby's naked skin as they crossed the threshold. Her head drifted, letting her eyes take in everything.

She was happy to find that the minimal size of the decorations on the mask allowed her eyes and her peripheral vision to pick up on almost everything she might normally see. The room's décor followed the hallways; warm, classical, antique. Most of the furniture comprised of long loungers or couches with an assortment of high-back chairs. Ruby noticed the assorted clusters of large bean bag style chairs took up the corners. The light from the torches didn't fall here, perhaps purposefully to block light for the corners. From her vantage, she couldn't see much of what filled those spaces.
Long rectangular tables at the center of the 'U' shaped room, just inside the door, offered food to the guests. A very elaborate spread of fruits, cheeses, meats and breads covered each table. Two smaller tables nearby presented crystal carafes of various refreshment while waiters and waitresses circulated through the room with silver trays of champagne and other sorts of drinks. Each waiter or waitress wore a classical white and red Victorian style dress outfit.

Ruby counted about fifty people in the large ballroom scattered around the various chairs and sofas. Like those in the hallway, many were in various states of dress or undress. She couldn't help but feel a twist in her belly as she glimpsed a man and a woman passionately engaged on the back of a sofa in the middle of the room in plain sight of everyone.

That was the point where Ruby's mind actively noticed the overt sex acts around the room. A woman on her knees servicing two men sitting on a sofa. A woman perched on a high-back chair slowly riding the man sitting in the chair as another woman kneeled on the floor behind licking both. All of this displayed open and free in a way that Ruby never experienced. The overt nature of the sex in the room fed the fire that Miss. Ash set to simmer in her belly.

"You must be Blackbird's friend." A woman's voice caught Ruby's attention, causing her to turn from the surrounding sex to an older woman who approached. She wore a long flowing purple and blue patterned dress bound at her waist by a corset that stopped just below her firm grapefruit sized breasts. Those breasts sat free and exposed above the corset. The woman's straw blond hair sat up on the top of her head in a loose bun. Her skin was taunt and softly tanned, gently flush from what appeared to be an abundance of champagne judging by the half empty glass in her hand. The deep lines at the edges of her eyes and mouth told Ruby she was much older, but the firmness of her body gave her a young radiance.

"I'm Abigail, please call me Abby. Welcome to my home."

"Thank you Abby, I'm Victoria, this is my pet." Bianca replied making it a point not to reveal any information about Ruby which she both accepted but found rather strange. She understood that this was a very exclusive and private event, likely something you needed references and referrals for.

"It's a pleasure to meet you Victoria. Your pet is most amazing, she has certainly caught the attention of many of my guests."

"Thank you for saying so. I felt considering the pains you took to make this happen for us, it was only fitting that we make an entrance that would show our appreciation." The way Bianca talked and worked Abby, Ruby could tell this was not the first time she'd been to one of these.

"I certainly appreciate your attention. I have made the arrangements you requested. I set aside the Robeson guest room for you when you are ready to retire. You will not be disturbed."

Abby spoke softer as she related the guest room details, a hand softly on Bianca's arm. "Please, make yourselves at home. You are my guests, so I demand you enjoy yourselves. But be careful not to let this one wonder too far away, I may drink her up given a chance." Abby said with a mischievous grin before walking away to grab another glass from a waiter.

Both Bianca and Ruby watched as Abby moved away before Bianca folded up her arm and placed Ruby's hand comfortably in the crook of her elbow. "Do not worry my pet, I will keep you close. Tonight you are all mine." Bianca promised, guiding them deeper into the room.

Ruby felt the hungry eyes on her. Her mind raced. Lewd visions and sounds of sex all around them permeated both her mind and also her body. Bianca took two glasses of champagne from a roaming waiter and offered one to Ruby as they walked. It almost seemed as if Bianca was circling the room more to show Ruby off than to really mingle with the guests. Aside from Abby, they hadn't spoken or contacted anyone since they arrived, but circled the room at least once.

"If ever there was a vision of angels in front of my eyes, now I know I have died and gone to heaven." The voice was melodic and confident as it approached from behind. Bianca turned to see who addressed them, and her face quickly turned to a beaming smile behind the black mask.

"Todd!" She whispered leaning into him. "It's a pleasure to see you. I really appreciate you adjusting your schedule for this." Bianca spoke softly so only the three of them could hear.

The man standing before them was a client of Bianca's, Ruby knew that very well but never met him. He was handsomely attractive, his angular, muscular body filled out the dark tailored Victorian tuxedo. A half burgundy velvet red and half black doublet vest covered his hard chest. It ran down to a pair of tight black slacks and black boots. He wore a black embroidered jacket with burgundy accents on the wide lapel collars and tails that hung down to the backs of his knees. The black and burgundy mask hid his dark brown eyes, but not the heat Ruby saw in them when he turned his attention to her.

"And this must be your protégé." He said stepping forward, taking Ruby's hand in his and lifting it to his mouth to kiss. His eyes traveled the full length of her body from head to toe and back, taking in every inch. "You truly look like an angel." Todd said, letting her hand go. "Come with me, I have a nice place a bit more secluded to sit." He escorted each of them by the hand and guided them to the other side of the ballroom. Pushing through a set of double doors, they entered another room hidden from the gallery.

Darker by comparison to the main room, but more cozy in the way the smaller number of lamps warmed the room but left lots of shadow throughout. A few small groupings of chairs and loungers filled the room, square in design, wood paneling and green walls again with older looking carpets, paintings and décor. Todd led them to a table in the corner, around it two high-back chairs, a lounger and a sofa sat unattended.

"Come sit with me pet." Bianca said as she sat in one of the high-back chairs, slightly angled to one side, her hand patted the leg on the side with more room, motioning for Ruby to join her. Todd watched intently as she obediently sat on Bianca's lap. Her legs crossing her mistress's legs and Bianca's arm around her waist, Ruby leaned in on her shoulder.

"Are you enjoying yourself pet?" She asked, sliding a hand up across Ruby's belly until it found the soft roll of her breast. Her hand cupped the breast through the dress, her index finger and thumb trapping the hidden nipple between each other.
Bianca mashed the nipple firmly between her two fingers, sending a flash of erotic pain shooting from Ruby's nipple straight to her already smoldering belly.

"Yes, Mistress." Ruby bit her bottom lip, a sharp gasp, her mind flush with the already heavily built up arousal.

Todd watched intently, sitting in the other chair so he had a good angle. Bianca leaned in, her lips opening slightly as she ran her hot pink tongue up along the nape of Ruby's neck. Fingers rolled the nipple without remorse. A fog of desire sent Ruby's mind swimming as her mistress filled her with a mix of pleasure and pain.

"Open your eyes pet, tell me what you see." Bianca ordered and Ruby did as she was told, not realizing she'd closed them. Her mouth hung half open as she breathed in sharply. She fought against the quickly building arousal to keep her heart from pushing her over too fast.

Looking around the dark room, shadows from the lamps made discerning activity in the room from this angle interesting as her eyes focused. Although she had trouble making out details, she was certain there was a group close to them, four or five men and women, all practically naked intertwined with each other.

Before she could answer, the profile of a younger skinny man rose over the top of a lounger, hands holding the backrest as another, larger heavily muscular man rose behind him. The large man held the smaller man, almost a boy compared to his partner, by the shoulder. Judging by the shadows dancing across his face, his expression was one of deep pain and bliss all wrapped up together. The man behind held a look of stern concentration and pleasure.

"Two men, a smaller skinny man and another, larger, muscular, behind him." Ruby answered, not realizing how vacant her response sounded as her mind watched, filling her body with lust. So lost in the scene Ruby hadn't realized Bianca's hand had moved down between her thighs, softly rubbing across the light sheer fabric at the triangle of hair just above her sensitive folds.

"Is he enjoying it?" Bianca whispered, her mouth practically kissing Ruby's neck. Her tongue traced a line along her jawbone.

"He seems to be, yes." Ruby replied practically in a trance as if the act of watching two men enthralled with each other was hypnotic. The heat in her belly flared.

"Do you see something else that might explain why he seems to be in such bliss?" Bianca asked, her fingers slowly pulling at the long dress, drawing it up along Ruby's legs, causing it to bunch at her hips.

Ruby looked longer, studied harder. Her mind raced, trying to reconcile the fog of lust with noticing details her mistress apparently saw. Then she saw it, movement under the skinny man. An arm, a skinny arm, a woman's arm sliding along his torso until it reached his skinny white hips.
The longer she looked the more detail she noticed. Finally seeing that the woman's face was in line with the man's crotch. Every time the larger man pushed into him, the smaller man's hips pushed down, driving him into the woman's mouth.

"There's a woman. She's sucking him as the larger man is driving him into her." Ruby's body tingled now as her arousal spread from her belly outward along her skin. The sudden cool touch of Bianca's fingers on her naked skin drew a sharp breath from Ruby, her teeth biting softly on her lip as her eyes closed at the energy of the touch. Her legs unconsciously spread, giving her mistress access to her heated slit

Between watching the trio on the lounger and the tender caress of Bianca's fingers on her lips, Ruby's hips unconsciously gyrated in unison with the thrusts of the larger man. Every time he pushed into the smaller man, Bianca ran her finger over Ruby's swollen pearl at the apex of her lips, causing her hips to thrust in answer.

The rhythm of moans and movement in the room became one between the four of them. Ruby arched her back, leaning against the back of the chair as her mistress claimed control over her body once again.

"I think you're aroused my pet." Bianca whispered, her fingers keeping up the rhythm. Ruby could only nod as she fought to keep her mind in control of her body. "Do you think watching you has aroused our friend?" Bianca added after Ruby's nod of agreement.

"I... do... Mistress." Ruby murmured between breaths as her

arousal grew closer and closer.

"I think you should show him how much you enjoy being the object of his arousal." Bianca whispered, the suggestive sensuality of her tone flowed like honey into Ruby's ear, the suggestion being all she needed.

Without question or hesitation, Ruby pulled her legs together and slid from Bianca's lap. The dress fell back to the tops of her feet as she walked. Her body dripped with sensual energy, a sultry flowing gait toward Todd.

Eyes locked from behind masks, Ruby let Todd drink in her movements as she drew closer. Never having a reason to exude sensuality with anyone, Ruby let her arousal and her confidence take over, enticing Todd's attention to hang on her body as she walked.

Her hands went to his chest, excited to feel the powerful muscles behind so much fabric. Slowly, her hands removed his tie and unbuttoned the top of his shirt; her eyes never leaving his as she worked. Pulling the bulk of her dress up her legs until she could kneel at the edge of his seat, Ruby's hands went next to the vest in front of his shirt. Unbuttoning each button as slowly as possible, she kept up the passion of the moment.

Free of the vest, Ruby opened the shirt, exposing the smooth muscular skin behind. Leaning in, her tongue blissfully teased at his hardening nipple while her hands eagerly worked the belt blocking her access to opening his slacks. She trailed licks along his chest to the other nipple as her fingers freed the belt and eventually the button keeping his slacks closed to her. Tenderly rolling his nipple with her tongue, one hand slid down his pants along his thigh, tracing the bulk of his manhood through the fabric.

Beginning a trail of licks down his chest toward his belly, Ruby's fingers freed him from the cloth prison in time for her mouth to greet it. The musty scent of his arousal and manly sweat filled her nostrils as Ruby's tongue traced the length, exploring each vein and bump.

Working her way back to the tip, Ruby pulled back away from his belly, so the mask wouldn't interfere with her need to swallow him. She worked him slowly, over and over, hoping to reach an agreement that would give him to her whole. At least until she felt the hand at the back of her head pushing her deeper.

"That's it pet, he needs to really feel how dedicated you are." Bianca's voice pierced the fog, the fog of running on automatic since planting the suggestion in her mind. The shaft pierced the back of her throat with Bianca's push.

Unable to breathe for a split second, Ruby pulled back abruptly. Again and again Bianca pushed her down, and each time she fought back until finally she held herself deep on him.

The guttural moan surging from his manly chest told Ruby she'd found the spot Bianca was trying to reach.

"Good girl." Bianca whispered into her ear as her palm softly guided Ruby's face from his saliva drenched shaft. "Stand up pet." Ruby did as she was told while Bianca held the folds of her dress. "I want you to straddle him." Bianca ordered gently, driving Ruby forward as Todd worked the slacks down over his knees.

Placing her knees on either side of Todd's thighs, Ruby grabbed onto the back of the chair. She looked down into Todd's eyes, dark brown globes that didn't seem able to pull themselves away from her body.

Expecting things to go a different way, feeling her mistress pull the jewelry from her ass surprised Ruby. She found the absence disconcerting, like an old friend who was suddenly not there.

That sensation didn't last long once the tip of Todd's thick head pierced the ring and bit by bit filled the walls deep inside. "Go slow pet," Bianca whispered from behind. "Let's see if my little whore can keep from coming." She teased as Ruby gyrated her hips.

Arms above his head, hands using the back of the chair as leverage, she groaned at the feeling of him filling her dark canal. His eyes never left hers as she rode him. The sensuality of the moment shocked Ruby. Here she was riding a strange man at the behest of her mistress, and somehow she felt closer to both Bianca and the man because of the moment of closeness they were sharing. Ruby realized after a long moment that Bianca referred to her 'little whore' but it suddenly became clear she meant Todd and not her.

It would seem that some aspect of the game had started already, and she was perfectly happy to play.

Bianca's hands slipped up behind her, cupping, kneading her breasts, rolling her swollen nipples between her fingers as she rode Todd. He was having trouble and Ruby could see the look in his eye, the strain on his face. She tried to change the rhythm, or tension of her ass on him, but Bianca kept the pressure, using the hold she had on her pet's breasts to keep the movement going.

"Don't you dare come whore or I'm going to punish you all night." Bianca hissed from behind Ruby. As if on cue, she felt Todd clench and tense beneath her, and then suddenly the warm heat of his seed spraying into her dark canal caused Ruby to groan with lust. On any other occasion, not insisting on a condom would draw disgust or anger from Ruby, but for reasons buried deep in her consciousness at the moment, Ruby accepted and trusted Bianca's game.

"Are you enjoying yourself pet?." Bianca asked moving to the side of the chair, taking Ruby's chin between two fingers before turning her head to a long passionate kiss that seemed as much to punish Todd as it was to show her appreciation to Ruby.

"Yes, mistress." Ruby replied as the kiss broke. Bianca held her dress up as she pulled herself up off of Todd's shaft. Suddenly the cool metal of the butt plug being pushed into her stretched hole caught her off guard as she stepped off the chair. As Ruby stood, Bianca walked over to the side of the chair so she was close to Todd's head. "I want you to go lay down on that lounger whore, put your head at the foot of the lounger facing up." Bianca ordered, the recognizable cold, distant tone in her voice.

It was strange for Ruby to hear that tone used with someone other than her. Todd did as ordered, stepping out from in front of Ruby and walking to the lounger. Now in clear view of the other group of men and women that started everything, Todd lay down on the lounger, his head at the foot.

"Come pet. It's time for your reward for being so obedient and focused." Bianca helped Ruby to the lounger, still holding the folds of her dress as she walked. Her butt muscles straining to keep the plug tightly sealed with the increased amount of lubrication now pushing at the edges.

"Open your mouth whore." Her teacher growled at the man on the sofa who quickly did as ordered, his mouth open as wide as it could go. Guiding her protégé to straddle the lounger, the valley of her thighs now squarely hovering directly over Todd's mouth. Bianca's hands guided Ruby until she as was practically in the man's mouth before slowly pulling the butt plug from its location.

Ruby couldn't see what had happened, but judging by the contented sigh Bianca gave, she was certain Todd received his punishment. "Now clean her thoroughly until she comes all over your face." Bianca ordered. The sensation of his tongue lapping and exploring the two holes with hunger and lust caused an almost instantaneous rush of her need and lust.

Bracing herself against the lounger, Ruby's legs quivered with strain and intensity of his assault on her molten furnace. Bianca stepped up in front of her, hands gently kneading at her breasts. She leaned in, pulling Ruby into a heated, searching kiss. Bianca's lips nipped and pulled at her own. It was the first time Bianca kissed Ruby in a way that wasn't hungry or lustful. This was the emotion and connection they shared in the car.

A hand went to Ruby's cheek, holding her face as the kiss grew more and more passionate with the intensity of raging fire in her belly. Tongues danced like ancient lovers finding each other again over the ages. Suddenly the fire in her belly flared. That simmering fire kindled the first time Ashley touched her in the tub now and inferno. Ruby's body lurched with the force of unbridled wild horses as she pushed herself into Todd's mouth and gripped at the lounger as if holding on for her life. Bianca held her with the kiss as the fire flared through her body, burning away any last vestiges of the girl she used to know.

Spasms and aftershocks tore across her body as Ruby fought to support her weight. The orgasm faded gradually. Bianca broke the kiss with a throaty moan, holding her close enough for their eyes to connect. "I'm falling in love with you, Ruby." Her teacher whispered so softly Ruby barely heard it. At that moment though, she didn't need to hear the words, she could see it in her teacher's eyes, feel it in her touch.

"And I you, Mistress." Ruby could barely contain the words. Bianca held her there for another minute before pulling away.

"Get up whore." Bianca ordered, kneeling beside the prone man on the lounger. "You've pleased me." She added before turning to help Ruby over the lounger. It surprised Ruby at how compliant a man like Todd was with Bianca. Their shared energy felt like equals regarding confidence and self-assurance, but for someone like him to give away that control seemed at odds with Ruby. "Meet us upstairs in the room."

"Yes, Mistress." Todd replied, pulling up his pants before turning to a door in the corner that led deeper into the house.

"I see the questions on your expression. We'll discuss them more later. For now, I need you to understand what is about to happen." Bianca explained, sitting down on the lounger Todd left empty. Ruby followed suit, sitting down next to her teacher to keep the conversation they were about to have as private as possible.

"I will serve you any way you need, Mistress." Ruby replied softly.

"I know you will pet." Bianca took Ruby's hand in her own, holding it in the most tender way Ruby ever felt Bianca hold her since they'd been together. "Once we are upstairs, you will be nothing more than a tool for me to use, to abuse him. I may ask you to do things that seem harsh or degrading, please realize this in no way reflects my feelings for you or our relationship. You've come a long way pet and I think for this to work you can handle more intense domination from me. My clients are mostly men and they want and accept a different level of domination than I've ever given to you. If you are to be my partner in this and other things, you need to learn to accept and want a similar level as the men we will meet."

Ruby was silent for a long moment. What Bianca asked wasn't anything she wasn't willing to accept, especially if it meant they could be together. Seeing that the dynamic between them might become more intense on both sides was something for Ruby to process.

"I understand Mistress." She finally said, her fingers pressing the ruby at her throat between them. "I've accepted this fully understanding what being yours meant. I'd rather suffer humiliation wrapped in the blanket of your security than be free of any abuse and be without you." Something in Ruby's unwavering acceptance seemed to pierce Bianca to the core. Even hidden behind the mask and the dark shadow of the room, Ruby could see her teacher's eyes glint with a swell of emotion.

Bianca could have sat there staring into her young lover's eyes all evening. The words permeated not just her mind but her soul, leaving her frozen in the new woman who sat before her. This was not the girl Bianca met in class so many months ago, timid and scared. She was a new woman, one who found something in herself no one could take away.

Ruby endured sexual abuse beyond what most people would consider extreme and accepted it. More dedicated than she was before, Bianca wondered how far was too far.

They followed the path Todd took out of the room into a small dimly lit hallway leading to a staircase. One floor up, it wasn't hard to find the room allocated to them. Nestled at the end of a hallway away from the others, it would serve as their private sanctuary for the night.

Stepping into the room, Bianca took pleasure at seeing Todd kneeling on the floor, legs folded under his hips, arms stretched out in front of himself as he bent forward with his forehead on the floor between his arms. The view sent a warm expression over her face. The boisterous and confident man in the main ballroom now kneeled naked on the floor, submissive and pliant.

"Get undressed pet." Bianca whispered, her hand pulling down on the zipper that kept the light sheer fabric pressed tight to Ruby's body. She led them both to a freestanding wood cabinet, throwing open the double doors. A set of hangars waited along with two outfits she'd sent in with the driver and prepared by their hostess.

Reaching to her mid-back, Bianca worked the zipper to her own dress down as Ruby slowly slipped her down over shoulders. Her pale naked skin glowed in the low torch light as its shadows danced around the room.

"You can remove the mask and there is a bathroom over there for you to wipe off the paint." She showed with a hand toward the back of the room. She watched as Ruby did as she was told without word or question. Slipping out of her dress, and hanging it up beside the sheer white dress.

Bianca's eyes wandered to the young nubile backside of her lover as she washed her face. It was a shame to wash away Ashley's handiwork, but it would likely smear during the night. She smiled, her eyes taking in the curve of Ruby's body and how soft it seemed in the dim wavering light.

When Ruby turned and walked back to where her mistress stood, her movements were slow and deliberate. Bianca held a breath as the ripe, nubile body sashayed toward her, those cool blue eyes shadowed in a sultry gaze by the shadows. "I'll help you put your outfit on." Bianca gently slid a finger down Ruby's breastbone to her belly as she spoke before pulling the outfit from the cabinet.

Holding up a black shiny latex full torso corset, Ruby stepped into the leg holes while Bianca tightened the straps and buckles on the front. The latex stretched tight against Ruby's body, the half cups at the top pushing up her naked breasts. Next, a pair of thigh length latex boots with short heels and a pair of mid-arm latex gloves. Bianca backed up to look at her pet with an adoring gaze.

"Go kneel beside my slave and wait for me pet." She ordered.

"Yes, Mistress." Ruby obediently walked to the opposite side of Todd, still splayed out in his kneeling pose, and kneeled beside him. Wrapping her latex clad arms behind her back, hands folding into her elbows, she waited obediently. Bianca's mind raced at the possibilities presented to her. There were no limits outside of a request by Abby to leave by noon. They had more than enough time to explore this dynamic.

Todd seemed overjoyed at the idea of using this as a chance to train Ruby and never once shied away from adding a bonus to his usual fee to cover the extra expense and the new participant.

Bianca pulled her own outfit from the dresser, a black bodysuit with sheer front and back exposing her from her breasts to her belly. An open collar made of latex provided a zipper, fully exposing her ample chest from beneath the smooth black tinted fabric. Shoulders and arms covered in latex to the wrist and hips and crotch shaped in a wide 'V' at the front and forming into a thong in back. An inconspicuous velcro flap between her hips provided access to her inner thighs. Latex boots rising above her knees, with more pronounced stiletto tips clung tightly to her toned legs.

Her deep green eyes scanned the reflection in the mirror to make sure that every piece fit properly and gave the sense of sexual strength this evening would require. Satisfied in her appearance, Bianca pulled three items from a shelf in the cabinet and turned to her waiting slaves.

"Sit up whore." She growled at Todd from behind. Instantly the man's tone muscular body moved, his warm tanned skin darker than the two of them even in the dim light. He sat up on his haunches, his hands on his lap as Bianca moved up behind him, pulling a black leather hood over his face.

She checked to make sure that his eyes, nose and mouth were all correctly placed before tightly clasping the straps at the back of the hood. A soft whimper escaped Todd's throat as she worked the buckles. "I can make it tighter." Bianca hissed, swinging a hand down across his chest until it contacted the hard, muscular breast with a resounding crack.

"Thank you, Mistress." Todd mumbled through the mask as she cinched the last strap. Saying nothing else, Bianca snapped a leather blind over the eyes of the mask, then pushed another leather piece with a small protrusion into Todd's mouth until she could snap the corners into grommets at either side of his mouth hole.

"Can you hear me whore? Nod your head." She ordered.

Todd nodded as ordered. "Show me how you signal to invoke your safe word!" Bianca asked as Todd held up a hand with three fingers from his middle to pinky into the air.

"That's a good whore. Put your arm down and wait quietly." Bianca chided, reaching over his shoulder, her fingers pulled roughly on the nipple opposite the one she smacked. A grin crossed her face as she noticed the red imprint of her hand was still visible on his tan skin.

Walking up behind Ruby, she put a hand on her shoulder. "Don't be scared pet." She whispered, before slipping a black latex hood over those strawberry blonde locks and down over her freckled face. Pulling at the latex until it wrapped the neck just above the collar and left the mouth, nose and eyes open.

"Open your mouth." Bianca commanded sliding a black leather strapped harness over her head. A blind, resembling the one Todd wore, covered her eyes. She fitted a ring a couple inches wide between two straps into Ruby's mouth, between her teeth, locking her mouth open. "You must be starving pet. We'll feed you soon." She said as her hands tightened the straps.

Pulling Ruby's arms together, she slid each arm into a leather loop connected to a larger leather strap that ran across her back. From that leather strap hung a conical harness that Bianca pushed Ruby's arms into before tightening the leather around her arms, binding them to her back.

"Stand up whore." She commanded after making sure that the

restraints on her partner's arms would keep them stationary. Todd stood straight up in a fluid motion without his hands. Bianca guided him to a space in the middle of the room where a chain hung from the rafters.

At the end of the chain hung a pair of studded leather cuffs into which she latched Todd's wrists. At his feet, connected to 'U' rings bolted to the floor were two more chains with studded leather cuffs. Spreading his legs, she latched his ankles into each cuff so his feet spread a few feet apart.

Stepping up to a shelf on the wall behind where Todd hung, Bianca selected a large metal hook with a bulbous round tip at the end and an eyehole at the top with two pieces of nylon rope. Without any preparation, she pressed the bulbous tip between his cheeks. The round tip slowly push into his puckered hole until the metal from the hook pressed tightly between his perfectly toned as cheeks.

She ran the nylon rope around his waist and up along his chest, over his shoulders and along the back of his head until the hook at the end of either length connected firmly into a ring on the back of the hood.

Walking back to the shelf, she picked up two shiny metal chains with clips on either end. Connecting one clip from the chain to the nylon rope along Todd's shoulder, the other end clipped firmly to each nipple. A muffled groan filled the hood as each clip caused his body to flinch. She tested the tension of the chains to make sure they would apply pressure on the nipple clips if his head moved.

Walking back to the shelf, Bianca pressed a button on a large rectangular panel. A low hum from the rafters filled the silent room as Todd slowly rose until he barely stood on his tiptoes. Satisfied with the proper placement of her slave, Bianca walked back over to where Ruby still sat silently on her knees.

Taking her by the armpits, she urged Ruby up, guiding her across the room to stand in front of Todd. A furled frown crossed Bianca's face as she realized her issue with their placement. After some searching she found a square wooden box a few feet away large enough for someone to kneel on comfortably.

"Step up pet and kneel." She said after sliding the box in front of Ruby so it was partly between Todd's legs and supporting her arm as her pet stepped up onto the box. Ruby kneeled carefully until her face sat perfectly in line with the strung up slave's manhood.

Guiding her bound body forward, Bianca slipped Todd's limp

manhood into the ring in her mouth until her lips pressed against his crotch.

"There you go pet, enjoy." Bianca said before stepping around the back of Todd and walking to the shelves where she selected a rather long cat-of-nine tails with very thin leather strips. "I told you I would punish you for coming without permission." Bianca hissed sternly before her hand lashed out with the whip. A resounding crack of leather on skin preceded the muffled complaint of the bound and strung up man. His groans filled the room as dark red impressions formed at the middle of his softly tanned skin.

Again and again she struck him, two at a time, her wrist spinning back over itself to let the original momentum carry the second strike. His body flinched every time, his legs fighting for some leverage to brace against the whipping. After about eight or nine strikes, Bianca walked around the side, happy to see that he had grown to fill the awaiting mouth.

Each strike forced his body to lurch forward, pushing him in and out of that hungry slobbering hole. A stream of saliva ran down her chin and splashed over her full pert breasts each time his body withdrew even a small bit.

Bianca wondered what was going through Ruby's mind as she kneeled there, unable to effect anything, only able to accept his full thick manhood filling her mouth.

"Are you enjoying your meal pet?" she whispered to her bound toy, admiring the flood of saliva running between her chin and mouth. Ruby only nodded, Todd still firmly embedded between her lips. "If I remove the ring, will you promise to keep him in your mouth?" Her lust filled husky tone met quickly with a nod of the hungry pet's head. "Very well, don't let it fall out or you'll be next, do you understand?" Another quick nod firmed the contract, creating a new plan in Bianca's mind.

Unbuckling the strap that held the ring in place, she guided Ruby's head back until Todd's shaft was no longer in her mouth. Letting the ring drop from her mouth to hang under her chin, Bianca's mind spun mischievously. "Close your mouth around it and don't let it fall out pet." Bianca ordered, holding him against her lips.

"I understand Mistress." Ruby replied pliantly before his meaty pole disappeared into her mouth, her chin less than an inch from his balls. Bianca moved to the side, so she could assault her slave, and watch Ruby's progress. Moving from side to side, she started striking him just above his firm rounded ass.

Each time his hips jerked, pushing him forward. Another couple of hard swats on the top of her slave's taut ass and Bianca shifted to swatting up at his cheeks. A number of the leather straps penetrated between his legs and cheeks to strike at his sensitive underside and the sensitive sack of nerves below his shaft.

The bound slave jumped as the leather bit into tender skin. A heavily muffled cry of pain erupted into the air as his body jerked, pulling his hips up and back. Bianca sneered as she watched the head of his shaft pull past Ruby's lips and hang precariously at the edge of her chin.

"Oh, pet." Bianca feigned disappointment walking over to Ruby. Her hand deliberately rubbing the thick saliva slathered across her breasts before roughly kneading the pert globes. "I'm afraid you need to be punished pet. You promised you wouldn't let it fall out."

"Yes Mistress. I deserve punishment for failing you." She replied delicately, but loud enough for Todd to hear.

"Very well, it seems my pet will take your place whore." Bianca's tone was almost sad, as if she wasn't happy about stopping the punishment of her slave. Walking to the panel on the wall, she reversed the process that pulled Todd up in the first place, letting him slowly come back to stand on his feet.

Grabbing a long metal bar with rings welded at either end from the shelf, Bianca returned to her man whore and began freeing his legs, then his arms. "Stand there." She commanded moving Todd a few feet back as she disconnected the cuff's attached to the chain and replaced it with the bar.

"Stand up pet." Bianca ordered, helping guide her to a standing position on the box, then helping Ruby step down onto the floor. "Now sit down." She commanded, guiding her to a sitting position on the box. Returning to the panel, she ran the chain out until a clank of the bar hitting the floor filled the room.

Picking up the bar, Bianca carried it over to where Ruby sat. She carefully attached each metal cuff lined with fur to Ruby's ankles, spreading her legs to an almost uncomfortable distance.

"Lay back", Bianca guided her onto her back, bound arms under her. Reaching between those soft pale tender legs, Bianca pulled at two snaps where the corset met the hip, pulling away a piece of the latex to expose her glistening wet womanhood.

Bianca moved to the panel and retracted the chain until it started pulling her bound legs up into the air. She walked over to Todd. Still standing obediently where she placed him, she led him by a ring at the throat of his hood over to where Ruby lay.

"You will hold her until I tell you to let her go!" Bianca commanded, taking him by the hands and guiding them to Ruby's armpits. Each hand slipped between arm and body as Todd straightened, lifting Ruby off of the box.

Bianca pulled it out of the way and walked back to the panel, retracting the chain more until Ruby lifted into a vertical position. "Let her go whore." Bianca directed as Ruby reached a point where she was hanging a few feet from the floor. Todd moved with her until told to release her. Now she hung before him a head short of his hips, prompting Bianca to raise her up more.

Stepping up to the curious duo, Bianca moved Todd closer. Removing the gag from his mouth, she pushed his head forward with a hand on the back until his face pressed against the dew moist flower. "You will lick her until she comes, but you will not come, do you understand?" Bianca hissed at him.

"Yes, Mistress." His tongue slipped out of the hood and began softly licking at her blooming flower. Bianca kneeled beside her inverted lover, her hand taking the engorged shaft in her hand and pressing it to Ruby's soft lips.

"Try again pet." She offered as his thick head pressed onto Ruby's lips, prompting her to open her mouth and accept it. Bianca's hand pushed on Todd's ass to move him forward, feeding her more of him. "Now I need to punish you for disappointing me." Bianca said loudly, walking around behind, picking up the cat-O-nine tails she'd dropped.

Without warning, Bianca struck hard at Ruby's ass and spread legs. A muffled yelp escaped her throat as each consecutive strike bit into her. By the time she administered ten or fifteen strikes from the whip, the pale tender skin glowed red with welts and both of them moved in unison with their combined arousal. Todd gently thrusted into her mouth and his tongue worked tirelessly at cleaning the nectar from her flower.

Bianca walked around behind Todd and smacked him on the ass with the whip. "No coming whore. I want her to come now!" Bianca demanded. The more amusing aspect of the whole situation for Bianca became the hesitation to let his head move. While he licked Ruby, the movement of his head pulled on his nipples and the hook pulling on his ass.

Walking back around behind Ruby, she continued whipping at her ass and legs, remembering how Ashley's whippings caused her to orgasm. As if on cue, her tender body convulsed in her immobilized state as an orgasm spread like a wild fire set in her belly.
Her yelps replaced with groans, her movements grew erratic and powerful as her body searched unsuccessfully for some way to brace. Bianca continued the assault on her ass, letting the random leather strap contact the tender skin between her legs until finally her whole body went limp. To Ruby's credit, the man whore's still idly penetrated her mouth.

She walked back around to the front, her slaves still connected in their embrace. Kneeling beside her lover, Bianca removed the thick saliva drenched phallus from her mouth. "Pet, are you ok." She questioned softly.

"Yes, Mistress." Ruby replied with a content whisper as she hung from her feet, gasping for air. Bianca smiled widely at the situation before turning to Todd.

"Hold her up whore." Bianca ordered, guiding his arms to her armpits. Ruby hung horizontally as Todd held her. Bianca walked back to the wall. Letting the chain out until her feet touched the ground, Bianca unlatched the cuffs, then helped her pet stand, then guided her to her knees.

Looking up from Ruby, she realized how hard and aroused Todd was from the deep wet hole of her mouth. Bianca sneered, thinking of how this could go before picking a thin rubber cased wire from the shelf.

Wrapping the wire around the base of his throbbing pole and tightening it with the associated hardware, his already engorged manhood swelled with a dark red hue.

Taking Todd by a hand, she led him to a low sitting bench with metal cuffs on either side. "Lay down whore." Bianca demanded, watching him carefully lower himself onto the bench, laying on his back.

Locking his wrists into the cuffs, Bianca pulled a pair of leather straps from a nearby table and wrapped them around his arms and across his body, pulling his legs back until they pressed against his chest. Tightening the straps with buckles, Bianca immobilized his legs, putting his ass at the edge of the bench, the thick member jutting out between his bound thighs.

Bianca walked back over to the shelves near the panel and picked up a thick black dildo attached to a leather strap with a large section of spongy leather on the opposite side.

Walking up behind Ruby, Bianca gently put a finger along her lips until she opened her mouth. "I need you to do something for me pet." Her Mistress said as she slipped the spongy leather piece between her teeth, making her close her mouth around it before wrapping the straps around her head and tightening them with buckles.

"Crawl this way pet." Bianca guided Ruby by the shoulder across the floor. The movement was slow, but gave her a chance to enjoy the demeaning position as her blindfolded, bound and gagged pet crawled on her knees with a large black dildo protruding from her face. Finally reaching the man whore laying prone on a bench, Bianca grabbed a bottle of lube from a shelf and slathered the tight hole after removing the metal hook still buried in him.

"Be thankful I'm using lube whore. This is a big cock." She teased mischievously. Reaching for Ruby, Bianca guided her forward until the head of the dildo poked his puckered hole. With a hand at the back of Ruby's head she pushed until the dildo disappeared and her mouth pressed against Todd's ass cheeks.

"Very good pet. Now, I want you to rock back and forth like this." Bianca demonstrated with her hand on those soft shoulders, until Ruby was moving on her own.

Pleased Ruby would continue, she stood and walked to the head of the bench, picking a riding crop from a shelf before climbing up onto the bench. Pulling the flap from over her pulsating core, Bianca lowered herself down onto Todd.

"Lick your mistress whore. I want to come like you made her come." She ordered, pressing herself into his face until his tongue dragged across her engorged nub. It surprised her how wet she was as he licked her dripping lips. Bianca began slapping at the swollen member between his legs, causing his body to jump, pushing his tongue up into her.

Bianca watched Ruby's hooded head bobbing, her thick dildo filling his slutty ass with rubber. The whole experience inflamed and arousal deeper than Bianca ever felt with any of her clients. Even though she likely spent more time during the evening putting people in places versus actually doing anything, none of that mattered. Ruby showed herself as committed and resilient as she professed, which only turned Bianca on more.

It didn't take long for Todd's attention to bring her off. Burning with need long before they met him, his tongue jutting into her moist folds set her off. Every time she smacked his oversensitive shaft or Ruby pushed against his prostate, Todd fought to keep himself from coming forcing him to put his attention in other places.

Her flower buzzed as his tongue pushed her over the edge. Arms supporting her weight by leaning on his chest, she ground her drenched flower against his face as she came. Her moans filled the room without a care who heard. Like some lioness asserting her dominance over a pride. Bianca groaned through her shuddering orgasm until the waves of need washed away.

Taking a moment to catch her breath, his continuing attention on her lips caused Bianca to grin. *At least he's as dedicated as she is.* She marveled before finally pushing herself up off of him. Walking down along his body, her fingers trailing along his toned body. Ruby still gently pistoned into his ass. Bianca's eyes went to his manhood. Deep red and swollen from the wire keeping the blood from leaving, the slightest touch made his body jump.

"You can stop pet." Bianca whispered, guiding Ruby's head back until the dildo slipped from the now loose hole.

Unstrapping the dildo gag, Bianca laid it on a nearby table along with the harness that held the blind and gag. Needy cool blue eyes looked out from the inside of a black latex hood. "Pet, please clean him for me." She said, his quivering and stretched asshole staring her in the face.

It was a test more than anything as she wanted to see how Ruby would respond to being asked to lick someone's ass. Without hesitation, Ruby leaned in and licked around the hole, suckling softly on the ball sack hanging close by before returning to the edges of the broken hole.

With a reassuring smile that spread over her face, Bianca pulled the girl away from his ass. "Very good, come here." Bianca urged, guiding Ruby on her hands and knees to where Todd's head lay. "Please lick my juices from his face." Her teacher ordered. Obediently, Ruby crawled up to Todd and licked his face from chin to nose and cheek to cheek. She was diligent and attentive, making sure to even lick trails of liquid that ran down his neck.

While she licked him clean, Bianca unstrapped his legs, letting them fall back over the end of the bench where she locked his ankles in cuffs to hold his legs secure.

Certain every drop licked clean from his face, Ruby sat back on her haunches waiting for further directions. Bianca sat on the edge of the bench near Todd's shoulder where her pet sat. Looking down coolly, she considered the blossoming woman before her without speaking. Finally she reached down and took Ruby's chin, guiding her head up to catch the gaze.

"I think our man whore has an overloaded cock that we should probably release before he gets hurt. I'm happy to let him stay like this for another hour, but I want to give you the choice." Bianca let the words sink in. She knew Todd could hear this and wondered how he would describe the differences in dynamic between them when the games ended. "You can leave him like this, or you can give him release. I give you the choice pet."

Ruby sat silent for a minute, a minute that seemed to drag on forever. There was something going on behind those eyes that caught Bianca's curiosity. She wasn't trying to figure out what her mistress wanted. It almost seemed as if she was considering how far she really wanted to take it, or what she felt he could endure.

"Mistress, if it pleases you, I believe he's earned the chance to release. He gave me a very powerful orgasm." Ruby's response came tempered and thoughtful, and Bianca found her body warming to the confidence in her response.

"Very well pet. I am pleased to let him come. How do you suggest we bring him off?" Bianca was curious where this would go.

"Would Mistress allow her pet to take him in her pussy without a condom?" The request surprised Bianca in more ways than one. To be sure, Ruby already had Todd's seed in her ass, but she figured getting him off with her mouth would top the list. Doing this without protection concerned Bianca to no end. Todd was tested regularly. It was part of their contract. And while Bianca couldn't remember if she'd ever told Ruby that in the past, the complications with the request still carried a lot of weight.

"I don't think that's a good idea pet. It's not safe." Bianca reminded her, kneeling down to be closer and get a closer look into those eyes to understand what was going on in her head.

"If you believe it's not a good idea, I will follow your direction, but I can tell you it's safe Mistress. Believe me." Ruby explained, more confident than ever, as if there was something that bore weight in this discussion that Bianca was not aware of. Bianca regarded her. A silent tension between them as she attempted to decipher the situation without getting into detail and destroying the fantasy they had built up around them.

"I will trust you pet, but you must promise to explain to me why." Bianca knew that the trust between them needed to go both ways if this relationship were to develop in the direction she believed it was going.

"I promise Mistress." Ruby replied without hesitation in her voice, which Bianca couldn't argue with.

"Very well." She replied, pushing herself up before helping Ruby stand. Leaving her arms bound, Bianca helped Ruby climb up onto the bench till she was straddling her whore's hips. Sliding back as Bianca guided his head to her, Ruby's expression changed, twisted as the need to feel him inside finally hit. Head arched back, mouth open, a shudder pouring across her skin like water as she settled down onto him, her hips and ass against his thighs.

Unable to support her weight with her arms, Ruby braced her legs and slowly moved her hips against his shaft, slowly building speed as confidence, balance and need grew inside her.

"How does that feel whore"

"It feels wonderful, Mistress."

"Is she hot and wet for you?" Bianca questioned, leaning on the bench next to Todd's head, watching her lover ride his manhood with only her hips. Ruby's face was a visage of focus and lust. Eyes still closed, mouth open, her moans and whimpers soft but deep, growing from her chest. Her breasts bounced as she ground her hips harder and harder with each shift.

"Do you want to come inside her? Do you think you deserve to fill my pet with your dirty seed?" Bianca chided Todd as his chest rose and fell faster, his moans growing more and more intense.

"Please, Mistress… may… may I give her my seed?" her man whore fought through breaths and concentration to keep himself from coming until told to.

"Well, since she's asked for your dirty whore seed inside her, I guess it's only fair that you give it to her whore." Bianca hissed at him as she watched Ruby ride him. Her pearl was rubbing along his pelvis every time she ground down onto him. Her chest rose and fell in unison with his, and both of them had trouble keeping their focus.

"May I come Mistress?" The request from Ruby surprised Bianca as she had been expecting a reply from Todd. That they were both synced together was very amusing to Bianca as she watched the two of them move.

"You may come when he fills your twat with his dirty whore seed pet." Bianca responded, wondering if her man whore thought her reply hadn't been permission to actually come. "Come for her whore. Give her your dirty whore seed." Bianca ordered Todd, her finger reaching over to tweak the clip still attached to his nipple.

As if on cue, Todd's body tensed, his back arching up, fighting against his restrained arms and legs. His head shot back as a groan ravaged his chest. Whatever happened inside his body and between the two of them in the sexual connection they shared, Bianca couldn't tell.

Ruby's eyes shot open at the very moment Todd's body clenched. The look in her eyes made Bianca wonder. The moan and sigh of contentment from Ruby's throat a second later told Bianca this was something she'd been wanting for a long time. Her body continued to grind and gyrate and shook on top of Todd, not having any other way to brace or release.

Suddenly Ruby collapsed onto Todd's torso as both of them fought to catch their breath and stop the pulses of ecstasy radiating through their limbs. Savoring the final release, Bianca remained still, watching and enjoying how natural the interaction between the two of them was.

Eventually, she stood, walking along the table, releasing the cuffs on Todd's arms. Her hands started unbuckling the straps holding Ruby's arms behind her before unlocking his legs. "When you two have recovered, why don't you wash up and come join me in the bedroom." Bianca suggested before walking through the room to another door leading into a medium-sized room with a king-size bed and a full bathroom.

But what am I to do?

Catching her breath wasn't the hard part, nor was it the never ceasing aftershocks that were rippling out from her belly every few seconds; the hard part was finding the strength, desire or energy to push herself up off of Todd's warm masculine body.

The click of heels on the wood floor disappeared deeper into the room. Ruby could only guess there was another room somewhere with a bed and a bathroom. She sighed softly at the sound of Todd's heart in his chest slowing. It was soothing to feel his heart under his skin, so close to her head, it was relaxing her too as reality came back to her senses.

"If you can find the energy to push yourself up off my hips, I'll gladly slide off the bench and carry you to the shower." The suggestion made Ruby laugh at first. Bracing sore arms and quivering legs in a way that let his hard muscular body move beneath her. Todd slid swung his legs over the edge of the table.

True to his word, Todd slid an arm across her back and another under her legs, cradling her head on his shoulder. He carried her through the dungeon to a door with warm orange flickering light behind it. Using her feet to push open the door, Ruby snickered at being carried but appreciated the chance to recuperate.

He set her down at the door to the bathroom. Holding onto the door jam, she made sure her legs would work before moving any further. Certain she had control, Ruby slowly moved into the bathroom. Much like any other guest bathroom, the sink, toilet and enclosed shower were nothing special, outside of the fact that everything in the room was new and modern, unlike the rest of the house. Stripping out of her outfit, she turned on the water in the shower. The speed of hot water to the spout surprised her, filling the small room with steam.

Testing the temperature, Ruby stepped in, letting out a sigh at the feel of the hot water washing away the abuse to her body. She wasn't trying to wash away some vile thing that happened to her; she was letting the heat sooth the things she accepted as a part of her life now.

"Save some for me." Lost in her thoughts, she'd barely noticed Todd step into the bathroom until his words penetrated her mind.

"Sorry, lost in my thoughts." Ruby replied, her eyes slowly tracing the lines of the man standing outside the glass enclosure. She realized this was the first time she'd ever really seen Todd in all of his magnificence and desirable light. Grabbing a towel at the back of the shower, she opened the door, leaving the water running as she stepped out and let him in. Drying off, her eyes lingered on him longer than she probably should have, but considering what they just shared, she was sure he didn't care. With a towel wrapped around her torso, Ruby walked into the room while drying her hair with another towel.

"Come here, pet." Her teacher held a loving softness in her eyes, a hand patting the edge of the bed where she was lying. Spread out in the middle of a king-sized bed too large for the room; Bianca already stripped out of her outfit and wore a simple sheer black lacy robe tied with a black rope at her waist. The robe didn't hide much of anything.

"Yes, Mistress." Ruby did as asked, climbing up on the bed, working the ends of her hair through the towel.

"For the rest of our time here, you are my lover, not my submissive. You may call me whatever you desire." Bianca pressed a hand on Ruby's cheek pulling her in. Their lips crushed together as Bianca's tongue sought her own. The fullness of the older woman's lips on her drew Ruby in. She suckled gently on Bianca's lips, nibbling with teeth and letting their tongues dance until Bianca broke the kiss. Her eyes went immediately to Ruby's cool blue orbs, searching deep into her soul to ensure she hadn't damaged something fragile.

"Are you ok baby?" Bianca questioned, concern spread across her face like a billboard. It was apparent to Ruby that she worried something may have pushed Ruby too far.

"I'm great Mi- I'm great." Ruby smiled, catching the chuckle her teacher stifled at how ingrained her responses became.

"You're happy? Not hurt in any way?" Bianca added obvious concern in her words and eyes.

"I'm very happy. Nothing we did could make me question the choice I've made." Ruby tried to reassure Bianca.

"I'd say that was about medium for what Bianca is capable of." Todd's voice drew their attention to the doorway of the bathroom. He stood leaning against the wall, naked, drying his wild chestnut hair. Ruby couldn't help but drink in his body as he stood there. He was flaccid now, but still hung three to four inches out from his body against a large sack between his muscular tan legs. His stomach showed the angular cut of a man who took very good care of himself.

"Very few of my clients want it really hard." Bianca corrected as Todd walked closer to the bed. Stepping up to the side of the bed Ruby settled into, Todd's hand reached out, pulling the bundle of towel twisted between her breasts. The towel fell to the side as his hand pushed it away. His eyes drank her up the way she'd looked him over.

Ruby's gaze went from him to Bianca, who was watching the two of them interact with a familiar predatory look on her face and in her eyes.

"I think she could handle anything you throw at her." Todd replied, the back of his hand sliding down along Ruby's arm. The sensation sent goosebumps along her skin, causing her to gently suck in a breath as her eyes moved back to him. Ruby fought the urge to reach out and take him in her hand or lean in and swallow him again. He charged her body for more, but she wasn't sure of her energy level for more.

Bianca must have sensed the growing sexual tension in the room as she pulled sensually at the bow keeping both sides of her robe closed against her body. The sheer lacy fabric fell from her ample breasts as she reached and palmed Ruby's cheek, pulling her to the middle of the bed.

Leaning in, Ruby forced a kiss, fueled by the need to be one with her mentor, her lover finally in her arms. Her hand crossed the divide between them, slipping under the black robe to the soft curve of her teacher's thigh. Bianca pushed into the kiss also, one hand sliding past the pillows to pull Ruby's head closer, while her other hand tantalized Ruby's swelling breasts with light tender touches. Fingers crept through her hair, sending warm energy coursing along her skin as their kiss grew more intense and passionate.

Before she knew it, their bodies came together, their kiss a series of licks, pecks, sucks and brushes with the occasional giggle of sidelong look. Ruby always imagined what it would feel like being entangled with her teacher, but now she was. A leg between hers, the motion fanning the flames that she thought put out by the hot shower, while breasts crushed together seemed to feed the heat of their bodies. Hands explored where there was space to break in.

Ruby's only other experience with a girl ended in kissing. She never even considered being this enthralled by another woman, but something about this seemed right. The feeling of soft, feminine fingers exploring her body sent ripples of ecstasy out from her belly to every inch of her being.

What she hadn't expected was the sudden sensation of movement behind her. The hot thick pressure of Todd's growing arousal pressed against her butt as soft sensual kisses found her neck and back. Ruby let out an uncontrollable moan as her body became overwhelmed with sexual energy. Hand's caressed her from both sides, sliding along her curves, fingers tracing the lines around her breasts and along her inner thigh.

Bianca's kisses slipped from mouth to chin, then along the tender spots on her neck to the nape and the shoulders. Todd's kisses moved along her neck and down her back. Desire swirled into her mind confusing reality as they enjoyed her body.

Todd's hot, swollen flesh fell into the space between her legs vacated by Bianca's thigh as her kisses slowly work their way to Ruby's breasts. Her eager mouth kissing, biting at supple, electrified flesh. Her tongue traced the gradual curves of Ruby's plump mounds. She left a cool wet trail of tingling pleasure in its wake. Her mouth found Ruby's swollen, erect nubs yearning for attention. Lips closed around them as her moist tongue teased and flicked along the sensitive pink tips.

Ruby inhaled sharply at the first touch of her lover's mouth on her aching nipples. This was the first time Bianca explored her body out of desire rather than domination, and the difference made her body float.

Before long they had Ruby on her back as both of them took a breast in their mouths. Her hands played in Todd's nappy hair, pulling him into her as her body writhed in unison with their attentions. Bianca shrugged the robe from her shoulders exposing her full voluptuous body to Ruby. This wasn't the first time seeing her teacher fully naked before, but the moment added a glow that flared her desire.

As his mouth sucked hungrily at her breasts, her body tensed and shuddered at the feeling of another mouth trailing a path of licks along her side and belly until finally landing at the apex of her tender thighs. A deep moan escaped her throat, her back arched softly as Bianca's hungry mouth explored the tender flesh between her legs.

She avoided Ruby's flower, teasing as her tongue skirted the edges, her breath blowing on hot embers. She could feel herself tighten, pushing out above her lips as they moistened with need. Looking down, she marveled at seeing those curled red locks moving between her legs, kissing along the insides of her thighs.

She saw Bianca look up along her belly, catching her own gaze. Ruby felt the deep connection in their share gaze and for the first time she saw a need to please instead of being pleased.

Ruby's mind swam at the euphoria of it all, and the second she felt Bianca's tongue on her moist petals her deep groans filled the room as the reality of what was happening finally galvanized in her mind.

"Todd, fuck me." Bianca demanded as her mouth tenderly kissed Ruby's nether lips. Not one to deny a request from the woman between her legs, Todd gave her breast one last lick before rolling off the bed and positioning himself as Bianca lay with her belly on the bed.

Kneeling, straddling her hips, Todd angled himself down and slowly pushed the length of his manhood into her teacher. Ruby watched her face as he entered her. She felt the subdued moan on her lips before the gentle motion of his thrusts drove her tongue deep between Ruby's wet lips. She grinned through a whimpering moan. Her hand gently kneaded her aching breast, fingers pulled at her nipple as the motion of their desire flowed from Todd to Ruby through Bianca.

They moved in harmony, the symphony of their grunts and moans filling the room. Time and space vanished around them as only the sensation of pleasure in her body and the connection she felt with the other two people became real. Before she knew it, Bianca crawled her way up her body, kisses and licks trailing in her wake until she came to hover above Ruby. Her deep green eyes filled Ruby's soul as her lover leaned in with a deep open mouth kiss.

Ruby could taste herself on those lips, on her tongue. She was tangy, sweet and heated. Moaning into the kiss her mind raced. Always coming back to the flood of emotions filling her body in the embrace of the one woman who showed her more about life than she'd ever known.

So enthralled with the deepness of the kiss between them, Bianca melted into Ruby, their bodies pressed into a soft embrace as two women became one. The rest of the world slipped away between them. Ruby felt her body floating as she and Bianca wrapped together. Hands lightly slid across heated skin as kisses turned into nibbles or licks, occasionally shifting to an ear or neck only to return the center of their world in each other's mouths.

Their moans were soft whimpers and sighs as the heated desire between them changed to tender love, at least until Bianca's level of arousal changed. Ruby noticed it as her lover's breathing grew more erratic and her movement more controlled.

She noticed Todd behind Bianca. A hand slipped past her belly and drove her legs wide as her hand found Ruby's womanly heart. Fingers caressed Ruby's downy mound, crept between her damp petals like snakes in the garden. Three of her teacher's fingers filled her, the sensation made Ruby arch her back, purring. They pressed against her swollen pearl and worked closer to her magic button. Ruby's body curled around her tormenter, her mouth seeking solace.

Bianca's breathing grew heavier to match the intensity, her hands worked at bringing Ruby closer along with her. Lips and tongue tantalized her sensitive breasts as Ruby quickly reached her peak. Before she knew what was happening, Bianca's mouth jumped to her own as fingers urged her to climax.

A heavy throaty moan filled her mouth as they kissed, her lover's body writhing in a dizzying explosion of emotion. Wildly riding the waves of passion tearing through her, Bianca's hands concentrated some of that energy into Ruby's core.

Crashing over the wall, her teacher's wild energy set her own body off as it convulsed into a chain of spasms. Regardless of the tidal wave of orgasmic power that over took the both of them, they remained centered in each other; their mouths letting the passion and energy flow until they were both calmly caressing each other's faces between soft kisses.

Ruby's head ended up in the crook of Bianca's shoulder as exhaustion overtook her, the joy of being so close and free with her mentor quieted her thoughts for sleep.

Bianca breathed deeply, taking in the cool river air. Leaning on a metal rail, she stared out over the Mississippi river as the Creole Queen floated by. The muffled churn of the boat's large paddle wheel in the water behind it, and soft jazz music circulating became white noise for her thoughts.

The weekend became more than she ever imagined. Waking up with Ruby's warm soft body cuddled against her own crystallized feelings she hesitated to accept. The thought made her smile, knowing that this blossoming woman she'd committed herself to felt just as deeply.

"Well, that's the look of a woman who's gone through a life changing experience." The voice of her best friend barely broke through her thoughts until the touch of a hand on her shoulder drew Bianca back to reality.

"Wha…. Oh, Hey Ash. I didn't see you." Bianca stammered, embarrassed at being so lost in thoughts. Giving her friend an adoring look, they hugged until Ashley replied.

"It's ok. You were obviously deep in thought." The suggestion turned Bianca's thoughts back to what had been on her mind.

"I was thinking about last night. Thank you again, by the way. I don't know how to repay you for what you made happen." Bianca gushed. She'd likely never know what kind of favors Ashley spent or incurred to make it happen, but she was sure there would be a way to pay her back some day.

"Seriously, Bee. It's nothing. The look in your eyes tells me it was more than worth it." Ashley put her arm over Bianca's shoulder and gave her a squeeze, the enamored look in her friend's eyes reminding her that Ashley would do anything for her happiness.

Bianca turned and walked along the concrete path that followed the river through town. They strolled in silence for a few minutes, never needing to fill an awkward silence between them.

"I take it Todd liked her?" Ashley finally asked, breaking the silence before taking a sip from a coffee cup she'd been holding. Kieran and Todd were the only clients her friend knew by name. She knew Todd mainly because he'd been the closest thing to a male lover for Bianca in a number of years, and he was more than a client to either of them. It was also the reason she'd wanted him to be the first they played with together. If the chemistry between Todd and Ruby worked, it would be a signal to Bianca that her heart and her desires were in sync.

"It was more than I could have ever imagined Ash. They connected the moment they came together, like two planets caught in each other's gravity." Bianca's body tingled as her mind replayed the image of them in the side room.

"Were you rough on her?" Ashley asked after a moment. She'd noticed the flush of reminiscence in her friend's eyes as they walked. The emotion in Bianca's eyes quickly changed to warm mischief at the question.

"Apparently not as hard as I could have been." Bianca chuckled to herself. "I could have probably wrapped her up in Japanese knots, hung her in the center of that ballroom and let your friend's guests have their way with her and she would have begged for more." The imagery made her mischievous smile grow even more when she saw the look of dismay on Ashley's face.

It took Ashley a moment to collect her thoughts after the powerful image of their youthful student being the main attraction at one of Abby's events. Ashley finally swallowed hard before asking.

"Do you really think she's that committed?"

"To me, yeah, I do. I believe she'd endure just about anything I asked her to." Bianca's tone became harder as the realization of what she'd just said hit her. Beyond the budding love between them, Ruby came into her own as a submissive at the hands of her mistress. Confident and self-assured, her student was quickly finding her strength, but how much of it was her feelings for Bianca and how much was truly who she was. "But I think she truly believes and accepts what she's becoming. You should have seen her at the meeting on Thursday. She took to it like a fish to water once she got past the hesitation of her doubts."

"You're really in love with her now, aren't you?" Ashley asked, putting her arm back across Bianca's shoulders. The question shouldn't have surprised Bianca. They had been inseparable since they met in college, and things grew more powerful over the years. On some level they were still together, still lovers, but deep down they were two souls bound through pain and joy, forever connected.

"When we finished playing with Todd, I let the dynamic change. The fantasy ended, but the evening didn't. I brought her into the bed, I brought both of them and we made love in a way I haven't done in a long time." The memory swelled in her chest, her throat tightened as moisture welled in her eyes. Ashley stopped and turned to hold Bianca with her gaze.

"What's wrong Bee?" Her friend asked, surprised by the sudden well of emotions to overtake someone she knew had a reputation for being hard and cold. Bianca stared through Ashley before her gaze fell to the supportive arms that held her shoulders.

"Yes. I'm in love with her Ash." Bianca finally choked out against her tight chest. "… and it scares me." Her mind finally processed the hesitation she'd felt over the past few weeks.

"Why does it scare you?" Ashley already knew the answer, it was obvious to a woman who was forever Bianca's first lover. But Ashley also watched that young girl she fell in love with grow into the hard, confident professional who found strength in being able to distance and detach herself from the world around her. It was the one thing that made Bianca so successful both publicly and privately, her ability to approach business dealings with cold objectiveness.

Not growing emotionally attached to her clients, but being able to put on a believable face gave her an edge and gained her respect. Todd was the one anomaly, but he started as rebound sex after Randall and was the first to sign up at the suggestion of her business proposal. She wasn't in love with Todd, but there was an emotional connection between them that didn't exist with any other client. He also knew where the boundary was and what it would cost him to cross it.

"Being with her makes me hesitate." Bianca said after a minute, wiping tears away from her eyes. Walking to the metal rail, she leaned over, looking to the river like she had been when Ashley found her.

"Hesitate? How?" Ashley questioned, her tone unconvinced by the admission. Bianca turned and caught her gaze, as if that one question shattered the entire premise of her argument.

"I… I'm finding it hard to reconcile how I feel about her with how I treat her. I don't know how to be her mistress and her lover at the same time." She sighed as Ashley reached across and placed her palm on Bianca's face, turning her head.

"You've never been very good at this." Ashley teased. Bianca laughed out a sarcastic, sad laugh.

"Every relationship includes aspects of Dominance and submission. The difference is you both have established the roles and boundaries. You don't have to make her sleep in a cage at night to establish your dominance over her, you've already got that. Oddly enough, I imagine she'd do it if you asked." Ashley added her laugh to Bianca's. "She's coming into her own as the woman you had a hand in creating. A large part of that is the submissive you've shown her is part of who she is."

"Why didn't it work with us?" Bianca asked softly. There was a lot of truth in what Ashley said, but at one time she was the one in Ruby's place and the dynamic of their relationship changed, eventually ending the deeper aspects of their exploration into fetish.

Ashley's mouth turned down into a thin frown, as if she felt Bianca was trying to compare the two relationships to understand her failings.

"Bee, after all this time do you really believe it didn't work between us?" Her question flooded memories into her mind as Bianca considered what she'd asked. She didn't believe that things hadn't worked between the two of them. They shared the most amazing connection and relationship that two people could ask for, but the dominant/submissive relationship withered.

Part of the reason being their inexperience with that kind of relationship. The other part was more to do with Bianca and Ashley being more evenly balanced as dominants, making it hard for either to submit to the other.

"No," Bianca shook her head, embarrassed that she'd implied things didn't work between them. "That's not what I meant Ash, I guess I'm just worried Ruby's growing confidence will override the submissive side of her much the same way you came into your own." Ashley's lips curled back up as she leaned in and gave Bianca a kiss on the cheek.

"You forget Bee, I always had a dominant side, but I wanted to explore. We've both spent enough time with her to know she's submissive by nature. Think about your clients, some of the most confident, powerful businessmen in town, but the minute you put that collar on them they bow down without hesitation or question." There was a reason Bianca loved Ashley, and she again reminded her of that reason in this single moment in time.

"Do you think I'm crazy for falling for her?" Bianca asked quietly.

Ashley's face warmed, her eyes glinting with that adoration she'd shown the first time she'd met Ruby.

"I think you'd be crazy for rejecting it. It's been a long time since I've seen you this focused and full of emotions." Ashley replied, her hand sliding back along Bianca's head to push a thick drape of hair back from her eyes. "Strangely, I'm crazy about Ruby too. Mainly because I see how she affects you, but also because I enjoy being with her. I like the dynamic that has grown between us."

A flurry of thoughts and images ran through Bianca's mind at the suggestion of the dynamic between the three of them. The fact that Ashley felt the way she did about Ruby made falling in love with her much easier. Her friend never approved of Randall, and the reasons remained hidden to Bianca till it was too late. Approving of Ruby, regardless of the situation between them, carried a lot of weight for where the relationship could go.

"I think she really likes you too. I saw the way she responded to you when you were getting her ready." Bianca's lips spread into a smile. "Which by the way, you outdid yourself putting that whole thing together. The looks Ruby got from the guests, I honestly could have offered her to the room and they would have eaten her alive." The suggestion that the ensemble Ashley put together for Ruby created such a powerful response, sparked a flood of emotion inside her friend. Her normally light tan skin grew dark red as goosebumps rippled along her arms.

Even though Ashley eventually became a lawyer, she'd started college out with an interest in art and fashion. While those who mattered never recognized her talents, prompting the reason for going into law, she never lost the touch or the taste for it. "How did she do with it?" Ashley inquired, finally composing her emotions.

"She gave your vision life Ash. Her poise and confidence gave no thought at all to all of those eyes cutting through the strategically placed embroidery. She could have walked into that room naked and wouldn't have been as alluring." Bianca gushed, remembering the look of the two women and the man in the alcove, so taken by Ruby, they stopped their intimate interaction to drink her in. "Honestly, I wonder if she was more proud of being on my arm or being in your outfit." Bianca teased her friend with a tender squeeze of her hand on Ashley's shoulder.

Ashley chuckled out loud as they both pushed off of the rail and started walking back towards home. "How did the latex outfit work?"

She hooked Bianca's arm into hers as they walked.

"Pretty well. I think we'll need to work on a better plan for access to her lower torso. That flap works ok, but doesn't open up access to her rear." They walked in silence for a few moments, then Bianca continued. "I had her upside down, ankles bound by a spreader bar connected to a chain, arms bound behind her. Todd was licking her while he was in her mouth. I must have whipped her fifty times on her ass before she came. She never once complained." Bianca marveled at what Ruby accepted. It was nothing compared to what Veronica and Cain put her through, but she didn't seem phased by any of it, which made Bianca beam with pride.

"If you really want to push her, take her back to Mulroney's and offer her to the room." Ashley said with a wicked look in her eye. Bianca gave her friend a questioning look, uncertain why Ashley of all people would suggest something so severe.

"You know what that would entail Ash." Bianca's dismay at the suggestion resounded in her question, but the look on her friend's face told her she was completely serious.

"Of course." She almost dismissed the question. Both Bianca and Ashley became involved with the circle of people who regularly attended Kieran Mulroney's events for a time. Both of them experienced the extremes of where some of these people could take fetish behavior, and exposing Ruby to that didn't sit well with Bianca. "You said yourself you could have probably offered her up to the room and she would have accepted without question."

"That's different, Ash." Bianca countered. "Tying her up and offering her to Abby's guests would be like putting a piece of meat on the table to be sampled. Tying her up and offering her to Kieran's guests would be like throwing her in a medieval dungeon." She shook her head. There was also a good reason her feelings for Ruby caused Bianca to hesitate, to make sure she didn't do anything that might test the trust and limits they created. Ashley was right, this did not differ from any other romantic relationship where one person was more dominate than the other, the difference was that Ruby accepted the way her mistress used her sexually.

"I know Bee, I was simply suggesting the most extreme scenario where you could push her. If you would prefer to offer her to Abby's guests, I can work something out." Ashley replied, her eyes closing slightly as she raised an eyebrow at the suggestion of turning to Abby again.

"It's a possibility, Ash, but right now I want to focus on establishing the softer side of our relationship." Bianca answered with a shrug as they walked.

"Where is she?"

"At work, I may have her come over after and spend the night. I'll need to figure out with her on how to move forward." Bianca's mind was racing with how she would change the dynamic between them. They needed to discuss how things would change and the things they could keep as well as the changes Ruby would accept and the ones she might think odd now that walls between them were torn down.

"You can still maintain much of the domineering personality, I don't think she would question or rebel. I think she is probably as in love with being free to surrender control to you as much as she is in love with you. Remember, a true submissive wants to please and accepts giving up control." Ashley explained as they walked. "What did she do that first morning when you let her sleep in your bed?" She asked

"I woke up to her licking my pussy." Bianca said warmly, a flush of excitement filling her cheeks at the memory of that first night.

"Did you ask her to?" Ashley asked with a sultry tone to her voice fanning the heat Bianca was suddenly feeling.

"No, I just woke up to the feeling of a hot wet mouth working me to a climax."

"Did she seem to enjoy it?" Bianca realized with the question they really didn't discuss that first day after the night in the playroom. Discussions about the tender moments between the two of them seemed unnecessary to share with Ashley. Now as things became so much clearer between them, those events came rushing back into her mind.

"She was playing with herself, and by the taste of it, she was very much in heat." Bianca reminisced. It was surprising thinking back to the innocent girl she'd convinced to step out of her comfort zone and offer herself to strange men for a night of sex. How far they'd both come since that night. Ruby blossomed into a very different woman, but Bianca changed in that time too because of her.

"See, she would probably be content with sleeping on a large dog mattress on the floor like a puppy. All she would need was permission to be on the bed in the morning making love to you." Ashley teased putting ideas in Bianca's head. Bianca needed to see how the relationship could stay dominant and submissive without removing the tender closeness of two lovers.

"Well, like I said, it's going to be a learning process for both of us." Bianca answered, leaning over to lay her head on Ashley's shoulder.

"As usual Bee, I'm here for you… or now I guess it's the both of you." Ashley replied softly, turning her head to kiss Bianca on the head.

"Will you come over? I'll make dinner." Bianca asked her arm over Ashley's shoulder, her head still on the other one. "I need to decide if I want her to brief Martin."

"Sure, we can discuss ideas." Ashley replied, taking Bianca's hand as they turned back toward the main streets of town.

Ruby was beaming as she walked across the quad to her biochem class. The lunchtime sun was high, but the days turned steadily cooler as the end of the semester drew to a close. The past few days rushed by like a dream after waking up in the arms of her lover and Mistress Sunday morning. Somehow, going to work seemed pointless to Ruby, but she still had her life to live. And then there was the meeting on Tuesday with Bianca's boss and one of the managing partners of the firm.

True to their agreement, Bianca refused Ruby the opportunity to see her Monday night to go over the meeting. Regardless of the change in their relationship, her teacher was still trying to keep the image of propriety for anyone that might try to turn this into an inappropriate relationship. They still had two weeks till the semester was over and Bianca was no longer her teacher.

Unlike the last time she'd been told to brief the team, this time Ruby received details of the meeting the night before, giving her time to prepare.   From the way Bianca gushed the evening after when she called Ruby, it seemed she'd done a good job and caught the attention of some very important people in the company.
There was something almost erotic about her mistress praising her that made Ruby flush. She'd played with herself after the call, even though she'd been told not to orgasm until they were together again. Ruby complied, but it didn't stop her from bringing herself close.

Lost in her thoughts as she entered the medical building, she barely noticed the tall, balding older man dressed in a gray jacket and slacks coming toward her. "Ruby do you have a minute to talk?" The man asked, pulling her from her thoughts. Looking up at the scruffy graying goatee and soft smile lines around his mouth, Ruby realized it was the department head, Dr. Lewonzi standing over her.

"Uh, I, I have class in like five minutes." She replied trying to figure out why the Medical school department head would want to talk to her.

"It's ok, I'll give you a pass. We can talk in my office." The older man said in a light medium pitched tone as he turned toward the administration offices of the medical school. Realizing she didn't have much of a choice, Ruby followed in silence, trying to figure out if she'd come up short on her grades prior to finals. As far as she knew, she had a strong B in every class. Regardless of her recent distractions, Bianca had insisted that she needed to keep her grades up, and something about the shift in her world had instilled a new focus on classwork.

Leading her into his office, Dr. Lewonzi waited till she was in the room before he closed the door behind her. "Have a seat Ruby." He offered walking around behind his desk. Covered in a chaotic assortment of books, papers and folders all stacked up in some less than organized way, the desk gave off the impression of a very busy or unorganized man working behind it. As he sat down, he leaned back in his chair, his eyes sizing up the look in her face as silence filled the office. "How are things going this semester Ruby?" He finally asked, leaning forward with his elbows on the desk.

"Good, I guess. I struggled a bit in the beginning with all the new upper level classes, but I seem to have caught up." She replied confidently, fishing for a reason to explain the meeting.

"Are you finding the new business curriculum we started requiring this year difficult?" He asked. The fact that his next question had gone to Bianca's business class sent up a flare. Thankfully, her training over the past few months taught her to keep her emotions and reactions in check, enabling her to keep from showing fear to a man who was clearly looking for a reaction to something.

"It was difficult at first. I couldn't quite understand the need for nursing students to have business classes, but the internship has given me a whole new perspective." She gave him as much truth as she could to keep from letting anything show that might give her away.

"And this internship, you're working with Bianca Ristretto?" He asked directly leading her to understand that something was coming she would not like.

"Yes sir. I understand they chose three other students who are working in other areas of the company." She added, having been told by Bianca a few weeks after she started. As far as Ruby knew, there was nothing improper about the internship and nothing ever happened at the office that might create a conflict.

"Yes. And from the reports I've received you all are doing very well." He answered, not hinting what he was getting at. "Do you ever see Ms. Ristretto outside of class or your internship?" The question wasn't a surprise. The direction things were going, it was the obvious next step, one that she'd prepared for ever since she and Bianca talked about cooling things off until the semester was over.

"I've joined her for dinner a few times after working late." Ruby kept her answer short, making sure not to say anything that he could turn back on her if he had information to the contrary.

"So if I told you I have been told by a professor on campus familiar with you and Ms. Ristretto, that two people closely resembling the both of you were seen at a party in some very compromising situations, you would stand by your assertion that you do not spend time with Ms. Ristretto outside of class or your internship?" Keeping his question vague, couched in a hypothetical, told Ruby whoever believes they saw the two women couldn't be certain. Bianca and Ashley went through a lot of trouble to keep their identity hidden for the party, so Ruby could only assume whoever said something saw them at the Mulroney house. The problem with that premise was that then they could positively identify them.

"Sir, I don't know who thinks they did or didn't see the two of us together, but if they did, it was on campus or at her office." Ruby's mind ran back over the answer she'd given and made a note to chuckle to herself later. Six months ago, she would have turned into a puddle of mush at being charged with having an improper relationship with a teacher. Today she barely blinked at the question.

"Very well Ruby. I'm putting you on probation with a clause to expel if the school determines that you have been engaged in a relationship with Ms. Ristretto outside of class or your internship. Also, removal from the internship program with her company is necessary and you will take your final next week with a proctor. As long as she is an instructor at this school, we forbid you to see her. If you don't abide by this, we will expel you. Do you understand?" The force and finality of his statement caught her like a cat-o'-nine-tails strike to her exposed sex, causing a sharp pain to shoot through her body.

Everything in her life that meant anything over the past six months, everything that defined that woman, Dr. Lewonzi stripped away from her without warning. Ruby fought back the fear and emotion welling up inside as she simply stared across the desk, her blue eyes cold and hard. Before she might have turned into a blubbering mass of emotions, but now she felt the poise and confidence steel her against the storm.

"You have no cause to remove me from my internship. I've done nothing that warrants removal and you have no proof aside from a vague rumor that I've done what you accuse me of." She replied coldly, feeling Bianca in her mind and understanding now how she became the woman she did.

"Unfortunately, Ruby, even the image of impropriety gives me the authority to do this. If you don't agree, you're welcome to take this to the University. Until that happens, the probation stands." Realizing Dr. Lewonzi wanted her to give up the truth, she stood without another word, and walked to the door.

"This isn't over." She said cold as ice as she walked out of his office and out of the building, completely forgetting about Biochemistry. As soon as she was out of the building and halfway across the quad, the cold hard shield she'd erected to hold herself together collapsed.

Crashing to her knees on the side of a building, tears streamed down her face as her body shook from shock, fear and loss. *How could things explode like this?* Her heart pounded against her chest as her thoughts went to Bianca. Kneeling on the grass, sobbing, a steady stream of tears ran down her pale face.

Ruby eventually found the strength to push the pain and the fear from her mind long enough to pull out her phone. *Miss. Ash, I need to see you. It's urgent.* She typed a text message and pressed send. Uncertain if Dr. Lewonzi might have someone watching to see if she ran back to Bianca, Ruby sought solace from the one person she knew would understand.

Driving back to the office from a lunch with a client, Ashley's mind ran over the client's discussion when the message came in. Seeing a message from Ruby wasn't so much a surprise as the timing. While Ruby rarely reached out to her, Ashley never had an issue with Ruby contacting her. In fact, she wanted her to, but the urgency of the message caught her off guard.

Pulling over into a parking spot on the side of the street, she read over the message before selecting Bianca's number. Her friend picked up after two rings, which meant she was likely still in her office. "Hey what's up?" Bianca asked, her voice coming through the speaker in Ashley's car.

"Did you and Ruby have a fight?" It was the first and only reason she could come to why Ruby would come to Ashley before going to Bianca for anything.

"No, why?" Her friend asked, a new tone of concern in her voice.

"I got a message saying she needed to see me urgently, did she message you?" Ashley inquired, looking at the GPS in her car to figure out the best route to the college.

"No, what's going on?" Bianca's tone turned serious.

"I don't know. If she didn't come to you first, there must be a reason." Ashley replied.

"Where are you?" Ashley could tell by the tone that her friend was off balance now. The only thing to do was figure out what was going on and to do that she needed to confront Ruby.

"St Charles near Lee Circle. I was coming back to the office from lunch. I'll head to the campus and get her and find out what's going on." Ashley said, turning her sleek black Audi around in the middle of the street. "Don't worry Bee, I'll let you know as soon as I know what's going on."

"Thanks Ash." Bianca hung up. Ashley quickly dialed Ruby's phone back, hoping she wasn't in a situation where she couldn't answer. The phone rang once, twice, three times as tension pulled at her neck.

"Miss. Ash?" Ruby's voice, broken and choked, followed the click of a call received.

"Ruby, what's wrong? Where are you?" She asked, hoping

Bianca's lover would give some indication of what was so urgent.

"Can you pick me up? I'm outside the books store near the visitor center on the south end of campus." Hearing the pain and sorrow in Ruby's voice did not reassure Ashley.

"I'll be there in ten minutes." She replied realizing it was a straight shot being on St. Charles already.

"Thank you." Ruby said almost sobbing as the line disconnected. That she was crying, and Bianca did not understand what was going on, meant something else had happened. Whatever happened, it was hard enough to break down the cold confidence Ruby developed over the past few months.

The drive was quick, traffic after lunch wasn't as heavy, putting Ashley on the side of the street outside the designated bookstore a few minutes early. Pulling out her phone, she sent Bianca a quick message. *Picking her up now. She's been crying. Will call when I know more.* Just as she hit send, Ruby stepped out onto the sidewalk, looking around. Ashley tapped the horn, catching her attention. Judging by the redness and bagginess around her eyes, Ruby had been crying fairly hard until recently.

Opening the door, she climbed in and immediately leaned in to hug Ashley.

"Whatever is going on Ruby, it'll be okay." Ashley wrapped an arm around the young girl and held her close.

"No, it won't." She said sobbing and wiping tears from her eyes before closing the door.

"What is going on little one?" Ashley's use of her pet name would hopefully add a little urgency to understanding the problem. She sat and watched patiently as Ruby pushed away more tears.

"Can we go somewhere quiet to talk?" The request surprised Ashley. She'd assumed they would talk in the car, but as there seemed to be a reason for wanting to be more comfortable, Ashley pulled the car out into the street, finding her way through the city to a local coffee shop.

Eventually, seated in the back of a rustic college coffee shop a few miles from campus, Ashley turned her attention from the few students scattered around working on homework, to the solemn, flushed young woman. "Okay, little one, let's have it." She demanded in a soft but serious tone.

"The Department head for the medical school pulled me into his office today." She fought for words through sobs, the emotional toll heavy. "He accused me of having an inappropriate relationship with Bianca after some professor supposedly saw us together at a party." The accusation from a department head at the school carried a lot of weight, but Ashley wasn't sure it was enough to cause this level of anguish.

"What proof does he have?" She asked, the lawyer in her stepping into the conversation.

"I don't know, it seemed like a vague insinuation from someone who knows both Bianca and I. But he apparently doesn't need proof as long as there's even the image of impropriety."

"So why the tears? What else is going on?" Ashley pleaded, still not sure she knew the whole story.

"He's put me on probation. He's threatening to expel me. He removed me from the internship and forbade me from seeing her in any capacity. He's even going to make me take my final with a proctor so I can't be in class with her." The bucket of bricks came crashing down, and it was crystal clear now why she was so distraught.

"He can't do that without some hard proof." She replied. She wasn't certain of this. University rules were very different regarding burdens of proof and due process.

"I can appeal to the school, but who knows what that will do." Ruby lasted just long enough to get the last few words out before the emotional toll hit her again and she started crying. Ashley pulled her in, holding her close. *How appropriate that this happens now as things are coming together.* She thought as Ruby sobbed into her shoulder.

A buzzing pulled her attention from Ruby once she noticed her phone was going off in her purse. "Hey." She said answering the call. "Yeah, she's right here crying on my shoulder." Ashley answered, running her fingers gently through Ruby's hair in an attempt to soothe her. "Something about the department head putting her on probation and threatening to expel her if he finds out she's been in an inappropriate relationship with an instructor at school."

She paused for only a second before responding, making sure her conversation was vague enough for anyone listening to not tie the conversation back to Bianca. "Apparently some professor at a party reported he saw her with this instructor and just the image that the rumor might be true is enough. The department head has removed her from her internship and will make her take her final with a proctor." Ashley could hear the anger growing in Bianca's voice but did her best to keep the tone of the conversation even. It didn't do either of them good to let this elevate until they knew more about what was really going on. "She's pretty distraught right now. I'll take her to my apartment for the night so she won't be alone." Ashley gently shook her head, knowing that Bianca was climbing the walls right now. "Don't do anything rash, Bee. Let's think this out and do it right so it hurts more." She said calmly, hoping to cool Bianca off a bit. "I'll call you later once she's resting." She sighed before turning off the phone.

Gentle sobs shook Ruby's body as Ashley held her. "It'll be ok little one." She knew what Bianca was going through, she could feel her own anger and frustration growing. She'd warned her friend about the possibility of this many months ago. To have it all come crashing down now, just when they were coming together and the world was making sense for both of them, riled Ashley's emotions as well.

"How the hell did this happen?" Bianca demanded, walking in through the front door of Ashley's apartment. Down the entry hall she strode anxiously into the open layout kitchen living room, slamming her purse and keys down on the black marble countertop. A careful mix of modern décor and old style wrought iron and wood floors made the kitchen warm and cozy. Ashley followed her friend into the kitchen, pulling two wine glasses from a black wrought iron hanging rack.

"I don't know." Ashley sighed, pulling a bottle of white wine from a shelf in the door of her refrigerator, before pouring each of them a generous portion.

"I called Kieran after I got off the phone with you. As far as he knows there aren't any current or previous professors or anyone affiliated with the university attending his parties. Besides, no one would risk losing their place for something this trivial." Bianca was fuming. The cool tingle of the wine in her mouth and throat helped slightly, but did little to settle her anxiety.

"There are only a few places this could have come from and it had to be recent or we would have heard something much earlier." Ashley talked through the situation as she pulled her own glass from her mouth.

"Do they really have the right to do this?" Bianca asked through a sigh as if the weight of the whole thing was threatening to crush her into the floor.

"I called a friend of mine who works in Tulane's law school. She said the school is on shaky ground without real proof, but they probably assume the image of impropriety argument and the threat of expulsion is enough to scare her into compliance." Ashley walked around the island of her kitchen and sat down on a bar stool, her eyes watching Bianca.

"What about the internship? That's not a school decision." She asked knowing that Ashley's law firm acted as counsel for her company's interests. Ashley's connection with M&K was how Bianca met Randall and gained her foothold with the company. Now she was relying on the connection with the company to at least save part of her lover's future.

"It's sticky. She signed a contract with the company for the semester with a clause for her contract to extend at the end of the semester if the firm deems her services in demand." Ashley took a sip of her wine.

Bianca could tell she was trying to figure out how to word the next part of her assessment. "The problem is that regardless of the company stance, because the internship counts as 'credit' toward graduation, they have a bit of leverage in deciding if an internship is in the best interest of the student's progress."

"And if the company requests that the school let her continue?" Bianca was running through points of leverage of her own.

"Hard to say." Ashley shrugged. "Depends on how much the school is willing to play hard with whatever proof they have." Bianca groaned softly, closing her eyes as she twisted her head from side to side, stretching her neck and shoulder muscles.

"Where is she?" Bianca asked, after a minute of silence as she tried to stretch strain out of her neck.

"Guest room." Ashley replied, tossing back the last of her wine then standing and leading Bianca down another hallway to a door. She looked into the medium-sized rectangular room with a whitewashed brick wall at the head of a low-set bed. On a bed with a grayish blue headboard and base covered in a white comforter, Ruby lay on the bed silently sleeping. The white walls of the room gave off a warm shadow as the day's sunlight waned through the window.

Bianca sat on the edge of the bed. Ruby was curled up in a ball in the middle of the bed. Wrinkled school clothes, hair splayed out in every direction above her head, The only sign of life being the gentle motion of her back as she breathed. She lightly brushed a hand along Ruby's soft reddish blond locks, her normally hard expression faltering as she watched her lover sleep.

"Thank you Ash." Bianca said standing and walking back to the door, laying her head on her friend's shoulder as they stood and watched Ruby sleep.

"I was my pleasure Bee. She needed us and we're here for her." Bianca stayed still, head on Ashley's shoulder as she watched Ruby. Her eyes welled with tears as she tried to imagine what she'd do now without this radiant presence in her life. Ruby became such an integral part of their life over the past months, and it was hard to think how this could destroy the personality they worked so hard to build up.

Lifting her head up off of Ashley's shoulder, Bianca turned back down the hallway to the living room. Picking up her wineglass and walking into the open living room, Bianca stopped at the window to stare down at the street below. Still in the middle of the French Quarter, Ashley's apartment was far enough from the center to give her a quiet cozy feeling even during the busy season. She turned around to see Ashley sitting on her dark gray leather couch with the half empty bottle of wine in the middle of the coffee table.

"I want to go to campus tomorrow afternoon and talk to this Department head." Bianca said frankly. "I'd like counsel from the company with me." She added. Her eyes watched Ashley's reaction, knowing there might be a conflict she'd need to work through.

"Is that wise? I mean no one at the company has authorized this." She responded exactly how Bianca expected. Regardless of their connection and friendship, the woman in front of her held professional ethics very close and would be hard pressed to cross the line.

"We pay your company a retainer to have an attorney's available for legal matters that arise, right?" Bianca argued, having already worked her plan out as the day crept along, unable to see her lover or her friend.

"Yes, Bee, but I'm not sure this counts." Ashley countered.

"We have a contract with an intern to be available to the company for a determined period. That intern is not being allowed to fulfill that contract because the school has an unfounded accusation of impropriety they are using as justification." Bianca walked closer to the couch, her eyes and Ashley's locked as she talked. "There is no complaint of inappropriate behavior coming from the company or any of the people she's worked with. As a matter of fact she's received great praise regarding her skill and support of the company."

"Isn't it going to look rather odd if the woman she's accused of having an inappropriate relationship with, shows up with a lawyer to argue the case?" Bianca grinned, softly nodding her head to the side at the question. Her lawyer was right, but in reality she was also Ruby's supervisor and the head of the division, which meant bringing someone else in would require Martin or another partner.

"What do you think Martin or Doug Keen will say if I bring this to them and request they intervene?" Bianca asked a bit more sharply than she had planned.

"They're going to say that you need to take care of it." Ashley admitted with a shrug as her shoulders sank at realizing Bianca was right in how this would play out.

"Do you agree that this is something counsel retained by M&K should be involved with?" Bianca pushed at her friend's admission.

"I can see the merit of the case, but I'm not sure the company will want to justify the billed hours for an intern." Bianca walked over and sat on the couch, her hand on Ashley's thigh.

"As junior partner and head of Mergers and Acquisitions, I have freedom to use the companies retained counsel for legal issues that effect my division." Bianca grinned softly, patting the warm, firm flesh under her hand. "This effects my division, especially after the brief Ruby gave to Martin the other day."

"You know, she said there was a stipulation this department head offered to this whole mess." Ashley's curious timing of this admission chipped away at Bianca's confident repose.

"What?"

"She told me that as long as you were an instructor at the university, they forbade her from seeing you." Bianca felt a flare of anger boiling up in her chest just as a familiar tingle at the back of her neck drew her attention away and pulled her back. That tingle, the one she'd felt as a young woman coming into her own every time someone told her she couldn't do something or that she would fail.

If there was one thing everyone learned quickly about her, it was never to tell Bianca she can't have or do something she wants. For some administrator at the college to tell her she can't be an instructor and be with Ruby was like telling her no.

Calling first thing that morning, Bianca broke through the usual bureaucratic crap that filtered the people from administrators. Not accepting no as an answer for an appointment with, Dr. Lewonzi she finally forced the department secretary into accepting an afternoon meeting.

Dressed in a white button up blouse with a flared collar and long sleeves, a knee-length black skirt, ankle wrapped heels and her hair hanging free and flowing over her shoulders; as one of Bianca's power outfits, she wanted this college administrator to understand he was playing with fire.

Ashley was more conservative, exuding the air of a serious lawyer. Dressed in a light gray blouse and skirt, her hair in a French braid against her head and a pair of burgundy wire-rim glasses. She oozed knowledgeable attorney, something her friend appreciated.

"Miss. Ristretto, I'm Dr. Brian Lewonzi." The tall Department head met them at the entrance to the department offices, telling her he at least understood the gravity of the situation. Bianca took the offered hand firmly, a show of strength to the man in front of her.

"This is Ashley Vanderbilt, she's here as attorney for Melantris and Keen in this matter." Bianca watched Lewonzi at introducing the firm's lawyer, wondering how he'd respond.

"Ms. Vanderbilt, It's nice to meet you." He said, extending a hand before inviting them into his office. "I'm not sure why you feel an attorney is necessary, but we can discuss that in my office." The three of them walked into his office, disorganized and disheveled as it was, he walked around to his chair and sat down after closing the door behind them.

"I understand that you've removed a student that our company has contracted as an intern from the program." Bianca kept her voice cold and impersonal, removing any possible connection with her feelings for Ruby.

"Yes, Ruby Phillips is on probation and as part of that means removal from the intern program. I'm not sure that you've been informed yet by the business department, but she will also take your final exam with a proctor next week. She won't be returning to your class." The man's tone seemed overly jovial as he discussed the punitive measures he was throwing at a student who had done nothing but follow her heart.

"May I ask what the reason you removed her from the internship is?" Ashley asked in an even, inquisitive tone.

"There are rumors of an inappropriate relationship with Ms. Phillips and your client, Ms. Vanderbilt." Lewonzi replied with an almost accusatory tone that burrowed below Bianca's skin.

"Is there proof of this relationship?" Ashley was quick to respond, setting the tone.

"We have reason to believe the accounts we have received have merit." The administrator in him kicked in as the political cross talk slipped into the conversation.

"If this is the case, why has my client not been censured or removed? Surely if you have enough evidence to accuse and punish a young student of an inappropriate relationship, you must have enough evidence to accuse the instructor she's supposedly in the relationship with." Bianca could see the older man's forehead twitch slightly. His hands went to a pen on the desk, nervously spinning it in his fingers.

"We did not feel there was need to ruin the reputation of a valued instructor. We have dealt with the matter." He retorted, having taken a moment to construct his reply.

"But you have no problem ruining a young student's reputation. A student who has garnered praise and recognition for her ability and poise in our company." Bianca countered, feeling the ire of the situation smolder inside her. Ashley's level and supportive hand on her shoulder pulled Bianca back, her dark brown eyes staring out from behind those burgundy wire-rim glasses at the man behind the desk.

"It is the position of Melantris and Keen that Ruby Phillips has met all requirements and obligations of her contract. We intended to offer a contract extension at the end of the semester for a paid internship. With that in mind, is it still the position of your department to keep these punitive measures in place?" Ashley handed Lewonzi a live grenade with one chance to receive the pin to turn it off. They both looked at the man, wondering if he would do what he needed to save himself or if he would let the grenade go off.

"I'm sorry, ladies." He finally said after a long silent contemplation. "Until such a time as the president of the university and the ethical review board direct me to change my decision, I must uphold the principles of our university, which means stopping activity that we deem inappropriate." Before heat of Bianca's anger could melt the cold facade she'd put up for the meeting, the reassuring hand of Ashley on her arm returned her focus.

"I see. I'm sorry you feel things need to go to that level." Ashley replied, cold and even keel as she rose and opened the door to the office. Bianca bit her tongue, letting the shrouded threat from an attorney carry more weight than anything she could throw at him.

They walked tall and quiet to the parking lot where Bianca's car waited. Once in the car Bianca couldn't help but growl at the top of her lungs, the reverberations shaking the solid German made car, and her friend at the same time.

"I guess we shouldn't have expected him to crumble that easily." Ashley waited until her friend expelled the rage bottled up inside before saying anything, and Bianca appreciated the fact she knew enough to expect it.

"I'm not sorry." Bianca grumbled. "After everything he's putting Ruby through with this, I'd be disappointed if he'd given in." She started the car and pulled out of the lot, back onto the streets of New Orleans. "Now he'll get to see what happens when you try to hurt the people I care about."

Somehow Ruby found walking soothing, more soothing than moping around in her apartment or walking through campus. *Two days!* she thought to herself, two days since she'd been told by Dr. Lewonzi that they forbid her to see or have any interaction with Bianca. Ashley told her that Bianca came by the apartment to talk and be close, but she slept through the night without being woken up.

Ruby was cold and broken, and it didn't matter how many clothes or how much heat she turned on; it lingered, filling her body. She meandered through the French Quarter, making the cab stop on Canal Street to keep any question of her destination a mystery.

She'd been able to audit her Trigonometry and Biochemistry finals due to her grades, which opened up a lot more time this week for studying, but the last thing on her mind was studying. On any other day she would have been at Bianca's office working on some project. Today was the first day the removal from the internship program really hit her. It created a void in places she'd grown accustomed to over the past few months. Work the day before seemed dreary and meaningless, and the entire world looked decidedly darker and gloomy compared to a few days ago.

Ruby wandered the streets aimlessly, partially trying to remember which crossroad was Ashley's apartment, the other part was to make sure no one was following her. Ashley's message asked her to come over after class, but warned her to keep her eyes open for anyone watching. She honestly doubted the university would dedicate those types of resources to make sure she was keeping to her probation, but who could say anymore.

Certain she had the right building, Ruby entered the external doorway leading up to the apartments above local shops. Walking down the hall, she kept looking back to make sure no one was watching before knocking on the door. Her heart warmed slightly when Ashley opened to see who was there.

"Oh little one, you look heartbroken." She said with a firm warming hug as Ruby stepped into the apartment. "Let's liven your spirits a little bit." Ashley said, closing the door and walking her into the apartment.

Ruby's heart nearly jumped out of her chest seeing Bianca standing up from the couch. "Mistress!" She yelped happily, running to

Bianca, crashing into her, arms wrapping her in a loving hug.

"I missed you too pet." Bianca chuckled, giving Ruby a soft kiss on her reddish blond head before backing away slightly. "Are you ok?" Her teacher asked, guiding Ruby to the couch before running the backs of her fingers over her cheek. Ruby's head leaned into the touch as her eyes closed, cherishing even the momentary contact.

"No mistress, I'm devastated. This couldn't have happened at a worse time." The youthful exuberance of her personality gone as she replied, her tone hollow and empty.

"It'll be okay love." Bianca pulled her into another hug. Holding her for a minute then pulling back. Bianca placed a hand on either side of Ruby's face and gave her a tender, loving kiss. As Bianca broke the kiss, she stared into Ruby's cool blue eyes now ravaged by redness and sorrow. "Baby, until we are back together and this is all over, you are free of any submission to me. You don't need to call me Mistress. Right now, I am your friend, your lover, and in some ways your equal. Do you understand?" Her teacher held her gaze until Ruby nodded her head.

"I understand." Ruby's voice cracked with emotion as she felt a weight shift from her soul. Ashley stepped up to the two of them with two glasses of white wine before sitting on the couch beside Ruby, sandwiching her between the two of them.

"We wanted you here so that Bianca could explain the situation." Ashley explained, putting a warm hand on Ruby's shoulder. Her eyes still lingered on her teacher, who sipped at her wine. The look in her eyes told Ruby she was trying to find a way to tell her something bad and couldn't find the words.

"Ash and I went to speak with Dr. Lewonzi yesterday to see if we could break the top off this can of worms and get you back into the internship at least." Bianca started.

"Unfortunately, he felt his position was being threatened by backing away from the decision, so he's holding firm." Ashley finished seeing the anger building in Bianca's eyes.

"I appreciate you trying." Ruby said turning from Bianca to Ashley and back. The two of them had clearly been working hard in her defense without telling her. She hated that either of them were in a position where they needed to defend her, but considering the both of them had made this choice, Ruby was appreciative.

"Oh, don't you worry, love. We're not done by any stretch of the imagination." Bianca scowled. "The problem pet, is we will need to work some magic to make this go away, and that could take time." Bianca added, finally getting out the concern Ruby saw in her eyes.

"What do you mean? How long?" Ruby felt her eyes swelling up again and the tightness in her throat building.

"We don't know little one." Ashley interjected, leaning in and kissing Ruby on the neck. "I'm filing a motion with the school ethics board to have them review your case, but being the end of the semester it could take time."

"And I'm calling in a few favors, but I don't know how much leverage they'd be able to bring." Bianca added taking the hand Ruby wasn't using to hold her wineglass in her free hand, fingers intertwined. The tenderness of her touch felt nice to Ruby, comfortable, warm, stable.

"I assume we won't be able to see each other until this is over?" Ruby asked as tears and sobs spilled out of her, prompting Bianca to pull her into a hug.

"No pet. I can't risk you being expelled for me." Bianca sighed.

"I'll drop out!" Ruby exclaimed between sobs as hard and confident as she could muster, considering. Bianca pulled back with a scowl on her face, her brow turned down and ruffled as she regarded the statement.

"You'll do no such thing, Ruby!" Bianca admonished her. The reply surprised Ruby, considering her teacher used her first name so sharply. "You dropping out of school is as much out of the question as me quitting as an instructor at the college. And if either would happen, I will quit before you drop out. Do you understand me?" Bianca's eyes were hard but not cold like she'd seen them before when the woman berated or admonished her. This was a warm hard. A fiery emotion in that look, no matter how hard it was.

"Ruby, you aren't cut off, You're welcome here for as long as you want." Ashley was turning out to be the anchor rock for Ruby and Bianca, a role she was certain they both appreciated without end.

"If a resolution doesn't appear by Christmas, I'll speak with Doug Keen personally and step down as an instructor at the school. Hell, they'll probably want to rotate us around, anyway." Bianca tried joking about the situation, but her weak laugh only caused Ruby to want to sob more.

"I… I don't know how to do this. Everything was so amazing now it's falling apart." Ruby felt the hopelessness of the situation fill her body. The things that had changed in her, and the direction that defined her life now seemed an impossible void to fill.

"Ruby baby, nothing is falling apart." Bianca pulled her close into a hug. "We've reached a crucial point in our relationship and conflict is part of the process. You'll never be alone, Ash will always be available for you and you'll always know where I am even though we'll be apart.

"Little one, I hope you don't think we brought you over here to give you bad news." Ashley caressed her arm with a gentleness that sent sparks jumping along her skin. Ruby looked up to see that look on Bianca's face that telegraphed she was about to be very naughty.

"I don't understand." Ruby looked to both of them, uncertain where they were going with this line of discussion. Bianca's hand brushed along her cheeks, pushing the gently curling reddish blond hair away from her face. Her hand slipped to the back of Ruby's head, pulling her closer. Her teacher's mouth opened, greeting Ruby with the first real kiss they'd shared since the morning she briefed Martin on the Peterson account. That kiss had been for luck, this was for love.

As she leaned into her teacher's kiss. She let the energy of their connection fill the void in her soul left vacated by her lover being ripped from her life. At the same time, Ruby felt luscious full lips kissing her neck, a heated tongue tracing the pulse under her skin. Her kiss with Bianca went from a deep, loving dance to fleeting nibbles and pecks and tangling tongues. Suddenly hands entangled her body as both women fondled her without hesitation. The heat in her belly she believed snuffed out by her dreams being destroyed flared in her heart. It spread across her skin like wildfire causing her to whimper. Her head fell back onto Ashley's shoulder.

Hand's pulled at her top, lifting it up over her head exposing her pink lacy bra. Whimpers changed to short shallow gasps as lips sought out flushed, exposed skin. Every inch received attention as the straps of her bra fell down her arms, shortly followed by the release of lacy fabric.

Cool air brushed along her now free and firm creamy breasts, Ruby's teeth caught her lip in response as her nipples jutted out, aching for attention. It wasn't long before Bianca's mouth gave them that attention, suckling one up between her lips as her tongue circled the areola. Flares of heat radiated out from her breast, creeping into her belly.

Ashley followed the trail of heat spreading through Ruby's body. Her fingers slipped undeterred into her pants. Crossing the curly mound of fur above the growing dampness of her womanhood. Her fingers hunted the heat building inside her as they pushed further. While her hands explored, her mouth laid loving kisses along the creamy smooth regions of Ruby's back.

Ruby found her legs spreading freely to accommodate the eager hand. As those fingers found her radiant jewel, her back arched as the shock of contact pushed the air from her lungs. It didn't take long before her pants opened. Bianca pulled at the fabric, while her tongue rode tempted the curvy roundness as the bottom of Ruby's breast. Unwilling to resist the attention, Ruby hitched her hips, letting the pants slip down her legs until they were a bundle on the floor.

She should have seen it coming. Bianca being the one to pull her pants down, but the intensity of Ashley's fingers on lips and the mouth on her back had Ruby's mind floating. It wasn't until she felt fingers slip away and hot wet tongue push between her folds that Ruby's body realized Bianca kissed her way between her creamy thighs. She sucked in a quick breath as her teacher's mouth descended over her dripping sex. Ashley's hands shifted to her breasts, kneading and pulling at her nipples as the woman's mouth moved over Ruby's neck.

Ruby's body buzzed with desire, but to her amazement there wasn't any lust in her heart. Contentment and passion filled her. The true nature of her relationship with these two women made itself manifest as they made love to her. In her heart, nothing would stop them from keeping her safe and a regular part of their life. With that, once again, Ruby surrendered herself to the what may come.

ACT THREE

Boundaries

Bianca's mind wandered watching the rainy skyline of the city outside her office window. The view matched her mood in so many ways, dreary, foggy, bleak. Almost two weeks since that night at Ashley's apartment, since the last time with Ruby. She and Ashley loved that young woman in so many ways that night before Bianca took her to bed alone. It was the first time alone as lovers and equals in their relationship, and while tears of sadness flowed that night, just as many tears of joy flowed.

In the past two weeks Bianca powered through the entire list of individuals around the city who wielded even some power and influence. She hoped at least one of them might pull a string or whisper a word to make this all end. Their night together lifted Ruby's spirits enough for her to get through finals, but just like her teacher, the positive energy was waning fast.

The buzz of her phone lying on her desk broke into plodding thoughts, forcing her back to reality. Her eye caught Ashley's name on the screen as she picked up and answered. "Hey Bee, you busy?" Her friend's voice was lively, but Bianca could sense an undercurrent in her tone that made her worry.

"Not really, we close on Peterson tomorrow, I was going over last details but my mind is wandering." Bianca complained, thankful her friend was the one person in the world that would listen.

"I know, mine is too. I heard from the school. The dean is at their Chicago campus for a conference and won't be back till after the new year. But they will review it then and there's a good chance it will be over turned." A sigh loud enough to be heard by the secretary made her body go limp in the chair.

"Ash, you know I'm going to have to quit teaching out of principle if we can't figure something out before then." Bianca promised Ruby it would be over by Christmas one way or another. It wasn't quitting that bothered her, she'd do it for Ruby in a heartbeat if she asked. To Bianca, letting the school win was unacceptable to her.

"I know, Bee. We see Abby later this week to at least find out if our professor was at the party, but I'm not sure where that will get us." Putting pressure on the person who started all of this had always been a long shot, but it was looking like a last resort.

Just then a text message divided Bianca's attention as she pulled the phone away to read it. *'You needed to see me?'* Her eyes went to the name, and she felt a swell of energy surge through her.

"Ash, Kieran just texted me. He's in town. I need to go."

"Talk soon!" Ashley didn't hesitate at ending the conversation. She knew all too well this was likely their last chance to end it their way. As soon as they disconnected, Bianca quickly wrote back.

'Are you in the city? Can you meet for lunch?' She'd have run to his office in an instant if she thought it would help, but this didn't seem like something she wanted to do over the phone or in a business setting.

'Meet me at Emeril's near LeMieux Galleries in an hour?' The response came quick, which surprised Bianca. Not being Kieran's style, but it pleased her nonetheless.

'Perfect, see you there.' She replied looking at her watch.

Deciding to walk and let her mind go over the discussion they'd have, Bianca left the office early. Kieran was the type who could be fairly predictable in business dealings, but Bianca wasn't sure how he might respond to this sort of request. Considering his past meeting with Ruby, she felt he would be the one to take an interest in the situation. Unfortunately, as she'd seen in the past two weeks, using clout and influence wasn't something you just pulled out of your wallet.

The rain tapered off to a soft mist, which Bianca was fairly certain was not an improvement. The umbrella she carried did little to keep the mist out of her face as she walked. Thankful she'd worn it, even though hats weren't usually her thing, the newsboy hat Ashley gave her last Christmas came in handy today.
Stepping through the door to the restaurant, pulling her long wool coat

and hat off, her eyes searched the dining room. "May I help you ma'am?" A woman's voice pulled her attention. An early twenties, slim female hostess with chestnut brown hair pulled into a ponytail, looked up at Bianca with dark green eyes. Dressed in a black button-up shirt and slacks, she matched all the staff in the swanky modern restaurant. Warm and cozy with lots of oak trim and floors, dark metal accents, this definitely seemed like a place Kieran would choose.

"I'm here to see Kieran Mulroney." Bianca responded, watching the woman check her book before stepping out.

"This way, please." She led Bianca deeper into the restaurant. The smell of food reminded Bianca she skipped breakfast out of disgust today. The low murmur of voices told her this would be a good place to talk privately about her problem.

"Bianca, so glad we could get together." Kieran jumped up from the table as soon as he saw her approach, pulling her into a warm hug. The hostess politely took her hat and coat, letting Bianca sit unencumbered.

"Kieran, it's good to see you too. Thanks for seeing me." Bianca gave him a warm smile as they broke the hug and she sat down across the table from him.

"A glass for my friend, please?" Kieran caught the waiter walking by before turning his attention back to her. "It's no problem, dear. You are by far one of my favorite business women in this town. There's very little I couldn't do for you." He added as they set menus down in front of them, along with a matching glass of white wine.

They ate first, politely discussing his business trip and her current accounts. Kieran was the one person Bianca was open to discussing work with, mostly because he brought her more business than she brought him. Being a man of influence in the business community, he knew a lot of the goings on and knew details about their accounts that weren't public knowledge, anyway.

"So, how is your little assistant these days? I'm very much looking forward to seeing how she complements you." Kieran wiped his mouth from the last of his meal, his steady green eyes assessing her. Bianca was sure that he could see the torment in her. The past few weeks she'd found it hard to keep up her usual cold, businesslike image.

"She is actually what I wanted to talk to you about." Bianca paused, taking a sip of her wine, her eyes also watching him for a response. When nothing of consequence appeared, she continued. "There were some rumors we were having an inappropriate relationship. And while the school doesn't have actual proof to punish me, they are punishing her based on the suggestion of impropriety." Kieran was silent, a gentle curl at the edges of his thin lips turned down.

"And now they have forbidden her to have any contact with you as long as you're teaching at the school?" He asked coldly. Bianca nodded solemnly, as if she was explaining bad grades to her parents. "And we both know it's not in your nature to quit." He added, the down turned edges of his mouth twisting back up into a grin.

"Exactly." A slight relief filled her at her friend's conclusion, realizing he was processing.

"I assume things have developed between the two of you since the last time we met?" He asked, with a glint in his eye that she knew well. Her mind jumped back to the night at his party. The way he lit up when he met her. The way he insisted on letting Veronica and Cain play with her so he could see how pliable she was. He called Bianca first thing the next morning to insist she join them when he returned from his trip.

"Very much so, yes!" She beamed at the thought. "I'm not ashamed to admit it, I'm in love with her, and any submissive nature she might have aside, she's in love with me."

Normally Bianca wouldn't have admitted that to anyone outside of Ashley, but seeing Kieran's interest in her, it seemed a way to personalize the situation. His eyes shifted to the room as he thought. Not looking at any one thing, but thinking, letting the motion and white noise of the room fill him.

"What is it you hope I can do?" Asking as he turned his attention back to the subject.

"You have contacts in the medical field, you have contributed to the endowment at the medical school. Hell, you're on the board of directors for both Loyola and Tulane." Bianca paused for a moment, turning her gaze off to the side. The emotional toll of this whole situation was more than she'd dealt with in many years. Composing herself, she continued.

"At the very least I want this to go away and I want her to pursue her life without restrictions. What I'd really like is for the school to take a black eye over this." She'd changed the emotion to anger, letting her frustration slip into her words. She could see the impact they had on the man across from her as his eyes shuttered slightly and his face grew more serious.

"This isn't a small favor, Bianca. We have a lot of history and god knows this has been a mutually beneficial relationship over the years, but look at this from a business sense. Is the price worth the product? Wouldn't simply walking away from the school be enough?" She could see what he was doing. In that moment of contemplation he decided what his price would be and deep down in her soul, Bianca knew she would not like it.

"Kieran, you know if I thought there was a better way, I'd never have asked this of you. We gave the department head the opportunity to back off. We tore up his flawed excuse for evidence and threatened a breach of contract with my company, and he still insisted. I'm prepared to swallow my pride and walk away, but not before I know I've done everything in my power to remove the stain on a young woman's future and bring her a little happiness."

Bianca was flush with fire now, her focus translated through her eyes, along with her mind. Conviction and confidence carried a lot of power with her, and she brought both to bear in her argument.

The sly, unassuming look on his face was a change from the serious demeanor before which was a good sign. Kieran always found her fire arousing. It brought them together in business and when he found out about her lifestyle, it created the connection for a powerful relationship. Now it was the reminder of that fire pushing his decision.

"Ok, I'll help you." His worn Irish and Creole accent flaring with excitement. "… but I have one condition." His eyes watched her, as if wondering whether she'd prepared for the eventuality of this. "I want her to offer herself as the main attraction at one of my parties."

The suggestion hit Bianca like a kick to the back of the head. It wasn't so much that the demand surprised her; it was the fact that she predicted the condition and the answer already. Bianca always knew she and Kieran thought in very similar lines, and if he didn't have a submissive streak, they likely would have been competitors, not friends, but to hear him offer this caught her off guard.

This was the point where the hesitation that caused fear and anxiety previously reminded Bianca of why she hesitated when it came to Ruby. "Anything else Kieran, but not that." Bianca snarled. Her response, or the fierceness of it, caught him unprepared. His eyes went wide with surprise at the rebuke.

"That's my price Bianca." He didn't back down or even offer an alternative, which scared Bianca.

"Well, thank you for your time, Kieran. I'm sorry we couldn't make this work." Bianca's fire smothered as she watched the last chance to win on her own terms dashed away.

"Wait," Kieran grabbed her hand as he expected Bianca to stand and leave. "Why is that request so out of bounds?" His voice softened and lowered. Bianca's eyes stared intently at the large, powerful hand on hers, letting the fire flare through her again.

"That's not her path." Bianca turned her eyes up and caught his gaze. They were both in business negotiations, leverage and influence. Kieran knew as well as she did when someone was willing to walk away from the table, there was a reason which they hadn't considered. "Yes, she endured an evening with Veronica and Cain, but what your guests would do to her would break her forever." He could see the consideration behind the request. Kieran was smart enough to realize Bianca wasn't just acting out of emotion. She thought this through before arriving in anticipation of the possibility.

"She's a natural Bianca. When I saw her that night, her strength drew me in. She accepted it without question." There was a very real look of admiration in those yellow-brown eyes.

"Ruby accepted it because I asked her to. I asked her to trust me, I told her that everything would be okay. I didn't want to give her to Veronica and Cain because I know what they are capable of. I know the depths of their depravity and if I offered her to the dungeon, they would carry Ruby into those depths because I asked her to."

Kieran blinked as if he hadn't considered her perspective on the request.

Bianca sighed, understanding now her conviction with this request. "It's not the path I want her to walk. I've seen how that level affects the slaves who go there. She's my lover, not a plaything, so no, I won't agree to that."

The look on his face was that of a man who suddenly realized a secret about the world long hidden to him. Deep contemplation filled his eyes as he regarded her understanding of the world he played in.

In truth, one reason Bianca went into business catering to men like

Kieran and Todd was that the fetish world tasted like ash in her mouth after seeing the things others endured in the dungeon. After her break with Randall, Bianca followed that path. She let the anger and pain of what happened fuel her desire to dominate those who accepted her. After punishing and abusing a slave so hard it hurt him, Bianca walked away.

Thomas Rutherford and Todd Jefferies were first to bring her back, but on her own terms, her own levels of intensity.

"I respect your position Bianca. Can't say I blame you. As much as I enjoy it sometimes, I have found my age and wisdom makes me hesitate when the darker guests attend my parties. I still wish to have her join us, but I'm curious to see how far she can go. Unfortunately, if we don't clear this up, I don't get the feeling either of us will see how far she can go."

Her mind chased ideas on something that would meet Kieran's grandiose standard but not put Ruby in a situation where she might break. Then her thoughts ran back to the conversation that had started this.

"What if I could put her in a situation I was more comfortable with? With a lower level of abuse, but you would get a chance to see her pushed?" The simple suggestion widened his eyes and his dark red tongue sliding across his upper lip told Bianca she'd whetted his appetite.

"I'd be open to it." He sat back, one arm across his torso while the other balanced his elbow on that arm and his hand stroked the short stubble growing along his jawbone.

"It may take me a day or two to get an agreement and we wouldn't be able to actually pay your price until we fix the matter. But if I can get the agreement, I will."

"Bianca my love, I trust you both as a friend and a colleague that you will do whatever you must to best make this deal happen." Leaning back toward the table, he placed his hand on hers again. "I will start making inquiries today. Once you have the agreement, I'll implement a plan." Her eyes lit up like stars realizing her way, and the whole plan rested on two women. A woman known for certain levels of sexual proclivity and a woman who had surrendered to her more times than Bianca could count out of trust and love.

Life was slowly becoming a broken record, the last few weeks a gloomy slog of wash and repeat. Ruby sobbed to herself, her head against the door of the office in the coffee shop she managed when she wasn't in school. As soon as finals ended, the void in her life became more apparent, driving a push for more hours at work. Of course that had only filled the void and the hours with pointless activity, making the yearning to fill the void worse.

She'd started spending her evenings she didn't work at Ashley's apartment. Ruby was glad for the company, especially since her roommate was never there anymore. The two of them slowly drifted apart over the summer after she met her boyfriend, and being involved with Bianca didn't help matters.
Ruby could at least be thankful her job paid well enough to pay for the apartment if her roommate moved out, at least for the time. Ashley's apartment allowed for occasional phone conversations with Bianca. Those helped lift the mood, but as the days dragged on, even phone calls stopped having as much effect.

A knock at the door startled Ruby. She jumped at the noise, stifling a sob. "Ruby, there's someone out here asking for you." The voice of Clarice, one of the baristas called through the door prompting a raised arm to wipe tears from eyes before opening it.

"Thanks." She said with a sniffle before following the other girl back to the front of the store. Her mood lit up mildly when she saw Ashley standing at the edge of the counter holding a fresh cup of coffee. "Hi Ash." Ruby appreciated Bianca giving her the freedom to greet Ashley with more familiarity after their night together, it made the time spent over the past few weeks more comfortable.

"Hey Ruby, you have a few minutes to talk?" Those warm brown eyes were smiling with cheerfulness lost to Ruby for weeks. She nodded, leading Ashley back to a worn couch in the back of the shop, away from the bulk of the customers seeking shelter from the cool gloom outside.

"Is everything okay?" Ruby asked as they sat down, Ashley sitting close.

"Everything is very good little one." The way she said it gave Ruby the impression that something concerning the situation changed. Ruby wanted to hope. She wanted to feel the fire burning inside her body again, pushing the cold void away. "I won't be home tonight, so I wanted to talk to you." Those youthful pink lips turned down in a pout at the suggestion that Ashley wouldn't be home, which meant there wasn't a reason to go to her apartment tonight.

"That sucks, I was thinking about making shrimp scampi tonight." She teased, hoping maybe the suggestion of food might convince a change of plans.

"I appreciate the offer." Ashley giggled to herself, placing a hand on Ruby's back to give her a reassuring pet. "Are you doing okay?" The question was fairly moot. They all knew where the emotional heartbreak barometer was at the moment. Ruby exhaled, looking down at her hands in her lap.

"I'm okay. I'm still randomly crying whenever I look at the clock and realize I should be at my internship, or my hand accidentally brushes the collar." At the suggestion, her hand reached to the ruby hanging at her throat, her thumb and forefinger pressing it between them. "… but considering the situation I'm stable for now." Ashley watched her finger the ruby before sliding her hand from the back to the shoulder and pulling Ruby into a hug.

"It'll be over soon, little one. If we have any say in the matter, one way or another it will be over soon." She whispered, the finality of the statement caused Ruby to pull back and look up at the woman's face.

"What happened?" Her tone filled with concern and questions worried that Bianca gave in to the suggestion she step down. Bianca swore to step down by Christmas, and they were growing dangerously close to that point.

"I won't go into details now, until things are in motion, but there's a request for you that could end this." The wording of the answer only seemed to add more concern and questions to her mind as they circled.

"A request?" Ashley cocked her head to the side and gave Ruby a very cryptic, amused look.

"I'll put it this way, what would you be willing to do or give of yourself to make this all end as soon as possible?" Ashley's question was quiet enough only Ruby could hear it, but the implication pierced her mind like electricity. She wondered if Bianca offered her up as a bargaining chip, or if one of her clients requested her as the price to play her game?

Ruby's mind chased the answer to her own questions. Apparently for longer than she'd thought when the expression on Ashley's face changed. There was a hint of concern on her face that the answer Ruby would give might not be what they wanted.

"I have sworn and surrendered myself to Bianca more times than I can count, and nothing in that has changed. I know she loves me, and will always keep me safe, to answer your question, anything either you ask of me, I will do."

The delight returned to Ashley's face. It told Ruby that whatever it was they were planning, there was a glimmer of hope it would be the end of everything. Ashley started slowly nodding before speaking. "That's what Bianca said, but we weren't going to make any inquiries without you choosing for yourself. I wanted to be certain." Ashley looked at her watch, then reached in to take Ruby's chin between two fingers. "Head high little one." She said before leaning in and giving Ruby a kiss on the cheek. "I'll give Bianca a kiss for you. She sends her love."

Ashley whispered into her ear away from where anyone could hear before pulling away and standing up. "We should know more tomorrow afternoon. Bianca and I are going to speak to the last piece of the puzzle after work. I'd suggest you use the spare key and come over after class tomorrow." Leaning down, Ashley pressed her lips to Ruby's forehead in a loving peck. "Love you little one, I'll talk to you tomorrow." She said before walking out, leaving Ruby sitting on the sofa.

There was a tingle of excitement moving up along her spine at the implications of the conversation. She stared off toward where Ashley sat a minute before, her mind ran through the conversation again.

A request could mean anything from anyone. Only a few of Bianca's clients knew anything about Ruby, and only a few more who traveled in those circles did either. In reality, she decided, it didn't matter who had requested her, or what they had requested, if Bianca asked it of her, she wouldn't hesitate.

Anxious energy or excitement? Bianca was having a hard time telling the difference. She and Ashley drove along the highway toward the last piece of the puzzle they needed in place to bring an end to this entire problem.

"Would you stop that?" Ashley chided the bouncing leg, an outlet for Bianca's nervous energy. Being this anxious was very unfamiliar for Bianca. Usually the cold, calculating personality used anxious energy to put things in other places, not channeled to her legs. Being a passenger in a car didn't help, but Ashley insisted on driving since it was her friend they were going to see.

"Sorry Ash, I'm having trouble not letting this whole thing stress me out." She apologized knowing her friend felt it too, she just wasn't showing it. "I just need this to be over. I had to cancel a session with one of my clients. He's been on my schedule for months. I wasn't sure if I'd even be up for it, let alone not hurt him."

"I understand Bee," Ashley's calm demeanor on some level became an anchor over the past few weeks, but Bianca felt her patience slipping. Ashley showed amazing poise considering this threw all of their lives into chaos.

"How was your date last night?" The question forced a sidelong glance, which immediately changed with Ashley rolling her eyes. Though she vehemently denied that the man she joined for dinner the night before was a colleague from work, Bianca relished that at least one person's life wasn't on hold because of this whole affair.

All three of them were suffering on some level, and Ruby was likely the hardest hit by it all, but it would be over soon one way or another. "He's a friend. He started as criminal counsel about six months ago. There's nothing more too it." She tried to deny it, Bianca knew her better than that. The distraction of everything going on clouded her judgment slightly. Maybe it was just seeing things where they weren't because she wanted them to be there.

"Well, I hope you had a good time. How's Ruby doing?" Why not change the subject to something more pressing on their minds? It was apparent that Ashley had nothing juicy to say about the man, so there was no point in pushing.

"She's not doing well. I'm afraid if this goes on much longer we're going to lose what we created in her." The tone in Ashley's voice conveyed much more than her words ever could have. Of the two women, she'd spent the most time with Ruby over the past month and knew her moods well by now.

"Well, let's end this then." Bianca declared not accepting defeat anymore. "She was ok with the plan?"

"Yeah, for the part that we could tell her." Ashley disagreed with keeping the details of the plan a secret. It wasn't as much about keeping Ruby in the dark as it was to preserve the deal. Being told about the request as the price for the favor would open her imagination of too many things they could ask her to do. If this worked, Bianca wanted her ready for anything.

"I know it was hard not telling her Ash."

"It wasn't hard, she barely blinked at the suggestion." Ashley smiled as she turned the car off onto a long winding driveway. "Honestly, I believe you now when you said she would take on Abby's whole house without hesitation. If it pleases you, there's nothing that girl wouldn't do for you." This was the point Bianca, tried to convey to Kieran. Even if she thought it would please her Mistress, she would do it, no matter how it destroyed her.

Pulling to a stop in front of the large Victorian mansion, Bianca harrumphed in amazement. The Gothic Victorian design looked much more magnificent in the daylight, even as gray as the weather was today. Abby stood on the middle of three balconies along the front of the house under peak arched roofs. Straw blond hair spilled over a black off the shoulder sweater which hung down to a pair of worn denim pants. She a friendly wave as they exited the car and moved up the steps.

It surprised Bianca that the large doormen were not still guarding the door as they approached. A young black woman dressed in a button up gray blouse and black skirt greeted them warmly, ushering them in with a smile.

"Ms. Abigail will be down in a moment." The woman's creole accent was thick. "Please wait in here." She urged them into a lounge to the left of the front door, looking out to the property through tall thick pane windows. The lounge was warm from what afternoon sun hit the house, but also from the soft blues and tangerine colors, giving it a feeling of being more a solarium in Florida than a Victorian house in Louisiana.

Ashley took a seat on the sofa in the middle of the room, as

Bianca strolled, looking at the random antique items displayed around the room. "Ladies, it's such a pleasure to see you again." Abby walked into the room, a glass of what Bianca assumed was scotch or rum in her hand. "Ashley, it's been far too long my sweet blackbird." The older woman greeted her with a hug and kisses on each cheek.

"Abby, you're absolutely right, it's been way too long." Ashley replied, sitting back down on the sofa.

"Bianca, I trust your visit was everything you hoped it would be?" Turning to greet her other guest, Abby also gave Bianca a hug and kisses on both cheeks.

"Beyond anything I could have hoped for. Thank you again for your hospitality." Bianca gushed, following suit and greeting their host similarly before taking a seat beside Ashley on the sofa. Abby moved to a single seat facing the sofa.

"It was absolutely my pleasure. My little bird here is one of the founding members of this party, it was the least I could do." The comment reminded Bianca of the years after college when Ashley took the exploration they'd started and branched out. She used her art skills to help a few of her new friends establish an erotic costume party before being introduced to Veronica and the darker side of Kieran's parties. Though her participation in Abby's parties over the years waxed and waned, she always kept close contact with Abby and always had an open invitation to attend.

"Your message said you believe you've had a problem with a guest and also a proposition for me." She seemed very laid back about the whole situation, which Bianca found reassuring as they were about to ask her for a strange favor.

"Do you have any guests who teach or have positions at Tulane or Loyola?" Ashley asked inquisitively, not wanting to accuse anyone before there was reason. Abby looked at the both of them, her lips pursed and her brow furled softly as if she was thinking through a list.

"Marissa…" She yelled, her head turned to send the call down the hall outside. A moment later the young black girl arrived at the door.

"Yes, Ms. Abby?"

"Can you bring me the guest list for the twenty third please?" With a subtle nod, the young woman disappeared only to return a minute later with a medium-sized leather-bound journal already open to the page she wanted.

Her eyes scanned the list, flipping a couple of pages until she found what she was looking for. "Ah, yes we do. A professor David Mathis, he's been coming for a little over a year, I believe. Why?" Her curiosity peaked now.

"We have reason to believe Dr. Mathis or someone associated with him divulged information regarding our young friend who attended Bianca at that party. This information, though vague and unsubstantiated in order to keep himself from blemishing his reputation, has put her in a place of blemish to her reputation."

"I certainly hope you are wrong about this." Abby grew visibly agitated, her soft tan skin radiating a shade of red. "The first rule of this party is that who you meet and what you see is a secret. To share with anyone outside of the guests is grounds for removal." Ashley was nodding in agreement.

"I remember Abby. I don't wish to bring any undue attention on you or your parties. Unfortunately, as long as Dr. Mathis maintains his belief that our friend was here in the compromising position he is saying she was in, she cannot live her life the way she wishes."

It was Abby's turn to nod at the statement. Bianca wasn't sure what Abby could do to convince Mathis of his error, but she was certain by the expression on her face, that this professor would recant without issue.

"I will take care of it in a way that removes any blemish on your friend." Abby reached out, touching Ashley's hand, her tone softened. "She was absolutely ravishing. Many of my guests could barely take their eyes from her." The older woman was obviously one of them by the look of her face as she gushed over Ruby.

"That outfit was all Ashley." Bianca reported proudly causing a flush of red to spread across her friend's cheeks

"I recognized her handiwork." Abby replied with loving admiration in her face, looking across the sofa at Ashley.

"Actually, our young friend is the other matter we wished to speak to you about." Bianca interrupted, not wanting this to devolve into a love fest between the two women.

"Oh? How so?" Abby asked, shifting her weight back in the seat.

"We have a friend who has a particular taste. To help with our little situation he has requested to see how far Ruby, our friend, will go to please her mistress." Bianca tried her best to spell this out without sharing too much too soon. "His original plan would have put Ruby in the hands of guests who I don't believe we could have controlled or who would have treated her well."

Her gaze turned to Ashley who placed a reassuring hand on her thigh. "We would like to propose a scenario where you select a group of your most trusted and respectful guests, maybe twenty men and women for an exclusive party. Ruby will offer herself to the group for the evening and they can enjoy her as long as they abide by a few simple rules." Bianca felt her dominatrix confidence starting to flood back into her soul. The tingle of power in her limbs and mind felt refreshing as she watched how Abby would respond to the proposal.

"What are these simple rules?" Abby asked sipping at her drink, the naughty look on her face telling Bianca she was more curious about the rules to know what they couldn't do than what they could.

"Ruby has a safe word. I will announce that word or the signal that she will use to show she wishes to use the word. In the event she uses the word, all activity stops until such a time that she is willing or able to continue. At no time will anyone do anything with Ruby where I am not there to monitor her." Bianca paused, looking to Ashley for a second as if questioning her next step, then she looked back to Abby. "I assume everyone who attends your parties are required to provide test results?"

"Every six months if they are regulars and within twenty-four hours of attending if they are last-minute invites or new members." Abby nodded.

"Very good. So last two rules then, no one will ever penetrate Ruby without protection. And I will be the final authority. If I say stop or say no to something, there will be no questioning or arguing. If there is, that will be the end of the event." Abby didn't reply, even though Bianca stopped talking.

The older woman's green-blue eyes regarded them. Bianca knew they just laid down rules for her own party. Abby, to Bianca's amusement, held a look not of disdain or anger, but with desire in her face.

"And your friend?" Abby asked almost dismissively.

"He may join, he will probably watch." Bianca could tell she was processing.

"Will she roam or will she be in a central position everyone can enjoy and watch?" To be fair, Bianca hadn't thought out this point very far. The whole thing happened so fast, there wasn't time to think that far ahead. Her mind ran back to the night in Abby's torture room, the night at Kieran's house and the evening in the playroom with the cage. Ruby seemed to enjoy being bound and unable to decide what happened to her. The thought caused her own naughty grin to form.

"She'll be presented in a central place where everyone can enjoy the show." Abby nodded slowly.

"And she's ok with this?" There was the question Bianca had expected to be the first one. Abby knew they used her torture room that night, so she knew Ruby was on some level her submissive.

Bianca only let her grin grow.

"She will do whatever I ask of her." The answer seemed to make Abby pause, realizing that while Bianca answered the question, she'd not actually answered the question.

"Abby…" Ashley interjected, realizing there would be a disconnect. "The connection Ruby and Bianca have is much more than some Dom/sub game. Ruby's commitment to Bianca reaches many levels. I have spoken to her about this, and if this is what Bianca wishes of her, she will happily oblige." The clarification seemed to set Abby's mind at ease as her face lit up with excitement.

"When would you like to do this?" She said after a long pause. The question sent a rush of emotion over Bianca's body. The emptiness they endured over the past month would fade soon as she sensed the end of their turbulent time.

"We will need to make sure we clear up the problem with Ruby and the false accusation first. They're restricting her movements until then, but I suspect it will be soon." Bianca explained.

"I will do what I can to bring about a reckoning for Mathis. That should help I hope. But please give me about two weeks to prepare for the party once you know you can." Abby said standing, implying that the meeting was over.

"Thank you so much Abby," Ashley stepped up to give the woman a hug. "You have no idea what this means to all of us." The woman hugged Ashley back, her eyes on Bianca who stood behind her.

"I think I have a good idea of the impact this will have on at least two very interesting people." Abby said with a wink before breaking the hug with Ashley and moving to Bianca. "Keep both of them safe, you have something very special here." Abby whispered as they hugged.

"I will, thank you." Bianca replied before moving away to the front door of the house. The elation and euphoria of the quest for a solution finally being over had Bianca grinning from ear to ear as they walked back to the car. Until it was done, they would keep Ruby ignorant of the details. But once it was done, there would need to be changes for the better in their situation.

Silence! Ruby hated the silence. She stared at her phone. Sitting in the student cafe across the quad from the nursing building where her clinical indoctrination for next semester was. Ruby's eyes shifted to the scene outside the window. She watched the flow of people moving here and there, living their lives and dreams, stressing about school and relationships, but living. All of the fury and bluster of the week before from Ashley about there being a chance to end this, a chance to get things back to normal, and there was silence.

When Ashley returned to her apartment that afternoon to find Ruby waiting as told, the news was less than amazing. She only said that they spoke to friends they thought could help and were waiting for an answer. Ruby knew there was the chance that they didn't want to get her hopes. There was always the fear of things not going their way, or things hadn't gone well and they were trying to figure out their next step.

The more Ruby thought about it, she just wanted someone to tell her what was going on. Just because she was by nature a submissive in Bianca's eyes, and would happily follow her mistress into the gates of hell, didn't mean she wouldn't like to be told that was the plan.

With a heavy heart and emotional exhaustion weighing her down, Ruby picked up her bag, determined to walk across the quad to her indoctrination and get on with her day, no matter how trite it seemed. Walking into the building, shaking off the cold, she pushed on, despite the numb aimless emptiness within.

Climbing up to the second floor and turning down the hall, she walked to the auditorium. At the door, a man leaned against the wall, his eyes on her as she approached. Thoughts raced trying to remember if she knew his face from somewhere, but she kept coming up blank. It was apparent to her that he knew her the second he pushed up off the wall when she neared.

"Hi Ruby, I'm Dr. Sills. Do you have a minute?" Anxiety streaked along her spine at those words. It had been the same way that Dr. Lewonzi had lured her into his office to put her on probation.

"I need to get to Indoctrination Dr. Sills." She pointed out the auditorium door he'd been standing beside with a nod.

"I know, I've already spoken to Ms. Blanchard. She's aware you'll be late." He smiled, with his hand urging her toward an empty classroom across the hall. Ruby shrugged before turning to join him as he led her to the classroom. "Take a seat." He offered with a gesture of his hand, his tone much more friendly and genuine than Dr. Lewonzi had been.

"What's this about Dr. Sills?" Her tone short as she took the offered seat. Considering how Dr. Lewonzi treated her, who could fault her for being short with him.

"I thought you should know, that Dr. Lewonzi has transferred to the campus in Chicago. He is working on a project at the medical school there." His face grew more serious, hazel eyes never leaving her face. "I am familiar with your situation, as the new head of the department I want to apologize for any misunderstanding or anxiety this whole affair might have caused you." Ruby felt her chest tighten. It suddenly became hard to breathe, as tears slowly welled in her eyes. A rush of fear, pain, excitement and relief swirled in her mind like so many colors as her mind swam in what this man was telling her.

"It would seem that the individual who reported the alleged incident amended his statement and recanted any belief that involved you in any inappropriate relationship." Ruby was barely following what he was saying, trying to fight through the rush of relief and emotion filling her like an overflowing bucket.

Sills couldn't help but recognize her struggle, which was likely why he abruptly wrung his hands together and stood.

"So, effective immediately, I have removed any restrictions or probations from your file. Please accept my apology on behalf of the school. If you need some time to collect yourself, I think Ms. Blanchard will excuse you from your orientation." She looked up through tearful eyes at the man's heartfelt, genuine smile as he put a gentle hand on her shoulder before leaving her to her thoughts.

For weeks she'd been sobbing in pain and emptiness, now she found herself with her head in her arms crying tears of joy. No matter how she tried, the bucket of emotion was overflowing now, spilling out of her onto the floor until the pressure subsided, leaving her filled.

A half hour must have passed of Ruby crying into her sleeve before the rush subsided. Sitting up and wiping wet red eyes, she blinked through the fog of tears pulling out her phone.

'Mistress, there's news. May I attend you tonight?' She messaged Bianca as quickly as she could, erasing and retyping many times before the message said what she wanted. There hadn't even been time to set the phone down before a message came back.

'I would love to have you pet. Please arrive downstairs at five and be ready to attend me like my beautiful pet.' Ruby's heart skipped. She hadn't expected Bianca to jump straight into things after everything that happened. The warm serenity began filling that void in her soul at once again serving the woman whose collar circled her neck.

Dry-eyed and free of the sniffles that plagued her for another thirty minutes, Ruby walked through campus as if the sun hung over her head, following her wherever whim carried her. The difference in mood was night and day compared to the morning, and she couldn't help but beam at how Bianca and Ashley had kept their promise.

Dr. Lewonzi leaving for Chicago seemed to her like a punishment rather than a promotion. In the grand scheme of things, what did it matter as long as the probation and restrictions vanished. Pulling out her phone as she walked, Ruby's thumbs furiously typed out a message to Ashley. 'I don't know what you did, but thank you from the bottom of my heart.' She added a heart and kiss emoji to the end of the message and hit send.

Walking through campus to her apartment, her phone buzzed.

'There's nothing we wouldn't do for you, little one. See you tonight.' The message lit up Ruby's face like a spotlight. She wasn't sure what she'd done to cause Ashley and Bianca to grow so close to her through all of this, but she was glad to have them in her life.

The remainder of her day passed in a blur of commotion, her mind barely registering. Thoughts drifted to being with Bianca, finally being free of the stigma she carried for over a month without reason. While the accusation was absolutely true, everyone to include Dr. Lewonzi knew the accusation stemmed from inaccurate accounts that never would have held up during an inquiry.

The events of the past months raced in her mind as she walked along the streets of the French Quarter to Bianca's apartment. Walking through the city to avoid being seen going to Ashley's became a habit, and now she walked because she wanted to. The crisp cool evening air had the spirit of the coming holidays. Decorations and lights were out in small bits here and there, adding to the already festive atmosphere of the French Quarter.

Walking up to the door, Ruby felt that anxious nervousness she'd felt the first time well up along her back, up to her neck. This was a much different anxiety, knowing what to expect it wasn't fear but anticipation. Pressing the app on her phone and keying in the code, the familiar circle of green around the knob and resounding metal click of the door opening made her heart skip. Butterflies circled in her belly as she stepped into the foyer. She was uncertain where Bianca was, so she decided to present herself right off the bat.

Quickly stripping the multiple layers, her rosy flush skin hummed with nervous energy. Goosebumps spread across it as she pulled her panties down and folded them on top of the pile of clothes. Ruby ambled down the hall, listening for voices of any hint there was anyone else. She'd checked her watch before she opened the door, a few minutes before five, with more than enough time to strip.

The playroom was quiet, candles arrayed around the room giving the usually soft lit room a darker, almost erotic feel. On the large square bed in the middle of the floor, a ball gag, the red ball and black strap she'd grown very familiar with, lay beside a thin black remote and note on a folded card. *Put this on, tightly, and put yourself on the sybian level 2. No coming. I will check on you when I'm ready.*

Her eyes went to the black half circle sitting in the middle of the room with what looked like two rubber dildos protruding vertically out of it. One of the rubber nubs was thick and about four inches long, the other was thinner and curved but much longer. Doing as directed, Ruby picked up the gag and placed it between her teeth, tightening the strap around her head until the leather bit into her lips. Forcing herself to breathe through her nose, she picked up the remote and walked to the sybian. Grabbing a small bottle of lube nearby, Ruby spread the slick liquid over each dildo then across her holes.

Guiding the longer thinner one to her tight puckered hole, muscles protested and clenched as the rubbery head pushed into the depths. *How long?* She wondered, the further it went, the more her body protested until more rubber pressed against neglected sensitive folds.
Pushing in like an intruder unconcerned with protest or argument, the thick rubber pierced her heated canal, filling her until the sensation of small rubber nubs against her pearl declared the end of her journey.

For over a month Ruby felt the void, the emptiness deep in her heart and soul at the missing aspects of her life torn away for no reason. As she settled against the machine and pressed the button to activate it, any complaints of filling that void washed away with the sudden power of desire overwhelming her. Eyes closed, a whimper of ecstasy escaped her throat with muffled intensity as Ruby succumbed to the pleasure.

"There's my good pet." Ruby's eyes shot open at the words. She didn't know how long she waited since putting herself in place. Based on the volume of saliva spilled over her chin and down across her neck and breasts, the realization that she had zoned out struck a very surprising chord.
For a moment she forgot about the intruders or the gag in her mouth when she saw Bianca standing over her, a very form fitting latex corset, leggings and gloves that looked almost painted to her body. The corset stopped at the rise of her perfect mounds, holding them in.

Behind her Mistress stood Ashley, dressed in a similar latex body suit except for the fact that it covered her body from shoulders to feet. Beside her stood another woman, shorter but slender with long mixed Asian features and raven black hair flowing down one naked shoulder. She dressed in a red leather corset, latex leggings and gloves. She held what looked like a very thick bundle of rope.

"Are you enjoying yourself pet?" Bianca asked, stepping up and leaning in close, licking the slobber from Ruby's chin.

She kneeled down before her pet, fingers spreading the slobber on her pert breasts before harshly pinching Ruby's swollen, aching nipples. It all happened faster than Ruby could respond, only being able to let out a high-pitched but muffled yelp from behind the gag.

Her body jumping suddenly reminded her of the full penetration. "Answer me pet, are you enjoying yourself?" Bianca hissed, her finger twisting the same nipple again. Ruby nodded as colors swirled in her mind. She thought the harder her mistress tweaked her nipple, the hotter her need became.

"Good. You didn't come, did you?" Bianca asked. Ruby immediately shook her head, knowing all it would take was a finger slipping into the cleft between her legs to prove her wrong. "Very good." Bianca gave Ruby a naughty look before taking the remote and turning it off.

"I need you warmed up for tonight." She added, taking her pet by the arm and helping her up onto uncertain legs. "Get on your knees and prostrate yourself" Bianca ordered, leading her pet to the bed. Ruby did as ordered, kneeling on the bed before leaning forward, her face on the mattress and her arms across her back.

"She's very good." Came a voice Ruby didn't recognize, which she assumed was the new woman.

"This one is very special. And it's been a very painful period since the last time she could service her mistress, so there is a lot of eagerness there." Ashley's voice was unmissable as her praise filled Ruby with pride.

Bianca untied the gag, pulling it from her mouth.

"Ok, pet, this is Ms. Raven. She is here to help me plan something with you, but in order to do that, she will bind you up in a rope. You will not speak unless asked a direct question, and you will do whatever she tells you. Do you understand?" Bianca walked up to Ruby with a blind, pushing it down over her eyes and tying the silk strap around the back of her head, checking to make sure there was no light coming in.

"Yes, Mistress." Ruby replied confidently. She'd seen images of rope bondage a few months ago when she was trying to figure out what game Bianca was playing. It always looked so beautiful and symmetric. She remembered wondering if being bound up like that hurt. It looked like answers to those questions would come soon.

"This will be uncomfortable for a time but it will not hurt." The voice of Ms. Raven came soft and silky, almost reassuring and sultry as Ruby felt her move up on the bed.

Time became a blur in the darkness of the blind as the slowly building rope design circling her body neared completion. Rope encircled her legs and chest with her arms bound behind her back the same way that Bianca bound them with Todd.

Binds bit into her skin whenever Ms. Raven made her move to tie a new section. Over her shoulder and down the middle of her torso, between her legs, around her legs, around her chest even binding her breasts rope trailed. The only part of her body not bound was her head and Ruby suspected there was a reason for leaving that free.

Suddenly all activity ceased, then abruptly she felt tension on the rope. Pulling at every fiber, something lifted her up. The fabric of the bed fell away, leaving only the sense of hanging as the strain of the rope held her. Curiously she found the erotic aura of the ropes bite and tension touched her deep down in her gut.

Before there was a chance to become accustomed to the sense of floating bound up like this, something thick and warm pushed into her moist sheath and dark entrance, burrowing deep into her.

At the same time, she felt hands hooking soft cold metal at the edges of her lips and over her teeth before tightening a strap against her head. A memory from the night at Kieran's house reminded her of the gag they used. Now she couldn't close it if she wanted to. Next, cool rubber pushed between her teeth set against her tongue. The sensation from her tongue spoke to a dildo based on the shape of the head and the ridges and bumps molded into the rubber.

"Ok, pet. We're going to leave you like this for a while and let you enjoy Ms. Raven's bindings. If you feel you absolutely cannot keep from coming, use your signal and we will come check on you." Her mistress's voice was calm and adoring, which in its own way spread calm through her own body as the pumping began. First the dildo intruding from behind thrust deep together, then her mouth. All three intruders began slowly alternated the pumping.

The level of degradation at being a piece of meat hanging on a hook used as three warm holes, initially filled Ruby's thoughts. At least until the pleasure of the motion against her body reminded her of who she really was. From the first day when she'd offered herself to those two men, Bianca knew the button to push with her, what she was and what she was capable of. No matter how humiliating some would see this, Ruby knew what it was. Humiliation was something to tear at one's self-esteem, Ruby knew surrendering to Bianca only fed her self-esteem.

Ruby lost track of how long the slow methodical pumping continued, but she knew that her body was on the verge. Unfortunately, aside from admitting defeat and asking for help, there was little she could do anymore to stop it. Her cheek and thighs were dripping wet with saliva and her arousal. She could feel how wet she was as the dildos moved.

"I can't believe she's still at it." The sultry voice of Raven broke the moaning, panting and electronic pumping silence in the room.

"She's going to explode." Ashley's voice joined, a finger running across her inner thigh.

"You've pleased me very much pet. Would you like to come for me?" Bianca's voice whispered with the sweetness of honey in her ear as Ruby tried to nod around the intruder pushing in and out of her throat. "You need to do one more thing for me and I'll let you come."

Hands touching her body, pulled at the ropes as her position slowly shifted from being on her side to hanging with her back to the floor. Her head hanging. The dildo in her mouth slipped out while the pumping continued. Just as she wondered what the one more thing was, she felt the warmth of skin against her cheeks and smelled the wet, heated scent of arousal over on her nose.

"Now pet, I know you are close to coming. Ms. Raven is hot from watching you please your Mistress. You must get Ms. Raven off before you come. But if you come first, Miss. Ash will punish you." Suddenly the straps on her head slipped off, allowing the hooks keeping her mouth open to fall free.

Ruby's mouth closed around the offered tender flesh just as she felt the dildo at the other end pick up its pace. Anxiety spread through her mind as she realized what Bianca meant. They were pushing her to the point she can't fight it, and she had to be faster and better.

Her tongue lapped feverishly at Raven's slick folds. Her mouth sucking and nibbling hungrily at the small lips. Her body shuddered at the intensity of the building orgasm. Ruby could hear Raven's soft panting and whimpers growing more erratic as her tongue lapped against Raven's slippery softness. The fear of her body growing too close too fast filled her.

Ruby's tongue slipped up into Raven's soft petals, penetrating her. Immediately small velvety fingers clenched against the side of her head, pinning Ruby, pulling her tongue up deeper. She shuddered as the final threshold of passion tore through her body.

Unfortunately, at the same time Ruby's convulsed against the attention. The speed and intensity of the pumping grew steadily faster as Raven's orgasm pushed them both over the edge. They both exploded at the same time.

Again and again the thick rubber filled her as muscles clenched and pulled at both. Ruby was sure she felt liquid spray against her perpendicular legs tied to her hips. Raven finally released her head, Ruby gasped deeply for air as her own body struggled to recover. Clenching spasms still rocked her body, helplessly suspended in the air, unable to grab onto anything.

The intruders slid out of her with a wet, sloppy release. Silence fell over the room, the only sound was slow panting of Raven and Ruby. The sensation of velvety leather sliding along her body from crotch and up along her torso grabbed Ruby's attention, still unable to see anything. "Tell me something little one." Ashley questioned, her voice sultry but eager. "You came at the same time as Ms. Raven. Do you feel that I shouldn't punish you?" Ruby fought to catch her breath, needing to sound confident in her answer.

"Mistress told me to get her off before I came. We came at the same time. I failed the challenge Mistress laid out for me, so yes I should be punished." Ruby was confident in her conviction. If there was one thing she'd learned in their time together, it all came down to pleasing Bianca. Arguing a different outcome would only displease them both and would likely result in a much harsher punishment.

"I agree completely. Thank you for accepting your failure little one. Please keep count for me." Ashley announced out loud as if she had stepped away. That instant, the familiar sting of leather striking her body caused Ruby to jump and yelp. The thing she'd failed to take into account with her punishment was the increased sensitivity of her skin as the ropes slowed circulation and built up blood in certain areas.

The strike hit her bound breasts. The sensation was like an electric shock tearing through her body. "One Ms. Ash." Ruby counted through gritted teeth, realizing the strikes would be ten times more powerful than normal. Again and again, each strike hit a different part of her body. Her legs, her breasts, her sensitive flesh, her ass and each time she counted gritting her teeth and trying to surrender her body to the assault.

"Fif… fifteen." Ruby cried, tears streaming down her cheeks as the last strike bit into her swollen and over worked lips and ass. Tensing for another strike, the touch of a soft hand against her now painfully swollen and abused pussy replaced the expected whipping.

"Very good pet. You were very strong." Still hanging with her back to the floor and her head hanging below her shoulders, a soft loving kiss pressed to her open mouth as Bianca's hot silken tongue slipped in and danced with her own tongue.

The kiss was erotic, hungry, full of lust, but Ruby didn't care. She wanted Bianca to use her in whatever way she wanted, slave, slut, lover. The point had long passed when Ruby distinguished between her personality, and her needs compared to Bianca.

"Ms. Raven will untie you. When she finishes, please collect your clothes and join Miss. Ash and I in the apartment. I wouldn't recommend getting dressed." Bianca murmured after breaking the kiss.

"Yes, mistress." She exclaimed with contentment in her voice as she hung used and bound without worry or complaint about her life. Things were right side up again and after seeing how the two of them fought to get her back, Ruby knew nothing in the world would tear them apart again.

Evolution

The scent of garlic and spice filled the kitchen. The faint sound of sizzling created a comfortable white noise in the background as Bianca and Ashley laughed together. Slipping a green olive between her teeth, Bianca watched her friend cook. There were many things that Ashley was deft at and finding her way around a kitchen was marvelously one of those. Never having picked up cooking as a skill, Bianca relied heavily on her friend's skill more than she wanted to admit.

Tonight was no exception. Bianca would have more likely ordered from one of the many gourmet restaurants in town for a dish ready to eat. Tonight demanded a more personal touch. "I can't believe she lasted that long." Bianca beamed, admiring her young lover's stamina. "She made a mess though."

The words came out just as the elevator door opened. Turning to look, a toothy grin spread across her face before catching Ashley's eyes and nodding toward the lift. They both walked out of the kitchen to look, fascinated to see Ruby kneeling in the elevator, her clothes folded neatly in front of her knees, waiting patiently.

"Oh, my gawd. She's so adorable." Ashley whispered, looking back at Bianca. "Little one, you may enter the apartment." The direction registered immediately as Ruby picked up her pile of clothes in one hand while slowly crawling into the apartment on two knees and one hand. Bianca moved to the submissive girl with tender grace.

"Pet, you've pleased me in many ways tonight." Bianca said kneeling and lifting Ruby's head up by a finger under her chin. "For the rest of the night you are an equal among us. Please go clean up and join us when you are finished. Take your time and let the hot water relieve the abuse you've taken." Bianca leaned in and gently sucked on her lovers lower lip before standing and helping Ruby up by her hand. "Don't worry about getting dressed."

"I'm so glad to be home." Ruby whispered before she turned to the master shower. Bianca watched her walk away, her eyes lingering on the curves of her body. The red lines of the ropes and flush of her arousal were still prominent on her usually pale silken skin.

"I am too my dear." She whispered to herself as Ruby disappeared into the bath. Both Bianca and Ashley had stripped out of their latex outfits, wearing nothing but cotton panties and sports bras.

260

There didn't seem a reason to get dressed again after abusing Ruby since they would most likely end up naked again.

"Is Raven not joining us?" Ashley asked from the kitchen, cutting an assortment of vegetables she was using to cook.

"No, she needed to meet her boyfriend." Bianca picked up a glass of rose wine from the counter and enjoyed a sip of the cool fruity liquid on her tongue.

"She did a great job. I think they're going to love her." Ashley was noticeably giddy about the whole thing, a state Bianca had not seen in a long time. The two of them were considerably closer because of the events of the past month with Ruby spending so much time at the apartment.

"Is her outfit still in one piece?" Her mind was racing on how to present Ruby to the audience Abby was assembling. Bianca wanted something that would grab their lust long before they ever presented her.

"Yeah, I had both of the dresses dry cleaned that week." Ashley nibbled on a piece of cheese, her eyes staring as if contemplating something. "She needs to do it!"

"Do what?" Bianca questioned, uncertain where her friend's mind was.

"Even though we already agreed, she needs to walk out into the crowd of guests all assembled and offer herself to them for the night." The simple suggestion kindled heat in Bianca's belly. Her mind leapt back to the night with the two men. The level of fear and uncertainty in Ruby's eyes as she understood what she was being asked to do. How far she had come since that scared girl, Bianca thought to herself as she considered it.

"I'll do it." The statement stopped Bianca's response cold. She turned surprised to see their radiant student leaning against the wall between the bedroom and kitchen. Wrapped from chest to knees in a large white wool towel, her strawberry blond hair hanging in a tangled mess along her shoulders. The skin on her shoulders and arms returned to their alluring pale tone, but she glowed simply from being where she was, and Bianca could see it.

"Come here, baby." Bianca said holding out her arms, pulling Ruby into them to hold her firmly. "I missed you so much. No one will ever take you away from us again." She could feel the tears in her eyes as she tenderly kissed that wet hair.

Ashley stepped out of the kitchen and joined them, surrounding Ruby in a hug that spread to Bianca.

"You're home now, little one. I think things will be much different now." Ashley also kissed Ruby on the head before Bianca pulled back.

"Did you say, I'll do it?" Ruby's agreement finally connecting with her thoughts. "You don't even know what we're asking of you." The tranquil contentment in her cool blue eyes told Bianca everything she needed to know.

"It doesn't matter. Whatever you want me to do was part of the price for bringing us back together. I don't know what you had to promise or favors you burned to make this happen, but I want to do it. For you, and for Ash because it's what you want." Ruby paused, turning to reciprocate the hug Ashley tried to give. She held on tight, and Bianca could see the love in that thoughtful face. "Besides, you both swore to do anything to end this, why should my commitment be any less?"

Bianca regarded Ruby for a long few moments as she and her best friend held each other close. "I can't help but marvel at the woman you've become Ruby. That uncertain girl who didn't want to be in my class." She cocked her head to the side with a smile on her face. "Now look at you."

"Can I get some of that?" Her abused lover nodded toward the glass of wine as she gingerly sat at one of the bar stools. Ashley walked back into the kitchen, grabbing a glass and the bottle from the refrigerator before handing both to Ruby. Pouring a generous helping, both women glanced at each other with knowing looks.

"How did you blossom so fast little one?" Ashley wondered, checking on the dishes around the stove.

"I had a good teacher." Ruby teased, the color coming back into her face as she sipped at the wine. "So would someone like to explain to me what happened?"

Ashley shook her head. "We'll talk at dinner. You enjoy your wine. It'll be ready in a minute." Bianca took her friends cue to pull plates and silverware out of their respective places around the kitchen. Setting the plates where Ashley could put food on them, she walked around the table setting down silverware and napkins.

Her eyes watched Ruby as she sipped at her wine. She was watching the two of them move around the kitchen with fluid familiarity.

The look on her face was contemplative but peaceful. It made Bianca wonder.

There was a fondness in her eyes as Ruby looked to Ashley. Bianca appreciated the fact that the two of them grew to much more than simple friends during this ordeal. Of all the people in the world she'd want Ruby to latch onto, Ashley topped that list. At least she knew Ashley would always be there for them.

Ashley broke her deep contemplative thoughts, handing over a plate of penne pasta in a red sauce with a torn piece of warm Italian bread on the edge of the plate. Bianca jumped slightly before accepting the plate. Ashley carried a plate of food and a large bowl of salad over to the table. Bianca refilled each glass of wine while they sat.

"To family and doing whatever is necessary to keep the family safe." Bianca raised her glass. From her point of view, after everything they had been through, this was the closest any of them had to family.

"To family and the bonds that grow from it." Ashley added taking a sip of her wine.

"To family." Ruby whispered. Bianca regarded her response as a sign of something on her mind.

"What's wrong Ruby?" Bianca reached over and put her hand on Ruby's hand, giving it a light affectionate squeeze.

"Nothing… sorry. I'm just still getting used to the idea that this is more than me being your pet." Ruby took a sip of her wine, likely as a chance to collect her thoughts. "When this whole thing happened, we just declared our feelings for each other and it was all fresh. Then things fell apart. While there were a few of situations where I was an equal, I was only ever really your lover, girlfriend, whatever for a couple of days."

Bianca nodded at the admission. She was right. While life mostly continued for the two of them, life that she begged to understand came to a screeching halt for Ruby. Bianca looked to Ashley who was purposefully staying quiet in this discussion, letting her take the lead in what was really her relationship.

"You're right baby. We will take it slow and get back to where we would have been before this all started. But for now, know that you are with me because I want you as a friend and a lover before I want you as a pet to dominate." Bianca paused, trying to gauge Ruby's response before her eyes looked to Ashley again, then back. "What do you want Ruby?"

The silence that hung over the table after that question could have shattered the solar system. It dawned on Bianca that regardless of the things they'd spoke of regarding her submission and devotion, they'd never talked about what she wanted as a friend and lover.

"I want to be yours for as long as you want me. I want the three of us to become the best of friends. I want to feeel that mystical connection that the two of you have that allows you to move around each other in a kitchen, feeling each other's thoughts and emotions without speaking."

The assertion that she and Ashley had such a powerful connection caught Bianca by surprise. She'd never thought of it that way, but from the eyes of an outside observer, she was right.

"Ruby baby," Ashley reached over and took her other hand. "You're part of our family now. You've woven yourself into both of our hearts and souls too tightly, we never want that piece of us taken away again." Bianca nodded at her friend's description of the situation. Ashley had always been much better at those aspects of interpersonal skills.

"That's why we have a few changes to the life you've known for the past few months if you're interested." Bianca interjected, causing Ruby's attention to shift with surprise in her eyes. "You can totally decide how much or how little of this you want to accept, you are under no obligation to accept any of this." Ruby could see the earnest look on her face causing her to nod softly as if telling her she understood and should proceed.

"Starting next week…" Bianca continued, "… You'll finish out the year as my intern. After the New Year starts, my division is taking on a new account with a focus on the medical field. You'll come on as a paid intern understanding that your class schedule will come first." Ruby's cycs blinked, astonishment fell over her face as she turned to look from one woman to the other.

"You apparently impressed someone important." Ashley added with a smirk. In reality Ruby's presentation to Martin regarding the Peterson account came out so confidently presented and defended, he presented the offer and the company jumped on it. Bianca nodded softly in agreement.

"Ash mentioned you said the dynamic with your roommate wasn't what it once was and you weren't sure the two of you would keep the apartment though the lease." Ruby nodded, finishing her mouthful of food.

"She's always with her boyfriend, our time off never crosses and with work and everything going on neither of us has really had time. We were never great friends, more roommates of convenience."

"Well, Ash wants to let you continue to use her apartment to live until we can come up with a more permanent solution. We want you close, but I never planned my apartment with guests or roommates in mind unless you want to sleep in your cage down stairs." The suggestion made Ruby smile with a mouthful of food. Bianca was sure the possibility of spending the night sleeping bound up in the cage crossed Ruby's mind on more than one occasion. That would never serve as a way to live life.

"I don't know Bee, that smile seemed to be an affirmation of approval."

"Seriously? Could we at least put it at the foot of the bed?"

"Don't tempt me pet... Ashley at least suggested a large dog pillow."

Bianca gave her an impish look before the whole table broke out into flowing laughter. "Of course being close to school and your friends and classmates is important," Bianca added after the laughter calmed down.

Watching Ruby pick absently at her plate now, Bianca realized her focus had shifted to something more serious as she stared at the fork moving around her half empty plate. Looking at her friend then back to Ruby, Ashley shrugged.

"What's wrong, baby?"

"So what happened?"

Bianca understood when she heard the two of them talking that they weren't going to be able to keep things from her. The more she thought about it, she realized there wasn't any need to keep Ruby in the dark or questioning. The whole time this rollercoaster ride kept Ruby in the dark, which only caused stress.

Whenever Bianca spelled things out, set the boundaries for things, Ruby accepted without question. It occurred to her that understanding and being able to decide for herself was what made things work with Ruby.

"If you must know." Bianca saw Ashley looking at her with a raised brow, her head half-cocked to the side. Bianca knew they had agreed not to go into detail, but Ruby needed to hear it. "We were running out of options. No one was invested enough in the situation to burn that pricey of a favor, at least until Kieran Mulroney, anyway."

Ruby's eyes turned up intently, listening to the story now. "Thankfully Kieran has a lot of connections in the medical field and the college. I don't know what he did, or who he talked to, all I know is that he convinced the school to move Lewonzi and replace him with someone sympathetic to us."

"Why was Mr. Mulroney so much more invested than everyone else?" Ruby's curiosity filled her face, not understanding her benefactor.

"You apparently impressed Kieran by how you handled yourself at his party."

Memory flashed across those cool blue eyes as a soft scowl creased her brow. "It wasn't like I could get up and leave. They had me strapped to a bench."

Bianca laughed at the visual. "Not that baby, but your poise and determination. You walked into that room without the first clue what would happen to you, without being able to see who or what was happening to you. You accepted every bit of abuse they gave you without complaint. That's what impressed Kieran." Bianca could see the change in Ruby's face at the assessment, as if she was uncertain how those traits impressed anyone. Bianca leaned closer and took Ruby's hand between both of hers.

"Ruby, do you understand why that impresses a man like Kieran?" Ruby shook her head.

"It's the same reason you earned a paid internship at the company. I had nothing to do with that. You impressed Martin with how well you presented our case. Your poise and confidence filled the room and you didn't back down when he threw a hard question at you. Some junior associates who've been with the company for years don't have that."

"But you had something to do with that." Ruby countered, a gentle twinkle of realization in her eyes.

"I made no recommendations to Martin about your position. He offered that to me the afternoon you presented to him. He'd just ended his call with the Peterson representatives and he was so excited they'd accepted our offer, he told me to hire you as a paid intern once the fourth quarter was over." Bianca could see Ruby growing anxious as if she needed to clarify her thought.

Her eyes lit up now. "No, I mean you helped me become poised and confident and determined."

"How? What did I ever do besides beat you and abuse you and make you surrender yourself to others for my pleasure?" Bianca knew the answer to her question, but she wondered if Ruby realized it. The sparkle in her eyes, the furled brow of uncertainty, threatened to push away understanding she knew was there.

"I… I don't know." Ruby looked like someone who had the answer on the tip of her tongue but couldn't articulate the words. Ashley clucked softly, prompting Bianca to push harder.

"When I first met you, all I saw was a timid, uncertain young girl who let the flow of the world carry her along. What was the first condition I ever set with you, the one that defined everything that we did together?" Bianca's push turned into a pull to force Ruby to understand.

"It was my choice. Walk away or attend, agree or don't, you made me choose my path."

"How do you think that turned a timid, uncertain girl into the blooming confident young woman I've fallen in love with?" The words came out soft but strong, meant to lift. A thin smile formed across Ruby's lips before they curled up in a deep grin at the edges.

Her eyes turned back to her teacher.

"You made me decide who I wanted to be and what I wanted. Making my own choices, no matter how hard, drove me to want more." Both women slowly started nodding at the realization.

"So now do you understand Kieran's interest in you?" Ashley questioned, hoping to ride her realization back to the original question.

Ruby tried hard for a minute, then shook her head with more uncertainty.

"Kieran Mulroney, David Keen, Me, Ashley, Todd, the circles we walk in, they all respect strength and confidence. Kieran saw that in the proud girl who walked into the middle of his dungeon and basically said 'do your worst'

"So I assume Mr. Mulroney was the one with the request?" Ruby asked after a long silence.

"He was." Bianca admitted honestly.

"What did he request of me?" Ruby's look hadn't changed, her confidence was there, but there was a need to understand behind her eyes.

"Actually, I denied his request knowing it would likely hurt one of us. But we provided him with an alternative he accepted." Bianca tried to sidestep answering the question, but she could see Ruby not having it.

"What did he request?" She asked again, more sharply.

"He wanted you to offer yourself to his guests in the dungeon." Bianca replied coldly, letting the weight of his request carry to her young student. Ruby's eyes looked to Ashley, whose face slackened into a mask of almost fear at what Ruby might say. "I told him no because Ashley and I have seen the levels of depravity that go on in his dungeon, and our love for you wouldn't let us take you down that path."

"Ruby, Bianca knows you would have done anything she asked, no matter what. And if she said yes, you eventually would have followed her in a hell neither of us want to know again." Understanding washed over Ruby as her whole body relaxed slightly.

"And what was the alternative?" She finally asked, realizing that Kieran's influence still carried some weight in the price they'd paid.

"Ms. Abby agreed to let you offer yourself, under my very strict rules, to a select group of her guests for one night." They could have cut the silence at the table with a knife as Ruby seemed to work through the idea. A soft flush tinted her skin from the exposed shoulders to her face and Bianca couldn't tell if she was angry, scared or aroused at the idea.

"That's what tonight was about? The ropes, the multiple dildos?" The question broke a fog of silence over the table.

An almost undetectable motion caught Bianca's eyes as she realized the towel Ruby wore was moving gently. A naughty grin crossed her teacher's face, then realized Ashley saw it too.

Without warning Ashley reached over and pulled the tucked towel free, letting it fall to the sides of the chair, exposing their young pet's naked body. As they suspected, her hand was between her spread legs tenderly rubbing her exposed pearl.

"You are a naughty little slut aren't you pet?" Bianca teased seeing Ruby's smile grow at being caught. "So the idea of being served up like a piece of meat to be sampled and enjoyed by a room full of complete strangers turns you on?" She asked, sliding from her chair to kneel beside her horny lover. Her own hand pushed Ruby's out of the way, causing those cool blue eyes to close as her student's head rolled back with an exasperated sigh.

"Does that please you?" Ruby moaned, her head lifted to look deep into her teacher's deep green eyes. Bianca slid up, leaning in until her teeth clamped down gingerly on Ruby's nubile full lips, her lips closing around her teeth to suck against the biting pain.

"Would it be bad to say as much as I enjoy the idea of your body being used to pleasure other people, I don't want to share you?" Bianca's sultry question slid across Ruby's skin while her fingers rubbed at moist folds.

"I only want you my love, but if watching others take pleasure from enjoying what you own, then share me until you tire of it."

Bianca blinked, realizing Ruby used a term of endearment with her. She wasn't sure if it had been the dom/sub dynamic they'd created that kept her from feeling like an equal in the relationship, but the fact gave Bianca hope for things.

She'd had two weeks to prepare herself for tonight. The days passed like a blur between the holidays, her internship, and spending time with Ashley and Bianca. The time working in Bianca's office gave Ruby a chance to really come to understand the woman she was committing so much of her life to.

The dynamic had changed, with Ruby being treated more like a colleague and friend than the intern she was trying to train. It wouldn't have been fair to say Bianca didn't play games with her, or impose her domineering mode at times. However, the dynamic had become much more playful.

Outside of work and the office, things grew warmer between the three of them. Ruby moved a portion of her belongings to Ashley's apartment and spent the weekends using that as her 'home' instead of running across town. She could study or decompress when Bianca was with a client who hadn't bought into having her join. Ruby didn't mind, her mistress took enough time keeping her in check.

The temptation they talked about at dinner about moving the cage to the foot of the bed, turned out to be more alluring than Ruby imagined. She'd only been teasing, but att least one night a week, when Bianca was with a client or wanted to sleep in the bed alone, she locked Ruby up. She'd spend the night with dildos filling her holes and a blindfold over her eyes for the night. Strangely, Ruby was finding some serenity in those nights at least until she woke up. Then her mistress freed her and demanded Ruby service her, as numb hands and legs refused to move fast enough.

"Ruby, don't move." Ashley's hiss brought her back to reality.

"Sorry." She realized her zoning off caused her body to float as Ashley's deft fingers painted a new mask onto her face. The invitations sent out to Abby's guests requested soft or painted masks to accommodate any activity that they might get in the way. Ashley stood firm on Ruby wearing her mask, swearing it made the outfit what it was.

"It's ok. Just stay still. After I'm done with your face you're going to lie down on the massage table so I can make a few enhancements." The suggestion of enhancements drew a curious glance, which made Ashley smile. "Trust me, you'll love it."

As expected, when Ashley finished the face mask, Ruby moved to the long white massage table. Lying on her back, the shock of cool, silky soft paint sliding over her breasts made Ruby jump. She giggled a bit at Ashley's groan, feeling her other hand wipe along the soft roll of her mound.

"Oh Wow!" Bianca's voice broke the silence that fell over the room as Ashley worked. Ruby's eyes flickered around looking where she was until her lover came up to the side of the table standing across from Ashley. "Ash, my god! You just can't stop outdoing yourself, can you?" Her friend beamed at the admiration of her work.

"She's going to stun everyone into just wanting her to stand and be statuesque." Ashley teased as her brush slipped down her belly to the heated space between her hips.

"Remember, the ropes are going to smear that." Bianca was regarding Ruby's body with heated lust in her eyes, which made her want to jump up and look even more.

"This is a new paint, it's got a silicone base, the stuff they use for drawing clothes on naked women. It can take some punishment." Ashley pulled the brush away to review her work. "Besides, by the time we get to the ropes, no one will care how the paint looks." Bianca laughed softly before leaning down and giving Ruby a soft kiss on the lips, her tongue slipping between them quickly.

"How are you, baby?" Ruby loved that look in her eyes. She felt a swell of desire fill her chest as her pulse raced slightly.

"Couldn't be happier." Simple contentment carried her like lying on a cloud, her body floated with a radiant humming sensation of heat or electricity. Bianca smiled as a hand reached in to brush her lover's cheek.

"The car will be here in an hour." Bianca uttered, turning to walk out of the room, leaving the other two women alone to work.

The painting took another forty minutes so Ashley could make sure her masterpiece was perfect. As before, neither of them would let her see the final product until they dressed her fully, swearing it would ruin the image. To Ruby's delight this time Ashley spent a few minutes taking pictures with what sounded like a very expensive camera before they dressed her.

"Open your eyes little one." Ashley urged. Ruby opened her eyes, her mouth gaping open in astonishment. Dressed again in the same white embroidered dress, diamond earrings climbing up the lobe of her ear and a diamond icicle necklace that stopped above her breastbone. She felt more elegant, more bridal than sexual. The paint on her body was faint through the sheer cloth. Detailed with hues of blue, white and gray, it made her skin seem almost icy. Frosty patterns in varied shades of gray, blue and white emphasized her breasts and the apex between her legs under the white embroidered pattern of the dress.

The ornate white silver mask was the same one, but the painted mask underneath was more articulated. Ashley improved her visual using the same frost design and blue, gray and white hues on her face and neck.

The muted shades of the paint on her skin gave her both a frosty aura, but somehow the white of the dress made her glow. Ruby turned slowly in the mirror. Her eyes watched every rotation. She marveled at the way her movement exposed the sexual nature of the outfit but showed nothing directly.

"Oh Ash, I'm speechless." Ruby truly was at a loss for words. The look of appreciation in her eyes all the answer she needed. Her eyes caught Bianca enter the room. Dressed as she had the last time they went to Abby's party, but now there were burgundy accents in her hair, her mask, and sewn into the dress and on her fingernails. The reddish hues brought out more of Bianca's own red in her skin and hair.
Though dressed much as she had been before, this time the feeling was different as Ruby saw her lover in a much different light than she had the last time as her companion. "Just masterful Ash." Bianca murmured with delight as the shutter of a camera clicked behind Ruby, turning her attention.

She turned as Ashley snapped pictures, wanting to capture her art now that she'd perfected the look. "You're absolutely right, they aren't going to want to touch her for fear of ruining this." Bianca stepped up to Ruby, her fingers cautiously sliding down along Ruby's body, brushing her breasts and belly with long burgundy fingernails. "Are we ready?" Bianca inquired, looking at the clock above the vanity.

"Just a second." Ashley said grabbing a small bottle from the vanity and turning to Ruby. Carefully she spread a very subtle bluish gray gloss over her full lips, completing the frosty look. "Now she's perfect. I just wish I had thought to kiss her before doing that."
Everyone in the room laughed warmly as Bianca pulled the capes from the clothes rack. Slipping the white one around Ruby's shoulders before slipping her own cape on, Bianca completed the costumes. "I need ten minutes." Ashley turned back to the clothes rack as she quickly stripped off her tank top and sweatpants. Bianca guided Ruby out into the hallway.

Standing so she could see her lover's whole body. Ruby felt warmed by those eyes as they drank her in.

"Do you have any doubts pet?" Both of them knew the answer to the question, but Ruby knew Bianca wouldn't feel right with the situation until it was in the open.

"None." She replied confidently and proudly. "Thank you for helping me discover who I am. I realized I never really thanked you for that." Bianca's head cocked slightly to the side with a loving look on her face.

"You never need to thank me for anything Ruby, everything you've done, everything you've become was because you believed in yourself. I just provided the vehicle for you to find it."

"Well, thank you anyway." She wasn't going to let Bianca get out that easily. Ruby knew it was hard for her teacher to accept the softness Ruby added being in her life. She knew she had to keep pushing until it became natural.

"I will be there the whole time, keeping a watchful eye on you, as will Ashley. They all know the rules and will abide by them, or Abby will ask them to leave. No harm will come to you as long as you trust that I'm there for you." The realization that those were the same ideas she'd been told the first time here in the basement on the verge of being taken by two strangers seemed to bring her journey full circle. It all started here and now here she was a blossoming mature woman about to embark on a whole new adventure.

"I know, Mistress. I never doubted." The look on Ruby's face must have sparked a memory in Bianca too, as her face changed to one of recognition and joy.

Just as a comfortable unspoken understanding developed between them, a buzzer rang alerting them there was someone at the door.

"Ash, it's time." Bianca called into the dressing room just as Ash stepped out in a flowing black skirt that hung to her heels in the back but barely covered her thighs in the front. Above the skirt was a Victorian style corset with burgundy accents at her breasts and running down to her hips. She had lacy elbow-length gloves on her arms and black buckled knee-high boots on her feet. Her hair was straight, flowing around her shoulders, and she wore a solid black mask with ornately painted burgundy work on the front. Her lips also were a matching color of burgundy.

"Beautiful as always baby." Bianca admired, as Ruby found it hard to take her eyes off of the way she looked. Ashley grinned as they opened the door to a slim older man in a tuxedo and round cap standing by the door.

"This way Ladies, please." He offered an outstretched hand to the limousine that waited on the street. Much longer than anything Ruby experienced before, she couldn't help but smile thinking she was arriving to a party where she was the guest of honor in a limousine fit for the president.

Sliding into the cabin of the limousine, seeing Kieran Mulroney and Raven sitting together in the seats facing backward surprised Ruby. Kieran wore an outfit very similar to the one Todd wore the last time she saw him, except for a cane and a black top hat. Raven was almost unrecognizable. She had bluish white hair, closely matching Ruby's skin, pinned up in a very wild hairdo with two long locks of thick hair hanging down on either side of her face. Her corset was a pearl white with a lacey frilly skirt that looked very much like it matched Ashley's, short in the front and long in the back. The bust on Raven's corset was sheer, barely hiding her dark quarter size nipples. Her skin, normally a darker tone, looked like someone had dipped her in a vat of flour, pale and soft, matched with her hair. It almost washed out her Asian features. Her lips were black along with her eyes behind a pearl white lacy mask.

"Good evening, ladies. You all look magnificent for the performance tonight." Kieran said in a surprisingly easy and respectful tone, a hint of his Irish accent still lingering.

"It's very good of you to transport us like this Kieran, thank you." Bianca settled in on one side of Ruby with Ashley on the other side.

"Mr. Mulroney…" Ruby spoke but was quickly interrupted.

"Kieran, please, Ruby. Even though we have only met twice, I feel I know you as a friend and all of my friends call me Kieran." Ruby nodded politely before continuing.

"Kieran, I don't know what it cost you to help solve our little problem, but somehow I doubt my participation tonight will adequately repay you. I wanted to say thank you, and I hope one day I can repay you properly." Ruby noticed his eyes dart between Bianca and Ashley as if wondering how they might respond, but they both sat silently watching him.

"Well Ruby, first agreeing to meet my request, from what I understand without even knowing what it was in the beginning, is payment enough. I invested a little influence in a venture I thought was worth the cost. If you told me right now, you changed your mind and didn't want to go through with it, I would accept your decision and would speak nothing more of it." He paused shortly, leaning in with his hand on the top of the cane. His eyes pierced her soul. "Thankfully, I don't get the impression that you would walk away even though I just said it was your choice. So it would seem the return on my investment is well worth the cost, and I see a lot of potential here."

That he saw her as an investment was a new perspective for Ruby as he spoke. There was something in his words that led her to believe there was a deeper meaning to what he considered an investment in her, but she would not pry. Bianca's reassuring hand cupped her thigh through the light fabric, telling her that doing what she had done was enough.

They filled the ride to Abby's with idle chatter and small talk. Ruby stayed fairly silent during all of it as her mind split between what Kieran said and what she was about to do. This wasn't fear and she didn't have doubts, but to say she wasn't anxious or excited would be a lie. Kieran had offered them Champagne to celebrate, and Ruby was thankful for it to calm her mind and body.

As the car pulled up to the house, her heart raced against her chest, threatening to burst out as the door opened. "We'll see you inside ladies." Kieran said excusing himself followed closely by Raven who carried a large bag that matched her outfit. The door closed for a moment as Bianca and Ashley turned to look at her.

"We'll walk in much the same way we did last time, but the difference will be that Abby has everyone in the main room." Bianca looked to Ashley then back to Ruby. "Abby will bring the room to attention, but how we do this is up to you. I can set the stage if you wish." Ruby immediately started shaking her head, a look of determination on her face.

"I'm offering myself to the guests. It's up to me. You said yourself that Abby already sent out the rules, so there shouldn't be anything else to do but start." Bianca seemed surprised by the conviction she was showing in this decision.

"It will take Raven a little time to set up, so once you have made the announcement, we can walk around the room and give everyone a look before the show starts." Ruby nodded in agreement at Ashley's suggestion.

"You ready pet?" Bianca asked, untying her cape and letting it slide off of her shoulders.

"Yes, Mistress." Ruby let the cape slide from her shoulders as Bianca tapped on the window. The door opened a second later as all three women stepped out. Walking on Bianca's arm as before, Ruby strode up the steps to the house, tall and full of pride. She wasn't proud to be offering her body to a house full of horny men and women, she was proud of the woman she had become and she wanted everyone in that room to feel it.

Walking along the hallway, the absence of people seemed almost strange to Ruby. The soft flicker of lamps created dancing shadows on the walls as the soft orange glow at the end drew near. Strangely dressed as she was, Ruby felt as if she was being led down the aisle for a wedding rather than the real purpose. The strength and proximity of Bianca leading her, fed the heat of her resolve until they reached the door.

"Ladies and Gentlemen, please gather around. We have a guest who would like to make an announcement." She heard Abby call out before they reached the door. It dawned on Ruby that she hadn't thought to ask if the guests knew the nature of their party or their guest. At this point it didn't matter.

Stepping into the room, the contradictory black and white of her and Bianca together caused a stir. The murmur of the crowd when she stepped forward, and the hushed tones of excitement and admiration caught Ruby's ear. The heat of their admiration twisted in her belly. The murmurs faded, replaced by resounding applause, filling the air as Ruby stepped up to the middle the crowd. Many were sitting in chairs set in a circle around the center of the room. A table large enough for a person to lie on sat nearby.

Coming to a stop in the middle. The applause died down until there was silence enough for her to speak. Turning to review the crowd, she saw Kieran sitting nearby, relaxed and observant, watching events unfold. Ruby wondered if he would join. "Ladies and Gentlemen, thank you very much for coming tonight. I am here to show my appreciation and devotion to people who have helped me become the woman standing before you today."

Ruby's eyes first went to Bianca, then to Ashley, who was

standing beside Abby and then to Kieran. She spun in a full circle to catch the gaze of all four people before continuing. "So, in celebration of that devotion, I am here to offer myself to you for the night. As a thank you to my Mistress, my body is yours to pleasure yourselves with until you tire."

At the suggestion of what she was offering, a flared murmur of hushed discussion circled the room. "My friend Ms. Raven, will need some time to prepare, so I will walk around so you may feast your eyes. Once she is ready, the real entertainment begins." With a soft curtsie, the room exploded with applause and conversation as twenty sets of lustful eyes drank in her body. This would be a night to remember.

Taking flight

Bianca watched how the room responded to Ruby, how her simple presence and demeanor seemed to draw them in. Women whispered and pointed, the looks on their faces a mix of awe, lust and even jealousy. The men most stared uncertain of their luck as Abby's chosen few.
By the surprise on the faces of the guests, it was clear to Bianca that Abby left the nature of the parties festivities vague in her invitation, and only that there were rules attendees must follow if they wished to attend.

She also watched Kieran's face from across the room. He was hard to read, always had been, which was what made him being a closet sub so much fun. By the look on his face though and the way he stared at Ruby in the limousine, she impressed him still. The way she'd stepped out on the floor and announced her intentions couldn't have gone unnoticed by him.

"You won the room pet." Bianca whispered as Ruby came over and took her arm, letting her Mistress guide her around the room.

"Thank you for saying so, Mistress. I hope I represented you well." She was nodding politely to guests as they walked and talked, many of whom approached for a closer look. One woman sauntered up to them, without so much as a greeting. She placed her hands eagerly on Ruby's breasts, kneading and mashing them beneath the fabric of her dress. Her hands slid down along Ruby's curvy torso, slipping down to the waist. Then just as abruptly as she had arrived, the woman walked away with a chortle. Ruby and Bianca shared a snigger before moving on.

"I was very proud." Bianca replied as they walked, passing a cluster of chairs and sofas. Every set of eyes watched as they approached, each hungry to sample the offered dish not just look at it. A medium aged man dressed in a very common ruffled off white top and red tights sat in a chair surrounded by a group of men, his swollen member exposed and fully erect. His eyes caught Ruby's and Bianca watched to see how she would react. Without hesitation, Ruby knelt before the man, pulling her dress up to her knees. Hands behind her back, her mouth descended around his thick head, slipping down along the meaty pole.
His hand went to her head as she started bobbing up and down on him. Bianca hovered like a protective bird as the other men regarded the way their new toy attended to his manhood. Hands stroked and rubbed, even a few women stepped up to observe, whispering sentiments of desire.

After a few minutes of attending to the man, Ruby rose from her knees, nodded politely to something the man whispered and turned back to join Bianca. The heat of the lust in the room ticked up a few notches, and Bianca could tell it would be a feeding frenzy once Raven finished.

"I'm ready for you." Raven whispered indistinguishably to Ruby, stepping up next to the two of them. Ruby looked pensively to Bianca, who gave her a reassuring smile.

"I love you Ruby, sometimes I think I don't deserve your dedication to me. Enjoy yourself." She gave her lover a soft kiss on those gray and blue lips before releasing her hand for her to join Raven at the front of the room.

"Friends, could I have two volunteers to join us up here." Ruby's presence filled the room again, as all the guests moved to a place they could see the show. A man from the side of the room they hadn't made their way too, a younger gentleman also in and off white ruffle shirt and red tights with a half phantom of the opera mask stepped up.
Not surprising to Bianca, the older woman who fondled Ruby before, stepped forward, the hunger still in her eyes. "Thank you. Could you please remove my dress and my jewelry and hand it to Ms. Raven?" Ruby stood straight commanding the room. The dichotomy was curious to Bianca. The woman was a natural submissive but had a strong, confident personality, yet in submissive environments she still showed her confidence in a way that didn't clash with the expectation of submission.

The woman stepped around behind, unzipping the dress as the man took the shoulders in his fingers to hold it up. Both of them held a side of the dress as Ruby slipped her arms out, then they lifted the dress up over her head. The older woman took every chance to touch Ruby whenever she could. Carefully they unclasped her necklace and removed her earrings.

Naked before the crowd, Bianca looked to Ashley when the fury of murmurs filled the hall again as everyone could finally admire the painted handiwork on her body. Abby said something to Ashley and even from the side of the room Bianca could tell Ashley's skin grew warmer.

Ruby kneeled on the floor and prostrated herself the way she had the first night Raven came to test the plan. Hands behind and across her back, holding the opposite elbow. Regardless of what she may have said or done since entering the hall, her true submission to the room started now.

Unlike the time in the playroom, Raven made a show of her art. Much the way Ashley had gone to the extreme to display her talent; Raven turned the act of binding Ruby with her rope into one of the most erotic displays Bianca had ever seen. A practicing dominatrix herself, Raven knew the intricacies of control and arousal. Sliding the rope along Ruby's body as she moved the girl around to bind this point or that, she not only teased the person being tied, but the audience ate up every movement and touch.

The tension in the room intensified quickly as it became apparent that Raven was working the binding that would suspend Ruby from the floor. Somewhere in the room, a control similar to the one in the upstairs dungeon uncoiled and revealed a hook attached to a high tensile metal line. Raven silently urged a few men sitting close to help with a wave of her hands as three men stood up and lifted Ruby from the floor and onto the hook.

The rope suspended her so she was floating on her side only a few feet from the floor. Aligned perfectly at waist level for most people. Raven took her by a bound and swollen breast, her fingers on the nipple as she pulled to cause Ruby to spin slowly so everyone could see. Her head held by a rope around her hair placed her mouth at a very convenient angle and also ensured every time she pulled her head, the rope pulled at the other end of her body.

The rope at her crotch ran to either side of her warm, damp entrance, with plenty of room to enter, but enough so that the rope put tension on her labia and lips. The rope ran to the back across her cheeks, pulling them aside for better access.

One of Abby's female attendants wearing nothing but a pair of panties, leggings and garters walked into the middle of the room. Beside where Ruby hung, on a waist-high table, she placed a large fish bowl of multi-colored condoms and a few small bottles of lube. Bianca had expected a rush of people running up to get their taste, but something about the mood in the room created a much slower flow.

The man who Ruby had attended to, still stiff as a tent pole and one other man who had been watching nearby walked up. The one who she'd started sucking positioned himself behind her, pulling a condom over his thick member and squirting a little lube onto it before grabbing her bound legs and plunging himself into her.

Ruby let out a low moan as the first guest took her. The other man stepped up in front of her, feeding those cool blue lips his long slim manhood. The two of them together started pumping into her, forcing the swinging rope to push her back and forth between them until they were entering her in unison.

Bianca's eyes swept the crowd. More of the guests watched than seemed interested in taking part. Some had hands in their tights, or other people's. Bianca spied two men sitting off to the side, one on the hips of the other, his eyes intent on what was happening to Ruby. The motion of his hips spoke to enjoying his own entertainment.

Before she knew what had happened, the one riding stood up and sauntered over to her pet. Slipping a condom on with a large dollop of lube in his fingers, he pushed up beside the other man who was thrusting heavily into her, and worked his medium length thick head into Ruby from behind. Bianca watched Ruby's body jump at the thrust, before the man matched the rhythm of the other two men.

"May we cum in her mouth?" The man pumping into her mouth asked to Bianca, who he reasoned was protecting her by the way she watched. She walked up to where her lover was hanging, her body being ravaged by a constant cycle of men filling her.

"Pet, what do you want?" Bianca asked kneeling to be face to face with her Ruby. "I have assurances from Abby that they are all clean and tested regularly." Ruby was breathing raggedly as the men behind her continued to thrust. As they were talking a couple of women walked up and started sucking hungrily on her bound and blood flush breasts.

"It's… ok Mistress." Ruby replied breathlessly. "I told them to pleasure themselves with me in any way they wish as long as they abide by the rules." Bianca could tell Ruby's pulse was racing, putting her close to an orgasm.

"As you wish pet. And you are welcome to come whenever you need to." Bianca said with a wink before standing. "Those who wish to feed your seed into her mouth are free to do so." Bianca said firmly, making sure to be very specific about the body part. As she stood up, the man reinserted his throbbing meat. It didn't take long before it wracked him with spasms, thrusting into her mouth.

Pulling out of her mouth, he leaned in and whispered something before kissing her on the cheek, making room for a young woman standing nearby. The woman stepped up, presenting her womanhood to Ruby, obviously not concerned about the fact another man had just come in her mouth.

All it took was a few men stepping up before others gained their courage. The next hour was an almost constant round robin of men getting their fill of each hole until finally succumbing to their passion. Some came on her chest, or her belly, or her ass, instead of coming into a condom inside of her. There seemed to be an unspoken break as the movement around Ruby ceased completely. Abby walked up with a half full glass of her favorite liquor in hand. "Should we get her down, maybe give her some water now that everyone has backed off for a bit?" Bianca nodded to Raven who walked over.

"Can we bring her down for a minute, maybe put her on that table since it's what it's there for?" Raven smiled with a nod and walked over to a pair of nearby men. All three walked over to Ruby as the men lifted her up. Raven shifted the support rope, so it was now behind her as they sat her on the table. Ashley walked over with a small water bottle as Bianca joined them.

"How are you holding up little one?" Ashley asked, putting the spout of the water bottle into her mouth and letting her drink. Ruby sucked eagerly at the bottle like a hungry baby nursing. A minute later she nodded, pulling her mouth away, a small amount of water splashed against her chest now smeared with sweat, and paint and bodily fluid. Ruby jumped slightly at the sudden coolness on her hot flush skin.

"I'm doing good Miss. Ash." Ruby commented, noticing most people had moved into smaller groups away from the center. A look of concern furrowed her brow.

"Don't worry, they do this." Abby interjected, surprising everyone. They hadn't noticed her join the group. "Have some fun, take a break, have more fun. It's how the parties tend to go on all night for some." She waved dismissively towards the crowd with a broad grin on her face. "Shall we adjust the line so she's not lying on her side? I don't suppose Ms. Raven wants to untie her just to put her in a different position." Abby added again, surprising everyone.

"That would be wonderful, thank you, Abby." Bianca said approvingly. Before anyone could say anything else, two men approached the table.

"May we?" The lead man, tall and muscular, stripped naked, his semi-hard member bobbing between his legs asked for permission to take a turn with Ruby. The group of women backed away, letting the two men take advantage of the change in position. Tall and muscular lifted Ruby up while the smaller slimmer man slid under her and sat on the table. Her rolled a blue condom on.

They lowered their bound treat onto the man's lap, his well proportioned rigid flesh pressed between her cheeks, burying itself deep. Ruby let out a throaty groan. The hands of the man on the bottom cupped her swollen orbs while the tall, muscular man, slipped his own sleeve on and pushed into her from the front. Bianca grinned at the way her body responded, melting into the penetration, her mouth open and her eyes closed.

The man on the bottom used his grip on her breasts to move her on him while the other man's thrusts added to the momentum. Her hips ground as much as they could as the man on the bottom leaned back until he was lying down. Both men sawed into her, alternating thrusts. A woman close to Ashley's age and build walked up, her flowing red dress bunched up around her waist as she stepped onto the table and lowered herself onto Ruby's face. By the almost instant way the woman rolled her head back, mouth open in an aroused moan, their young play thing wasted no time pushing at the woman's center of pleasure.

Bianca enjoyed watching how the guests pleasured themselves on Ruby's body but didn't abuse it. There wasn't the usual man handling or vicious fucking, and smacking so hard it left welts. Abby's guests were respectful of the gift she had given them.

The woman came within minutes, crying out, her body ravaged in a series of spasms. As she lifted herself off, Bianca had to stifle a laugh when she saw Ruby's drenched face, liquid running freely down her cheeks and neck. Shortly after the two men lost control, groaning long and hard as both pumped with reckless abandon into her. Tall and muscular's skin, flushed red and tension rippled every ligament until finally both men's bodies released in unison.

After the rough, powerful climax they'd shared with her abused pet, the men tenderly lifted her up, pushing the table back, leaving Ruby to hang with her back to the floor. A moment later three women sauntered over, Bianca watched with curious interest as they circled, fingers swept across her skin, hungry eyes chose the most enticing parts.

What happened next surprised Bianca, her mind racing back to the thoughts of Abby's respectful guests. One woman kneeled between

Ruby's exposed legs and began licking her abused tender flesh with the most gentle touch, as if she was trying to lick away any pain. Another of the women softly licked at the blood strained skin of her breasts, her mouth a feather's touch against what Bianca imagined was fairly sensitive skin by now. The woman not only seemed to provide a little pleasure, but also gave her student a tongue bath from all the sweat and bodily fluids covering her now destroyed paint job. The third woman, surprised Bianca even more when she kneeled at Ruby's head and softly kissed her mouth as if they were lovers.

Bianca watched the women intently, not noticing a man and woman approach from the side. "Excuse me." The woman spoke, pulling Bianca's attention away.

"Yes?" She blinked away her distraction, turning to the couple.

"The group would like to release her from her bonds and clean her up. We have another way that we would like to enjoy her if you allow us." The gentle way the woman asked almost concerned Bianca, uncertain if this was some sordid plot. Eventually she nodded in agreement, waving Raven over.

"They want to remove the binds and clean her up. Can you do it quickly?" Bianca asked of the other dominatrix.

"Very easily." Raven replied with a skip in her walk, moving with the couple over to where Ruby hung. The woman spoke to the three women on Ruby. They stepped back helping Raven release Ruby from the hook. Bianca had no idea where this sudden shift in activities started, and realizing she was quickly losing control of the flow, stepped back and watched.

"What's going on?" Ashley's voice drifted across her consciousness, pulling her attention partly from Ruby. They watched as Raven deftly untangle the ropes.

"I have no idea." Bianca's tone was almost awestruck. She felt a warm hand press against her hip, the thin fabric of her dress barely blocking the heat of the hand settling where the soft rise of her butt started.

"I get the feeling someone planned this." Ashley commented. Bianca was about to ask how she knew just as four very stout men, wearing only tights and masks carried a large copper tub into the room. Their muscles rippled against the strain, finally setting the tub down off to the side of the circle created by chairs and sofas. As Raven removed the last of her extensive rope bind, the group of women and the one man who started this picked up their guest of honor and carried her to the tub. Bianca couldn't help but feel a swell of emotion choke her throat as a hand jumped to her mouth. Watching the lines crisscrossing her body where the ropes had bit into her.

"It's ok. She's fine." Raven must have seen her reaction as she stepped up beside the two of them. It dawned on Bianca The last time she never saw Ruby immediately after being released by Raven. Somehow, the smeared paint made it look worse than it was.

With delicate and deliberate motions, they lowered Ruby into the water. A few female guests who stripped out of everything but tights descended on the tub with what looked like large sponges. Their hands worked tirelessly below the water of the tub. Ruby's eyes were closed, her mouth partially opened letting the warmth they could all see steaming up out of the water soothe her body. The women eased her forward, holding her hair up as they cleaned her neck and back.

Before long, two of the women helped Ruby to stand by holding her arms and supporting her weight. A blue, gray white film hung to her skin, but the lines were vanishing quickly. As the two women held her up, two others walked over with large clay jugs and gracefully poured water from the large spouts. Starting on either side of her body, the splash of water ran her body, washing away the last of the paint and grime.

Supported by two women, Ruby stood in the middle of the tub, the mask still on her face. Her body glistened wet and clean. Like some ancient Egyptian goddess stepping out from magical cleansing waters as slaves attended to her perfect wet skin. Bianca could see a soft smile form on her lover's face as the women rubbed and washed away the few remaining areas of stubborn paint. "Was this your idea?" Bianca inquired, noticing Abby stepping up to watch. The older woman shook her head, those perfect straw blond strands locked in place on top of her head.

"They must have worked this out with my staff earlier." She replied absently, her eyes admiring the ritual her guests were going through. The women holding Ruby's arms helped her out of the tub as the women who poured the water from jugs approached with large white cotton towels. As they dried Ruby off, a few others removed the table. Then the four men from before carried a massive folded pillow surely measured ten feet square. Setting it down on the floor and letting it spread out, the pillow's thickness rose at least a foot and a half above the floor.

The women pulled away the towel to reveal Bianca's magnificent naked pale lover clean and radiant. Surrounded by a small group of now naked guests, the women who had cleaned her quickly stripped. It hadn't occurred to Bianca before, but the core of the guests thinned out considerably in the past hour. Only maybe ten remained and at least half were simply lounging around the center watching the show.

One very sultry looking woman as tall as Ashley with full natural breasts and a gait that would have made models jealous took Ruby by the hand. Looking back as she walked, making sure her body radiated every ounce of sexual energy she could, she led Ruby to the large pillow. Pulling her in for a deep passionate kiss, they both slowly descended back into the middle of the pillow where the group of naked guests quickly joined them.

Bianca felt herself grow wet, that familiar knot in her belly and a new pain in her chest as she watched. Letting her lay at the middle of the pillow, hungry mouths and eager hands suckled and explored her body like lovers yearning to learn everything about their new partner in one night. Teeth nibbled softly at her rosy nipples, licked at the roll of her breasts. Two women shared the space between her legs, their mouths and hot breath meticulously working up between her creamy thighs. A man and a woman shared her neck and mouth as they kissed and licked above Ruby's shoulders, the woman's tongue seductively sliding along those full lips Bianca so enjoyed kissing.

She suddenly recognized that pain in her chest and felt guilty. "What's wrong?" Ashley must have seen the change in her face prompting her to ask. She wrapped an arm over her shoulder, pulling Bianca close.

"I suddenly feel jealous." Bianca admitted solemnly. She could see the friendly look of amusement on Ashley's face out of the corner of her eye.

"Because you don't want to share her in such an intimate way or because you want to join?" Ashley teased. Bianca knew well enough, there was more to their relationship than simple jealousy at watching her lover being ravaged like this. She could see the way Ruby was panting, her body moving with the motion of her handful of lovers. It was like watching some unsuspecting woman being seduced by a coven of vampires right before they devour her and the imagery was powerful.

"Because," Bianca paused trying to understand her feelings. "…

because I never expected it to go this way. I'm torn between wanting her for myself when it comes to intimacy like this and letting her enjoy the appreciation of her guests for what she did." It was obvious to everyone standing and watching that was what this became. It only reinforced her decision to turn Kieran down on his request. This would have been a very different scene had this been in his dungeon.

"Go join her." Ashley prodded with a naughty grin on her face. Bianca watched as the two women who had been working on her thighs finally reached the damp petals of her womanhood. Their combined mouths kissing Ruby's lips caused her back to arch, her legs shuddering. Ruby's hips and body writhed with fluid movements to match the passion flowing over her skin. Her head turned to the side, accepting the man's thin but long uncut manhood, the woman with him helping Ruby by licking his shaft. They occasionally shared kisses or his slick tip when it came out of her mouth.

"No, this is her moment." Bianca replied with warm emotion in her voice. "I can have her whenever I want her… and so can you." Bianca added whispering to her friend, squeezing her hand as Kieran stepped up.

"Definitely an investment worth keeping my eye on." He said cryptically, his eyes taking one last look at the pile of naked skin on the pillow. A sly grin crossed his lips as he turned without further word and walked to the main door, Raven beside him, her arm on his shoulder.

"Now I know Kieran can be rather eccentric, that that was downright cryptic." Ashley said with a chuckle. Bianca shook her head and chuckled herself, her attention turning back to her pet. By her own decision, Ruby found her way on top of the man she'd been sucking on a minute before, the woman who had helped her was sitting on his face and the two of them were kissing. Another man had slipped up behind and pushed himself into her. The other women continued to lick and explore her breasts and her neck. One woman's hand vivaciously rubbed Ruby as she rode the two men, the red, pale skin telling of the heat building again in her body.

"He's not wrong though." Bianca finally replied. Accepting that regardless of what happened, deciding to take a chance with that meek uncertain girl pleading for her grade had paid dividends they still didn't realize. She pulled Ashley in close, laying her head on her friend's shoulder as they watched the woman who had grown out of that meek girl mature into something amazing.

EPILOGUE

Upelkuchen

Ruby groaned with frustration, leaning back in the tall bar chair, hands rubbing her eyes before sliding back along her messy bob cut hair. "You okay, baby?" The voice of Bianca broke the frustration. She warmed at the feel of lips on the back of her neck and a hand circling around in front of her, pressing against her belly. Bianca kissed her softly several times, her hand slipping up from her belly to her breasts free and naked under her shirt. A soft squeeze of her round globes made Ruby purr until the hand released it. Walking around the bar into the kitchen, Bianca had a flirty look on her face. "What are you working on?"

Dropping her pen to the spine of the thick book, closing it. "I need to be ready for the GMAT by next Friday if I'm going to get into the program." Almost a year working as a paid intern, and eventually a part time junior associate on Bianca's team at M&K gave her a whole new appreciation for business. Only six months away from receiving her nursing degree, Tulane's MBA program offered a spot in their program as long as she scored well on the Masters entrance exam.

"I'm sure you'll do fine." Bianca picked a large green grape from a bowl and bit it in half, her red lips surrounding the round orb to catch the juice before sucking the rest into her mouth. Ruby couldn't help but stare. There was something painfully erotic about the way her lover did some things, and looking away didn't help. She felt a bit of wetness pooling between her legs, realizing half a day passed since the last time they'd done anything together.

She'd attended her Mistress the night prior during an evening with Todd. Her mistress made it a point to keep her on the verge all night without the slightest hint of release. After Todd left, Bianca turned her attention to harshly abusing her, still keeping her on the edge until Ruby begged, tears streaming down her face. Bianca took her at that point, making love to her and bringing out a body draining orgasm that left Ruby near unconsciousness for almost twelve hours.

"I'll do ok, but I'm not sure I've got everything covered." Ruby ruminated. It wasn't that she was uncertain or worried, she just realized there were aspects of the exam she didn't know.

"My love, the GMAT is testing how well you can think for yourself and articulate your answers. I think it's fair to say you have that covered." Bianca was right in some regard, but she'd worked way too hard over the last year to let this slip away.

"I know sexy, but if there's one thing you've taught me, it's never accepting good enough." Ruby stuck her tongue out playfully.

"You're right of course love, but ten cocks is a bit overkill isn't it slut?" Bianca teased back winking at the tongue play. Though Abby's party was the last time anything of that magnitude happened, Bianca made a point occasionally to bring up the event. It became a playful reminder that sometimes taking things to the extreme isn't necessary. Ruby kept her word and remained available for everyone at the party to enjoy, and enjoy they did.

By the time the last couple, the one who started the plan to free her for the masses, gave her one last kiss and left the party, the twilight sky was lightening. Bianca and Ashley fell asleep on a nearby sofa, never leaving her side. Ruby was certain on more than one instance she dozed off, wracked with exhaustion with whoever she was tangled up, only to be awakened by a new friend.

She could barely walk for the next few days, Bianca made sure not to do anything more rough than fingers or the sybian for a week. The way the guests took her from a piece of meat to their favorite lover in a few hours still choked Ruby up when she thought of it. They'd returned to Abby's parties a couple times since. Ashley found her way back into that world apparently with her old mentor's help. Ruby never knew that Abby was one of Ashley's art professors in college, which was how she'd found that world in the first place.

"You're staying here tonight?" Bianca asked, picking absently at the plate of salad she'd made for lunch an hour ago and forgot to eat until now.

"Of course. Ash is out with Peter, and they'll probably want the apartment to themselves tonight." Ruby joked, rolling her eyes. As expected, her roommate moved in with her boyfriend and eventual fiancee halfway through the spring semester. This left Ruby to decide if she could justify staying alone on the other side of town. She helped the lady who rented the apartment to find a new tenant to fill the last three months of the lease. Ruby moved in with Ashley more permanently. Six months of sharing time between living with Ashley and spending weekends and nights during the week with Bianca worked out fairly well, always giving Ashley the freedom to use the apartment when she wanted it.

"Are you still considering finding a place of your own?" Bianca asked.

"I guess it'll depend if I pass this test." She sighed. "If I get into the program, I wouldn't be able to pay the rent and pay for my program without a loan."

"Well pet, you know there's no hurry to go anywhere. My offer still stands though if it means having you close." Ruby adamantly shook her head, her short strawberry blond hair flying around like a mop.

"Absolutely not. If there's one thing you've taught me it's working to earn everything I have." Ruby flatly denied the offer the first time. Of all the things Bianca gave her, she'd never given Ruby anything she hadn't earned and Ruby wasn't about to let that change now.

"Well, I can always get you a big doggy mattress and lay it at the foot of the bed when you need to let Ash have the apartment for Peter." Bianca teased remembering a conversation with Ashley when she was trying to come to terms with the new dynamic. Ruby rolled her eyes and sighed. Though she wasn't rolling her eyes in opposition to the sleeping arrangement, the revolving door of boyfriends over the last year was getting old.

"I liked Mark better." Bianca joked.

"So did I, but Peter is a lot more respectful of the space at the apartment." Ruby laughed at the fact that she and Bianca were discussing their best friend's dating history. Neither Bianca nor Ashley could figure out why she'd had so much trouble finding a guy that worked out or completed her in some way. But then Bianca and Ashley had the benefit, or the disadvantage of history and understanding each other. Ruby knew the problem, but wasn't sure if it was her place to say anything.

"She goes through another guy I'm going to suggest she goes for girls next." Bianca laughed under her breath, pushing a fork of spinach and cucumber into her mouth.

"That won't help." Ruby replied dismissively, picking up a glass of water and taking a large gulp, her eyes watching Bianca to see how she responded. As expected, her brow wrinkled as she ate, slightly frustrated she couldn't respond immediately.

"What do you mean?" She finally choked out, trying to swallow and talk.

"Do you guys really want to know?" Ruby dangled the answer like a piece of cheese. She knew Bianca would say yes, but she dangled it anyway.

"You're a little tease. Of course I want to know." Bianca sighed. Ruby still found the new dynamic of their relationship curious. Despite still being Bianca's sub, still wearing the collar proudly and letting Bianca use her whenever, the two of them developed a much more equal and confident flow between them. Ruby felt comfortable using endearing terms or questioning Bianca and her lover became much less cold and much more open with Ruby.

The dynamic shift was fun, but scary at times. "She can't find someone out there who gives her what being a part of our life gives her. I think deep down inside she realizes that if she finds someone who is good enough, he will take her away from what she really wants."

"What does she really want?" It must have seemed strange for Bianca to hear an analysis of her best friend from someone else. They'd been together for so long and knew each other's quirks and thoughts without question, but Bianca truly seemed bothered she hadn't seen this.

"Us." Ruby said with love in her voice. "For the longest time the two of you were together. Maybe not dating or living together, but the friendship you have is essentially an evolved relationship. You go to lunch, have dinner dates, meet for drinks. You are so comfortable sexually with each other you give no thought to the idea of providing each other comfort and pleasure." Ruby stared off through the windows looking out over the city, trying to decide how to word what she wanted to say.

She let a long breath out through her nose as she looked back at Bianca. "Then suddenly you are infatuated with some young girl you see as a project, a distraction, a potential plaything, and now the dynamic has shifted slightly. Little did Ash or you or I realize how things would turn out between us. Events created a situation where I grew much closer to Ash, strengthening the bond and bridging the gap she felt was growing between the two of you. Now life has settled out a bit, and she sees the two of us together, me splitting time between our place and yours and she feels a need to let you and I grow together, so she's trying to find something to fill that void."

The slack, contemplative look on her lover's face told Ruby she'd hit on something neither of them considered. A thought running through her mind tripped an intense realization in Bianca. Ruby could see the emotion welling up in her face as she walked over to the other chair at the bar and sat down.

"How did you become so intuitive?" Bianca ran a thumb over Ruby's lower lip. "Sometimes love, I fail to recognize how aware of the world you are. It never dawned on me that we both might have unconsciously treated what we had as a relationship. And now she unconsciously feels like I dumped her for you." It wasn't necessarily how Ruby would have described the situation, but the question caused her to shrug in agreement.

"That's my feeling. I get to see a lot more of her day to day than you do, and I can see the difference in the way she is when we are all together and when she's with her dates. Something is missing with them that shines bright when we're all together. She's in love with us, and I know you love her, I love her too." Ruby put her hand on Bianca's giving her a reassuring squeeze. The act made her chuckle softly to herself realizing it had usually been her needing the reassuring squeeze.

"What do we do?" For all of Bianca's confidence and poise, Ruby realized the woman struggled with relationships, which was probably how things between Bianca and Ashley developed so strangely. Ruby appreciated that Ashley's guidance brought her lover as far as it did, allowing her to do the rest. Taking a page from the dominant supporting the submissive playbook, she reached over, pressing her palm to Bianca's cheek before leaning in for a soft loving peck on her lips.

"We become what we all want, the big happy family you spoke of last year." She looked into her lovers emerald orbs, gazing deep into her soul. "We're not exactly your typical couple as it is. So how would the three of us coming up with a more permanent arrangement where we can love each other and share our life together be that strange?" Ruby knew it was a tall order that would likely involve a fairly intense change in their life, but after everything they'd been through what would it matter.

Before any further plans evolved, Bianca's phone buzzed. Walking over to the counter, Ruby saw Bianca's eyes go wide when she read the message. "Kieran wants to know if we are free this evening. He would like to talk to all three of us." Ruby shook her head, her eyes going wide in surprise. Before she could say anything, Bianca already dialed Ashley's number. "Hey, can you cancel or postpone your date tonight…. Kieran sent me a message asking if the three of us were available tonight... no, not a party… He wants to talk to us… You sure?... Positive?... Ok, See you at six?... Ok… love you too."

"I guess Peter's not that important!" Ruby joked, considering the conversation they'd just had. Bianca shrugged and rolled her eyes this time. After Bianca confirmed with Kieran, they could be there around six thirty, further conversation about their family plans faded. Ruby tried to dive back into her studies, but the question around what her recent benefactor might want with the three of them divided her thoughts.

Not wanting to show disrespect, both of them started early to make themselves up nice. It was a good thing they'd given themselves the extra time since showering together always turned sexual with Bianca forcing her sub to pleasure her.

Ruby finished drying her hair when Ashley stepped into the apartment. "Hey baby." She greeted Ruby, walking over, a quick kiss on the lips. "There's a car downstairs waiting, where's Bee?" Just as the question came out, Bianca stepped out of the bathroom, hands pushing earrings into her ears. "Well, I'm glad I wasn't the only one who thought we should look nice for Kieran" Ashley joked.

"Did you say there was a car waiting downstairs?" Bianca asked. Ashley nodded, causing her to check her watch. "Sometimes I hate how much of an alpha he is." Bianca growled through her teeth. "You look fine, your hairdo is meant to look messy. Leave it!" She joked at Ruby, still messing with her hair as she sat on the bed to pull on a pair of boots.

"I think it looks great." Ashley chimed in as Ruby glared playfully at Bianca before throwing the towel over the bathroom door.

"Ok, let's go." Bianca ordered, grabbing her coat and opening the door to the apartment. The other two followed her out. As mentioned, there was an expensive sedan sitting on the curb waiting when they came down. It wasn't as long as the car they'd rode in to go to Abby's party, but it was still nice.

"So Ash," Bianca started in as the car turned down the street toward the highway. "Ruby and I were talking, and we think there's something missing in our relationship." The assertion surprised Ashley.

Ruby knew her mind was racing, trying to remember if she'd heard either of them mention anything wrong with the relationship.

"What?" Finally breaking the tension and silence. She couldn't stand not understanding what was going wrong. Bianca tried her best to keep her face serious. In her defense, Bianca has amazing control over her emotions and her poker face, but the emotional weight of the conversation made fighting a smile difficult.

"You." Ruby finally said breaking the silent tension Bianca was trying and failing to hide with the smirk on her lips. Ashley only blinked, uncertain what that one word response had to do with anything. "We realized that last year when the three of us were inseparable with everything going on, we were all in love with life. You and Ruby became much closer while we were separated and once we were back together, the three of us fed off of each other."

"I'm still confused. What changed?" Ashley looked at both of them like they were high on something, expecting to find out this was all a hallucination.

"You remember we were talking a few days ago about your having problems finding the right man?" Ashley nodded. "Ruby figured out why." She felt Ashley's eyes burrowing through her now as if digging for the answer without asking.

"Please listen and don't judge my impressions until I'm done." Ruby wanted assurances Ashley wouldn't bite her head off.

"Oh little one, I'd never judge or berate you for an opinion." Ashley's caring motherly tone came out letting her relax.

"You're in love with us and what the three of us together represent." It was the most succinct way she could say it without going through the long diatribe she'd shared with Bianca earlier.

"But of course I love you both." Ashley replied.

"Not love Ash, you're in love with us and the connection we all share." Bianca corrected, changing the perspective of the response. Ruby could see the change in her eyes as she considered the new information.

"Ash, have you ever really stopped being in love with Bianca?" Ruby hoped to define the questions in Ashley's thoughts. Her contemplative expression softened as her eyes went to Bianca.

"No, not really." The admission didn't surprise Ruby, especially after what they'd talked about already. Judging from Bianca's expression it didn't surprise her either.

"Could you truly be happy just being good friends with her having someone else to spend your life with?" Ashley shrugged.

"I don't know, probably not." Which as far as Ruby could tell spoke to many of the problems that plagued Bianca's relationships over the years.

"All I've ever known was the two of you being there for me, loving me, supporting me. How could I not want our family together?" By the look on her face, Ashley's mind fought to work through the image of what they were suggesting.

"We haven't thought it through exactly…" Bianca interrupted. "Mainly because we just only… well Ruby explained it, this afternoon."

"But I imagine we'll need a bigger place, or a remodeled place." Ruby continued.

"Ruby, are you suggesting we all live together?" Ashley still seemed a little dumbfounded.

"As lovers, friends, whatever." Ruby replied warmly, knowing once it was out in the open there was no turning back.

"You're ok with this?" Ashley turned to Bianca, who had a bigger than life grin on her face. The expression was enough to answer her own question. "Who am I to argue? Dating was becoming so stressful." She laughed, causing the both of them to join her as they all leaned in for a family hug in the middle of the car's cabin.

About the same time they started breaking the hug, the car turned up Kieran's drive and came to a stop in front of his house. The door opened to Kieran standing at the top of the stairs to his porch. He looked much like he the way he greeted them the first time, a bright friendly look on his face as the three of them slid out of the car.

"Ladies, it's always a pleasure to see you." He called down, waiting for all of them to reach the top of the stairs. "Bianca, as radiant as ever. Thank you for coming so soon." He gave Bianca a hug and kiss on the cheek.

"Kieran, always a pleasure to see you. You know I can't deny a request from you" Bianca gave him a smirk, returning the hug and kissed him back before he turned to Ashley.

"Ashley, I definitely don't see enough of you anymore. I hope you are well." Like Bianca, he gave her a hug and kiss on the cheek.

"Can't say I miss the parties, but I miss you, Kieran." Ashley returned his embrace, giving him a playful wink. Then his eye fell on Ruby, who had slowly walked up the steps, giving her girls a chance to greet him.

"Ruby, my angel. I trust you are well?" Ruby blushed at the way he looked at her. She and Bianca spent a few evenings in private with Kieran and she'd seen a side of the man very few people ever see. It hadn't changed her opinion of the man, but it definitely made seeing him the way the public saw him strange.

"I'm very well thank you Kieran." She gave him a tender hug and a kiss on the cheek before moving to Bianca's side.

"Come in, ladies." He ushered them inside, following him into the lounge at the front of his house. "Charles, can we get three glasses of the Malbec please?" He asked the young man in his mid-twenties who stood at the entrance to the lounge when they approached. Before they sat, Charles walked in with three glasses and a bottle of dark red wine. Presenting a glass to each of them, he poured generous portions, leaving the bottle corked on a table beside the high-back chair Kieran sat in.

"To the value of smart investments." Kieran offered a toast of his own glass, his eyes watching the three of them. While Ruby nodded and put her glass up to accept the toast, her mind was having trouble understanding Kieran's words. By the look on the faces of her companions, regardless of their mind for business, they were uncertain as well.

"To family." Ashley replied, the look on her face turned happier. Bianca, Kieran and Ruby all echoed her toast and drank. When the red liquid hit her tongue, Ruby's mind perked up. The undertones of fruit and oak warmed her body. As they all drank a little, their host shifted in his seat, leaning forward to pull their attention.

"So I know you three are dying to know why I called you here." Kieran's exuberant eccentricities aside, he was an amazingly astute and empathic person. The whole situation riveted Bianca and Ashley's attention, which Ruby was certain was the reason for the way he said it. Reaching into his coat pocket, he pulled out a fairly thick legal-size envelope and handed it to Ruby.

"What's this?" She asked, staring at her full name written in beautiful cursive print on the front.

"Open it and see." Kieran urged, his face still full of energy but unreadable as he sat back in the chair.

Ruby's fingernail caught the corner, ripping the fold until she could push her finger through to the other end. Inside, a very thick packet of folded paper fell out into her hand. Unfolding the papers, she could feel the eyes of everyone on her, eager to understand. As she turned the paper to the front, she saw the letterhead for Kieran's company at the top. It was a handwritten letter in the same script as her name on the envelope.

> Dearest Ruby,
> There are things and people in life where investments in time, energy and money are realized to be a great waste of all three. And then there are investments that cost a person very little, but bring the greatest returns.
>
> I believe you are an investment beyond money or influence. In you I see great potential, that guided by the right hand can achieve greatness. With that in mind, I feel it is necessary to continue my investment in your growth.
>
> 1st Attached to this note you will find documents detailing a trust fund I have set up in your name. The sole purpose of which meant to cover your current student loans as well as any tuition costs you will incur in pursuit of your MBA.
>
> 2nd: Upon conferment of your graduation from your nursing program, there will be a position waiting for you at a new division of my company. The focus of this division is on developing medical technologies to help nurses diagnose and treat patients faster and more accurately. You will work as the assistant to the division manager until such a time that you understand the intricacies of the business.
>
> This is only the start of your journey,
>
> Sincerely
> Kieran Mulroney.

Ruby's mouth hung open as she reached the end of the letter. The look on her face, her mind racing in a hundred different directions. Trying to understand the words, her body suddenly thrumming with anxious energy radiating across her skin. There had to have been confusion in her eyes as she sat unmoving, trying to make sense of it all. The stillness of her body must have worried Bianca and Ashley who sat close, waiting for some answer to the contents.

"Wh… why?" Ruby finally stammered out, looking up at Kieran. Concerned with what the letter might say, Bianca took it from Ruby as she looked to her benefactor for an answer.

"Oh my God Kieran!!" Bianca looked up from the paper dumbfounded, her eyes wide with disbelief. The man shrugged, his demeanor that of someone who has spent a life not caring what others think of him or his actions. Bianca handed the letter to Ashley, letting her read. To Ruby's surprise, Kieran still had not answered her question.

"Why Kieran? What's she to you?" Ashley was the only one who questioned him without disbelief in her voice. Being the lawyer in the group, she was most likely to see the logical side of the issue.

"Why not?" He responded absently. "I've followed Ruby's path since Bianca introduced me to her that night and everything that I've seen says she is bound for great things. She has two very supportive and loving women in her life to keep her on track, but what she lacks is a path."

He took a sip of his wine, those hazel eyes staring across the top of the glass at Ruby. "As a nursing student, there was little I could do to provide a path. As a nurse who is working on a background in business also, I can influence that greatness. Once before I used my influence to help a young, scared woman from losing something she held dear. She repaid me by selflessly surrendering herself to strangers because she knew it was the price she needed to pay for what she truly wanted. Now I get a chance to use my influence to ensure she never has to make that choice ever again."

Without warning, overcome with emotion, Ruby broke out into sobs as tears streaked down her face. It had been the first time in almost a year she'd cried for any reason other than Bianca or Ashley's whipping pushing her too far. This time the tears and sobs were tears of joy, just like the day she'd learned the case against her had fallen apart and she was free to see the love of her life again.

"Oh baby, baby." Bianca pulled Ruby into her shoulder, her voice calm and whispering as a hand stroked her hair.

"I take it that's a good thing?" Kieran asked with a raised eyebrow and concern on his face. Both Ashley and Bianca sat still, watching Ruby's body shake with sobs, hesitant to answer with any understanding. A short time later, Ruby lifted her head up off of Bianca's shoulder, her hand wiping tears from her eyes.

"Yes…" Ruby finally said, rising and walking over to Kieran. She wrapped her arms around her benefactor, hugging him more lovingly than she'd ever hugged him before. "I am absolutely speechless Kieran." She whispered between sniffles and residual sobs before pulling back.

"No need to say anything Ruby. You are special and you have two very special women who love you very much. Don't let them go." Kieran winked to the two of them. "I'll be keeping a close eye on your progress and expect to see great things from you."

Ruby was still shaking from everything when they finally walked out of his house and slipped into the car. There was a lot to do in the coming months between graduating school and getting accepted into the program. All of that on top of finding an answer to all of them living together. It would be a busy year, but somehow she knew the three of them together could meet any challenge with confidence.

About the Author

J. Scott, is an up and coming author who weaves steamy images of sexy love in contemporary and imaginary settings of fiction for discerning thoughtful readers who seek escape. This is her first published work, but she has been writing romance and erotica in short story and collaborative formats for years. She has at least two other novels in the works coming out in the next year, stay tuned.

Acknowledgements

Thanks to all of the wonderful beta readers who made sure that the story was solid from cover to cover. We couldn't have done it without your insight and willingness to share your time and energy to make this a success.

Other books by this author

Please look for other books by J. Scott coming to book retailers in the next year.

Fox and Hare - An interracial contemporary Lesbian Romance - Coming Soon.

Connect with J. Scott

I really appreciate you reading my book! Here are my social media coordinates:

Friend me on Facebook: https://www.facebook.com/J_scott_author

Instagram: https://www.instagram.com/jscott_author/

Twitter: https://twitter.com/j_scottauthor